Also by Val McDermid

A Place of Execution
Killing the Shadows
The Distant Echo
The Grave Tattoo
A Darker Domain
The Vanishing Point

TONY HILL NOVELS

The Mermaids Singing
The Wire in the Blood
The Last Temptation
The Torment of Others
Beneath the Bleeding
Fever of the Bone
The Retribution

KATE BRANNIGAN NOVELS

Dead Beat
Kick Back
Crack Down
Clean Break
Blue Genes
Star Struck

LINDSAY GORDON NOVELS

Report for Murder
Common Murder
Final Edition
Union Jack
Booked for Murder
Hostage to Murder

TRICK OF THE
DARK

VAL McDERMID

HARPER
WEEKEND

Trick of the Dark
Copyright © 2010 by Val McDermid.

Published by Harper Weekend, an imprint of HarperCollins Publishers Ltd.

First published in Great Britain by Little, Brown: 2010
First published in Canada by HarperCollins Publishers Ltd: 2011
This Harper Weekend paperback edition: 2012

HarperCollins books may be purchased for educational, business, or
sales promotional use through our Special Markets Department.

HarperCollins Publishers Ltd
2 Bloor Street East, 20th Floor
Toronto, Ontario, Canada
M4W 1A8

www.harpercollins.ca

Library and Archives Canada Cataloguing in Publication
McDermid, Val
Trick of the dark / Val McDermid.

ISBN 978-1-55468-751-0

I. Title.
PR6063.A168T75 2012   823'.914   C2012-903382-0

Typeset in Meridien by M Rules
Printed and bound in the United States
RRD 9 8 7 6 5 4 3 2 1

This book is dedicated to the memory of Mary Bennett (1913–2005) and Kathy Vaughan Wilkes (1946–2003) – friends, teachers and supporters. I'm still walking through the doors they opened.

Acknowledgements

This book has deep roots. It started with Mary Bennett and her colleagues at St Hilda's College, Oxford, who spotted something that deserved a chance. By delightful coincidence, I was writing it when the present Governing Body appointed me to an Honorary Fellowship, a distinction of which I am more proud than I can say.

Specifically, I owe thanks to Manda Scott and Leslie Hills who talked me through various climbing scenarios; to Professor Sue Black, whose powers of explanation and description were invaluable as always; my editor, David Shelley, whose insights show me how to make it better; Stephanie Glencross, whose instinct for story is second to none; my copy editor, Anne O'Brien, who keeps me on the straight and narrow; and my agent Jane Gregory and her team.

I don't think I could do this without my wife Kelly and my son Cameron. I suspect I am no fun at all when I'm in the thick of it, but still they give me their love, indulgence, support and most importantly, their laughter. Only another thirty-five to go, guys . . .

I had been told about her.
How she would always, always.
How she would never, never.
I'd watched and listened
But I still fell for her,
How she always, always.
How she never, never.

from 'Her'
by Jackie Kay

Prologue

What's your earliest memory? I don't mean something you've been told so many times it feels like a memory. I'm talking about the first thing you remember through your child's eyes. A knee-high memory, a don't-understand-the-words memory, an honest-to-god slice of emotion that can still fell you like a tree. The recalled moment that is the key to what shapes you for ever.

Mine has narrow wooden bars running vertically through it. A cot or a playpen, at a guess. I can't picture what I'm standing on. I can see my hands clutching the bars tightly, small fingers still chubby like toddlers' are supposed to be. My nails are crusted with dirt and there's a very particular smell. Over the years, I've worked out that it's a mixture of stale urine, marijuana, alcohol and unwashed bodies. Even now, when I walk among the homeless who inhabit the invisible hinterland of the world's great cities, I feel comforted by the smell that repels most people. The homeless smell like home to me.

I'm stalling. Can you tell I'm stalling? Because the heart of the memory still makes me shiver to my soul.

In front of me is a movie cut into slices by the bars. My mother is wearing a bright tangerine blouse and the man has the front of it bunched in his fist. He's shaking my mother like one of the dogs would shake a rat or a rabbit. He's shouting at her too. I don't know what he's shouting, it's just a jagged cascade of violent sound. She's sobbing, my mother. Every time she tries to speak, he slaps her hard with his other hand. Her head jerks like it's on a spring. There's a thread of blood trickling from one nostril. Her hands try to push him away, but he doesn't even notice, he's so much stronger than her.

Then one of her hands slips down and presses against the front of his trousers, stroking him through the stiff dirty denim. She lets herself fall against him, close so it's harder for him to hit her. He stops shouting but he doesn't let go of her shirt. He pulls up her skirt and pushes her down on the floor and carries on making her cry. Only in a different way.

That's my first memory. I wish it was the worst one.

Part One

1

Tuesday

U nder normal circumstances, Charlie Flint would have consumed all the media coverage of the trial of Philip Carling's killers. It wasn't quite the sort of murder that was right up her street, but there were good reasons why this particular case would have interested her. But nothing was normal right now. Her professional life was in shreds. The destruction of reputation, the prohibition against doing the one thing she'd ever been any good at and the continued threat of legal sanction alone would have been enough to distract Charlie from the news stories. But there was more.

The headline news in Charlie Flint's world was that she was in love and hating every minute of it. And that was the real reason she was oblivious to all sorts of things that normally would have fascinated her.

The needles of the power shower on her shoulders and back felt like deserved punishment. She tried to change the subject, but neither mind nor heart would play along. This morning, like every morning for the past six weeks, Lisa Kent was the only item on Charlie's mental bulletin. As the day wore on, Charlie could generally drag her attention back to the things that actually mattered. But first thing, before she'd hammered her defences into shape again, top of the dial was Lisa bloody Kent. And here are the bullet points, she thought bitterly. Bad timing, nothing in common, wrong bloody woman.

Seven years she'd been with Maria. Now, as if it wasn't enough to be wracked by guilt, Charlie had the additional mortification of living a cliché. The seven-year itch. She hadn't even known it needed scratching until Lisa had glided into her life. But this had gone far beyond an itch. It was a ferocious irritation, an obsessional derangement that had invaded her life indiscriminately. No apparently innocuous event or remark was immune from a sudden takeover by the image of Lisa's assessing eyes or the echo of her languid laughter.

'Fuck it,' Charlie said, savagely pushing her silver and black hair back from her face. She jerked the shower switch to the 'off' position and stepped out of the cubicle.

Maria caught her eye in the mirror of the bathroom cabinet. The sound of the shower had masked her entrance. 'Bad day ahead?' she asked sympathetically, pausing in the act of applying mascara to emphasise eyes the colour of horse chestnuts.

'Probably,' Charlie said, trying to hide her dismay. 'I can't remember the last time I had a good one.' What had she actually said out loud in the shower? How long had Maria been standing there?

Maria's mouth twisted in wry sympathy as she worked moulding paste through her wavy brown hair, a critical look on her face. 'I need a haircut,' she said absently before returning her focus to her partner. 'I'm sorry, Charlie. I wish there was something I could do.'

'So do I.' A churlish response, but it was all Charlie could manage. She forced herself to deal with reality as she rubbed the towel over her hair. The trouble with falling in love – no, one of the *many* troubles with falling in love when you were already in a loving relationship you didn't actually want to end – was that it turned you into a drama queen. It had to be all about you. But the truth was Maria had heard nothing more than the complaint of a disgraced forensic psychiatrist staring an uncertain future in the face. A talented professional who'd been shunted into a dead-end siding for all the wrong reasons. Maria suspected nothing.

Swamped by a fresh wave of guilt, Charlie leaned forward and kissed the nape of Maria's neck, obscurely glad of the shiver she could see running through her lover. 'Pay no attention to me,' she said. 'You know how much I *love* invigilating exams.'

'I know. I'm sorry. You're worth better than that.'

Charlie thought she heard a trace of pity in Maria's voice and hated it. Whether it was real or her paranoia, it didn't much matter. She hated being in a place where pity was possible. 'What's worst about it is that it's so undemanding. It leaves too many brain cells free to fret about all the things I would rather – no, damn it, *should* – be doing.' She finished drying herself and neatly folded her towel over the rail. 'See you downstairs.'

Five minutes later, dressed in crisp white cotton shirt and black jeans, she sat down at the breakfast table she'd laid earlier while Maria was showering, their morning routine still a reassuringly fixed point in Charlie's emotional chaos. Even on the days when she didn't have work, she still made herself get up at the regular time and go through the rituals of the employed life. As usual, Maria was spreading Marmite on granary toast. She gestured with her knife towards a large padded envelope by the bowl where Charlie's two Weetabix sat. 'Postman's been. Still don't know why you gave up cornflakes for those,' she added, pointing at the cereal bars with her knife. 'They look like panty shields for masochists.'

Charlie snorted with surprised laughter. Then guilt kicked in. If Maria could still make her laugh like that, how could she be in love with Lisa? She picked up the envelope. The computer-printed address label revealed nothing, but the Oxford postmark made her stomach lurch. Surely Lisa wouldn't . . .? She was a therapist, for God's sake, she wouldn't drop a grenade on the breakfast table. Would she? How well did Charlie really know her? Panicked, she froze momentarily.

'Anything interesting?' Maria asked, breaking the spell.

'I'm not expecting anything.'

'Better open it, then. Given you don't have X-ray vision.'

'Yeah. My Supergirl days are long behind me.' Charlie contrived to free the flap of the envelope without giving Maria any chance to see the contents. Puzzled, she stared down at a bundle of photocopied sheets. She inched them carefully out of the envelope. They appeared to offer no threat, only bewilderment. 'How bizarre,' Charlie said.

'What is it?'

Charlie thumbed through the pile of papers and frowned. 'Press cuttings. A murder at the Old Bailey.'

'An old case?'

'Still going on, I think. I vaguely noticed a couple of reports already. Those two city slickers who murdered their business partner on his wedding day. At St Scholastika's. That's the only reason it stuck in my mind.'

'You mentioned it. I remember. They drowned him down by the punts or something, didn't they?'

'That's right. Not the done thing in my day.' Charlie spoke absently, her attention on the clippings.

'So who's sent you this? What's it all about?'

Charlie shrugged, her interest pricked. 'Don't know. Not a clue.' She fanned through the papers to see if there was anything to identify the sender.

'Is there no covering letter?'

Charlie checked inside the envelope again. 'Nope. Just the photocopies.' If this was Lisa, it was completely incomprehensible. It didn't fit any notion of therapy or love token that Charlie understood.

'A mystery, then,' Maria said, finishing her toast and standing up to put her dirty crockery in the dishwasher. 'Not exactly worthy of you, but a chance at least to put your investigative skills into practice.'

Charlie made a small dismissive sound. 'Something to mull over while I'm invigilating, anyway.'

Maria leaned over and kissed the top of Charlie's head. 'I'll give it some thought while I'm torturing the patients.'

Charlie winced. 'Don't say that. Not if you ever want to treat me again.'

'What? "Torturing the patients"?'

'No, suggesting that your mind is on something other than drilling teeth. It's too terrifying to contemplate.'

Maria grinned, revealing an appropriately perfect smile. 'Big girl's blouse,' she teased, wiggling her fingers and waggling her hips in farewell as she headed out of the kitchen. Charlie stared bleakly after her until she heard the front door close. Then, with a deep sigh, she put the two Weetabix back in the packet and her bowl into the dishwasher.

'Fuck you, Lisa,' she muttered as she scooped the papers back into the envelope and stalked out of the room.

2

Coming home against the stream of humanity heading for work reminded Magdalene Newsam of her years as a junior doctor. That feeling of dislocation, of living at odds with the rest of the world's timetable, had always buoyed her up at the end of another grinding stint. She might have been so tired that her fingers trembled as she put the key in the door, but at least she was different from the rest of the herd. She'd chosen a path that set her apart.

Thinking about it now, she felt pity for that former Magda. To cling to something so trivial as a marker of her individuality seemed pathetic. But at that point, there had been so many roads not taken in Magda's life that she'd had to grab at whatever she could to convince herself she had some shred of independence.

She couldn't help the smile. Everything was so different now. The reason she was weaving through the head-down pavement crowds heading for the Tube couldn't have been further removed from the old explanation. Not work but delight. Awake half the night not because of a patient in crisis but because she and her lover still found each other as irresistible as they had at the start. Awake half the night and not tired but exhilarated, body weak from love instead of other people's pain.

The surface of her happiness wobbled slightly when she turned into Tavistock Square and confronted the imposing Portland stone façade of the block where she still lived. A three-bedroomed mansion flat in central London, only minutes away from work, was beyond the wildest dreams of her fellow junior registrars. They were resigned either to cramped inadequate accommodation in the heart of the city or marginally less cramped housing in the inconvenient suburbs. But Magda's home was a luxurious haven, a place chosen to provide a comfortable and comforting escape from whatever the outside world threw at her.

Philip had insisted on it. Nothing less would do for his Magda. They could afford it, he'd insisted. 'Well, you can,' she'd said, barely allowing herself to acknowledge that accepting this as their home implied that she also accepted her dependence. And so they'd viewed a selection of flats that had made Magda feel as if she was playing house. The one they'd ended up with had felt least like a fantasy to her. Its traditional features were more of a match for the rambling North Oxford Victorian house she'd grown up in. The aggressive modernism of the others had felt too alien. It was impossible to imagine inhabiting somewhere that looked so like a magazine feature.

Accustoming herself to living here had turned into something very different from Magda's first imaginings.

12

Philip had barely had time to learn the darkling route from bed to bathroom before he'd been killed. The breakfast conversations and evening entertainments Magda had pictured never had the chance to become habit. That she occasionally allowed herself to admit that this was almost a relief provoked shame and guilt that triggered a dark flush across her cheekbones. Transgression, it seemed, was not something she could wholeheartedly embrace yet.

She was trying, though. If she was honest, she liked coming home to her flat after a night with Jay. There was something a little sleazy about rolling out of bed and putting on yesterday's clothes, something sluttish about crossing central London unwashed on the Tube, knowing she smelled musky and salty. They'd agreed long before the trial that they couldn't start living together until that was all done and dusted. Jay had pointed out that they didn't want anything to muddy the waters of other people's guilt. There was no suggestion that they should try to hide their relationship. Just a sensible acknowledgement that there was no need to trumpet it from the rooftops just yet.

So in the mornings, Magda came home alone. Dirty clothes in the laundry basket, dirty body in the power shower. Coffee, orange juice, crumpets from freezer to toaster then a skim of peanut butter. Another demure outfit for court. And another day of missing Jay and wishing she was by her side.

It wasn't that she had to brave the oppressive grandeur of the Old Bailey alone. Her three siblings had worked out a rota which meant one of them was with her for at least part of every day of the trial. Yesterday it had been Patrick, dark and brooding, clearly away from his City desk out of wearisome obligation to the big sister who had always taken care of him. Today it would be Catherine, the baby of the family, abandoning her graduate anthropological studies to be at Magda's side. 'At least Wheelie will be pleased to see me,' Magda told her hazy reflection in the bathroom mirror. And there was no denying that Catherine's perpetual lightness of spirit would carry her through the day. Too much isolation made Magda uneasy. Growing up as the oldest of four children close in age, then student flats, then hospital life had conditioned her to company. Among the many reasons she had for being grateful to Jay, rescuing her from loneliness had been one of the most powerful.

Magda swept her tawny hair into a neat arrangement, her movements expert and automatic. She stared at herself judiciously, bemused that she still looked like the same old Magda. Same open expression, same direct stare, same straight line of the lips. Amazing, really.

A stray tendril of hair sprang free from its pins and curled over her forehead. She remembered a rhyme from childhood, one that had always made Catherine giggle.

There was a little girl
Who had a little curl
Right in the middle of her forehead.
And when she was good
She was very, very good.
But when she was bad, she was horrid.

For as long as she could remember, Magda Newsam had been very, very good indeed.

And now she wasn't.

3

Subject: Ruby Tuesday
Date: 23 March 2010 09:07:29 GMT
From: cflint@mancit.ac.uk
To: lisak@arbiter.com

Good morning. The sun is shining here. A blurt of blue irises that wasn't there yesterday hit me when I opened the front door this morning. Almost dispelled the gloomy prospect of watching over 120 Legal Practice students to make sure they're not cheating in their conveyancing exam. But not quite. Every crappy little job I have to swallow right now reminds me of what I should be doing. What I'm trained to do. What I'm best at.

Strange package at the breakfast table this a.m. with an Oxford postmark and no covering letter. Is this your idea of fun? If so, you're going to have to explain the joke. Your Scorpio sting in the tail, I don't always get it.

Wish I was in Oxford; we could walk from Folly
Bridge to Iffley and say the things we don't write down.
I might even sing to you.
    Love, Charlie
    Sent from my iPhone

Subject: Re: Ruby Tuesday
Date: 23 March 2010 09:43:13 GMT
From: lisak@arbiter.com
To: cflint@mancit.ac.uk

Hi, Charlie
<The sun shines here> but sadly not here, so even if
you were in Oxford, we'd have to find something more
appealing than a damp river walk. I don't imagine we'd
find that too hard, though. You always manage to cheer
me up, even on the grey days.
    <a blurt of blue irises> poetry like that, maybe you
should be petitioning the Creative Writing department
for work. All those novels about serial killers and
profiling – you've got the inside track, you could teach
them how to get it right. Poor you. Poets shouldn't have
to invigilate exams!
    <strange package> is, sadly, nothing to do with me.
You must have another secret admirer here among
the scheming spires. So what did the package
contain?
    Nothing much to report here. This morning, I am
supposedly working on The Programme. When I first
envisioned 'I'm Not OK, You're Not OK; Negotiating

16

Vulnerability' I had no idea it would come to consume my life.

Thinking of you. Wishing we could run away and play.

LKx

Subject: It's a mystery
Date: 23 March 2010 13:07:52 GMT
From: cflint@mancit.ac.uk
To: lisak@arbiter.com

Another secret admirer? I don't think so. :-} One would be more than enough anyway, as long as it was the right one.

If not from you, then from whom? The only other people I 'know' in Oxford are the few remaining dons at St Scholastika's who taught me, and I can't think why any of them would be sending me a package of newspaper clippings about a current murder trial. Unless someone mistakenly thinks it might interest me professionally because of the Schollie's connection? If so, then it's someone who isn't very current with my present status as the pariah of the clinical psychiatry world.

I've scanned in a couple of the articles for your edification. Just so you know what I'm talking about.

Hope the seminar programme is going well. I don't know where you find the energy. If I end up teaching students how to do what I used to do best, I will send them all on one of your weekend courses to teach them to develop empathy.

Sorry about the weather.

Love, Charlie

From the *Mail*

THE BATTERED BRIDEGROOM

Two city whiz kids callously murdered their business partner on his wedding day then enjoyed a night of wild sex together, the Old Bailey heard yesterday.

The evil pair smashed Philip Carling's skull then left him to drown just yards away from the Oxford college garden party celebrating his wedding, the court was told.

Shocked wedding guests taking a romantic stroll by the river found the bridegroom's body floating by the landing stage where the college punts were moored, blood from his shattered skull staining the water.

Paul Barker, 35, and Joanna Sanderson, 34, are charged with murder and fraud. They owned a specialist printing firm in partnership with their victim, which gave them unique access to sensitive City information. Carling, 36, had allegedly threatened to expose Barker and Sanderson as devious fraudsters who were lining their pockets by insider trading.

The prosecution alleges that the two conspirators silenced him within hours of his marriage last July then spent the night in an orgy of noisy sex.

Carling's widow, Magdalene, 28, was in court yesterday as Jonah Pollitt QC outlined the details of the double-crossing conspiracy that her husband's partners carried out at the society wedding in the grounds of St Scholastika's College, Oxford.

While the friends and family of the happy couple celebrated with champagne and smoked salmon, the cold-hearted pair were murdering the groom. Carling went missing shortly before he and his wife were due to leave for their Caribbean honeymoon.

The court heard how Barker and Sanderson had been introduced to each other by Carling three years ago. They soon became lovers. A year later, Sanderson quit her job as a merchant banker to join Carling and Barker's company as sales and marketing director.

According to the prosecution, the scams that may have cheated genuine investors of hundreds of thousands of pounds began soon afterwards, using contacts of Sanderson's to set up the money-grabbing trades in stocks and shares. Philip Carling was kept in the dark. Discovering the truth cost him his life.

The trial continues.

From the *Guardian*

INSIDER TRADING REVEALED

Two directors of a printing company specialising in sensitive documents relating to city take-overs used their inside knowledge to perpetrate a series of frauds that netted them hundreds of thousands of pounds without the knowledge of their business partner, a court heard yesterday.

Paul Barker, 35, and Joanna Sanderson, 34, stand trial at the Old Bailey charged with fraud and the murder of their partner Philip Carling, who was threatening to expose them to financial watchdogs and the police. Carling, 36, was killed within hours of his marriage, with the reception in full swing only yards away.

Yesterday, giving evidence for the prosecution, Detective Inspector Jane Morrison of the Serious Fraud Office told the court that the conspiracy had come to light as the result of information received from the widow of the murdered man.

Magdalene Carling and a friend had been dealing with the dead man's personal effects following his tragic death when a computer memory stick came to light which contained details of Barker and Sanderson's frauds, along with draft letters to the DTI and the police outlining the insider trading and Mr Carling's desire to clear his name even at the cost of implicating his partners.

DI Morrison said, 'The letters expressed his shock at discovering what his partners had been doing. They referred to his wedding and said he wanted to start married life with a clean slate. As far as we can discover, he was killed before the letters could be sent as part of a cover-up by Barker and Sanderson.'

For the defence, Mr Ian Cordier, QC, asked if it were possible that Mr Carling could have been ignorant of so large-scale a fraud in so small a firm where he was also a partner.

DI Morrison said that given the way responsibility was

structured following the arrival of Ms Sanderson at the firm, it was very unlikely that Mr Carling would have uncovered what was going on in the normal run of business. It had not been a particularly clever or complex scheme, she added, but it was clear that Mr Carling was not involved in that side of the business.

The case continues.

From the *Mirror*

CALLOUS KILLERS MADE LOVE FOR HOURS

Two company directors accused of murdering their business partner on his wedding day spent the night after his death in a noisy sex romp, the Old Bailey heard yesterday.

Steven Farnham, a fellow guest at the fatal wedding of Philip and Magdalene Carling, stayed in a hotel room next door to the one occupied by the alleged killers, Paul Barker, 35, and 34-year-old Joanna Sanderson.

He said, 'There was a connecting door between the rooms, so the soundproofing wasn't very good. Paul and Joanna were obviously having sex, very loudly and over a period of a couple of hours.

'I was disgusted. Philip had been brutally murdered only a few hours before. Paul and Joanna weren't just his business partners. They were supposed to be his best friends. But they didn't seem to be grieving at all.'

Asked by the defence if sex were not a common reaffirmation of life after a death has occurred, Mr Farnham replied, 'I'm a stockbroker, not a psychologist. All I can say is that I was devastated by Philip's death. The last thing I felt like was having sex. And they were supposed to be really close to Phil, so I don't see how they could act as if everything was normal and nothing had happened.'

The prosecution alleges that Sanderson and Barker killed their business partner during his wedding at St Scholastika's College, Oxford, to prevent him exposing their illegal insider trading activities which netted them a fortune.

The trial continues.

Subject: Re: It's a mystery
Date: 23 March 2010 14:46:33 GMT
From: lisak@arbiter.com
To: cflint@mancit.ac.uk

Hi, Charlie
Fascinating stuff. Makes me glad I've given up newspapers! It must be pretty bewildering for you, though, getting all this strangeness in the post. What an interesting life you lead. I suspect you'd find me very dull by comparison.
    <If not from you, then from whom?>
    I can't help thinking you're looking at this through the wrong end of the telescope. If the package came from someone who was interested in you professionally, wouldn't it have gone to the university? I think this is something that connects to you personally. Which make me think it must be something to do with your old college. Anyone connected to Schollie's could get hold

of your home address through the alumnae office, couldn't they?

One of the things I've learned from NV is that hardly any of us has mastered the art of asking the right question. Perhaps you should consider what your correspondent has failed to send you? I always like the answer that's not there . . .

I have three one-to-one NV clients this afternoon. My colleagues tell me I should throttle back on the f2f stuff now the programme is doing so well, but I don't know. I still like the feeling that comes with making a successful intervention in someone's life. You understand that, I know, even if they're not letting you do it right now.

Till tomorrow.

LKx

4

My mother disappeared when I was sixteen. It was the best thing that could have happened to me.

When I say that out loud, people look at me out of the corners of their eyes, as if I've transgressed some fundamental taboo. But it's the truth. I'm not hiding some complicated grief reaction.

My mother disappeared when I was sixteen. The guards had walked away from the prison leaving the door unlocked. And I emerged blinking into the sunlight.

Jay Stewart leaned back and read her words, head cocked critically to the side. It did exactly what it needed to do, she thought. Arresting and intriguing. Pick it off the three-for-two table, read that intro and you couldn't not want to carry on. That was the secret of getting the punters to part with their money. Simple to understand, hard to do. But she'd done it once already. She could do it again.

When she'd decided to write her first book, Jay had done what she always did. Research, research, research. That was the key to any successful endeavour. Check out the market. Consider the opposition. Acknowledge the potential pitfalls. Then go for it. *Preparation is never procrastination.* That was one of her key PowerPoint presentation slides. She'd always been proud to say she'd never plunged headlong into anything.

That was just one of the things that wasn't true any more.

Not that she was about to admit so fundamental a change to anyone except herself. When her literary agent had taken her to lunch the week before so he could reveal that her publisher was dangling a new contract before them, Jay had made a point of appearing as cautious and noncommittal as ever. 'I thought the bottom had dropped out of the misery memoir business with the market crash,' she'd said when Jasper had raised the subject halfway through their finicky starters of scallops with mango salsa and pea shoots. As she waited for Jasper to marshal his reply, Jay stared at the food and wondered when exactly it had ceased to be possible to find simple well-cooked dishes in expensive restaurants.

'And so it has.' Jasper beamed at her as though he were the teacher and Jay the favourite pupil. 'That's why they want something fresh from you. Triumph over adversity, that's what they're interested in. And you, my dear, are well set to be the poster girl for triumph over adversity.'

He had a point. Jay couldn't deny that. 'Hmm,' she said, dissecting a scallop and putting a delicate forkful in her mouth. An excuse not to say more till she had heard more.

'Your story's an inspiration,' Jasper persisted, his lean and wary face uncharacteristically kindly. 'And it's aspirational. The readers can relate to you because you weren't born with a silver spoon in your mouth.'

Jay swallowed, raised an eyebrow and smiled. 'The only silver spoons around when I was a baby were those cute little coke spoons my mother's friends wore on chains round their necks. Not many of my readers came from that universe either.'

Jasper gave a tight professional smile. 'Probably not, no. But your publisher's market research indicates that readers do feel close to you. They feel they could be you, if things had just been a little bit different.'

No chance. Not in a million quantum universes. 'Tangents,' Jay said, her attention on her plate. 'The facts of my life touch the edges of their lives in enough places for them to feel a shivery sort of connection. I see how that worked with the misery memoir. The readers can snuggle under their duvet, all smug and cosy because they escaped my descent into the procession of hells my mother dragged me through in the first sixteen years of my life.' She drew her breath in sharply, hearing it whistle through her teeth. 'But triumph over adversity? Isn't that a bit like rubbing their noses in it?'

Jasper frowned. 'I'm not sure I see what you mean.' Somehow, he'd managed to clean his plate with predatory efficiency while Jay was still barely a third of the way through her food. It was one of the reasons Jay had chosen Jasper as her agent when she'd first decided to write her misery memoir. She liked the people with appetite to be ranged on her side.

'*Unrepentant* gave them the chance to feel sorry for me. To be glad that they had escaped what I went through. But an account of how I triumphed at Oxford, set up a successful dotcom company, sold out before the bubble burst then went on to found a niche publishing business while knocking out a bestselling misery memoir . . . Well, it seems to me that all I'm doing is providing them with reasons to hate me. And that's not a recipe for selling books, Jasper.'

'You'd be surprised,' Jasper said, his voice dry as the Chablis they were drinking. 'People who know about these things tell me the punters love to read about people like them who have made it.'

Jay shook her head. 'What they love reading about is vacuous celebrity. Talentless show-offs who will do anything for their moment in *OK* magazine. Idiots who think appearing on *The X-Factor* is the pinnacle of achievement. *That's* people like them. I am not people like them.'

'You do a good job of pretending.'

'Only up to a point. Then there's the lesbian thing. By ending the book where I did, I managed to keep my adolescent yearnings more or less off-stage. But writing about Oxford and after – it's hard to see how I can avoid it.'

Jasper shrugged. 'The world's moved on, darling. Lesbians are cool now. Think Sandi Toksvig, Sam Ronson, Maggi Hambling, Sarah Waters.'

'You still wouldn't want your daughter to marry one.' She finished her appetiser and placed her cutlery neatly together on the plate. 'At best, they'll think I'm a lucky bastard.'

'They certainly will if they find out the size of the

advance,' he said, his eyes narrowing in pleasure. 'Half as much again what we got for *Unrepentant*. Which is terrific in a flat market.'

A waiter whose designer suit had patently cost more than Jay's outfit whisked their plates away. 'Do you think they only hire staff who fit the suits?' she said absently as she watched him swagger back to the kitchen.

Jasper ignored the question and stuck heroically to his pitch. 'But you're a TV face now too. Ever since they started inviting you as a special guest investor on *White Knight*, you're on the radar.'

Jay scowled like a disgruntled teenager. 'And that's the last time I let you talk me into going against my better judgement. Bloody *White Knight*. I can't buy a packet of spaghetti in the supermarket without someone trying to pitch me their brilliant business idea.'

'Stop pretending to be a curmudgeon. You love the attention.'

'I *am* a curmudgeon.' Jay paused while artfully arranged slices of pink lamb surrounded by neat piles of Puy lentils interspersed with perfectly carved miniature root vegetables, all set on massive porcelain plates, appeared in front of them. 'I meant what I said the other day. I really don't want to do any more *White Knight*.'

She could see Jasper biting back his frustration. 'Fine,' he said, his smile thin and his voice tight. 'I think you're crazy, but fine. So why don't you do something instead that gives me a legitimate excuse to keep everyone at arm's length? "Sorry, she's writing. She's got a deadline." Plus you know you enjoyed the process of writing *Unrepentant*. And you also discovered you have a talent for writing memoir.'

28

Jay couldn't deny that she liked the idea of Jasper telling the world to go away. Bar the door and keep the barbarians out while she gorged on love. She knew enough about the arc of relationships to understand that the rush of emotional and sexual intensity between her and Magda would pass soon enough. You couldn't postpone the first flush till you could create a window in the diary. It came and went on its own timetable. And this had come so instantly, so unexpectedly, so unpredictably it was hard not to fear it might fade just as fast, though it was hard to imagine how it could fade when Magda's beauty made her heart flip every time she cast eyes on her. Having an excuse to hide from the world so she could bind Magda closer to her only had an upside. Never mind that in the long run the book wouldn't make her any friends. She had enough of those.

She sighed. 'Oh, all right, then,' she said, more grumbling than gracious.

Jasper's grin was naked delight. 'You're not going to regret this.'

'For your sake, I hope not. You know how bad things happen to people who cross me.' There was a moment of chill, then Jay smiled. 'Only joking, Jasper,' she said.

His smile was a shaky echo of hers.

5

Before they met, Charlie Flint had expected to despise and dislike Lisa Kent. Even though Charlie had been the one flying under false colours that first time, she'd been convinced she was the one on the moral high ground.

Her passion for her profession meant she was constantly alive to opportunities to extend her knowledge and experience. So when it became clear that there was a new trend in self-help programmes that tiptoed close to cult territory, she wanted to check the phenomenon out for herself. The one she'd chosen from the three or four she'd been aware of had been Lisa Kent's 'I'm Not OK, You're Not OK: Negotiating Vulnerability'. NV to its acolytes; groups always had to establish private language that set out the terms of their ownership.

Charlie had signed up under a false name for a weekend seminar. Her intent had been to use the experience as the basis for an incisive, devastating account of the whole phenomenon both for peer-reviewed academic publication and possibly for a three-page spread in the *Guardian*'s G2 section.

The fifty-odd audience members were pretty much what Charlie had expected – mostly mid-twenties to late thirties, undistinguished by individual style, nearly all bearing the taint of defeat tempered only by an anxious hope that this weekend would somehow transform their lives. What had taken her aback was the grudging realisation that Lisa Kent was neither shaman nor charlatan. What she was peddling was mostly sensible and practical. Mainstream therapeutic stuff. What made the seminar cult-like was Lisa's charisma. When she spoke, she held the room in her hands. They loved her. And Charlie was shocked by the realisation that she wasn't so different from the rest of them. Her training and experience hadn't immunised her to Lisa's charm.

But still, there might yet have been no harm done. What happened in the afternoon coffee break changed that. Charlie had been leaning against a wall, drinking tea and trying to look downtrodden enough to belong when Lisa made her way through the crowd and stopped in front of her. Lisa had peered at her name badge and given a wry smile. 'I'd appreciate a little chat, Ms . . . Browning,' she'd said, hanging enough scepticism on the name to make sure Charlie understood this shouldn't be taken as flattery.

Charlie followed Lisa into a small room off the main hall. Low modular chairs lined the walls and a water cooler hummed in one corner. There was no clue to its function in the arrangement. Charlie sat down without waiting to be asked, crossing one leg over the other, wondering what was coming. Lisa leaned against the closed door, still with the twisted smile in place. Her eyes, Charlie thought, were hard to avoid. A greenish blue tractor beam that had transfixed a room full of people and now made her feel pinned down. 'This is an amazing experience,' she said, trying to imitate the enthusiasm she'd heard at lunch.

'Dr Charlotte Flint,' Lisa said. 'Charlie to your friends, I believe. First degree in Psychology, Philosophy and Physiology from St Scholastika's College, Oxford. Masters in Clinical Psychology and Psychopathology at Sussex. Qualified as a psychiatrist in Manchester, where you are now a senior lecturer in Clinical Psychology and Psychological Profiling. Home Office-accredited to work with the police as a profiler. How am I doing?'

'You missed out my campfire badge from the Guides. How did you spot me?'

Lisa pushed off from the door and got herself some water, turning her back on Charlie. 'I recognised you.' She turned back, shaking her head gently. 'You spoke very eloquently at the Forensic Science Society about the reasons for the choices you made in the Bill Hopton case.'

Bill Hopton. The man who had walked free thanks to Charlie's reluctant conclusion in the witness box that he hadn't murdered Gemma Summerville. The man who had walked free to murder four other women. Just mentioning his name was a gauntlet of sorts. The Hopton case had catapulted Charlie into the public eye. It hadn't done her many favours at the time. And now it appeared to have destroyed her career. But back then, that afternoon in

Oxford facing Lisa Kent, it was still a bomb waiting to go off, although it remained the one case everyone connected to law enforcement wanted to talk about with her. Deliberately, Charlie said, 'I didn't know you're a member of the FSS.'

Lisa sipped her drink, studying Charlie over the rim of the white plastic cup, dark eyebrows raised in amused arcs. 'I'm not. But I do have friends who are familiar with my interest in the way people's minds work. I thought it was you this morning, but I made some checks at lunchtime to be certain.'

'It's a free country.'

Lisa laughed. 'Don't be ridiculous. You're here to do a demolition job. You think I'm exploiting gullibility and weakness for profit. Though quite how it ties in with offender profiling, I'm not sure.'

Bang to rights, Charlie thought. 'I did think that. I don't now. As to the professional relevance – manipulation of others is how a lot of serial offenders get away with things for so long.' She got up and moved towards the door. 'It's been an interesting day. But I think it's probably best if I leave.'

'I should be angry with you, Dr Flint. But for some reason I'm not. You really don't have to go.' The words were innocuous enough; the tone was not.

Charlie shook her head. 'I think it's best if I do. I don't want to put you off your stride.'

'You're probably right. Knowing that you know that I know who you are would alter the dynamic in the room.' Lisa dug a card out of the pocket of her loose trousers. 'I seem to have confounded your expectations, which means this has been a waste of your time.' She smiled. 'Let me make it up to you sometime. I really do think we might have some interesting things to share. Here's my card. Let's stay in touch.'

As she walked back to her hotel room, Charlie tried to unravel the nuances in Lisa's voice, but she could never be quite sure that what she thought she'd heard had really been there. Had Lisa been flirting? Was it some kind of professional challenge? Or did she simply enjoy the cat-and-mouse game? Whatever it was, Charlie was snagged on the hook of Lisa's charm.

Puzzling over the exact meaning of Lisa's words had become a familiar experience for Charlie. Since that first encounter the ether had hummed with their electronic interchanges, the professional usually making way for the personal exchanges of two people building a connection.

In Charlie's experience, clinical psychiatrists fell into two groups. The ones who deliberately chose never to question anything about themselves and the ones who subjected every aspect of their lives to the same scrutiny they applied to their patients. Charlie often wished she was not doomed to membership of the 'analyse this' crew. But it went some way to explaining her fascination with Lisa. The more inscrutable the woman's communications, the more Charlie yearned to unpick their meaning. What she was clear about was that they were flirting. Flirting with each other, flirting with ideas, flirting with danger.

Perhaps you should consider what your correspondent has failed to send you? I always like the answer that's not there . . . What exactly did Lisa mean by that, Charlie wondered, staring at her computer screen. Was she simply referring to the newspaper cuttings, or was this another instance of oblique suggestiveness? The way Lisa made her feel was like a family of termites burrowing through the solid foundation of her relationship with Maria. Charlie knew she had no business playing this risky game, but every time she resolved to leave it alone, there would be a text or an email demanding her attention and requiring a response. She was as hopeless as some of her patients. Unable to resist what she knew was bad for her. She couldn't even be sure the woman was a lesbian. Flirtation and obliquity might just be her natural mode. So little of their communication had been face to face and so much of it had been a teasing joust. Maybe Charlie was completely off the mark. Really, for all she knew, Lisa could be straight. This whole mess could be nothing more than pitiful wishful thinking. With a despairing moan, Charlie turned back to the contents of the envelope.

Clearly, the clippings were only a selection of what had been published in the media. Could it be that the answer lay in the missing stories? Impatiently, she called up Google News and typed in the name of the victim. In a fraction of a second, the search turned up a list of everything the media had produced about the murder of Philip Carling. There were dozens of them, even allowing for Google's winnowing-out of similar stories.

There were other, more urgent, calls on Charlie's time. Reviving her dying career, for one. But sometimes distraction was irresistible. Charlie called up the first story, determined to work through them methodically. The first revelation came in the second story she accessed, a *Daily Telegraph* article that referred to Dr Magda Newsam.

Shocked, Charlie realised that the widowed bride was no stranger to her. The name Magdalene Carling had meant nothing. But the alternate identity jolted Charlie from academic enthusiasm to dismay. She was appalled that she had somehow failed to register that the woman at the heart of this tragedy was someone she had once known. Suddenly, things began to make sense.

'Poor kid,' she said softly, pity in her voice. The realisation of Magda's place in the murder trial made one thing incontrovertible. Whoever had sent the mysterious package had almost certainly been part of college life all those years ago when Charlie had been an undergraduate, a pupil of Magda's mother Corinna and an occasional babysitter of her children. Was it Corinna Newsam herself, or had someone else sent the photocopies? And still the question remained: why?

Methodical as ever, Charlie continued through the archive material. She had almost come to the end when a photograph downloaded to her screen, appearing one slice at a time from the top down. The woman it revealed had the kind of beauty that made people stare. Even a snatched newspaper shot left no room for doubt on that score. Dark blonde hair and apparently perfect skin, the regular features of a fashion model, a mouth whose fullness hinted at sensuality. 'Wow,' Charlie said, admiring the shapely figure and undeniably good legs that gradually appeared.

The caption revealed that this stunning woman in the foreground of the photograph was Philip Carling's widow Magdalene. 'Look how you turned out, Maggot,' she said, amazed at this trick of the genes. But as she studied the wider picture, Charlie realised she needed no caption to recognise the woman at Magda's elbow. Age had not withered Jay Macallan Stewart's fine-boned beauty, nor custom staled her air of dashing danger.

Although it created more questions than it answered, Charlie felt sure she had solved the basic problem of the source of the cuttings. 'If my daughter was hanging out with Jay Stewart, I'd be doing something about it,' she said. And with a few keystrokes, she was in her email program.

Subject: More Questions Than Answers
Date: 23 March 2010 15:35:26 GMT
From: cflint@mancit.ac.uk
To: lisak@arbiter.com

I followed your advice. It was obvious I hadn't been sent all the press coverage, so I Googled news to see if I could figure out what was missing. Lo and behold, I discovered almost instantly that none of the versions I had been sent named the widow appropriately. Her real identity is not <Mrs Magdalene Carling>, it's <Dr Magda Newsam>. AKA Maggot, or at least it used to be when she was 10 and I was 21 and used to babysit her and her siblings. She's the eldest daughter of Corinna Newsam, the junior philosophy fellow at Schollie's who taught me and regularly used me as a babysitter until my final-year obsession with getting a decent degree and still managing to have some fun put a stop to it. Anyway, we've stayed in Christmas card touch since, though not so close that she mentioned Magda's involvement in this case.

Reading on, I came across a photo of Magda – who has grown into a drop-dead gorgeous beauty in the Princess Diana mould. And standing behind her was somebody else I recognised. She used to be plain Jay Stewart but now the world knows her as Jay Macallan Stewart. Dotcom millionaire and bestselling misery memoir author. Now she's the boss of 24/7, the web-based personalised travel guides. You might have seen her on *White Knight*, she appears sometimes in the guest investor slot. She was a couple of years behind me at Schollie's, but her notoriety was sufficient to overcome that handicap. Even among the dykes of Brighton, the stories about Jay Stewart galloped along the grapevine.

I remember her as ruthlessly ambitious, one of those working-class heroes who are determined to exploit every opportunity to the hilt and don't care whose faces they trample on in the scramble to the top of the heap. She was elected JCR president the year after I went down. Only after she'd secured the position did she come out, very spectacularly and stylishly, as the lover of a senior commissioning editor on one of the glossy fashion mags. Some of the college fellows wanted to throw her out, but she was always very careful never actually to break the rules.

So, I figure that if I was Corinna Newsam, and Jay Stewart was hanging round my daughter, I'd be looking to dig some dirt that could consign Stewart to the history bin. But she wouldn't want to approach me directly in case my lesbian solidarity was stronger than a very old loyalty to her and Maggot.

Now, having worked it all out, I'm not sure what to do. Do I want to get involved? Do I care? And doesn't lesbian solidarity count for something? All suggestions gratefully received.

Hope your clients didn't drive you to drink.

Love, Charlie

Subject: Re: More Questions Than Answers
Date: 23 March 2010 19:57:32 GMT
From: lisak@arbiter.com
To: cflint@mancit.ac.uk

Hi, Charlie,

If you were a dog, you'd be a Lakeland terrier, all dogged persistence, solidly reliable and wearing a grin that could melt an iceberg. Your discoveries are fascinating. Whatever the subtext here is, you're right, it's clear that it has something to do with Magda Newsam and Jay Stewart, and that the linkage to you is via Schollie's.

Your Corinna seems remarkably unsure of you, considering how well she appears once to have known you. In her shoes, I would have turned up on your doorstep and told you I needed you. You'd never have refused. Would you?

On the other hand, it may simply be that because she does know you, and understands how impossible you would find it to say no to her, she's asking for your help in the only way she can imagine that would allow you the possibility of refusal.

39

Or is it a test? Along the lines of, if you're not smart enough to work this out, you are no use to me.

Which is it, do you think?

<all suggestions gratefully received> I know you, Charlie. You need answers. You defined your options with that first decision to investigate the clippings; whether you acknowledged it or not, it tugged at your deep-seated affection for your old college. Now, it seems to me that you will not be able to rest until you have confronted Corinna and discovered what she wants from you.

Look on the bright side. Maybe you can wangle a trip to Oxford and we can spend some time together. It would be good to have some face time that isn't at a conference, don't you think?

Clients drove me to a delicious claret. If you were here, I would take the opportunity to wean you off those New World heavyweights you're so wedded to. I promise you'd enjoy the journey.

LKx

No doubt about that, thought Charlie. Lisa had chased thoughts of Magda and Corinna from her head with the suggestion of turning up on her doorstep and demanding her help. That was enough to set Charlie's thoughts flickering over the possibilities, both delicious and dreadful. The thought of Lisa and Maria face to face made her want to bury her face in her hands and weep with the impossibility of it all. She couldn't believe Lisa was unconscious of the effect her words would have; after all, the woman spent her days dealing with the innermost recesses of other people's minds.

'Grow up,' Charlie muttered. She forced herself to stop indulging in adolescent fantasies and to focus on the practical content of the message. Lisa clearly understood her well enough to know she could no more leave the cuttings alone than she could the charged communications between them. Corinna did seem the obvious candidate. There seemed no option other than to call her and settle the matter.

Charlie sighed. Finally she'd managed to find something even more daunting than the General Medical Council. Somehow, she didn't think it was going to be any easier to deal with.

6

'You can't argue with that,' Catherine Newsam said, ushering her sister out of the courtroom and down a narrow side passage towards the room the Crown Prosecution solicitor had arranged for them. 'The judge nailed it. I don't see how anybody could have any doubt that Barker and Sanderson did it.' She neatly interposed her body between her sister and a woman she'd seen on the press benches. 'Fuck off,' Catherine said sweetly over her shoulder as she followed Magda inside the room marked 'Private'. Being the youngest of the Newsam children had granted Catherine licence that sometimes made her siblings wince.

Two weeks since her first retreat there, and still Magda found herself surprised by the lack of comfort. Four not-quite-matching chairs with the tweedy upholstery worn smooth in patches, a table that was too large for the space and a metal bin that hadn't been emptied since they'd first dumped their used coffee cups in it. Someone had tried to lift the room's spirits by taping a couple of Spanish holiday posters to the wall, but the brilliant blue of the sky only made the grubby walls more dispiriting. But none of that mattered to Magda. What she cared about was having a refuge from the stares and whispers. 'You really think so? I don't know, Wheelie. Just because we want it to be that way doesn't mean you're right,' she said, tucking one leg beneath her as she perched on a chair.

Catherine nodded vehemently. She looked like a child's doll with her curly blonde hair, round face, bright blue eyes and pink cheeks. There was no physical resemblance between the sisters. Where Magda was tall, slender and effortlessly graceful, Catherine was average in every respect. What made her memorable was not her looks but her irrepressible bounce, currently pressed into service in defence of her big sister. Others might have resented Magda's beauty, but Catherine was proud of her sister and delighted that, for once, she could offer Magda the support and help that had always been at her own back. 'Trust me, Magda,' she said, adamant in her confidence. 'Especially after the way the prosecuting barrister rubbished the defence. They've had their last taste of freedom for a while.' She still gripped the door handle. 'Do you need something to eat? Or drink? Coffee? Muffins?'

It was amazing how often Catherine's eagerness to please manifested itself in food and drink. 'In spite of your conviction that it's all open and shut, I suspect the jury will be out long enough for you to do a commando coffee raid.'

Catherine checked the pocket of her jeans for change. 'I'll be back,' she said in a passable Terminator impersonation.

Magda couldn't help smiling, and Catherine's eyes lit up with gratification as she headed out the door.

For the first time since she'd arrived at court that morning, no other eyes were on Magda. The absence of attention was as tangible as the lifting of a physical weight. Being on show was exhausting. She wondered how Jay coped with being the focus of so much attention. Thanks to her appearances on *White Knight*, she was often recognised in the most unlikely of situations, stripping her of her privacy. 'I was so naïve about it,' she'd once said ruefully to Magda. 'I never appreciated how people assume possession of you simply because you appear on their TV screens.'

Magda wished they were together now; she never minded Jay's admiring scrutiny. But if Jay were here, the attention from the press and the public gallery would be even more oppressive. The attitude of the media would shift dramatically. From being the object of sympathy she'd become the subject of lurid speculation and diary-column gossip. Jay was right. They needed to avoid their relationship becoming public knowledge till the trial had slipped out of people's immediate consciousness. The one time they'd been photographed together, after Philip's memorial service, Jay had managed to put out the potential fire, making sure she was described as an old friend of the family. Having been taught by Corinna had turned out to be useful after all.

'We need to keep our private life private for now. You don't want them thinking of you as the merry widow,' Jay had said. 'Even though we haven't done anything wrong, there are plenty of people who would be only too ready to insinuate the opposite.'

She was right. Nothing they had done had been wrong. Quite the opposite. The more evidence Magda had heard in the courtroom, the more she understood how right Jay had been. If they hadn't done what needed to be done, justice would never have been served. But now Paul and Joanna were going to jail, where they deserved to be. And she was proud of the part she'd played in that process.

Magda clung tightly to that feeling of pride. She didn't have many unmixed feelings about Philip's death. It had been a terrible blow, no denying that. To lose your husband to sudden violent death on your wedding day was never going to be less than shattering. Even if you'd been tamping down your doubts about the marriage for weeks. But if it hadn't happened the way it did, she and Jay might never have found each other again. And that was a notion that filled Magda with horror. She hated herself for the thought, but in her heart she knew that losing Philip to gain Jay was a trade she'd settle for all over again. It shamed and appalled her in equal measure that she could even let such a thought cross her mind. Harbouring ideas like that made her cradle Catholic guilt kick in and left her feeling that her present happiness was not only undeserved but on the brink of being snatched from her.

Catherine shouldered the door open, a cardboard cup of latte in each hand, saving Magda from the darkness of her thoughts. 'That was quick,' Magda said.

Catherine grinned. 'I told you tipping the coffee-stall girl on day one would pay dividends. I don't even have to queue any more.' She passed a coffee over and perched on a chair, tucking one leg under her. 'I bet you're relieved it's nearly over.'

'Yeah.' Magda sighed. 'I'm just hoping that I'll feel some sense of closure.' She shrugged. 'A way to draw a line and move on.'

'Isn't that what Jay's about?' Catherine said. Magda searched for hostility in her tone and, finding none, decided her sister was only curious.

'Jay feels like a parallel universe,' Magda said. 'Not connected to my life with Philip at all.'

'But she is,' Catherine said. 'I mean, that's when you ran into her again. The day of the wedding.'

Her words sent an electric jolt through Magda's chest. 'No,' she said. 'It was after that. Remember? We met at a dinner party.'

Catherine looked puzzled. 'But she was there. At St Scholastika's. On your wedding day. I saw her.'

Magda gave a little laugh that sounded artificial to her. 'Well, she was there, it's true. She was speaking at a conference in college. But she wasn't at the wedding. I never saw her. I never even knew she'd been there till ages afterwards. It didn't come up.'

Catherine frowned. 'Oh. OK. I knew you didn't get together till later but I guess I just sort of assumed that you'd run into her. When I saw her, she was coming out of Magnusson Hall. Since we were using the loos there, and Mummy's office, I thought you must have seen her or something.' She gave Magda a tentative smile. Her big sister might have been protective of her, but when she thought Catherine needed slapping down, Magda had never held back.

But Magda had no intention of making an issue out of this particular conversation. 'Bloody social scientists,

46

always leaping to conclusions,' she teased. It was familiar territory, the hard scientists in the family grousing that the others had it easy, coming up with theories without the inconvenience of having to prove them empirically.

'That's not fair,' Catherine pouted. 'I try to keep an open mind. For example, I could have come up with all sorts of twisted reasons why you didn't tell the exact truth on the witness stand.'

There it was. Out in the open. What Magda had been afraid of for months. The milky coffee turned cloying and sour in her mouth. *It's OK*, she told herself. This wasn't some hard-faced cop or journalist. This was Catherine, the person who always wanted to think the best of her. Magda frowned, hoping it didn't look as fake as it felt. 'What are you talking about? Of course I told the truth.'

Catherine screwed up her face. She'd never been good at hiding her emotions, and Magda could see the progression of reactions on her face. Finally, she found the right form of words. 'I'm not saying you lied as such. Just that you said something that couldn't have been quite the case.'

Time to go on the attack. 'What on earth are you talking about?' Her forcefulness provoked the response she'd wanted. Catherine was embarrassed and apprehensive. But not so much as to back off completely. 'Well, you said you'd seen Barker and Sanderson leave the main wedding party and disappear round the far side of the Armstrong building.'

'That's right. I said it because that's what I saw. They slipped away towards the punt landing stage. There was no reason for them to go that way. You can only go to the landing stage or back up to the porter's lodge. And he didn't see them.' Magda stared down at the floor. 'That was when they killed him.'

'But you said you'd seen them from the window of Mummy's office. When you went up to get changed into your going-away outfit.'

'That's right. The office overlooks the Magnusson Hall lawn, where the marquee and the dance floor were. You know that.'

Catherine shook her head. 'But you weren't there, Magda. Not when you said you were.'

Magda felt cold, in spite of the stuffy warmth of the room. 'What are you talking about, Wheelie?'

Catherine's mouth twitched uncomfortably. 'I went up after you. I wanted to wish you luck. Give you a hug. Whatever.' One shoulder shrugged. 'Like sisters do. Only you weren't there. The door was unlocked but you weren't there.'

Magda forced a laugh, trying to sound warm and carefree. 'That must have been when I was in the shower. I took a quick shower, Wheelie. I was all sweaty and sticky from the dancing. I didn't want to put clean clothes on in that state. You must have come in then.' She leaned forward and rubbed Catherine's shoulder. 'Silly. Have you been worrying about this?'

'Not worrying, no. Just wondering.' Catherine's expression was still troubled. 'But, Magda . . . I don't think you can have been in the shower. Because, remember, when I couldn't find you I came back down the middle staircase in Magnusson Hall. And when I got to the ground floor, we met halfway down the corridor. Like you'd just come in the front door. And you were already in your going-away outfit. Remember?'

This was what she had dreaded. A witness who could challenge the version of events she and Jay had fixed on. But it was only Catherine, Magda told herself. Catherine, who had a vested interest in believing in the sister who had always been her hero. Magda shook her head indulgently. 'Well, of course. You don't think I was using the student bathrooms, do you? I had the keys for the Senior Common Room bathrooms on the ground floor of Magnusson Hall. Like I said, I'd just been in the shower.'

Catherine's face cleared in relief. Then it clouded over again. 'So when did you see them? If you were in the ground-floor bathroom, you couldn't have seen them from there.'

Magda gave an exasperated sigh. 'You missed your way, Wheelie. You should have been a lawyer or something. I saw them when I picked up the change of clothes from Mum's office. I stood at the window, looking down at the wedding. All the people I know and love, enjoying themselves. Thinking about the way my life was going to change.' She gave a bitter little laugh. 'Not that I had any bloody idea how it was really going to change.' She turned away from Catherine's gaze and studied the Spanish holiday poster. 'That's when I saw them.'

'Oh. OK.' Catherine smiled, uncertainly. 'I guess that clears it up, then.'

Magda sipped her drink and said nothing. She understood that labouring a lie was the very thing that undermined its credibility. 'Good coffee,' she said. 'Thanks for taking so much care of me over the trial. I appreciate it, Wheelie.'

Catherine shrugged. 'What else would I do? You're my sister.'

'I'm my mother's daughter, but she's not been near me.'

'She's struggling with the Jay thing, Magda. On top of losing Philip . . . well, it's been like a double whammy for her.'

'Thanks, Catherine.' Magda's tone was sharp. 'I didn't realise me being happy came in the same category as having your son-in-law murdered.'

Stung, Catherine stood up for herself. 'You've got to see it from her point of view. Philip was her dream son-in-law. He dies a horrible, violent death on the very day that all her dreams for you come true. And then you apparently turn into a lesbian without any warning. That's a bit hard for a committed Catholic like Mummy to take. You've got to give her time. You've got to talk to her. Make her realise you understand her point of view, even if you can't agree with it.'

Magda felt her throat constrict with emotion. 'And what about my point of view? When is she ever going to take that into account? How do you think I feel?'

'Like shit, I imagine,' Catherine said softly.

Before Magda could say anything more, the door opened and the familiar bald head of the court usher appeared in the gap. 'Jury's coming back,' he said.

'Already?' Catherine said. She turned to Magda. 'I told you it was open and shut.'

'As long as it's the right open and shut.' Magda followed Catherine and the usher out the door, praying that what she and Jay had done hadn't been in vain.

7

Once upon a time, Charlie had been more than a little in love with Dr Corinna Newsam. There were several very good reasons behind an infatuation that had lasted for most of her first year at St Scholastika's College. Corinna, the college's junior philosophy fellow, was the smartest woman she'd ever met. She was also the least stuffy academic, the most challenging conversationalist and the most demanding teacher Charlie had encountered. She was charmed by Corinna's Canadian accent, in awe of her mind and attracted by her sardonic smile. The husband, four children and adamantine Catholicism were mere details that barely impinged on Charlie's dreamy fantasies. And she never noticed that, like the family, she was entirely under Corinna's thumb.

The fascination didn't survive Charlie's first real love affair. Flesh and blood trumped dreams every time. Besides, by then Charlie had discovered Oxford was full of

51

bright, stimulating women who carried less complicated baggage than Corinna Newsam. Not that she stopped admiring Corinna. She just stopped imagining those moments when the brush of two hands would suddenly explode into something more. Probably just as well, since by then she was an occasional babysitter for the Newsam children. Feverish unrequited lust was a major impediment when it came to occupying the hands and minds of four independent and intelligent children.

Of course, Charlie also eventually worked out that Corinna was a control freak and that she was just another cog in the wheel of the machinery that made Newsam family life run smoothly. When she left Oxford, Charlie knew that, in spite of their mutual assurances, she would be out of sight and out of mind to Corinna. They'd exchanged notes with their Christmas cards for a couple of years, then that had tailed off too. The only time they'd met since Charlie's graduation had been her ten-year gaudy. It had been an awkward encounter, neither really knowing how to bridge the gap between past and present.

And now she was going to have to pluck up the courage to call her. It wouldn't have been such a trial six months before, when Charlie had still been someone with a decent professional reputation, albeit tinged with a degree of notoriety. But now? Charlie stared at the phone and sighed. It was no good trying to pretend that Corinna would know nothing of her disgrace. Oxford colleges were gossip factories, their Senior Common Rooms a buzz of speculation built on slender accumulations of half-truths and rumours. But in this instance, they'd only have had to glance through the neat stacks of daily newspapers on the

SCR table to fuel lengthy excursions through the moral maze of Dr Charlie Flint's professional actions.

'Oh, bugger,' Charlie muttered, reaching for the handset. This time of day, Corinna should still be in college. With luck, not teaching but reading. Or lying on the big green velvet chaise longue, thinking. The porter answered on the third ring. No such thing as a professional switchboard operator; the twenty-first century and still the college operated as if they'd barely made it out of the nineteenth.

'St Scholastika's College. How may I help you?' The burr of a local accent that sounded as if it had escaped from a BBC costume drama.

'I'd like to speak to Dr Newsam,' Charlie said, more brusque than she'd intended.

'May I ask who's calling?'

'Dr Charlotte Flint.'

'Dr Flint? How nice to hear you. One moment, I'll see if Dr Newsam's available.'

Bloody Oxford. Never lets you go. Charlie waited, hollow silence in her ear. Nothing as tacky as canned muzak for her alma mater. She'd almost given up when she heard a sharp click followed by a familiar drawl. 'Charlie? Is that really you?'

'Corinna,' she said, taken aback by the warmth she suddenly felt. 'But you're not really surprised, are you?'

'That depends on why you're calling.'

The joust was on. Charlie felt tired at the thought of it. She moved in a different world these days, and she preferred it. 'I'm calling because you sent me a package of newspaper clippings,' she said. 'About the trial of the two people who allegedly murdered Magda's husband on their wedding day.'

'Why would I do that?' Corinna sounded as if this were no more important than a routine tutorial inquiry about some detail of an essay.

'I think it was a challenge, Corinna. Given what you sent, would I be able to figure out who had sent it? And why? You did it because you're a philosopher. You've grown so accustomed to setting everyone tests and challenges that you've forgotten how to ask a straight question.'

'And what could my motivation for such a challenge possibly be?' Charlie thought she could hear tension in Corinna's voice now, but she couldn't swear to it.

'I'm not sure,' she said. 'But I did track down one photograph that gave me pause. I think if I was a mother and my daughter was running around with Jay Macallan Stewart, I'd be shouting for the cavalry. Now, I know I'm not everybody's idea of the cavalry, but I'm probably all you could think of at short notice.'

There was no humour in Corinna's laugh. 'I thought my memory was still reliable. You always had a gift for investigation and resolution. It's good to see the years have only sharpened it. Well done, Charlie.'

'What's all this about, Corinna? Apart from me being your self-fulfilling prophecy?' She didn't care that she sounded impatient.

'I need your help.'

Charlie sighed. 'It's seventeen years since I graduated, Corinna. You don't know anything about me.'

'I know enough, Charlie. I feel pretty certain you've got a burning desire to redeem yourself right now.'

Charlie closed her eyes and massaged her forehead. 'That's a little presumptuous, don't you think?'

A moment's silence, then Corinna spoke crisply. 'We know you here, Charlie. And there is a strong feeling among the senior members in college that you have been made a scapegoat. That you have in fact acted with honour and honesty. It may have been uncomfortable, but it was right to stand up for Bill Hopton's innocence when he was actually innocent. It's not your fault he went on his killing spree afterwards.'

'Some might disagree with you,' Charlie said, her voice weary. 'Some might say it was his very experiences at the hands of those of us involved in law enforcement that sent him over the edge.'

'Speaking as a philosopher, I find that an untenable proposition,' Corinna said briskly. 'Now, there's nothing we can do to help you professionally, obviously. Although I'm sure, where influence exists, it's being brought to bear. But what I can do is offer you the chance to be useful. To use your skills for good, if you like.'

Charlie didn't know why, but she felt like laying her head on the desk and weeping. 'I don't have the faintest idea what you're on about, Corinna. And I'm pretty sure I don't want to.'

'Charlie, we can help each other here. But a phone call isn't the way to do this. Come and talk to me. Come to Oxford for the weekend. Bring your partner if you like. I'm sure she'd find plenty to amuse her in the city. You don't have to come and stay with us if you'd find that awkward after all this time. We'll find you a room in college.'

'I don't think so, Corinna.'

'All I'm asking is that you listen to me, Charlie. No obligation. If you won't do it for me, do it for Magda. You and Magda were always buddies. Charlie, I understand the reason you do what you do. It's because you have a desire to protect the vulnerable. Right now, Charlie, my daughter has never been more vulnerable. Can your conscience really afford any more burdens?'

'That's a very poor effort at emotional blackmail, Corinna.'

'You said yourself if you had a daughter who was running around with Jay Macallan Stewart, you'd be shouting for help. That's all I'm doing here.'

'I understand that. But I'm not the person to help with this. I don't know how to break up Magda and Jay Stewart, even if I thought that was an appropriate thing to do.'

'I'm not asking you to separate my daughter from Jay Macallan Stewart,' Corinna said, sounding ruffled for the first time. 'I wouldn't be so crass. I know my Magda well enough to understand that finding out the truth about the kind of person Jay Stewart is will do the job perfectly well. What I'm asking is that you bring your talents to bear on uncovering that truth. At heart, this is about a miscarriage of justice. I thought you still cared about that kind of thing, Charlie.'

It doesn't take long for silence on a phone to loom large. After a few empty seconds, Charlie said, 'I don't understand.'

'Paul Barker and Joanna Sanderson did not kill my son-in-law, Charlie. The jury's out today, the evidence is stacked against them. They're going to jail. And it's wrong.'

'Haven't you left it a bit late to try and drag me into this? If it was really about avoiding a miscarriage of justice, surely you should have called me weeks ago.'

Corinna's exasperated sigh was not unfamiliar to Charlie. 'This hasn't exactly been easy for me. I thought it would be thrown out of court. I had no idea how far . . . Look, Charlie, what matters here is that the two people in the dock are innocent. They didn't kill Philip.'

Charlie couldn't help herself. 'Who did?'

'Some things don't work over the phone. Come and talk to me, Charlie.'

Hook, line and sinker, Charlie thought. Here we go again.

8

I left Northumberland Jennifer Stewart and arrived at Oxford Jay. A small thing, for sure, but the first stage of my transformation. A lot more was needed, that much was soon obvious. Years later, I still have vivid, humiliating memories of my first tutorial with Dr Helena Winter.

Helena Winter was one of the reasons I had chosen St Scholastika's. Hers had been the first book about philosophy that had fired my enthusiasm for the subject. When I'd come to the college for my interviews, I'd thought her the most stylish woman I'd ever seen. Impeccable in a charcoal pin-striped suit, she radiated calm composure. Her face was inscrutable, her hair a perfect chignon the shocking white of a new ream of printer paper. I desperately wanted to impress her.

I had prepared my first essay on the history of philosophy with her in mind and, as instructed, began reading it out. It may be hard to believe now if you've ever heard me on the radio or TV but back then I had a Northumbrian accent you could cut with a knife and spread on stottie cakes. I was barely into my stride when I became aware of Dr Winter's raised hand, like a genteel officer of the traffic police. I faltered to a halt.

'I'm so terribly sorry, Miss . . . Stewart,' Dr Winter said, not caring whether she sounded condescending or not. 'Your accent is positively splendid, and would be a great asset were you to be studying Anglo-Saxon and Middle English. But unfortunately I haven't understood a word you've said thus far. I wonder, could you possibly return to the beginning and speak a little more slowly?'

I was mortified. But at eighteen, I had no notion that a woman like Helena Winter was capable of being put in her place, never mind how to do it. So I started again, forcing my mouth round the sort of phonemes that would have earned scorn and mockery in my native Wearside. By the end of that first term, I was bilingual. BBC English for Dr Winter, Northumbrian when I was thinking and talking to myself.

The junior philosophy don was a powerful antidote to the formality of Dr Winter. Corinna Newsam was the polar opposite of most of the college's tutors. The list of differences was long and significant. She was Canadian; she was Catholic; she was married so she lived in a proper house, not a set of rooms in college; she had children of her own; she was no more than thirty-five, a mere child by Oxford's donnish standards; and she was informal, insisting we call her Corinna. Those were the tangible differences. But there were intangibles too. She was lively, making the ideas of Ancient Greek philosophers vibrant and relevant. She never patronised, and she wasn't a snob. Probably half of us were half in love with her.

Jay paused and reread the last paragraph. 'No,' she muttered. 'Strike the last sentence.' She had to keep reminding herself there were new brakes on candour. Magda would read this memoir. Most of what Jay didn't want Magda to know overlapped with what she wanted the rest of the world not to know. But there were more things that were off limits now. It was tacky to reveal to your lover that at the time she'd first had a crush on you, you were in love with her mother. So she erased the last sentence and took off her glasses, polishing them on her T-shirt while she figured out a new bridging sentence.

In short, she was the only member of the Senior Common Room who seemed to have friend potential for any of us.

What I didn't realise back then was that it wasn't friendship I needed. What was missing in my life was what had always been missing. I needed a mother. And somehow, Corinna Newsam picked up on that need.

Jay smiled in satisfaction. That would play much better with Magda. It also shone a benevolent light on Corinna, providing Magda with more ammunition against her mother's hostility. She could imagine Magda saying something to Corinna like, 'But she's so nice about you. She talks about how kind you were to her. Why are you being so unkind now?' Every little helped.

Jay checked the time in the bottom corner of her computer screen. Eighteen minutes till the next news bulletin.

According to Magda, the jury would be going out sometime today. But it would be tempting fate to expect them to come back with a quick verdict. Jay longed for it to be over so she and Magda could forge ahead with their lives without fear. But she knew from past experience that when you set a chain of circumstance in motion patience was the only ally worth cultivating. It would all be fine. The ball she had started rolling on Magda's wedding day would score a goal soon enough. The next news bulletin was irrelevant. Plenty of time to write more.

At the end of our third seminar, Corinna called me back. 'Are you in a rush?' she asked.

'No.'

She nodded and smiled. 'Fancy a beer? I'd like to have a chat about your work.'

I didn't know whether to be apprehensive or thrilled. I was only four weeks away from a world where adults didn't mix with those they considered children. We walked out of college and down to the nearest pub, hurrying against bitter driving rain that left no breath for small talk. One or two undergraduates glanced at us as we entered, doubtless recognising Corinna as she shook herself dry like a dog. At the bar, she bought two pints of bitter without asking what I wanted, then steered me to a corner table.

'I figured you'd prefer a pint,' she said, following her remark with a swallow that emptied the first inch of the tall glass. I decided it wasn't the time to remind Corinna I was under age or point out that I came from a teetotal Methodist background.

'Thanks,' I said. 'What was it you wanted to talk about?' I had no finesse in those days. I tasted the beer. It was thin and bitter and smelled of wet dog.

'Your essay was excellent. One of the best I've ever seen from an undergraduate. I think you might do well to consider the philosophy of language as a special option.' I tried to speak, but Corinna held her hand up. 'I think you've got interesting insights in that area. You'd probably be one of only two or three in the college doing it, so you'd get a lot more attention from your tutor. Which would be me.' She grinned. 'I like to steal the most talented undergraduates for my specialisms. It makes me look good when the exam results roll around.'

I had been sipping my beer while Corinna spoke and I'd managed to get it down to the same level in the glass as my tutor. 'I've already made a decision about my option,' I told her. I let Corinna wait long enough for the disappointment to show. 'I'm going for the philosophy of language. I've already read most of the set texts anyway.'

It was the right thing to say. It opened the door to unrivalled access to Corinna's intelligence and knowledge. And I was in love with that knowledge. Within a couple of weeks, we'd become regular drinking companions, meeting once or twice a week, usually around nine in the evening after Corinna had gone home from college, fed, bathed and bedded the children and eaten supper with Henry. I found her awesome; the idea of juggling a life like that was beyond my imagination. Corinna was awesome for other reasons too; no matter how much she drank, she was always coherent, always stimulating. Or perhaps it was that I was too drunk to notice anything different. We talked about our backgrounds and gossiped about people in college. Corinna complained about Henry, I complained about whoever happened to be the current man in my life. The men never lasted for more than a couple of weeks and all traces of their names have long since vanished from my memory. But Corinna used to laugh uproariously at my stories and regularly told me never to fall for a man just because he made me smile. I gathered it had been a long time since Henry had done that for her. From what she said, he'd grown more fond of drinking than of her. In the process, his world view had hardened into a hybrid of High Tory and hardline Catholic, where immigrants, lefties and homosexuals vied for top slot on his hate list. I had the distinct sense that if it had not been for her religious convictions Corinna would cheerfully have thrown Henry out of the house and their children's lives.

Jay paused again. It was all very well letting the prose flow, but she would have to edit her indiscretions before Magda got anywhere near the text. That last bit was certainly going to have to go. Henry had been as useless a waste of space then as he was now. But even though Magda knew her mother treated her father with all the disdain due to a feckless drunk, she wouldn't thank Jay for exposing Henry's failings to the rest of the world. She erased everything after 'different' and started typing again.

After the pubs closed, we would return to Corinna's rambling house in North Oxford and retreat to the sprawling basement kitchen. Henry never joined us, and I never thought that odd. If I thought about it at all, I presumed he wasn't interested in college gossip or the intricacies of philosophical speculation. Corinna and I would drink strong black coffee and talk about ideas and language till gone midnight, then I would throw my right leg over the crossbar of my step-cousin Billy's bike and wobble off into the night.

A couple of weeks after that first drink, Corinna asked me to babysit. 'The kids are all fed and ready for bed. All you have to do is read them stories in relays. I've threatened them with a fate worse than death if they play you up. Take no backchat,' she'd said, sweeping past me in a slinky black number and enough musky perfume to stun an ox.

I looked around the kitchen. Maggot, the eldest, eleven years old, so-called because Patrick couldn't manage 'Magda' when he was learning to talk, sprawled on an ancient chaise longue, supposedly reading a Judy Blume novel, but actually watching me like a hawk from under a white-blonde fringe. Patrick and James, nine and eight but looking like identical twins, were building something complicated from a kit, ignoring me and arguing about which piece had to come next. And four-year-old Catherine, the baby, known as Wheelie because she was born on Bonfire Night, was sitting in front of the TV, ignoring her *Thomas the Tank Engine* video and staring at me with a look somewhere between fascination and terror.

I took a deep breath and bent down, holding out my arms to her. 'Bedtime, Wheelie.'

Catherine scowled and folded her arms across her chest like a caricature of a Geordie matriarch. 'No. Stay here.'

I crouched in front of her. 'It's time for bed, Wheelie. I bet you're tired.'

'No,' she said mutinously, bottom lip thrust outwards.

I tried to pick her up. It was like wrestling a seal under water. 'No!' Catherine screeched, unfolding her arms and landing a punch on my mouth, smashing my lip against my teeth. I could feel the flesh swelling already. Now I began to understand how children get battered.

From behind me, Maggot said, 'Tell her you'll read her a story and she can choose. That usually works.'

I nodded. 'OK, Wheelie. Why don't you come upstairs with me and I'll read you a story? Any story you like?'

Half an hour and five stories later, Catherine's eyes closed. I watched for the best part of a minute, to make sure they weren't going to fly open again, then I crept downstairs. The boys were easier. I did a deal with them; they could watch some documentary about Isambard Kingdom Brunel provided they watched it in bed and promised faithfully to turn off the TV afterwards.

'They won't, you know,' Maggot informed me the minute the deal was struck.

'Maybe not,' I said, not caring. 'I'll check later.'

'They'll fall asleep eventually and you can turn it off before Mum and Dad get home,' Maggot said. 'Otherwise they'll only get stroppy with you.'

'And what's the deal with you?' I said. 'I take it you don't want reading to?'

'Hardly,' Maggot said with the superiority of someone who isn't yet in the tortured grip of adolescence. 'I go to bed at nine. I read till half past. I can be trusted. Until then, you can talk to me.'

I didn't have the first idea what nice middle-class eleven-year-old girls talked about. Where I came from, it was lads and shoplifting. Somehow, I didn't think either was on Magdalene Newsam's agenda. 'Can you play cribbage?' I asked desperately.

'No,' Maggot said curiously. 'What is it?'

So I taught her. There wasn't a cribbage board in the house, but I improvised with the boys' Lego. We talked too, but it was easier over a game of cards than facing each other across the scrubbed pine table and searching for something to fill the silence. There was nothing in that first encounter to predict what has come from it. But this isn't the place for that story. Not yet, dear reader.

By the end of that first term, I was babysitting for the Newsams about once a week. I still went out drinking with Corinna, and dropped in whenever I was at that end of town. For most of that term, I was homesick and lonely, cast adrift by geography and social class. But Corinna made me feel there was somewhere I belonged, somewhere I had value. There wasn't much of that elsewhere in my life in those days.

Jay paused. She knew what she wanted to say. Was there any point in even typing a line that could never survive the most cursory of edits? 'Yes,' she said. She wanted to see what it would look like on the page.

I would have cheerfully killed for Corinna Newsam then.

9

How to get to Oxford without Maria, without Maria ever realising: that had been the plan. That was the challenge for Charlie. If the stereotypes held, it should have been laughably easy; psychiatrist versus dentist, no contest. But Charlie knew Maria too well to rely on that. Maria often saw the bigger picture while Charlie was focused on the detail. Maria had been the first one to warn her of the dangers of the Bill Hopton situation. The first of many. The many she'd chosen to ignore because she'd been so fixated on pure principle over dirty practicality. And look what that had cost her.

She wondered now whether she could have done anything differently. She remembered their conversation the night before she'd delivered the report that had set the ball rolling. Although Charlie was scrupulous about not revealing confidential details to Maria, she'd always talked about the issues raised by her cases. 'Tomorrow I've got to write a report that's going to piss everybody off,' she'd said. 'They've got somebody in the frame for a particularly unpleasant murder. But I don't think he did it. I think he's a psychopath and I think there's every likelihood that one day he will graduate to a full-blown sex killer, but he isn't there yet. Some of my colleagues would say that's reason enough to put up and shut up, but I can't do it.'

Maria had probed her options and the depth of her convictions, then she'd sat at the dinner table looking worried. 'You need to not do this,' she said.

'I can't go against my principles.'

'Isn't there another way? Can't you excuse yourself from the case? Pretend you've got a conflict of interest?'

Charlie sighed. 'I don't see how.'

Maria considered. 'If you come up with this report, they won't use it in court, will they?'

'Of course not. It completely undermines what isn't a very strong case to start with. They might bring someone else in to see if a second opinion will come out differently, but there's no way the prosecution will use me now.'

'In that case, you have to persuade the police and the prosecutor to keep really quiet about your involvement. Let the court sort it out. Keep your nose clean, Charlie. You know what it's like when a prosecution fails. Somebody has to carry the can.'

And if things had played out the way Maria had suggested, things might have been OK. But they hadn't. They'd gone as wrong as they could. Someone had leaked her report to Hopton's defence team and they'd come looking for Charlie. They'd dragged her into the witness box and then it had been all over for the prosecution.

That would have been embarrassing but Charlie's reputation and career would have survived. If they'd listened to her recommendation that Hopton should be held in a secure mental hospital, it might even have been described as a reasonable outcome. But instead, Hopton had gone on to murder four women and nobody was looking past Charlie for someone to blame.

Corinna was right. She was more desperate than she could ever admit for something that would make her feel good about herself. Putting right a miscarriage of justice would do just that. And the chance to spend time with Lisa Kent might even be the icing on the cake.

Now Charlie drained the pasta and returned it to the pan, then tipped in a slug of the spicy salsiccia and tomato sauce she'd cooked earlier. 'Dinner,' she shouted, dishing it up and bringing it to the kitchen table. Maria arrived, still half-absorbed in the newspaper feature section. She found her chair by habit and sat down, the thin line of a frown between her eyebrows.

'Scary,' she said, setting the paper to one side and acknowledging her meal with a satisfied nod.

'What's scary?'

'Scary in a good way,' Maria said, helping herself to the bowl of Parmesan curls Charlie had prepared. 'This stem cell stuff. You know I told you a while back that we're going to be able to grow new teeth for ourselves from these little bundles of cells?'

Charlie, who generally paid attention to Maria because she was a trained listener as well as an instinctive one, nodded. 'I remember. You said the big problem was figuring out how the cells knew what kind of tooth to be.'

'Exactly. Because nobody wants a molar where an incisor should be. Not even if it's their own molar.' Maria gobbled a couple of forkfuls of pasta. 'Mmm, that's good. Well, there's a team of dental researchers who reckon they're close to cracking it.' She rolled her eyes.

'But that's good, isn't it?'

'It's good if you're the person who has a big hole where their teeth should be. It's not so great if you're the dentist who has invested time and money getting to be the best dental implant person north of the Severn–Trent watershed.' Maria reached for the glass of water sitting by her plate and took a swig. 'Here's hoping it takes them longer than they think to unravel the puzzle. Long enough for me to make my money and retire.'

Charlie laughed. 'You're barely forty.'

Maria's hand stopped halfway to her mouth. 'And just how long do you think I want to spend my days staring into the ruins of people's mouths?'

It had never occurred to Charlie that they should discuss retirement. She loved her job. No, strike that. She'd loved the job that used to be hers. When she'd had a functioning career, retirement had been for other people. They'd have had to carry her out kicking and screaming. She'd assumed Maria felt the same. Apparently she'd been wrong. Maybe her accusers were right. Maybe she wasn't much of a psychiatrist. 'I thought you loved your job.' It sounded like a dare.

Maria's eyebrows twitched. 'I love the challenge. I love the difficult cases. But the routine stuff? What's to love? What I always envisaged was giving up general practice in a few years and just doing a few days a month on the really specialist stuff.'

'You never said.'

Maria reached out and smoothed Charlie's hair. 'It never came up. Charlie, I don't know if you've ever noticed, but we hardly ever talk about the future. Or the past. I can't think of another couple who live more in the present than we do.'

'And that's a good thing.' Charlie pushed her food round.

'But that's not how it's been with you lately.' Maria's voice had softened and she laid her fork on the plate. 'Even since the Hopton business, you've been brooding over the past and worrying about the future.'

'That's what you do when the present isn't very rosy.'

Maria sighed. 'I know it's crap, having to get by on whatever crumbs you can pick up to keep you from going mad with frustration and boredom, but this is temporary, Charlie. Everybody says you're going to come out of this with a clean sheet.'

Charlie snorted. 'Professionally, maybe. But as far as the public's concerned . . .'

'It's not the public that hire you to profile and treat.'

'Maria, I'm no use as an expert witness if I'm so notorious that they can't find a jury that hasn't already made its mind up about me.'

Maria stared at her plate. 'You don't have to go to court. There's other things you do that satisfy you just as much. At least, that's what you always said.'

Charlie said nothing. There was no answer that didn't make her sound shallow and superficial, and that wasn't how it was for her. Giving evidence in court mattered because it was one of the few aspects of her work that had a concrete end product. If she did her job right, the guilty went to jail, the innocent walked free and the ill got treatment. Even if things didn't work out the way she believed was right, there was still a line that was drawn. An enclosure. When you spent your working life dealing with people whose mental processes were off-kilter enough to bring them to your door, anything that could be boxed off was something to be craved. Now she'd experienced the benefits of being an expert witness, she wasn't sure she could continue her work without them.

'There are still plenty of challenges for you,' Maria said, getting up and fetching a bottle of wine. She poured two glasses and put them on the table. Charlie recognised the gesture. Maria was drawing a line under a conversation she didn't want to continue because it wasn't going anywhere. Her next gambit would be a complete change of subject. 'Speaking of challenges,' she said, 'did you get to the bottom of those newspaper clippings? The ones that came in the post.'

Bingo. Charlie smiled. There was a lot to be said for living with somebody whose processes you understood. 'I did,' she said, letting herself be led to where she wanted to go. 'I looked online for other reports of the trial and it didn't take me long to work out that I knew the widow of the victim.'

'What? "Knew" as in personally?'

'As in personally and as in past tense. I used to babysit her when I was a student.'

'How come?' Maria absently picked up her fork and resumed eating.

'Her mother was my philosophy tutor. She had four

kids and a useless husband so she used to pick out one or two undergraduates every year to be her default babysitters. I was the lucky one in my second year.'

Maria looked aghast. 'Lucky? Taking care of four kids?'

Charlie lifted one shoulder in a shrug. 'They were pretty easy kids. And I got paid. Not to mention the extra tuition over the late-night glasses of wine. Corinna Newsam was always generous with her time and her booze.' She sipped her wine. 'And now it's payback time.'

'Payback?'

'She wants me to do something for her. Hence the lure of this morning's delivery.'

'She sent you the cuttings? This Corinna Newsam?'

'That's right.'

'But why? Why you? And why all the mystery?'

Charlie grinned. 'She's an Oxford don. It's like a bloody medieval quest. First you have to prove you're worthy of the task. Then you get to find out what the task is. Then you get to ride out against a legion of enemies and come back with the Holy Grail.'

Maria shook her head, bemused. 'I'm just a simple dentist, Charlie. You're going to have to explain that in words of one syllable.'

'You are "just a simple dentist" in the same way that Albert Einstein was a bit good at sums. Corinna sent me a puzzle. If I couldn't solve it or I wasn't interested, then obviously I couldn't be the right person to help. So she gets to eliminate the unsuitable candidate without ever actually having to lose face by asking for help. I solved it and I called her, so I passed the suitability test.'

'You called her?'

Charlie gave the one-shouldered shrug again. 'Well, yes. I mean, how else was I going to find out what's going on?'

'And what is going on?'

Charlie rolled her eyes. 'I wish I knew. But it's Oxford. So it's not as simple as ringing up and getting the full story. If I want that, I have to go and talk to Corinna face to face.'

Maria shook her head, bemused. 'Did they fuck your head up like this the whole time you were studying? No wonder you're so good at dealing with twisted minds. I presume you told her you weren't interested?'

'Not that simple, Maria. Corinna's smart. She knows what's been happening to me. And she baited the hook with the one phrase she knew would suck me in. "Miscarriage of justice," she said.' Charlie paused to take a drink, seeing the dismay on Maria's face. 'It might just be my chance at redemption. I can't say no at this stage. I have to go and find out what Corinna's problem is.'

'Charlie, you never get involved when people contact you directly. "Take it to the police. Or to a lawyer. If they think I'm the right person for the job, they'll come to me." That's what you always say. That's the line. I can't believe you're going to run off to Oxford on what's probably a wild-goose chase just because you used to babysit this woman's kids.'

'But nobody's coming to me any more, are they?' Charlie's anger burst suddenly, a boil whose surface tension couldn't hold any longer. 'I'm suspended from my clinical work, I'm suspended from the Home Office-approved expert witness list, the university's even suspended me from lecturing students. I'm stuck invigilating A-levels and teaching the occasional class at a sixth-form college. A wild-goose chase is better than no chase at all.' She squeezed her eyes shut and tried to breathe evenly.

'Fair enough,' Maria said after a long silence.

'I'm sorry,' Charlie said wearily. 'You didn't deserve that.' She paused momentarily, aiming for the right pitch of nonchalance. 'You could come with me, if you want.'

'To Oxford?'

'You make it sound like the moon.'

'It's another planet, that's for sure. It's your world, not mine. I'm a simple Northern lass, me.'

'You could keep me from getting involved in a wild-goose chase.' Charlie made a mock-piteous face. 'Save me from myself.' The best lies were always the ones closest to the truth, she reminded herself.

'I've got work.' Maria gathered the now empty plates and stacked them together busily.

'I'm not going till the weekend. I've got some more teaching and invigilating this week. Why not come? You've never seen St Scholastika's. You might even like it.'

Maria snorted. 'I'm too old to be seduced by those pretty buildings and glamorous minds. I like nice empty bits of nature to relax in, not cities. It's OK. You go, make a sentimental journey. See what your old teacher thinks you can do for her.'

'Then decline politely and come home?'

'Only if that's what you want.'

Charlie could see the worry in Maria's eyes and felt a quiver of guilt. It didn't matter that Maria was worried about the wrong thing. The dangerous adventure Charlie was embarking on was not the professional end of her visit to Oxford. Whatever Corinna might throw at her, it couldn't be half as risky as putting herself in Lisa Kent's way. But she was in the grip of something beyond her normal control. 'Thanks,' Charlie said, getting up from the table and turning away so Maria couldn't see her face. 'You never know. It might be just what I need.'

10

Her back arching, her muscles in spasm, Magda cried out once, a guttural sound that could as easily have been despair as joy. Her hands clawed at the sheet beneath her. Beyond conscious thought, beyond anything except the powerful surge of orgasm, she was incoherent, half-formed words tumbling from her mouth. Jay put her fingers over Magda's lips. 'I love you,' she murmured.

'Ungh,' Magda groaned. She'd never had sex like this. Wild, dirty, dark and never quite enough. That's how it was with Jay. Intoxicating and exhilarating. An excursion into discovery.

It wasn't as if she'd been dissatisfied with Philip in bed. Once they'd got to know each other, it had always been enjoyable. She'd liked it enough to initiate it more often than not. But with Jay, from the very first time they'd fallen into bed together it had been rapturous. Maybe it was something to do with accepting the true north of her sexuality. Or maybe it was the fact that her girlfriend was undoubtedly gifted. The sex alone would have been enough to keep her in thrall. But here there was so much more than that. Magda groaned again as Jay's fingers brushed her cheek and neck. 'Thank you,' she said.

'Again?' Jay's hand strayed over Magda's breast and down her stomach.

Magda shifted a little. 'No,' she said. 'I don't think I can take any more right now. I just want to enjoy being with you. To celebrate.' She stroked Jay's back, conscious that there were as many differences as similarities between their bodies. Skin colour and texture. Muscle tone and configuration. Body shape and contours. Hair colour and distribution. She'd heard people say homosexuality was a form of narcissism, but she couldn't see it herself. It was hard to imagine how she and Jay could look less like one another.

'You want more champagne?' Jay asked. They'd seen off a bottle when Magda returned from the Old Bailey, their relief making them knock it back like lemonade on a hot summer's day.

'I don't want to move. I want to lie here and savour the moment.' Magda sighed. 'I feel like a weight lifted off me today. It's like I can draw a line under the past and face forward.'

'I understand that.' Jay shifted so she lay on one hip alongside Magda, stomach pressed to hip, arm lying possessive below Magda's breasts. 'Justice has been done. Paul and Joanna are in jail for what they did to Philip. And you did your bit to make sure his death didn't go unavenged. So now you can be proud of yourself as well as feeling relieved.'

Magda ran her fingers through Jay's hair. 'I owe it all to you.'

'Don't be daft. I wasn't the one who had to stand up in the witness box and testify.'

'No, but there wouldn't have been any case to testify in if you hadn't given it a helping hand,' Magda said fondly, kissing Jay's forehead.

'Best if we put that behind us too, I think,' Jay said firmly. 'The less we talk about it, the less likely we are to let something slip.'

Magda was too besotted to be offended by the suggestion that she might not be capable of keeping her mouth shut. 'I'll never forget it, though. What you did, it was risky. And you did it for me. You did it for me when we'd only just got together. Nobody's ever taken a chance like that on me.'

'It didn't feel like taking a chance. I knew already you were the one for me. I knew how hard Philip's death was on you, and I had to do whatever I could to take the edge off the pain.' She snuggled even closer. 'Letting them walk free would have been an insult to his memory as well as an outrage to you. So I did what had to be done.'

'If I needed proof that you're the one for me . . .' Magda leaned back and smiled. 'And now we can stop hiding. We can go out together, do the things that lovers do without worrying that we'll end up in some gossip column.'

Jay chuckled. 'Chances are we'll still appear in some gossip column. But it doesn't matter now. It's not going to be a distraction in terms of the trial. We don't have to worry about some defence counsel insinuating that you had as much of a motive for wanting Philip dead as Joanna and Paul.'

'I always said that was silly. I mean, if I'd known I wanted to be with you, I'd never have married Philip, would I?'

'You might have wanted to be respectable,' Jay said. 'I know part of the reason you married him was because it was what everyone expected you to do.'

'And I was always the one who did what was expected of me.' Magda smiled, an unfamiliar feeling of mischief bubbling inside her. 'At least, until now.'

'Thank goodness. Of course, you might have wanted Philip's money. Just as decent a motive.' The lightness in Jay's tone was replaced by a more sombre note. 'Don't forget, it's still possible that somebody saw the two of us together on your wedding day. A meaningless encounter, they'd think. Unless they read some hack's innuendo and decided we were the evil plotters, not Joanna and Paul.'

'With an imagination like that, you should be a crime writer.' Magda reached over and tickled Jay's ribs. 'Nobody who knows either of us could imagine something so ridiculous. So, where are you going to take me for our first public outing?'

Jay pretended to think. 'I could get tickets for Arsenal at the Emirates on Saturday?' Magda pinched the skin over Jay's hip. 'Ow! I was only joking.'

'I know. But some jokes are beyond the pale. Come on, you're the publisher of the coolest travel guides on the planet. You must have thought of something.'

Jay leaned back on the pillows. 'I thought we might go

to Barcelona for the weekend. A lovely boutique hotel just off the Ramblas, dinner somewhere glorious . . . What do you say?'

'This weekend?'

'That's what I had in mind. Is that a problem?'

'I'm working on Sunday,' she said. 'And I thought I'd go up to Oxford on Saturday to see my parents. I need to tell them about us.'

'I thought your mother already knew? You said she kept digging away at you about me when you were home last month.'

'She knows because she's guessed. I've not actually told her. Not in so many words. And Dad is completely oblivious. He's going to be a nightmare.' Magda drew away slightly, tipping her head back to stare at the ceiling. 'I can already hear the Catholic fundamentalist rant. Honestly, he makes His Holiness Benny One Six look liberal.'

'Would it help if I came with you?' Jay reached up to stroke Magda's hair.

Magda gave a fake laugh. 'Not in any sense of the word "help" that I'm familiar with. Have you forgotten that my mother barred you from the house all those years ago when she discovered you were gay? No, I've just got to grit my teeth and get through it. Hopefully, the fallout won't be too horrendous. And Wheelie's coming up with me, so I will have someone in my corner.'

'Poor Maggot,' Jay said. 'Maybe I should sit outside in the car in case you get cast out like a Victorian fallen woman.'

'It's not beyond the bounds of possibility.' Magda propped herself up on her elbows. 'Enough of this. We're supposed to be celebrating. Is there any food in the house or do we need to order takeaway? I'm starving.'

'All that loving. It makes a woman hungry. How does pizza sound?'

Magda grinned. 'Perfect. We can eat it in bed. Then we don't have far to go afterwards.'

'That's right. We need to make the most of the next few days if you're going to abandon me for Oxford.'

Magda raised one eyebrow. 'Maybe you should sit outside in the car after all.'

11

Charlie hadn't planned to revisit St Scholastika's, but to get to the Newsams' house from the guest house she'd booked herself into meant passing the college gates. And she couldn't resist her old haunts. Some people, she knew, never quite cut the umbilical cord with their Oxford colleges, continually returning for whatever excuse they could come up with – a lecture, a guest dinner, a gaudy – but she had never been one of them. She'd mostly loved her time at Schollie's, but she'd been ready for the less cosseted world outside. The only time she'd been back had been for her ten-year gaudy, an event that had depressed her beyond words.

Returning to Schollie's then had been strange. Almost schizophrenic. Charlie had felt like her real-time self – a successful professional whose opinions were sought and respected by her peers, a woman who had made the transition from infatuations to love, someone at home in her own skin – and, simultaneously, like that awkward creature on the cusp of adolescence and adulthood, hiding uncertainty behind arrogance, desperately trying to figure out the shape of her future. Encountering people who knew only what she had been rather than what she had become had been a disorienting experience. She'd felt like a shape-shifter by the end of the evening, glad to escape to the Spartan college room with its grimly single bed. It had not been an experience that filled her with a desire to repeat it.

So wandering round her old stamping grounds hadn't been on Charlie's agenda. For most of the three-hour drive from Manchester to Oxford, she'd alternated between a fantasy that involved Lisa Kent and not much sleep, and castigating herself for even allowing the thought to cross her mind. What she couldn't deny was that she'd put herself in temptation's way.

As soon as she'd manoeuvred herself into a trip to Oxford without Maria, Charlie had texted Lisa. Am in Oxford Friday/Saturday, possibly Sunday. Get together? Lisa had simply texted back, Will email l8r, leaving Charlie in a ferment of impatience. The email, when it arrived, was a disappointment. But Charlie had to acknowledge that in her present frame of mind, almost any response would have been. According to Lisa, most of her weekend was regrettably spoken for: training sessions with those chosen to spread the Negotiating Vulnerability gospel to the people, meetings with conference organisers and a couple of one-to-one sessions with individual therapy clients. Charlie wondered if booking one of those sessions was the only way she'd ever get some face time with Lisa.

Then, hot on the heels of the disappointing message came a second. Charlie wondered if it was game-playing, but she didn't much care. At least she was playing with an equal. Now, Lisa was offering to meet her for a late drink on Friday evening. I should be free by nine thirty, ten at the very latest. Why don't we meet at the Gardener's Arms? Near where you're staying, right?

And so Charlie had arrived at the pub just after eight, setting up base camp with a view of the door in a bar that felt like a living room. She'd ordered a Thai curry from the vegetarian menu and made it last. She was on her third glass of wine by nine thirty, fighting the desire to knock it back and calm the clench of nervous anticipation that had her in its grip. Lisa would soon be sitting opposite her, the air crackling with the tension between them. Irresistible, that's what it would be, Charlie told herself. The guest-house bed would remain empty; they'd go back to Lisa's house in Iffley village. What would happen beyond the sleepless night and the dazed morning, Charlie had no idea. But it would cut through her life like a knife blade. The two parts would fall apart like a split fruit.

The hubbub of a Friday-evening pub seemed to rise round Charlie as time trickled past. The voices echoed in her ears, the laughter felt like an assault. Quarter to ten and no Lisa. She checked her phone every minute, but nothing appeared on the message screen. By ten, Charlie had started to feel sick. Her hands were clammy, her skin flushed and sweaty. She had to fight the urge to push through the crowd and into the fresh air. When the phone finally vibrated with a message at ten past ten, Charlie's whole body jerked.

So, so, sorry, everything running 18. Nothing 2 b done. Talk 2moro. Lx She read the words and felt the bile rising. She barely made it to the narrow street outside, vomiting her drink and dinner in the gutter between two tightly parked cars. Shaking and sweating, she leaned against the wall and swore at herself. Why had she let herself be sucked into this emotional game? With Lisa, everything was ambiguity. Was her message genuine? Had she got cold feet over embarking on an affair with a married woman? Was she playing the game for the hell of it? Or was it all on the level and Charlie just torturing herself out of guilt?

Back at the guest house, Charlie had lain awake, self-pity and self-disgust taking turns to beat her up. Then remorse had kicked in, making sleep impossible. Somewhere around one, she'd given up and gone online, reading everything she could find about the murder of Philip Carling. At least she would be prepared for her meeting with Corinna. Just like a tutorial. Old habits died hard.

By three, she was yawning. Before she signed off, she did a quick search on Jay Macallan Stewart, to remind herself of the headline public information. Wikipedia gave her a reasonable overview. After Oxford, Jay had used the economics element of her degree to take up a research post with a social policy think-tank. Within two years, she'd figured out where the world was heading and left to set up her own dotcom business buying up excess airline seats and self-catering holiday accommodation at rock-bottom prices and selling the resulting tailored packages on at a profit. Doitnow.com had been one of the runaway successes of the first online boom and Jay had had the wit to sell the business before the bubble burst. She'd spent a couple of years travelling, mostly under the radar, sending despatches home to various newspapers and magazines.

Her next venture had taken advantage of the second wave of internet business. With the explosion in short-break travel, what the world needed was a series of travel guides, constantly updated, available online and tweaked for the consumer's personal interests. And so the 24/7 brand was born. Available by subscription only, Jay's company boasted that there wasn't a major city in the world to which they couldn't produce a personally designed guide. Charlie herself was a subscriber, cheerfully handing over her £4.99 a month so she was never at a loss when travelling.

All of this had built Jay a reputation in the business world. Economics editors knew who Jay Macallan Stewart was. But what broke her out into the wider public consciousness had been a shameless leap on to the bandwagon of misery memoirs. Jay's upbringing had not followed the usual pattern. Her mother had been a hippie and a junkie. For the first nine years of her life, Jay had run as wild as it was possible to run. Then her mother had undergone a dramatic conversion to one of the more restrictive versions of Christianity and married one of the most repressive men in the North East of England. It had been, to quote Jay herself, 'like running headlong into a brick wall'. Factor into the equation Jay's gradual realisation that her burgeoning sexuality would make her even more of an outcast, and it was a recipe for precisely the kind of misery that sold in the millions. Charlie had no idea how truthful *Unrepentant* had been, but nobody had come out of the woodwork to contradict it, so nothing had interfered with the momentum that took it to the top of the bestseller lists.

And that was where the online story ended. There was nothing about Jay's personal life beyond the fact of her homosexuality. She was somebody whose name people knew without her actually falling into the dubious category of a celebrity. Charlie had to admit Jay had handled it impeccably. Somehow, she'd managed to airbrush the awkwardnesses out of history.

For there were awkwardnesses. Even Charlie knew that. She'd fallen asleep with an image of Jay Macallan Stewart in the front of her mind. Not Jay as she was now, but Jay as she had been when Charlie had first clapped eyes on her. Tall, rangy inside a baggy fisherman's sweater, hair a mane of chaotic dark curls, all wreathed in the blue smoke of a French cigarette. She'd made Charlie, two years her senior, feel gauche and adolescent. Even then, even though she had no valid reason for her instinct, she'd understood there was something dangerous about Jay Stewart.

Charlie had slept more soundly than she'd expected or deserved, and woke feeling groggy with barely enough time to shower and make it to breakfast. That left her with more than an hour to kill before she was due to meet Corinna. A wander through the gardens and the river meadow of Schollie's on a bright spring morning would at least have the advantage of dragging her down memory lane rather than through the tortured back alleys of what Lisa Kent was doing to her head. More importantly, it would give her a clear picture of the scene of Philip Carling's murder. She didn't imagine the college grounds would have changed much since she'd been an undergraduate. Oxford prided itself on its adherence to tradition, after all. But there would be differences, even if they were only subtle ones. If – and at this point it was a very big if – she was going to take a look at Corinna's supposed miscarriage of justice, she needed to treat it exactly as she would any other case and leave aside any preconceptions. And although she was a detective of the interior state, it never hurt to have a first-hand image of the scene of the crime.

Back when Charlie had been an undergraduate, Schollie's had still been a women's college, one of the last single-sex establishments. Along with St Hilda's, they'd resisted the pull towards admitting men, staunch in the belief that a collegiate university like Oxford should be able to offer a full range of choice to its students. They'd finally, ironically, been forced to give up their stand by the brutal economics of gender equality legislation. So now Schollie's was, like every other college in the university, open to both men and women. Unlike the former men's colleges, its buildings lacked beauty or distinction and, although the grounds were extensive and attractive, the college held no particular attraction for tourists. So there was no admission fee, no scrutiny of ID to establish whether a visitor was entitled to enter. Anybody, it seemed, could wander at will round the gardens and river meadow of St Scholastika's College.

Term had just ended so suitcases and blue IKEA bags were being hauled to cars while parents hovered and undergraduates tried to look cheerful about going home. Some who were paying to stay on for an extra week's residence lounged on benches, smug and still liberated from the old lives that lay in waiting to reclaim them. Charlie slipped through the porter's lodge and across the parking area outside Magnusson Hall to the part of the garden where the wedding reception had taken place. It was about the size of a football pitch, perfectly manicured lawn surrounded by a gravel path then herbaceous borders that looked bedraggled and unpromising in March. But back in July, when Magda and Philip had married, Charlie knew they would have been a luxuriant riot of flowers and greenery of every shade. In the middle of the lawn was a pair of cedars of Lebanon, taller and broader than Charlie remembered. On the far side of the grass was a bench where Charlie had often spent summer mornings reading or just staring, trying to get her head round her next tutorial as the fat brown river flowed sluggishly past.

Charlie crossed the grass, trying to conjure up the summer wedding that had ended so violently. There would have been a marquee, perhaps two. Tables on the grass. A band, a dance floor. People everywhere, shifting patterns of conversation, dancing. Hard to keep track of anyone's movements. Even the bride and groom.

The other thing about weddings in college was that there was no effective security. Just as anyone could walk in and out of college, so it was with private functions. Especially open-air events. There was no effective way to make them secure, not when there were other people on the site who had legitimate access to the buildings around the lawn. The side door of Magnusson Hall would have been open so guests could have access to the toilets. So anyone inside Magnusson could have walked straight out and joined the party as if they had a right to be there. Other buildings flanked the garden – the Chapter House, a small building that contained only seminar and tutorial rooms, and Riverside Lodge, another residential building. Charlie wondered whether the Chapter House was locked up on a Saturday. In her day, it would have been.

She came to her old bench and turned round to look up at Magnusson Hall. The Victorian building had once been an insane asylum, a source of much sardonic wit among students. In spite of that, it was decently proportioned, its yellow and red brick decoratively arranged. According to the court reports that Charlie had read, Magda had been in her mother's room when she'd seen Paul Barker and Joanna Sanderson slip away from the party. They'd disappeared round the bottom end of Riverside Lodge, between the building and the river, a route that led only to the landing stage where Philip's body had later been found. 'Unless the fire door from Riverside was open,' Charlie said softly.

She walked over to the corner of Riverside and stared back at Magnusson, trying to remember which room was Corinna's. It had a bay window, she recalled. On the second floor. There were only two possibilities, and both had a line of sight to where she stood. So, nothing wrong with what Magda said she'd seen, from a feasibility point of view.

Charlie turned away and walked the narrow flagged path between Riverside and the water. Tall iron railings topped the knee-high wall to keep the students from falling into the river. On her left, the gable end of Riverside rose, a sheer grey brick cliff punctuated by the square windows that had been fashionable in the 1970s when the building had been built. Halfway along was the fire door, a double square of glass with a deep band of black metal across the middle. In Charlie's day, the building had always been so stuffy in summer that the door was propped open more often than not. She wondered whether that was still the case. Everyone was more security-conscious these days. But if the people Charlie taught were anything to go by, students still liked to think of themselves as indestructible. They'd weigh the danger against the unbearable mugginess in the building and open the door. She'd put money on it.

At the end of the building, the path opened out on to a gently sloping concrete slipway. Beyond that was the sturdy wooden jetty where the punts were chained up. It was here that Philip Carling had been found. Smacked on both sides of the head with a heavy wooden paddle that shattered his skull, then bundled into the water and stuffed head first under a punt to drown. It wasn't a dignified way to go, but it was probably pretty quick. Any sound swallowed by the noise from the wedding party. Whoever did it would be wet, but if they'd had the presence of mind to stash a change of clothes nearby in Riverside or even further down the river bank in the college boathouse, they'd soon cover their tracks. Witnesses said that when Barker and Sanderson had returned to the wedding celebration, she'd been wearing a different dress and he'd changed his shirt. Their defence had been that they'd slipped away to have sex; that they'd been so desperate to get at each other that her dress had ripped and his shirt had been stained with lipstick and mascara, so they'd changed. It was one of those explanations that, although reasonable, was always going to sound contrived, especially since they were the only apparent suspects.

Of course, that was an argument that weakened if you knew about Magda and Jay. If Charlie was going to have anything to do with this business, there were a lot of questions she wanted the answers to. Like, when had Jay and Magda got together? Like, where had Jay been that Saturday night? And if you had a nasty suspicious mind, how long was Magda away from the wedding herself? Charlie gave a little hiss of a laugh. Oh, Corinna would love that question.

Charlie slowly turned and looked up the slope towards the Meadow Building. She'd lived there for three years, first in a tiny cubicle of a room sandwiched between a stairwell and a pantry, then in a big airy room on the top floor that she'd managed to swing because of her role as treasurer to the student body. She'd grown up in that building. She'd learned as much about herself as she had about her academic subjects. She'd fallen in love, had her heart broken then fallen in love all over again. Just like you were supposed to. She'd made friends and she'd changed her future.

Now that future she'd created for herself was sliding out of her grasp. Professionally, personally, she was on the skids. And here she was, back where it had all started. It would never have occurred to her to look for salvation here. But maybe Corinna was right. Maybe this was her chance to reclaim her life.

12

Jay stood at the window and watched Magda drive away. Allowing her to face so difficult a confrontation alone was hard for Jay. But there was nothing to be gained by getting into a fight about it. If Corinna and Henry chose to make Magda miserable over her choice of partner, that would be a ruck worth getting into. One Jay would relish. Still, in one sense, it didn't matter; Jay knew Magda was hers, regardless of what her parents might say or do. For now, it made her look better to step back and let Magda attempt to fight her own battle. And it freed the day for her to write. There hadn't been much time for that since the trial verdict. Jay made herself a coffee and settled down at the keyboard.

I only went home for a fortnight that first holiday. I didn't belong there any more. People I knew from school had lives that excluded me. Most of them had gone off to university with a gaggle of friends. Others were working, earning a wage that set them apart. The house where I'd spent half a dozen years before Oxford wasn't home either. My mother's disappearing act had removed any possibility of that. Mary Hopkinson next door took pleasure in revealing that nobody had heard a word from her since that chill winter night when she'd disappeared with a suitcase containing her best clothes, toiletries, and a framed photograph of me aged six. Any older and she'd have had to admit to her real age, I thought.

My stepfather's house wasn't a place where anyone would choose to be. He'd stripped it of anything that reminded him of my mother and now it was as icon-free as the chapel where I'd been forced to spend all my adolescent Sundays. Going back only reminded me of how liberating it had been to leave in the first place. I spent most of my time out of the house, even if that meant making a coffee in the local burger bar last three hours and a dozen chapters. On the second of January, I fled back to Oxford and slept for three nights in the Newsams' attic room before I could move back into college.

For the rest of my first year, Corinna was my rock and the children my occasional saviours. Of course I'd made friends among my fellow undergraduates by then. I'd even been elected as a representative on the JCR committee. But I could talk to Corinna more openly and more honestly than I could to any of my student peers. I felt as if I had nothing to prove with her. It didn't hurt my academic work either. I swear there was astonishment in Helena Winter's voice when she conveyed my

first-year exam results to me. I savoured it as I had
savoured few things.

The memory of the moment still made Jay smile. She'd
had plenty of glory since then, but that early triumph still
had the power to move her. It was strange how powerful
these recollections were. She wondered whether they
would have been so strong without Magda's reappearance
in her life.

There was no escaping the fact that Corinna had been
the centre of Jay's emotional life that year. She'd worshipped her, dreamed of her, fantasised about her and been
pathetically grateful to be allowed so close to the object of
her desires. But she'd always had to be careful, to guard
against word or gesture that might lead Corinna to suspect
there was anything 'unnatural' about her feelings. As far
as Corinna and anyone else was concerned, Jay took great
pains to foster the belief that she was merely an undergraduate Corinna had taken under her wing, not least
because she was good with the children.

None of which she'd be sharing with Magda. Jay sighed
and stood up. She needed to root herself in the past now,
not allow thoughts of Magda to drag her back to the present. She walked through to the kitchen and took a packet
of Gitanes and a battered brass Zippo from the drawer in
the big pine table.

Out on the terrace, Jay lit one of the pungent French
cigarettes and let the smoke fill her mouth. She hadn't
smoked properly for years, but she'd discovered when
she'd been writing *Unrepentant* that the taste and smell of
the strong tobacco were the best trigger for catapulting her

back into her past. She sometimes thought their choice of cigarette was the only thing she'd had in common with her mother. She let the smoke drift from her open mouth, watching the blue swirl dissipate in the chilly morning air. Even after all these years of abstinence, the cigarette felt completely natural between her fingers. She let it burn down, holding it near enough her face for the smoke to perform its magic. Now she could recall the urgency of those emotions, the rawness of experience that she wanted to translate to the page.

After the summer, things changed. Not between the Newsams and me, but between me and the rest of the world. The reason? My new next-door neighbour in college. A first year reading modern languages. Louise Proctor.

I was staggering down the corridor with a heavy cardboard carton when Louise emerged from her room. As we jockeyed to pass in the narrow corridor, our eyes met, and I felt for the first time the jolt and spark of instant attraction.

It was a moment of pure terror.

Somehow, I manoeuvred past Louise and stumbled into my own room. I virtually flung the box on the floor and collapsed on the bed, blood pounding in my ears. My senses were on overload. I could feel the weave of the bedspread beneath my fingers. I could see the coarse grains of dried plaster in the chips on the wall where drawing pins had gouged holes. I could smell dust and the cigarette butts in my ashtray and the bowl of orange-and-lemon potpourri that Corinna and her girls had brought round that morning as a 'welcome back' present after the Newsams' two-week package tour to Greece. And I could hear a voice in the room next to mine calling, 'Louise?'

I stumbled over to the window and pushed it open. At the next window, a middle-aged woman with wavy greying hair in a long bob leaned out, waving to the girl I had nearly collided with moments before. Louise looked up and saw us both at around the same moment her mother saw me. 'Hello!' Mrs Proctor greeted me cheerfully. 'Trying to get my daughter moved in!' Then she turned to look down again. 'Louise, bring up the grey suitcase next, darling.'

Louise nodded and opened the boot of a red Volkswagen Golf. Her gleaming dark head disappeared momentarily, then she reappeared with the suitcase. I suddenly realised I must look a complete idiot and retreated inside. I crossed the room and closed my door. Then I sat down on the bed again, trying to work out what on earth was happening to me. I didn't like the obvious answer, so I tried to carry on as if nothing had happened.

Louise's reaction made that easier. Whatever had hit me, Louise acted as if she hadn't shared it, in spite of my conviction that the moment of pure electricity had been mutual. After that first encounter, Louise seemed to steer clear of me. If we passed unavoidably between our rooms and the bathrooms or stairs, she scowled and her eyes dropped.

It took a force of nature to change everything.

Back in those days the idea of students having en suite bathrooms was laughable. Each floor had its communal bathrooms, with separate shower and bath enclosures. Unknown to each other, Louise and I were taking baths in adjoining cubicles. Outside, a prodigious thunderstorm raged, the rumbles and claps so loud that the windows rattled in their frames. Jagged forks of lightning skittered across the skies like fear shooting down the tree of the central nervous system. Then one thunderclap pealed louder than the rest; a crack, a scream of wood struggling against itself and suddenly chunks of plaster were cascading from the ceiling.

I yelled something incoherent and jumped out of the bath. Instantly, I was covered in plaster dust that stuck to my wet body. Grabbing my dressing gown, I wrenched the cubicle door open just as the other door also flew back. Louise's long black hair hung in strings round her frightened face, everything streaked with the same dirt that was clinging to me. We both stood gaping at the door leading from the bathrooms to the corridor. There was a roof beam crossing it at an angle of forty-five degrees. Since the door opened inwards, we were trapped. I looked up. Through the mess that had been the roof and the ceiling, I could see the heavy bough of the massive copper beech that was no longer shading the lawn outside.

'Oh shit,' I said.

'That's a word,' Louise replied drily.

'Actually, it's two, but this probably isn't the time to be pedantic,' I said, desperate not to be outdone in the cool stakes.

It took the emergency services most of the night to get the door cleared. Once we'd established that the groans and creaks of stressed timbers weren't life-threatening, Louise and I huddled together against the outer wall and started to talk properly for the first time. By dawn, we knew there was something unprecedented between us. Neither would acknowledge what it was, but we knew it was there.

Once we were freed, we were hustled off by the college nurse in spite of our protestations that neither was suffering from anything more than a few cuts and bruises. After we'd been liberated and had given our soundbites to the media, we retreated to a greasy spoon up the Banbury Road. Over bacon, eggs, sausages and fried bread, I finally said, 'I've never felt like this before.'

'I'm scared,' Louise said. 'I don't know what we're supposed to do.'

I shrugged. 'What comes naturally?'

'Yes, but what exactly is that?'

'I don't know. Play it by ear?' I seemed to be incapable of getting beyond cliché but either Louise didn't notice or she didn't care.

Louise dipped sausage in her egg yolk. 'I thought I was so sophisticated when I came up to Oxford.' She looked up at me, her eyes appealing. 'But I don't know anything about anything really.'

'We'll work something out,' I promised. I was only six weeks older than Louise, but I was an academic year ahead of her. Somehow, that made me responsible for whatever came next. It was the most frightening prospect of my life. Suddenly, I had lost my appetite.

I watched Louise finish her breakfast, then we walked back to college arm in arm. It was a slightly daring gesture, but everyone knew about our adventure by then, so it wasn't hard to place an innocent construction on the action. Back in my room, we stood facing each other. Then, inch by tentative inch, our faces moved closer until our lips touched.

What I remember most was feeling like there had been an explosion of light inside my head. Looking into Louise's eyes, I saw my wonder mirrored. Right then, I felt invincible.

Unfortunately, as I was to learn the hard way, that was never a feeling that lasted for long.

13

Charlie found it hard to believe how little Corinna had changed. She was still wearing the familiar heavy oval spectacle frames that might have been fashionable for fifteen minutes in 1963 in her native Canada, but hadn't had a single moment of glory since. Even now, her hair was pure 1960s: side parting, backcombed, flicked under her rather heavy jaw, the whole monstrous confection held in place with a layer of hair lacquer hard as shellac. It remained the same uniform dark tan of Cherry Blossom shoe polish. Charlie couldn't help wondering about the portraits in the attic. She smiled an uncertain greeting.

'Charlie. You came.' The same warm transatlantic voice. Corinna reached out and put a hand on Charlie's arm.

'I said I would.' Charlie let herself be drawn into the hall. Unlike Corinna, it was not as she remembered it. The scuffs and grazes of four young children had gone, painted over and erased. An Afghan runner on sanded and polished boards replaced the worn chocolate brown carpet. And there were proper pictures on the walls, not the garish splodges of kids' artwork. 'Wow,' she said. 'This has changed.'

Corinna's laugh was the familiar cracked cackle. 'That's what happens when your kids grow up and your husband grows old. There's no obstacle to having the place the way you always wanted it.' She led the way down the stairs to the basement kitchen. 'This hasn't changed much, though.'

She was right. The kitchen still had the air of a room through which a mild tornado had passed. Clothes, books, sports equipment, magazines, newspapers and CDs were strewn haphazardly over the sofas and armchairs that lined half the room. The dark red range still had one cream door, because the Newsams were accustomed to taking what was going, especially if it meant saving money. Radio 4 muttered in the background.

'Only the book titles are different,' Corinna said. She pulled out a chair at the kitchen table and waved at it. 'Coffee, yes?' She glanced up at the clock. 'We've not got as long as I hoped. Magda and Wheelie are coming for lunch. We can catch up on the small talk then.'

Small talk; my life to Corinna. 'Won't that be a bit awkward? Given why I'm here? Though of course, I'm still not entirely sure why I am here.'

Corinna gave her an odd look as she spooned coffee into a cafetière. 'Well, I wasn't exactly expecting you to interrogate Magda over the chicken-and-ham pie. I'd given you credit for a little more subtlety than that.' Then, more briskly, 'Besides, they're used to former students dropping in. The place has always had open-house lean-ings.' She brought the pot to the table along with a pair of mugs. 'So, how much do you know about what's been happening to Magda?'

'I know she married Philip Carling last July. They'd known each other three or four years, depending on which newspaper you read. The wedding and the recep-tion were held at Schollie's and late in the evening Philip Carling was found dead in the river by the punt station. He'd been beaten unconscious and stuffed under a punt. How am I doing?' Charlie was deliberately brutal, trying to provoke a reaction.

What she got was pretty much what she expected. 'Holy moly, Charlie. I see you never mastered the euphemism.'

'I prefer not to leave room for ambiguity. A few weeks later, Philip's business partners were arrested for his murder. They'd been using privileged information to make a killing on the stock market. Philip had found out and was planning to blow the whistle when he got back from his honeymoon. So they killed him. Magda found the key evi-dence that clinched the case against them. And this week they were both found guilty of his murder. And some-where in the middle of all that, you sent me a package of newspaper clippings.'

Corinna stirred her coffee mechanically. 'You haven't lost the gift for précis.'

'But why am I here, Corinna? What in God's name is all this about? Why do you care about the convicted killers of your son-in-law?'

She stirred some more, then sighed. 'This is going to sound crazy. I thought about going to the police, but I knew they wouldn't take me seriously, not when they had such a good case against Paul and Joanna. This is why I wanted to talk to you and not some stranger in a private investigator's office. You know I'm not a crazy woman.'

Charlie gave a sad, wry smile. 'You don't have to be crazy to have the occasional crazy fixation, Corinna. It happens all the time.'

'Trust me, Charlie. This is not a crazy fixation. I am convinced that Paul Barker and Joanna Sanderson did not kill Philip.'

Corinna clearly expected this to be a bombshell to Charlie, but she'd already worked out that she was going to hear something like that. 'The police got it wrong? The jury got it wrong?'

Corinna finally put her spoon down. 'It wouldn't be the first time.'

That was a well-aimed barb, and it stung. 'It happens less often than you think.'

'It nearly happened to Bill Hopton.' Corinna's voice was as level as her stare. 'I bet you wish it had.'

Charlie took a deep breath through her nose and counted to ten. She'd forgotten quite how challenging Corinna could be. 'No. I don't. I know it's not a popular position, but I still believe the legal system is worthless if we don't put truth at the heart of it.'

To her surprise, Corinna grinned. 'That's the Charlie I remember. That's why I wanted you on board.'

Charlie shook her head. 'A discredited expert waiting to be struck off? Nobody in their right mind would want me in their corner these days.'

Corinna flapped a hand impatiently. 'That'll sort itself

out. You'll see. In the meantime, you're the person to get to the heart of this.'

'To the heart of what? Why are you so sure this is a mis-carriage of justice?'

'Because I know who really killed Philip.'

Charlie knew this was the point where she should, like an investigative journalist in a massage parlour, make her excuses and leave. Knowing as she spoke that she was going to regret it, she said, 'Who?'

'The person who murdered my son-in-law was Jay Macallan Stewart.'

14

Sometimes it seemed to Jay that the past was more immediate than the present. She could lose herself in making love with Magda, but when they lay together afterwards, Jay often found her thoughts drifting away from the moment, sifting through memory before settling on one particular episode. It wasn't just because she was delving into her past to make sure her memoir leapt off the page. It had always been like this. It was as if she was constantly re-examining the past in an attempt to cast it in a shape she found acceptable. Jay wanted to look back down the vista of the years and see an unbroken, consistent upward path. Sometimes that took more effort than others.

By the time Louise and I were discovering just what it was that lesbians did in bed, I was already committed to running for President of the Junior Common Room — the quaint term for the undergraduate student body of an

Oxford college. It has always been one of those jobs that looks more impressive on a CV than it ever is in reality. But for me it was the next step in the reconstruction of insignificant Jennifer Stewart. Another measure of the distance I had travelled.

All it really involved at Schollie's in my day was making sure the other committee members did whatever they had been elected to do; meeting weekly with the college principal to thrash out any contentious issues and to drink the dry sherry I'd had to train myself to love; running college meetings and, depending on how Stalinist the holder of the office felt, altering the political and practical direction of life for the college's undergraduates. If, for example, one were so minded, one could persuade the JCR members to donate all their funds to the Society for Distressed Gentlewomen. Or some radical Marxist Central American guerrilla army. Depending on your point of view, it was either power without responsibility or responsibility without power.

My main rival for the presidency emerged as Jess Edwards, a geographer with a sharp line in rhetoric, a rowing blue and a disturbing degree of admiration for the historic achievements of Margaret Thatcher. The issues that divided us were practical as well as ideological. For example: I proposed a fund-raising programme aimed at the provision of a proper college launderette with state-of-the-art machines; Jess wanted to spend more on rowing coaches to improve the college's growing reputation on the river. The arguments between us had been hard fought, but soon after Louise and I became lovers, I realised my edge had blunted. Love had knocked the ginger out of me. Where before I would have cornered Jess and metaphorically ripped her limb from limb, now I was making more conciliatory noises than the most wishy-washy bleeding-heart liberal.

Jay leaned back in her chair, remembering her frustration when she'd realised it was all slipping away because she'd lost the relish for the fight. She'd never seen herself as someone for whom love would be enough. Her mother's fecklessness in the early part of her childhood, combined with the savage restrictiveness that had followed, had made sure of that. But with Louise, emotion had overwhelmed her, and the feeling of being at the heart of someone else's world was curiously intoxicating.

The problem was that she couldn't put her ambitions on hold. This was the fourth term of her three years at Schollie's. Soon her time would hit the halfway mark. It wasn't long to make an impression, to create a foundation for a life that was light years away from the grim and narrow prospects of her adolescence. For people like her, there was no second bite of the cherry. This was her chance and she had to make the most of it. Somehow, she had to find a way to turn it round.

Like a carnivore scenting blood, Jess fell on the weakness without mercy. Four days before the election, I was working in my usual spot in the college library when a shadow fell over my notes. 'A word,' Jess said quietly.

I followed her out into the garden and took the opportunity to light a pungent Gitane. The fact that I knew Jess loathed my cigarettes was merely an added pleasure.

'You've got as long as it takes me to smoke this,' I said bluntly.

'I won't need that long. I want you to withdraw your candidacy.'

I shook my head in disbelief. 'When you get back to planet earth, give me a call,' I said sarcastically.

'I'm making the suggestion for your sake. I don't want you to humiliate yourself. The JCR members won't vote a lesbian in as JCR President,' Jess retorted, smugness smeared across her face like dogshit on a shoe.

I had a moment of panic. We'd been so careful. Our embraces had all been inside the safety of our own rooms. I didn't think we'd ever done anything publicly that could be thrown in our faces; we'd never even been to a gay bar. Jess had to be bluffing, I decided. She couldn't know. Nobody could *know*. 'I'm sure you're right,' I said mildly. 'But why should you think that would bother me?'

'I spent ten years at boarding school, Jay. Give me some credit. I know you didn't have my advantages, but surely you're not so naïve as to think you and Louise could make kissy faces at each other over breakfast ever since the roof fell in on you without half the JCR noticing?'

I could feel my ears turning scarlet. Right then, I wasn't sure if I was angrier about our love being reduced to a schoolgirl crush or being reminded I was socially not up to snuff. Either way, it didn't matter. With that one speech, Jess had managed to undo all the softening I'd undergone at the hands of love. 'You're full of shit, Jess,' I snarled.

'I don't think so. As I say, I can't be the only one who's noticed. And unless you withdraw your candidacy, I suspect more people will know by polling day.'

'Are you trying to blackmail me?'

'Good lord, no,' Jess protested. 'But on my way out, I couldn't help noticing the election poster in the kitchen on your floor of the Sackville Building had been defaced. We wouldn't want that sort of thing to happen all over college, would we?'

There had been several times since I'd left the North East when I'd felt the urge to demonstrate my street fighting skills. Never more than at that moment. Somehow, I stopped myself, letting my hands relax out of their reflexive fists. Instead, I pushed past Jess and, leaving my books and notes behind for collection later, I made straight for the Sackville Building.

It was even worse than I'd imagined. The poster that this morning had read, 'Put a Stewart back on the throne' now had 'DYKE' pasted over my name. And added to the list of bullet-point promises I'd made were, 'Lesbian erotica section to be established in college library' and 'Coming-out workshops with professional counsellors'.

I ripped the sheet from the wall, tearing it to pieces. I dumped the remains in the sink and with a shaking hand spun the wheel of my Zippo and reduced its vileness to ashes. I leaned against the sink panting, my eyes smarting with more than the smoke. The knowledge that not many people would have seen it between first thing and now was no balm. I couldn't believe what Jess Edwards had done to me. I'd thought I was the ruthless one.

But I knew with stony certainty that, if I didn't back down, there would be a smear campaign the length and breadth of the college by next morning. And my chances of becoming JCR President would have vanished in the kind of humiliation that people would talk about for years afterwards. Whenever my name came up in conversation where there was anyone from my Oxford vintage, it would be, 'Oh, wasn't she the lesbian who thought she could be JCR President?'

And there was Louise to consider. Her ambitions were different from mine; she had no desire for power or notoriety. She'd been having difficulty enough adjusting to the idea of being gay without being humiliated by our fellow undergraduates. And make no mistake about it, I thought bitterly, humiliated we would be. Not much reality lay behind the romantic notions of the solidarity and supportiveness of a community of educated women. At St Scholastika's they were every bit as petty, envious and self-seeking as anywhere else. Thanks to Corinna's indiscreet gossip, I knew of two fellows of the college who had not spoken to each other for the best part of twenty years because of an irreconcilable disagreement over the true cradle of classical civilisation. No, my peers would barely tolerate Louise and certainly would never forgive me for thrusting the personal so very firmly into the public arena, even though I had had nothing to do with its dissemination.

For once in my life, I really didn't know what to do. I couldn't even turn to Corinna. I hadn't told her about Louise; some instinct had made me hold back. I knew the Catholic Church's line on homosexuality only too well, since it was the principal stumbling block between Louise and me. I simply couldn't trust Corinna to let her personal affections supersede her religious views. Wisely, as things turned out.

Jay cocked her head, considering what she'd just written about Corinna. She didn't think there was anything there that would upset Magda. After all, Corinna's subsequent behaviour spoke for itself, and Jay wasn't going to sugar-coat it when she got to that part of the story. However things turned out now, it was still valid. If Corinna welcomed her as a daughter-in-law now, it would play as a Damascene conversion; if not, Jay could take the moral high ground and stand tall under the weight of Corinna's continued disapproval. It might force Magda to a difficult choice, but Jay was convinced she would choose lover over mother at this point. And once that choice was made, there was no going back. Just as there had been no going back all those years ago.

I was sitting at my desk, staring out across the meadows when Jess reappeared. She knocked and stuck her head round my door. 'I see you removed the poster.'

'Wouldn't you?'

'Let me know what you decide,' she said, as casually as if she were asking me how I liked my coffee. 'I'll see you at breakfast.'

But she didn't. By breakfast time, Jess Edwards was dead.

Part Two

1

Charlie stared at Corinna, incredulous. 'You're sitting there and telling me you honestly think Jay Macallan Stewart is a murderer? Internet multimillionaire and misery memoir author Jay Macallan Stewart? Your family friend Jay Macallan Stewart?'

Corinna looked affronted. 'She's no friend of this family.'

'According to the newspapers she is. I know Magda's said nothing to the press, but I did see one photograph taken in the street where she was with' – Charlie made a quotation marks sign in the air – '"family friend" Jay Macallan Stewart.' She cocked her head to one side. 'I did wonder about that.'

'No way is she a friend. She's not welcome in this house. Hasn't been for fifteen years or more. Damn it, Charlie. Damned media and their lies.'

'But *Jay*? Why the holy fuck do you think Jay killed Philip?'

Corinna winced. Blasphemy or obscenity offended her, a prudery that had always amused Charlie. 'Because she's done it before. At least once, and almost certainly more.'

Until that point, Charlie had been willing to give Corinna the benefit of the doubt. But this was too much. 'Is this some kind of elaborate Oxford joke, Corinna? Some wind-up at my expense?'

'It's the truth, Charlie.' At least this intensity was familiar to Charlie from her professional life. It often accompanied the most sincerely held delusions.

Charlie held her hands up, palms outward. 'OK, let's just take this step by step. For now, let's leave to one side the suggestion that Jay Stewart is a serial killer and look at the case in point. Corinna, why on earth would Jay want Philip dead? What's the connective tissue here?'

She'd seen Corinna disappointed by her pronouncements before but Charlie would have said she was past being affected by it. To her surprise, she felt nettled when Corinna said, 'Can't you work it out, Charlie? You're the one who brought up the newspaper photo.'

'Magda? You're seriously suggesting that Jay killed Philip because she wanted Magda? Corinna, do you have any idea how bonkers that sounds? Even from the most besotted of mothers, that would sound mad.'

'Be that as it may, Charlie. But they're together. Jay is my daughter's lover. My beautiful, clever daughter. Magda hasn't had the nerve to tell me in so many words, but I know my daughter and I know what's going on. I've no idea how they met again, but I'm convinced that Magda's version of events is a lie. She says they ran into each other at the house of a colleague a couple of months after Philip died. But I think they were already seeing each other by then.'

Charlie frowned. 'But why on earth would Magda marry Philip if she was already having a relationship with Jay?'

Corinna shrugged in frustration. 'I don't think they were lovers then. Magda's too honest, too honourable. I can't imagine her cheating on Philip, no matter how attracted she was to Jay. And Jay's no fool. She must have realised that the only way she'd have a chance with Magda was to get rid of Philip.'

'That's a hell of a stretch. Killing the bridegroom on the wedding day in the hope you can move in on the bride? In my professional life, that's what I'd call grandiose thinking.'

Corinna refilled their mugs and started the stirring ritual again. 'Oh, come on, Charlie. You're a psychiatrist. You know how vulnerable people are to emotional predators when they've been bereaved. Jay would never have a better chance. She's a manipulator. You must remember that, surely?'

'I didn't know her that well. I was two years ahead of her, remember. That's a big gap in student terms. But Corinna, it's a huge jump from "I fancy her" to "I'm going to kill for her".'

'Not so big if you've killed before.'

Charlie held her hand up in a 'stop' signal. 'We'll come back to that, I promise. Just for the sake of argument, let's suppose that Jay had set her sights on Magda and she didn't care what she had to do to get her. But that's just supposition. It is – forgive me, Corinna, but it is – just a

fantasy. You've got to have something that vaguely quali-
fies as evidence before you can go around making
accusations like that.'

'You think I don't realise that? I do have some more to
go on. The wedding wasn't the only event in college that
day. There was also a weekend seminar on setting up
online businesses. And guess who the keynote speaker
was?'

'Jay?'

'That's right. She was there, on the spot, when Philip
was killed.'

'So were a lot of other people. At least two of them with
a confirmed motive, as opposed to a possible motive
you've just dreamed up.'

Corinna pursed her lips in disapproval. 'And speaking of
motive . . . do you know how the police came up with the
evidence against Barker and Sanderson?'

'According to what I read, there was a letter on Philip's
computer to the Serious Fraud Office and the Financial
Services Authority indicating how the pair of them had
come by their confidential information and how they'd
used it in an insider trading scheme to make themselves
very rich. Is that not how it was?'

Corinna looked pleased with herself, as if she'd finally,
incontrovertibly got one over on Charlie. 'That's nearly
right. Except it wasn't on Philip's computer. Not on his
desktop at the office, not on his desktop at home and
not on his laptop. It was on a back-up hard drive that
he'd left in Magda's old room here. He slept there the night
before the wedding, so supposedly he'd tucked it away in
her underwear drawer for safekeeping.' Corinna's voice

dripped scepticism. 'And Magda just happened to find it when the police were starting to get frustrated about ever nailing anyone for the murder.'

Puzzled, Charlie said, 'I don't understand what that has to do with Jay.'

'This letter is very detailed. It doesn't appear anywhere else in Philip's records. But apparently most of the information in it does. According to a very helpful detective I spoke to a while back, it could have been compiled by someone with accounting skills and computer skills and access to the office systems where Barker and Sanderson left their own digital trail. With the best will in the world, that is not a description of my daughter. But it does sound a lot like the skills Jay Stewart must have to have reached the pinnacle of business that she's achieved. Wouldn't you say?'

'Jay Stewart and a shedload of other people,' Charlie said. 'And it's not like somebody made this stuff up. They just made it easily accessible when it became clear the police weren't getting a handle on it.'

'Quite. But Magda made a mistake. The weekend before the trial, she drove up for Sunday lunch. Obviously, we were talking about the case, and Patrick said it had been a stroke of luck, Magda finding the back-up drive that gave the police their crucial leverage. And Magda said, quite casually, that it had been Jay who suggested there might be a back-up somewhere and that Magda should retrace his steps on the days before the wedding to see if she could track it down.'

'And why was that a mistake?'

'Because the discovery of the hard drive precedes the

occasion when Magda supposedly met Jay again by a couple of weeks.' Corinna kept her eyes on Charlie, a measured stare with absolutely no madness in it.

'It's suggestive,' Charlie said. 'But not necessarily suggestive of collusion to fit up Paul Barker and Joanna Sanderson. And presumably the police checked the internal information on the back-up drive to see when the file was created and saved.'

Corinna threw her hands up in the air. 'I don't know about stuff like that. But I've read about people fiddling with the dates on files. And Jay's whole professional life has been devoted to internet businesses. If anybody's got access to the kind of geeks who know how to alter digital information, it's her.'

'That's still not evidence. Corinna, there's nothing to attack here, in terms of a miscarriage of justice. Even if I got alongside Jay and became convinced, professionally speaking, that she was capable of doing what you suggest, there's still nothing you could call evidence.'

Corinna folded her arms tightly across her chest. 'I was afraid that's what you'd say. And however much I wish it was otherwise, I do understand there's little prospect of calling Jay to account for Philip's death. But she's got to be stopped, Charlie. This is my daughter we're talking about. Jay might want to pull down the moon and stars for her now, but what happens when that changes? What happens if she falls out of love with Magda and Magda doesn't want to let go? Or what if Magda comes to her senses and wants to leave her? Can you imagine what it feels like to know your daughter is spending her nights with a killer?'

'No, I can't. And I can see how concern for a child might make you build castles in the air.'

'This is not castles in the air.' For the first time, Corinna had raised her voice. 'There is a trail of bodies in her wake. Magda thinks I banned Jay from this house all those years ago because I discovered she was a lesbian. Now, you know me well enough to know that couldn't be the case. I never tried to keep you away from my kids even though I knew pretty much from the get-go that you were a lesbian. The reason, the real reason I froze Jay out of our lives was because I was convinced she killed Jess Edwards.'

Charlie was stunned into silence, the words echoing in her ears. She gave a tiny shake of the head. 'That was an accident,' she said at last, blinking hard to shift an image of Jess from her mind's eye.

'I didn't think so at the time, and I don't think so now,' Corinna said.

'What possible grounds could you have for saying that?' Charlie felt close to tears. Jess the bright and beautiful, the one with the glorious golden future she never got to live. Even though she'd only been a fresher in Charlie's final year, she'd made an impact. Charlie had not long left Schollie's when Jess had died, but it was a death that reverberated inside her, a denial of possibility that could reach out and touch any of them.

'The morning Jess died . . .' Corinna stared through the basement window, eyes level with the muddy winter grass. She sighed. 'Back then, I used to go into college really early. I'd get a couple of hours' work in, then run home and make sure the kids were clean and fed and dressed for school. That morning, I came in by the meadow gate around six. And I swear I saw Jay Stewart coming across the meadow from the direction of the boathouse.'

A moment of stunned silence, then Charlie said, 'Wasn't it dark that early?'

'It was dark. And kind of misty too. But I know what I saw. I knew Jay pretty well. Well enough to be certain it was her.'

'And you never said anything?' Charlie was trained to interview the most vicious of killers without letting judgement creep into her tone. But it was taking all of her professional skill not to scream at Corinna right then. 'You kept this to yourself?'

Corinna took off her glasses and polished them on her sweater. 'I told myself there must have been an innocent explanation. Maybe Jay was meeting Jess to try and take some of the sting out of the election campaign.' She glanced up at Charlie. Without her glasses, her face looked small and naked. Charlie wondered how calculated the move was. 'I had no reason then to imagine Jay was a killer. I thought I knew her. And think about it, Charlie. If I had told the police what I'd seen' – she spread her hands wide – 'it would have proved nothing. It would just have created a storm of rumour and suspicion that would have tainted the college. I didn't want Schollie's splashed over the tabloid press. And besides, there wasn't the slightest suggestion then or any time later that Jess's death was anything other than a terrible accident. Talking about what I'd seen would have achieved nothing. I didn't make the decision alone, either. I talked it over with Dr Winter and she agreed with me.'

Helena Winter, chatelaine of the legend of Schollie's,

Charlie thought. She would have agreed to anything so long as the college remained untarnished. Charlie willed herself to sit still, not to show how agitated Corinna's words had left her. 'Well, that's one suspicious death. What about the rest?'

Corinna replaced her glasses and glanced at her watch. 'We've not got much time. There's two others that I think should be investigated. Her business partner in doitnow.com, Kathy Lipson.'

'I remember that. It was a climbing accident.'

'Jay cut the rope.'

'And the verdict absolved her of any blame.' Now Charlie's voice was rising in pitch to match Corinna.

'That doesn't make her blameless. And the terms of their partnership meant Jay inherited Kathy's share of the business. Just weeks before she sold the company for millions.'

'This is crazy, Corinna. There's nowhere to go with this. There's nothing remotely approaching evidence.'

'Then there was a guy called Ulf Ingemarsson. I found out about him on Google. After I discovered Jay had been in college on the night Philip died, I started to wonder what other skeletons might be hanging around in her closet. And I found him. Ingemarsson was murdered. He was on holiday in Spain. He'd rented a villa up in the mountains above Barcelona. Very remote. And here's the thing, Charlie. He had the original idea for 24/7. He had the project in development. But Jay stole his work. He was about to sue her. He'd gone to Spain to get some peace and quiet to prepare the case. He was stabbed to death. He'd been dead for at least a week when they found him.

The Spanish police said it had been a burglary gone wrong. But his girlfriend didn't think so. His laptop was gone and so were the papers she said he'd taken with him to work on. They'd mean nothing to a burglar. But they'd mean everything to Jay Stewart.'

Charlie closed her eyes and sighed. 'And is there a shred of evidence to link Jay to this?'

'I don't know,' Corinna said. 'But it was an amazing coincidence, don't you think? Every time somebody stands between Jay Stewart and what she wants, they die. This goes way beyond coincidence, Charlie.'

Charlie felt very tired. She couldn't summon the energy to argue with Corinna any more. 'Maybe,' she said wearily. 'But I'm not a detective. And neither are you. You're going to have to let this go, Corinna. Otherwise it's going to eat you up and make you crazy.'

She shook her head vigorously. 'I can't let it go, Charlie. It's my daughter's life that could be at stake here. If you can't help me – if the law can't help me – I'm going to have to take this into my own hands. I'm not afraid of the con-sequences. I'd rather spend the rest of my life in jail and know that Magda was safe.'

Charlie had thought she knew Corinna. Now she realised how wrong she'd been. It didn't matter how intellectually able Corinna was, nor how capable of philosophical inves-tigation. When it came to her children, the primeval took over. There was no doubt in Charlie's mind that Corinna meant exactly what she had said. She would kill Jay to save Magda. And she'd calculated her mark perfectly. She under-stood Charlie's need to atone. Even though she'd done nothing wrong, people had died because of her. Now

Corinna was offering her the chance to save a life that possibly didn't deserve saving. With her head, Charlie knew there was no such thing as a redemptive trade-off, but her heart felt differently.

'I will kill her,' Corinna said. 'If that's what it takes.'

That was how stark the choice was. Unless Charlie could bring Jay to some kind of justice or demonstrate her innocence Corinna would at least make a serious attempt on her life. The trouble was Charlie had no conviction she could manage either goal. But at least if she agreed to help, she might buy enough time to talk Corinna down from this madness. 'I understand that,' she said quietly. 'And I can't let you do that.' She ran a hand through her hair, feeling more like ripping it out in frustration. 'I'll help.'

Corinna's smile was frail, her eyes mistrustful. 'I knew I could count on you, Charlie.' She reached out and patted Charlie's hand in a rare moment of physical contact.

Before Charlie could answer, she heard the front door opening. Footsteps clattering, then voices calling. 'Mum, where are you?'

'Hi, Mum, we're home.'

Corinna stood up. 'Thanks, Charlie. We'll talk again.' Then she swung round to face the stairs. 'We're down here, darlings.'

Oh Christ, Charlie thought. This is going to be some lunch.

2

Magda leaned across and opened the passenger door for Catherine, who jumped off the wall she'd been sitting on and hurried to the car. Magda turned down the Isobel Campbell and Mark Lanegan CD as Catherine climbed in. 'You're freezing,' Magda said, kissing her sister's icy cheek.

Catherine screwed up her face. 'You know I don't feel the cold.'

It was hard to argue with that, given Catherine had chosen to dress on a cold spring morning in black leggings, a cotton dress and a thin leather jerkin. 'You should have waited indoors, Wheelie.' It was the affectionate scolding of an older sister used to taking responsibility for the younger ones.

'I was ready. And it's always a nightmare trying to get parked round here on a Saturday morning, you know that. So I thought I'd be helpful and wait outside. Honestly,

Magda.' Catherine rolled her eyes and ran a frustrated hand through her tousled hair.

Magda, the perfectly groomed big sister, pulled away and threaded her way through the maze of streets below Shepherd's Bush Green. 'OK, OK. Have you had breakfast?'

'Of course I had breakfast, it's nearly eleven o'clock. And I'm twenty-two years old. God, Magda, I'd have thought taking up with Jay would have occupied all your mother hen instincts.'

Magda grinned. 'Hardly. Jay is more than capable of taking care of herself.'

Catherine groaned. 'Oh yes, how could I have forgotten? You only want to mother your siblings. When it comes to lovers, you always prefer someone who takes care of you. You bat those beautiful eyelashes and do that Grace Kelly smile and they're putty in your hands.'

'Thanks, Wheelie. You make me sound like a complete twat.'

Catherine giggled. 'Hey, did I say it was a bad thing? If I could find a bloke that ran after me like Philip did with you, I wouldn't be saying no, believe me.'

Magda's hands tightened momentarily on the wheel. 'If you ever find someone half as nice as Philip, you'll be doing just fine.'

Catherine twisted in her seat and studied her sister so pointedly that Magda glanced away from the road. 'What?' Magda said as she turned back to the traffic.

'You really did care about him, didn't you?'

Magda made an exasperated tutting noise. 'For fuck's sake. Of course I cared about him. I married him, remember?'

'Yeah, but . . .' Catherine's voice tailed off.

'There's no but, Wheelie. I loved him.' Abruptly Magda turned the music up.

They drove in silence for a few minutes, then the irrepressible Catherine picked up her thread again. 'See, you probably don't want to talk about this, but I'm going to ask you anyway because I want to know and you're the only person who can tell me.'

Magda groaned. She recognised the familiar overture to one of her sister's tenacious inquiries. 'You're right, Wheelie. Whatever it is, I probably don't want to talk about it.'

'I totally get that you loved Philip. Right up till you told me about Jay, it never crossed my mind that you didn't. But now you love Jay. And I mean, it's obvious to me that you love her and that loving her makes you happy. But that's what I thought about Philip too. Each of those things makes sense on its own. But together? I can't make sense of it.' Catherine hunkered down in the seat, pulling her legs up and wrapping her arms round her shins.

Magda tried to concentrate on driving. But Catherine's words drilled down too deep to be ignored. And if she couldn't deal with Catherine, who was on her side, how on earth was she going to deal with her parents? 'It's complicated,' she said.

'Well, duh. I got that much. What I'm trying to get at . . . is it that you're a lesbian and you've always been a lesbian only you were in denial, or is it just Jay?'

Magda felt like there was a stone in her stomach. Why couldn't she just get on with living her life? Why did she have to explain herself to anybody? Even as she had the thought, she knew the answer. Because she was the eldest. Because her life had never been her own. Because she'd grown up with three younger siblings who always wanted to know the why of everything. She'd grown accustomed to answering and they'd grown accustomed to being answered and now it felt like a divine right. 'I think I've always been a lesbian,' she said slowly. 'But I didn't want to admit it. Least of all to myself.'

'Why not? This is the twenty-first century, Mag. You can even get married now.'

'It took a long time to dawn on me, Wheelie. You know what it's like when you're a teenager, everybody has crushes on teachers, on other girls, on actresses, whatever. So there's nothing odd about being in love with your best friend except that the unwritten rule is that you don't talk about it. You have sleepovers and you snuggle and you talk till dawn but you never talk about any feelings you have for each other. And then you all start going out with boys, and it's what you do. You go with the flow. And you still feel the same about your best friend, only now it's clear you absolutely don't talk about it.' Magda ran into the sand, uncertain where to go next.

'Well, yeah. OK. Except the bit about still feeling the same. I stopped feeling like that when I started kissing boys.'

Magda gave a wry smile that twisted her beauty into something darker. 'Now, I get that. Back then, I didn't. I thought that was just how it was. And I was lucky. The boys I went out with were decent blokes.'

'Probably because you're beautiful so you got the pick of them,' Catherine butted in, pulling a sad clown face.

'Whatever. All I knew was they didn't make my chest hurt like girls did. They didn't make me breathe faster or count the hours till I would see them again. But they treated me well enough and I didn't dislike their company. It was easier just to go with the flow, Wheelie.' She pushed a stray strand of hair away from her face and checked her mirrors before moving over a lane.

'Why did you care so much about going with the flow?'

'Oh God . . . All sorts of reasons. I wanted to be a doctor working with children. I was too wrapped up in my work to be arsed with anything emotionally complicated. I didn't want to rock the boat at home. Things have been so grisly between Mum and Dad for so long, I couldn't bear the thought of throwing them another bone to fight over. And I was always supposed to be the one who was the good example. I didn't want to turn into the outcast, Wheelie.' She sighed. 'It all sounds really stupid now, but it was important at the time.'

'So you married Philip to keep everything sweet?' Catherine sounded incredulous. Magda couldn't blame her.

'It wasn't that cold-blooded,' she protested. 'I thought I loved him. I was genuinely fond of him, Wheelie. We had fun together. I liked being with him.'

'What about the sex? Didn't you *notice* you didn't fancy him? More to the point, didn't *he* notice?'

Magda winced. 'Straight for the jugular as usual. Look, the sex was fine. I'm not going into details, because it's none of your business. I got married to Philip with my eyes open. I knew I could make it work between us. It really didn't matter to me that it wasn't some earth-shattering grand passion. Frankly, I thought that kind of thing was overrated, judging by the mess most of my friends have made of it.'

Catherine let out a low whistle. 'And then you met Jay.' She laughed in delight. 'And she's turned you inside out and upside down. The gods are having their fun with you now, Mag. You've got your grand passion in spades.'

'Fuck you, Wheelie,' Magda said without rancour. 'Now it's my turn to ask you a question.'

Catherine raised her eyebrows. 'Fire away, sis.'

'Given you have no boundaries at all when it comes to other people's privacy, how come it's taken you so long to ask me the question?'

3

Jay smiled to herself. She'd learned from her first memoir that the closer she stuck to the structure of a novel, the more her readers would be drawn in. Cliff-hanging chapter endings and hints of what was to come, that was what kept the reader glued to the book. She'd been reluctant to revisit some parts of her past, but now she was getting into her stride, she was finding it surprisingly satisfying to see it take shape. And with the trial over, she found her focus was much stronger. Clearly, she'd been more stressed by what had been happening in court than she liked to admit to herself.

Acknowledging that made her wonder whether she'd had any understanding of her stress levels when Jess had died. At the time, she'd just kept her head down and done what she had to do. Thinking about it now, it must have had more of an impact than she'd realised. It was worth bearing that in mind as she wrote the next section. It wouldn't hurt to show a little vulnerability, a hint of grappling with grief.

I was eating breakfast alone in the dining hall when I heard the news. In spite of Jess's cruel barb, Louise and I had made a point of never coming in to breakfast together, though generally one would join the other as she was finishing her toast and coffee. But that morning, Louise hadn't appeared yet. I was sitting with a view of the entrance; after her threats of the previous morning, the last thing I wanted was Jess creeping up on me.

The news started as a murmur and gasp at the far end of the room, generated by the arrival of a handful of dishevelled rowers. They were normally among the first in to breakfast, desperate for calories to replace those they'd just used up in their early-morning exertions on the river. But today, they were late. And Jess was not among them.

The report snaked up and down the refectory tables, knots of people forming in the aisles. 'Jess Edwards is dead,' I eventually heard someone say in shocked and amazed tones a couple of seats from me. I dropped my fork with a clatter.

'Jess?' I exclaimed. 'Jess Edwards?'

'Yeah,' the woman who had just sat down diagonally opposite me confirmed. 'I just heard, at the serving hatch.' She jerked her head towards the rowers, now sitting hunched over cups of coffee, their shoulders angled to make themselves a self-contained group. 'They found her.'

'That's awful! What happened?' someone else demanded before I could ask the same thing.

'Nobody knows yet,' our informant said. 'They found her in the river. Face down. At the end of the meadow, by the boathouse. She was caught up in one of the willows. They were just launching the boat this morning when one of them saw her legs.'

'Oh my God. That must have been horrendous. I can't believe it,' I said, almost to myself. A complicated mix of emotions was swirling through me. I was appalled by the death of one of my contemporaries. No matter how difficult things had been between us, Jess was someone at the same point in her life as I was, and I was alive to the terrible tragedy of her death. But I'd be dishonest if I didn't admit to a sense of relief. Jess was dead but I was safe. Even if Jess's cohorts knew about the plan for the smear campaign, her death would thrust them into far too much disarray to capitalise on it.

I pushed my chair back with a screech of wood on wood and stood up. 'I just can't take it in,' I said, walking out of the dining hall like a woman in a dream.

Inevitably, my feet took me out of the Sackville Building and into the misty gardens. I scrambled down the rockery steps to the river bank and walked slowly towards the meadow. I didn't have to go far before I could see an area taped off and the dark shapes of police officers standing around by the boathouse. It was real. Jess was dead. She had been one of the golden girls of my generation, and now it was all over for her.

An event like that can be a defining moment for the group touched by it. I won't pretend we were friends, but the memory of Jess Edwards rises up before me several

136

times a year. Every University Boat Race, I think of her leading the college boat to victory. Whenever I watch young athletes, I remember the strength and beauty of her body. I regret the loss of promise, and I wonder what she would have made of her life. I look at the lives of the other golden girls and remind myself that most of them haven't done anything spectacular, as if that were some sort of consolation. It isn't, of course.

Was that the right note? The trick was to appear candid without actually indulging in candour. Jay knew that absolute honesty was a complete non-starter, not just for her but for anyone engaging in an enterprise like this. The truth was she'd been bloody glad when Jess Edwards had died. It had suited her at the time and even now she didn't think the world was any the poorer for the absence of another over-privileged Tory bitch with an overdeveloped sense of entitlement.

And that was an impossible thing to say. Maybe the structures of fiction were working so well for her because that was what she was really writing.

By dinner, the word was all over college. It looked as if Jess had gone down to the boathouse earlier than usual. According to one of her fellow oarswomen, she'd been complaining that her seat wasn't sliding freely enough, so the supposition was that she'd gone down to do something technical to it. It had been damp and misty, the ground underfoot slippery and muddy. Jess appeared to have lost her footing on the landing stage, hit her head on the edge of the jetty and tumbled unconscious into the water, where she'd drowned. A tragic accident, the consensus said, a verdict echoed in due course by the coroner. For my part, I promised my first task as JCR President would be to insist the college laid a non-slip surface on the landing stage. It was too little, too late, but it was the best thing I could do to honour her memory.

Because there was nothing to stop me becoming JCR President now. There were a couple of other candidates, but in truth, it had been a two-horse race between me and Jess. The election three days later was a walkover. There had been some murmurings about postponing it until after Jess's funeral, but tradition has always been a powerful argument in an Oxford college. And besides, the incumbent was determined to give up office at the end of term so she could concentrate on working for her finals. Her reminder that Jess cared about St Scholastika's and that she wouldn't have wanted her death to interfere with the proper running of the Junior Common Room was enough to make sure everything ran to the appropriate timetable.

So it was as President-Elect of the JCR that I contributed to Jess's funeral. I spoke about the importance of difference, the need for opposition so that ideas could be tested. I recalled Jess's wholehearted commitment to everything she did and how much we would miss her. And it came from the heart, even surprising me a little with its power. People who were in St Mary the Virgin that day remembered my address for years, or so they told me when they bumped into me at college celebrations or in real life.

Jay stood up and walked away from the computer. The next section would have to be perfectly poised and she wanted to think it through before she tried to put pen to paper. Once, she would have gone to a climbing wall and let her subconscious mind do the work while she was intent on putting together a sequence of hand- and footholds that would take her to the top of the wall with a degree of panache. These days, that was beyond her. The injuries she'd sustained in the incident that had claimed the life of her business partner, Kathy Lipson, hadn't seemed too bad at the time. Just torn ligaments in one knee, stiffness from the cold, a painful twist in the lower back. No big deal. But as the years had slipped away, it had become clear that the damage had plugged into genetic neurological predispositions. Her fingers lacked the strength to grip, her knees no longer wanted to crab across rock faces, her toes cramped in cracks. She was a liability on a mountain, bereft of the one physical activity she'd ever found any point in.

Now, she walked. There was no challenge in it, but there was rhythm and rhythm made her mind work. She loved to walk by the Thames, the river on one side and the traffic on the other. It was where she constructed business plans, resolved problems and built strategies for dealing with people. It was also where she practised her writing, figuring out how to tell the story that was in her memory in such a way that it made sense. Shaping and reshaping, organising her material in different arrangements, transforming the untidy into a pleasing form.

The next section she would write was about Corinna and it couldn't be dodged. There was no way to write this part of the story with full weight and resonance without including what had happened between her and Magda's mother. Of course it would be easier in some ways to ignore it altogether. Whatever Jay wrote, it was going to provoke unease between the two of them. She had to negotiate a way through the truth that they could all live with. And that wasn't going to be easy.

Jay made her way through the warren of tight little streets that brought her on to the Chelsea Physic Garden. Sometimes she walked from the Chelsea Embankment to Blackfriars and beyond if she was in the grip of a particular problem. But since Magda had arrived to fill so much of her life, writing time had become even more precious. She didn't want to spend any more time away from the keyboard than she needed to.

She walked briskly along the paths, paying no real attention to what she was seeing. As she walked, she munched Cox's Orange Pippins, her jaw grinding in counterpoint to her footsteps. There had to be a way of doing this that told enough truth so that nobody would quibble while at the same time disguising the darker side of Jay's real reactions and responses.

Rehearsing it as she walked, Jay eventually came up with what she hoped would keep everybody more or less happy. Her stride lengthened and her eyes sparkled as she retraced her steps at a brisker pace, eager to get back and try it out.

Not everything went as smoothly as my accession to the presidency, however. Inevitably, the ugly gossip that Jess had started did not die with her. People had begun to talk. There were times when I wondered if the feminist revolution had ever happened.

Some of you reading this will wonder whether I was paranoid. I know it's hard to believe I'm talking about 1993, not 1973. In the outside world, there were openly lesbian tennis players, actors and writers. Not many, admittedly, but some. Yet the world I inhabited was still fiercely homophobic even if it pretended otherwise. Oxford graduates tended to gravitate towards the kind of careers where gender equality was regarded with polite incredulity – never mind gay liberation. So nobody wanted to be branded as a lesbian, not even by association.

And yet, part of me wanted to believe I could dare to be different. Once I was safely ensconced as JCR President I refused to worry. Indeed, I even considered coming out and making a principled stand of it, but Louise had issued a panicked veto as soon as I broached the subject. If I came out, Louise had argued, then she would be forced into the open also. And unlike me, she was still firmly attached to her family and her home, where staunch adherence to the moral principles of the Catholic Church still held sway. To be lesbian in Louise's family would be to acknowledge that you were living in mortal sin, and she was not ready for that.

'It's all right for you,' she murmured in my arms in the early hours. 'You're gay. You know you're a lesbian. I don't. I know I love you, but that doesn't mean I have to be like you.'

So I held back. I reasoned that, if I ignored the rumour, it would fizzle and die when something more interesting came along. I was naïve; I didn't understand the damage that might flow from those poisonous words.

It had started seemingly innocently. The day of the election, I left a note in Corinna's pigeonhole confirming I'd meet her that evening as usual for a drink. I was eager to celebrate and in spite of my relationship with Louise, Corinna was still someone I wanted to share my moment of glory with. On my way out to our rendezvous, I checked my own pigeonhole and found a note from Corinna. 'Dear Jay, I'm going to have to take a rain check on tonight. Henry's mother is about to descend upon us, so I'm stuck at home. Apologies. Corinna.'

I was disappointed, but not unduly distressed. It wasn't the first time one or other of us had had to duck out of an arrangement. There would be plenty of opportunities to catch up, or so I thought.

I was wrong. The following day, another message from Corinna arrived. 'Dear Jay, with Henry's mother in residence, I won't need you to babysit Friday night. No doubt you won't be short of things to do! Corinna.' I felt mildly cross, having grown accustomed to the useful and regular supplement to my grant that babysitting for Corinna had become. But I knew relations between Corinna and her mother-in-law had always been awkward and that Dorothy would be insulted if I had turned up to take care of the children when she was in the house.

I waited for a note from Corinna to arrange our next evening out; she wasn't teaching me that term, so unless we bumped into each other around college, we communicated by notes. I waited in vain. Two weeks had passed since that initial cancellation, though I barely noticed the days slip by. There was the routine weight of academic work. There were the new responsibilities of office, where I had to bring myself up to speed with the current state of play and then develop my strategies for the changes I planned to institute. And of course, there was my relationship with Louise, still fresh, still exciting but also demanding.

Then, one afternoon, I was at an intercollegiate meeting of JCR Presidents in St John's. For once, the meeting finished earlier than I anticipated, and since I was less than five minutes by bike from Corinna's, I decided to drop in for tea. Corinna's car was in the drive, and I could see through the lit windows of the basement that the kids were home. I walked round to the side door and leaned my bike against the wall. As usual, I rang the bell and turned the door handle to walk in. To my surprise, it was locked. In all the time I'd been coming to the house, I'd never known Corinna lock the door in daylight hours.

I frowned and stepped back, feeling strangely rebuffed. I could hear footsteps on the stairs leading up from the basement, and moments later, the door swung open. Corinna stood there, looking faintly worried. Behind her, I could just see Patrick rounding the newel post at the bottom of the stairs. 'Oh. Jay,' Corinna said abruptly. 'You picked a really bad moment. We're just about to go out.'

'No we're not,' Patrick said. 'You just put a pie in the oven.'

Corinna flushed, half-turning to shoot a look at Patrick that sent him scuttling downstairs. 'That's for Henry,' she said crossly, clearly flustered. She took a

143

deep breath and arranged her features in an expression I had never seen before. It was the smile of someone who'd taken a course in facial expressions but had failed the practical. Her eyes stayed anxious, while her mouth curved unconvincingly upwards. 'Sorry,' she said. 'Some other time, huh?'

And the door closed in my face. It was as painful and as humiliating as if Corinna had actually slapped me. I felt weak in the knees, tears smarting my eyes. I was utterly bewildered by so uncompromising a rejection. For over a year, Corinna and her kids had been my family, my home. Corinna had trusted me with her children, with her complaints, with her dreams, and I had reciprocated. And now, with no warning, no explanation, no obvious breach, I was outcast.

Somehow, I turned my bike around and staggered down the drive on nearly steady legs. At the gate, I turned back for one swift glance. Patrick was standing on the window seat in the basement bay window, face blank, staring at me. When I caught his eye, Patrick half-raised one hand. He knew something had changed; it was a valediction, not a wave.

I have never been able to remember anything about the ride back to college except the blinding tears. I could think of only one reason for Corinna's defection. She'd heard the rumours and her affection wasn't enough to overcome her prejudice. Or, more likely, she'd told Henry about the rumours and he'd insisted that I wasn't to be allowed within molesting distance of his precious children.

If such a thing were to happen to Jay Macallan Stewart, entrepreneur and author, anger would sweep through her like a cauterising lance. But back then, I lacked the self-assurance for rage. However hard I'd tried, I hadn't managed to embrace gay pride yet, and part of me felt I deserved the scourge of Corinna's treatment, so guilt added to my devastation. I almost sympathised with Corinna, self-loathing piling one pain on another.

The final blow came a couple of days later, again via pigeonhole. I snatched my post greedily, seeing the familiar dashing scrawl on the college envelope. I ripped it open, staking my happiness on the forlorn hope that it was some sort of reconciliation. 'Dear Jay,' Corinna still dared begin. 'As you will recall, you had requested that I be your tutor next term for your moral philosophy option. Unfortunately, I now realise my teaching load will not accommodate this, so I have arranged for you to be taught by Dr Bliss at St Hilda's instead. She'll get in touch directly to make arrangements for you to meet. Yours, Corinna Newsam.'

I stood numb in the middle of the porter's lodge, desperately struggling to keep my composure. Corinna's denial of me felt like a physical wound deep inside. On either side, women jostled me accidentally as they went to check their own post. I saw none of them. All I could see was Patrick at the window, his bleak little face a pale shadow of my own sorrow.

4

Seeing someone else in the kitchen besides her mother, Magda felt cheated. She'd been screwing her courage to the sticking place all morning, readying herself for confrontation, only half-listening to Catherine's tales of student life, and now the moment would have to be postponed. Almost as soon as she'd had that resentful thought, it dawned on her that the woman rising from the kitchen table seemed too familiar to be a stranger. As her mother pulled her into a hug, Magda kept her eyes on the other woman.

'Darling, I'm so glad to see you,' Corinna exclaimed, drawing her so close Magda felt smothered. 'What a week for you.'

Magda patted her on the back, pulling away to let her sister greet their mother. 'Hello,' she said, with the formal smile of a woman who has been properly brought up in the kind of circles where outsiders at the lunch table were taken in one's stride. She eyed up the not-quite-stranger, taking in black hair stranded with silver and an overall impression of comfortable plumpness inside jeans and a nicely cut baggy blue shirt. A pleasant face with an air of mischief. But it was the eyes that tugged at her memory – calm, watchful, a startling pale blue with a darker rim. Like a husky, Magda thought.

The woman leaned one hip against the table, looking entirely at home. She nodded at Magda and Catherine. 'You don't remember me, do you?'

Catherine, freed from her mother's embrace, looked her up and down, frowning. She'd always had a much stronger visual memory than her sister. 'You're one of the minders, aren't you? I don't remember which one, but you're one of them.'

'The minders?' the woman said, sounding amused.

'What we called our babysitters,' Magda said. 'Mum's undergraduates. You were always temporary, therefore generic.' She shrugged an apology. 'No criticism implied. It's the nature of the thing. You were only ever in Oxford long enough to do a degree. None of you was ever in our lives for long.'

'So which one are you?' Catherine demanded, irrepressibly blunt as always.

Corinna groaned. 'What can I say? I did my best. Somehow, the whole manners thing didn't take with Catherine.'

The woman laughed. 'I'm Charlie. Charlie Flint. I used to read you *Winnie the Pooh*, Wheelie. You always liked Eeyore best.'

Catherine gave a little snort. 'Still do. Only sensible one

of the lot of them.' She stuck a hand out. 'Good to meet you again, Charlie Flint.'

Charlie shook hands. 'And you.' She cocked her head to one side, studying both Newsam girls. 'I wouldn't have recognised you, Wheelie. But I think I'd have been able to pick Magda out of a line-up.'

Magda acknowledged her comment with a raise of the eyebrows then turned back to Corinna. 'Where's Dad?'

Corinna crossed to the range and opened one of the doors, releasing a cloud of steam and the dense aroma of chicken, ham and pastry. 'He's got an Open Day at school. He's got to be there to show prospective parents round.' Magda's expression tightened but she said nothing. 'He'll be back around three, he said.' Corinna checked the pie, replaced it in the oven, then set a pan of potatoes to boil on the range top.

'Never mind,' Catherine said, pulling out a chair and sitting down. She grinned cheerily at Charlie. 'Mum, does Charlie know we have something to celebrate or are we going to have to go through the whole gruesome explanation?'

'Catherine, for heaven's sake,' Corinna said sharply.

'If you mean the court verdict, yes, I know about it,' Charlie said. 'And maybe I should leave you to it. I don't want to intrude.'

Magda caught the quick flash of annoyance on her mother's face, so she was surprised when Corinna said, 'Of course not, Charlie. You're not intruding.'

'Hardly,' Magda said. 'I feel like my whole life has become public property lately.'

Charlie smiled. 'It's never pleasant to be the focus of media attention.'

Catherine's eyes widened and her expression turned to astonishment. 'That's where I know you from,' she said with an air of satisfaction. 'Not just from being a minder. You're the one that was in the news.' She turned to her sister. 'You remember? The guy that got off with murder then went and killed those other women.' Then back to Charlie. 'You're the one that got him off.'

Charlie's expression didn't change from one of pleasant interest. 'That's not how I would describe what happened but yes, some elements of the media have chosen to express it in those terms.'

'Catherine' – Corinna dumped a bottle of red wine heavily in front of her younger daughter – 'Charlie is a guest in our home. We generally don't insult our guests.'

'Not until they've had a drink, at least,' Magda said, shrugging out of her jacket and bringing four glasses to the table. 'I apologise for my sister. I think I should just have cards printed so I can hand them out as I follow her through life. "Magda Newsam is very sorry about her sister's lack of tact."'

'Or we could institute the Catherine Newsam award for tact and diplomacy,' Catherine said. 'I'm sorry, Charlie. When I'm interested in someone or something, I tend to open my mouth without considering the consequences.'

'Keep working on the charm, then,' Charlie said. 'That'll probably save you from getting slapped too often.'

Catherine looked shocked for a millisecond, then she burst out laughing. 'Harsh,' she said, approving. 'So if that's not the way you'd describe what happened, what is?'

'Charlie might not feel like discussing it,' Corinna said, her tone repressive.

'Please, Charlie,' Catherine said. 'We've all been so wound up about the horrible trial, it'd be a welcome distraction.'

'Nothing like other people's problems to take your mind off your own,' Charlie said drily. 'It's really not that interesting.'

Magda had been following the conversation without taking her eyes off Charlie, wondering whether her newly discovered sexuality meant she'd be going through life seeing dykes everywhere or if it would wear off with time. Now she said, 'Wheelie's right. It would be so nice not to be constantly circling my own obsessions.'

Charlie puffed her cheeks up then let out a long noisy breath. 'All right. But I need that drink.' As Magda poured the wine, Charlie composed herself. 'I'm a psychiatrist. I have a particular interest in treating and studying psychopathic personalities.'

'What does that actually mean?' Catherine asked. 'It's one of those things you read in the papers but you're never quite sure what it actually consists of.'

'Psychopaths are individuals who don't have the capacity for empathy or remorse. How their actions affect other people is a matter of complete indifference to them. They lie, they try to control the world so it runs their way. The smart ones are glib and manipulative and learn how to fit in.'

Catherine groaned. 'Sounds like most of the men I know.'

'You've been unlucky, then. We reckon they only make up about one per cent of the population. Mostly I work with people who have been convicted of serious criminal

150

offences, but sometimes I deal with people who have other mental health issues. Their psychopathy is a side issue when I see them, but there is always a certain amount of concern that if they're released into society at large their mental state will lead to them committing serious violent crime. As a result of my professional experience, I ended up as a criminal profiler and an expert witness.' Charlie made a wry face. 'I was doing well. Just like Schollie's alumnae are supposed to.'

'And so you should,' Corinna said. 'You were one of my better students.'

Charlie laughed. 'I find that hard to believe, given how much time I sneaked off doing other things.'

'You're not here just to work.'

'You never said that at the time,' Charlie said. 'Anyway . . . I was called in by the Crown Prosecution Service on a murder case down near Leicester. They had a suspect awaiting trial and they wanted my expert testimony in support of their case. It was pretty much routine for me. I arranged to interview the suspect, a man called Bill Hopton. I ended up speaking to him on four occasions and by the end of our sessions I had some serious concerns. I asked for a meeting with the CPS lawyer.' She sighed and drank some wine.

'I told him that my professional opinion was that Bill Hopton was a psychopathic personality who was capable of sadistic sexual violence. That chances were he would go on to commit violent sexual assaults or rapes that would likely end in murder. But I was equally convinced that he hadn't committed this particular murder. It just didn't fit with the picture I had built of his personality type.'

'I bet that made you popular,' Catherine said.

'Just a bit. The lawyer tried to get me to change my mind, but I wasn't prepared to alter my professional opinion to fit their theory of the crime. So I was bumped off the case. Which would have been the end of it if the defence hadn't got wind of what had gone on. They came to me and asked me to be a defence expert witness. I said no, I can't, it's a conflict of interest, I only have the information I have because I was hired by the CPS, so technically it belongs to them. So they went away and I thought I was done with Bill Hopton. Which was fine by me, because he was a particularly unpleasant and scheming individual.

'Months went by and I forgot all about the Leicester murder. Then one morning I walked into the lecture theatre at the university where I teach and a process server slapped a subpoena on me. Whether I liked it or not, I was going into the box for Bill Hopton. And I was very uncomfortable about it, because I knew how circumstantial the prosecution case was. People think it's all like *CSI* these days, but it's not always that straightforward. This victim had been stripped naked and dumped in a pond, so the forensics were negligible.

'Bill Hopton had been seen hanging around outside the victim's workplace. There was plenty of CCTV footage putting him there. The defence argued that he liked sitting in that particular square because he could piggyback free Wi-Fi from one of the cafés without actually having to spend any money.' Charlie checked the point off on her finger. 'The murder weapon was a wheel brace from a Vauxhall of the same sort of vintage as the one Hopton drove, and his car was missing the wheel brace. The defence claimed there had been no wheel brace when Hopton bought the car, and they produced the woman who'd sold it to him, who said she didn't think there had been one.' A second finger joined the first. 'Hopton had given an alibi that turned out to be a lie. But the defence said he'd lied because he didn't want to admit being with a prostitute. They produced the hooker, who was a pretty pathetic witness, but she stuck to her guns.' A third finger. 'And then there was me.' Charlie ticked off the fourth finger then folded her hand into a fist. 'I couldn't lie. And the jury, quite rightly, found Bill Hopton not guilty.'

'I bet the prosecutors were fit to be tied,' Corinna said.

'They were furious and they let me know it,' Charlie said. 'I reckoned my days of being an expert witness for the prosecution were over. So I went back to the rest of my life. Interviewing psychopaths, lecturing in Manchester and hanging out with my entirely normal wife Maria.'

Magda tried to keep the startled look from her face. It wasn't that they'd been inculcated with homophobia; it had always been a case of hating the sin but loving the sinner. Nevertheless, she couldn't remember anyone ever being so casual about homosexuality in this house. Visitors who knew the Newsams knew better than to tread on their doctrinal toes. So nobody blasphemed in front of Corinna and nobody talked about being gay or having an abortion when she or Henry was around. Yet here was Charlie, openly referring to her lesbian partner as a 'wife' without being thrown out in disgrace as Jay had been all those years before. Maybe her parents were mellowing.

Maybe her own revelation might pass off with less drama than she'd feared.

She realised she'd missed some of Charlie's narrative and forced her attention back to their visitor.

'. . . at least two years later. But this time there was no doubt about it. It was exactly the kind of frenzied, careless attack I would have predicted. There was forensic evidence galore and digital evidence on Bill Hopton's computer. But because he was moving around, it took them a few weeks to track him down. And by that time, he'd killed three other women.' Charlie's voice dropped and she looked suddenly older, lines appearing round her eyes as they narrowed. 'I felt like shit, I'll be honest. I knew I'd done the right thing, but I still felt as if I should have been able to prevent what had happened.'

'Surely there was nothing you could have done,' Corinna said.

'I did recommend that Hopton should be sent to a secure mental hospital, but his lawyer screamed human rights abuse – his client had been found not guilty by a jury, he was an innocent man, the authorities were just trying to get off the hook. Nobody wants to get caught in the middle of that kind of aggravation,' Charlie said. 'So he walked free to kill four women.'

'And the media love a scapegoat,' Magda said. 'Is that why they ended up going over the top on you?'

'Partly. But it really kicked off when the family of one of the victims wanted somebody to pay for their loss. Literally. They decided to sue me for failing in my duty of care. Other relatives of the dead women got on the bandwagon and then one of them had the bright idea of complaining about me to the General Medical Council.'

'But all you did was testify in support of an innocent man,' Catherine said.

'Well, that's not how they see it.' Charlie drained her glass and reached for the bottle. 'Nobody else was ever charged with the Leicestershire murder, and the police are still happy to go off the record with journalists and tell them they're satisfied that they had the right man on trial. And that my testimony was the key to him getting off. And that's why I've been all over the papers.'

'So what happens now?' Corinna asked.

'I have to wait for the case to come to court. And for the GMC to hold a disciplinary hearing. Meanwhile, I can't practise. The university has suspended me on full pay. I'm picking up bits and pieces of teaching and stuff just to get myself out of the house. Poor Maria, she's the world's most down-to-earth person, and she's having to deal with me in all my anxiety and paranoia.'

'Is that what you're doing in Oxford? Teaching?' Catherine again, curiosity overcoming sensitivity.

'I wish. No, I came to visit a colleague. And since I was staying just round the corner, I thought I'd drop in on Corinna.' Charlie tipped her glass to her hostess. Then she turned to Magda. 'I didn't realise I'd be butting in at such an awkward time. I'll be honest. I'd seen the coverage of the trial in the papers, but I didn't make the connection with you.' She spread her hands in a gesture of apology. 'They didn't use your maiden name and I guess in my head I still think of you as Maggot.'

Magda felt the rising tide of a blush in her throat. 'It's

funny,' she said. 'Nobody called me Maggot for years. But you're the second person recently who's used my old nickname.'

'Really?' Charlie looked relieved that her shifting of the subject had worked. 'Some kid you used to know? Or another one of your minders?'

Magda looked at her mother, her chin rising and her shoulders squaring. 'Someone who used to be one of our minders until my mother threw her out of the house.'

Corinna rolled her eyes. 'Now who's going over the top? I presume you're talking about Jay Stewart. For the record, Magda, I did not throw Jay out of the house.'

'You told her she wasn't welcome any more. Because you didn't want a lesbian around your kids.' Suddenly the temper of the room had changed. All the emotion that Magda had been holding in check for months was bursting from its confines.

'I said no such thing.' All the warmth had drained out of Corinna's voice.

'Well, why else would you tell her to go? The only thing that had changed in her life was that she'd been outed on the college grapevine. What? Was it coincidence that that was the week you decided you didn't want her in the house any more?' Mother and daughter glared at each other, but Corinna said nothing.

Catherine turned to Charlie, shaking her head, and said, 'And they say I'm the one who puts her foot in it. I bet you're really glad you came.'

Magda seemed oblivious to the interjection. 'I'm waiting, Mum. If it wasn't because she's a lesbian, why did you cut Jay out of our lives?'

'Whatever you might think, Magda, I'm not homophobic. I've always known Charlie's gay and it never got in the way of our friendship. I was always happy to have Charlie take care of you kids.'

'So why?' Magda's voice was almost a howl. This wasn't how she'd planned today, but she couldn't figure out how to back down now she'd come this far.

Corinna glanced at Charlie as if she might have an answer. Charlie simply shrugged. 'I had good reason,' Corinna finally said. 'And it was nothing to do with who Jay chose to sleep with. I'm sorry, Magda, but I'm not going to tell you why.'

'You're going to have to do better than that, Mum.'

'No, Magda, I'm not. I'm entitled to my privacy. I don't have to tell you everything.'

Magda looked as if she couldn't decide whether to burst into tears or throw something. 'Well, whatever your stupid reason, you're going to have to lift the fatwa. Because if Jay's not allowed in this house, I won't be here either. I've been trying to find the right time to tell you this, but it's obvious there's never going to be a good moment. Jay and me, we're together. She's my lover.' She didn't wait for a response from Corinna, but turned to Charlie. 'I'm glad you're here. Maybe you can explain to my mother that this isn't the end of the world.'

'Oh, for goodness sake, Magda. Of course I don't think it's the end of the world,' Corinna snapped.

Magda's expression changed as something dawned on her. She rounded on Charlie, face scarlet with anger. 'That's why you're here. You're here because my mother realised Jay and I are more than friends. You're the token lesbian, the one she can use as a shield against the accusation of being a raging bigot. She had to dig back into ancient history, but finally she came up with one. You should be ashamed, letting yourself be used like that.'

'You're making yourself ridiculous, Magda.' Corinna had the implacable chill of an iceberg on collision course. 'Charlie, I'm so sorry.'

Charlie got to her feet, sighing. 'I think it's better if I leave. Magda, I'm really not here to give your mother some identity-politics Brownie points. For what it's worth, your mother has never had any apparent issue with my sexuality. I always reckoned she'd totally got that bit in the New Testament that says you can hate the sin but you have to love the sinner.' She picked up her coat and back-pack and headed for the door. 'I'll see myself out.' She gave them a sketchy wave and a lopsided smile. 'I do know the way, after all.'

'I'll be in touch,' Corinna called after her. As Charlie disappeared round the corner of the stair, she turned to her daughters and said, 'How gracious my children turned out to be. How dare you drive my friends out of my kitchen.'

'Same way you would cheerfully drive my lover out of my life,' Magda said.

'How can you be so certain about anything you've said today, Magda? We've never talked about any of these things. This is the first time you've even admitted Jay is your lover.' Corinna's voice had the edge of a steel blade.

'See? The very words you use are loaded: "admitted". Like I was pleading guilty to a crime. This is precisely why I've said nothing up till now. Because I knew it was going to be a nightmare and, frankly, the trial was enough for me to contend with.' Magda picked up her coat. 'I don't know. I had this crazy notion that the world had moved on. That when it came to their own flesh and blood, even my parents could step away from their bigotry and accept that love was more important than dogma.' She struggled to get her arms into her sleeves, violently yanking at her coat. She was close to tears now, but determined not to give way. 'I genuinely hoped you would say something like, "Forget about the past, anyone you love has a place in this family." Well, that just shows how bloody stupid I am.' She turned on her heel and half-ran for the stairs.

'Magda, wait,' Corinna said.

From the third step, Magda looked back. 'I don't belong in this family any more.'

5

Charlie had made a bet with herself. Five minutes before Magda emerged. She'd give it ten to be on the safe side, but she didn't think she would be on the losing end. She hoped not; it might technically be spring but it was still bloody cold. She settled down on the knee-high brick wall that separated the Newsams' garden from the pavement. It was a typical North Oxford street. Big redbrick Victorian houses that had been built for an era when everyone had servants. Set back from the street, mostly protected by dense shrubberies. Four storeys, with small rooms in the attics for maids and children, and kitchens in the basement. When Charlie had first been a regular visitor to the Newsam house, most of them had still been family homes and on summer evenings the gardens had resonated with the cries of playing children. Now, only a few remained as single units. The economics of property prices in the area had led to most of them being transformed into flats and bedsits, recognisable by their banks of doorbells and inter-coms. She wondered what sounds travelled now on the evening breezes.

She'd been sitting on the wall for a little over three min-utes when the door slammed and Magda strode furiously down the drive. Her eyes were heavy with tears, but she still had a grip on herself. Even in this state, Charlie thought, she had the kind of beauty that provoked a sharp intake of breath. When she saw Charlie, she stopped short. 'What the hell are you doing just sitting there?'

'Waiting for you.' Charlie stayed where she was. 'I'm going down to Schollie's to see Dr Winter. Do you want to walk with me? Or we could go for a drink, if you'd rather.'

Magda looked taken aback. 'You'd keep Dr Winter wait-ing just to buy me a drink? You must have forgotten what she's like.'

Charlie grinned and stood up. 'I don't have a firm appointment. I thought I'd just take a chance on finding her at home.'

Magda gave a little snort of laughter. 'Where else would she be? It's not like she's got any friends to hang out with.'

'I always thought your mum got on pretty well with her.'

'She's got more stroppy in her old age. Mum, that is. And Dr Winter really can't be doing with anything other than craven submission. So it's not as comfortable a rela-tionship as it used to be.'

'You sound like you should be in my line of work,' Charlie said. 'So, what's it to be? A walk to college or a drink?'

'A walk, I think,' Magda said cautiously.

161

Good choice for someone who wanted to be sure of her getaway, Charlie thought. She turned on to the street and Magda fell into step beside her. 'Why did you wait for me?' Magda said at once.

'I thought you might appreciate someone in your corner to sound off to.'

'And you're in my corner?'

'I've been out since I was twenty. People talk about coming out as if it was a discrete moment. One minute you're in the closet, the next you're out. Only it's not like that. It's a whole succession of moments. You come out to your friends. To your family. To your colleagues. To the faceless person on the end of a phone from the car insurance firm. To the mortgage broker. To the new neighbours. To the pub quiz team. These days it's mostly OK because even the raging homophobes know better than to show off their prejudices in public.' Charlie gave a deep sigh. 'But every single gay person I know has been on the receiving end of a vile and hurtful reaction at least once in their life. I suspect it's similar for black people, except they don't have a choice about confronting it. So yes, I'm in your corner. I know how hard this is. Especially since you've been rendered so very publicly straight by the terrible thing that happened to Philip.'

'I just want them to be pleased that I'm happy,' Magda said plaintively. 'I've had such a shit time since Philip died, you'd think they could maybe manage that.'

'It doesn't work like that. It actually makes them more protective. Corinna's desperate for you not to be any more hurt than you are already. She thinks that what you're doing is a recipe for getting hurt.'

'Why would Jay hurt me? She loves me.'

Where to begin, thought Charlie. Like so many doctors she'd encountered, Magda seemed to be an uneasy mixture of maturity and naïveté. Charlie put it down to an unnaturally prolonged time as a student combined with exposure to emotionally shattering moments. 'Our parents always want us to have the easiest, happiest life. Looking at it from the outside, being a lesbian doesn't promise that. Add to that the fact that, for whatever reason, Corinna and Jay fell out a long time ago. She's scared for you. That's what's at the bottom of this.'

'There's nothing to be scared of. I'm happier than I've ever been. I thought I loved Philip, but this is like watching a colour film after you've only ever seen black and white.' They turned a corner into another street which looked just like the one they'd left except that its different orientation meant the tree buds were further advanced.

Charlie grinned. 'Believe me, I know that feeling.'

'How long have you and Maria been together?'

It was, Charlie thought, the invariable question from the newly minted. 'Seven years. We did the civil partnership three years ago.'

'What does she do?'

'She's a dentist. She specialises in implants. Frankly, it would drive me completely nuts in about three hours, but she's fascinated by it.'

'How did you meet?'

The other inevitable question. 'At a wedding. One of her colleagues was marrying one of mine. We were both invited to the reception. Her gaydar twitched first and she chatted me up over the dessert buffet. I thought she was

163

very cute. Tell you the truth, I thought she might be a bit of a bimbo.' Charlie laughed, still rueful at her mistake. 'I could not have been more wrong. What about you and Jay? How did you meet?' She glanced quickly at Magda, who had her chin tucked down and her eyes on the pavement.

'Well, obviously, we met when Jay was still considered a fit and proper person to take care of us kids.'

'Of course. But I don't imagine you kept in touch all these years. How did you run into each other again?'

'There's a short cut here,' Magda said, indicating an alley fenced with high wooden palings that ran between the houses. 'It brings you out by the meadow gate.'

'I remember.' Charlie followed her, forced from her side by the narrowness of the path. 'So where did you guys meet up?'

Magda sighed. 'I know you're a friend of my mum's but, if I tell you, will you promise not to tell her?'

Charlie forced a chuckle. This was getting interesting and she didn't want to lose Magda now. 'Don't tell me it was somewhere disreputable.'

'No, nothing like that. But I just don't want her to get the wrong idea. Promise?'

'OK, I promise.' Charlie sidestepped a puddle, felt wet grass switch against her trouser leg.

'It's the most unromantic thing,' Magda said. 'We bumped into each other in the ladies' loo in Magnusson Hall. At my wedding. I came out of one of the cubicles and she was washing her hands at the basin. Our eyes met in the mirror, and we recognised each other straight away. It was amazing. Electric. But of course, nothing came of it. I mean, how could it? I'd just got married, it didn't make any sense to me.'

Liar, Charlie thought. Magda's insistence felt fake. Like a politician who finds five different ways to not tell the truth, she was responding to what had not been asked. 'But it was a connection.'

'Yes. A connection. Then, when Philip died, she got in touch. Asked if there was anything she could do. To be honest, the thought of spending some time with someone who hadn't known Philip was a relief. Can you understand that?'

The path broadened out and Charlie moved back to Magda's side. 'Completely. The death of someone close can assume an overwhelming presence in our lives. There's no hiding place from the dead. So yes, I totally get why that would appeal.'

Magda nodded. 'That's right.' She smiled and her whole face lit up for the first time. 'So I said yes, she could take me out for a pizza.'

It was a very different story from the version Corinna believed. And it would only serve to fuel Corinna's bizarre conviction that Jay was a multiple murderer whose latest victim had been her son-in-law. The trouble was, it unsettled Charlie. It made her instincts twitch. The encounter felt predatory and calculated and that made her wonder whether Corinna was quite as deluded as she'd thought. 'Nice story,' she said, giving no hint of her disquiet.

'Charlie?'

'Yes?'

'Do you know why Jay and my mum fell out? Was it really not just bigotry and prejudice?'

Charlie considered her options and decided she didn't actually have any. 'I don't know. All I can say is, your mum might not approve of homosexuality, but she's not a bigot. As far as I am aware, she's always been able to separate the general from the particular. I was in my second year when I started coming out to people and she was one of the first I told. And it changed nothing between us as far as I could tell. She certainly didn't stop using me as a babysitter. So whatever the reason for Jay being banished, I don't think it was because Corinna thought she'd be a bad influence.' Charlie gave Magda a gentle punch on the arm. 'Though, as things have turned out, it seems *I* might have been.'

Magda's smile was vague. 'That's a weird thought. But it doesn't make any sense. Jay says she can't think of any other reason why Corinna acted like she did.'

'It's a long time ago. Maybe they've both forgotten what was behind it. People do sometimes, you know.'

They reached a T-junction in the path and Magda pointed to the left. 'The gate's down there, just round the bend. It brings you into Schollie's meadow. I'm going back to the house.' She turned to face Charlie. 'I came to tell both of my parents about me and Jay. I'm not looking forward to telling my dad. He'll totally lose his mind. But I'm not leaving it up to Mum to break it to him.'

'You will be OK,' Charlie said. 'It's all survivable. You've got your woman to go home to. They can't take that from you.'

Magda suddenly threw her arms round Charlie. 'Thank you. It's been really helpful, talking to you.'

Startled, Charlie returned the hug. 'Any time.' She

stepped back, fishing a card out of her backpack. 'Here. Any time you want to get in touch. It would be good to hear from you.'

Charlie wasn't sure if the flush on Magda's cheeks was from the fresh air or the impulsive embrace. Either way, it emphasised her youth, reminding Charlie of the child she'd first known all those years ago. Magda took the card and tucked it into her pocket. 'It's weird. My minders coming back to take care of me.'

'I guess Corinna had good taste in babysitters.'

Magda groaned as she backed away. 'That's so not funny. Listen, I hope you catch up with Dr Winter.'

Charlie watched her swing round and run back up the alley to the street. It had been an interesting encounter. She turned round and started walking towards the meadow gate, hoping she could persuade Helena Winter into similar indiscretion, but doubting it.

As she opened the wrought-iron gate, her phone rang. Expecting it to be Maria, she was in no hurry to answer. But when she glanced at the screen, her heart leapt. She fumbled with the controls, almost cutting the caller off in her eagerness. 'Lisa,' she said, trying to sound relaxed.

'Hi, Charlie. How's your day so far?'

Charlie couldn't resist a dry little laugh. 'Interesting,' she said. 'In the Chinese sense.'

'Good. We all need the stimulus of interesting days. You can tell me all about it.' Lisa's tone was intimate, her voice seductive as ever. 'I am so sorry I missed you last night. I hated having to let you down.' She sighed, as if she'd been genuinely distressed. 'You know how it is. It's hard to say no when you think you might be able to help. It feels really selfish to walk away for the sake of my own pleasure. I'd rather have been with you, believe me.'

Charlie truly didn't care if Lisa was spinning her a line. It sounded convincing to her and as long as there was still a possibility that things could work out the way she dreamed of, she would go along with whatever Lisa said. 'I understand,' she said. 'Your time's not your own.'

'Exactly,' Lisa said. 'But I have managed to find some space today, if you're still around. I've cleared an hour, and if you could come over to my place, I wouldn't have to waste time going off to meet you then getting back here. Then we could make the most of what little time we've got. How would that be?'

Fabulous? A dream come true? Charlie cleared her throat. 'Which hour did you have in mind?' She shifted the phone to her other hand so she could look at her watch. It was just after one. Why was she even bothering? It didn't matter what time it was, she knew she was at Lisa's beck and call.

'Can you be here for half past three?'

Play it cool, Charlie, play it cool. 'That shouldn't be a problem. I'm on my way to see someone at St Scholastika's right now, but I'll make sure I'm free in plenty of time.'

'That's wonderful,' Lisa said. 'I can't wait to see you. I'm really looking forward to hearing all about your mysterious adventures.'

And that was that. Dead air. No endearments, no small talk. Just Lisa making her arrangements then moving on to the next thing. Charlie didn't care. She punched the air like an adolescent, grinning and doing a surprisingly graceful little pirouette on the tips of her boots. In the space of a couple of minutes, the world had shifted on its axis. Things were going her way. It didn't matter that she'd spent her entire undergraduate career in fear and awe of Dr Helena Winter. Today the tables would be turned.

Today, she would slay the dragon.

6

Walking into Helena Winter's den was like stepping through a wormhole in time. Nothing had apparently changed in the nineteen years since Charlie had sat down on the dark red sofa for her first tutorial on Aristotle. The walls were lined from floor to ceiling with books – and a quick glance suggested to Charlie that most of them were the same books, in the same slots – apart from the chimney breast, which was occupied by a large Victorian watercolour of Zeno holding forth to a rapt audience in a painted portico. The furnishings were Spartan: a sofa and an armchair, a plain pine table and chair by the window. The gas fire hissed and popped as it had all those years before, and Helena Winter herself seemed unaltered by the passage of time.

She had opened the door in response to Charlie's knock, looking as slim and straight-backed as ever. Dr Helena Winter, the Prescott Fellow in Philosophy, immaculate in tailored skirt and cashmere twin-set, a single strand of pearls at her neck, her white hair in the same perfect chignon. A bluestocking version of Audrey Hepburn, Charlie thought. There had been a fleeting moment of uncertainty in her dark blue eyes, then relief as she recognised her visitor. 'Miss Flint,' she said. 'Or is it still doctor?'

Straight for the jugular, as ever. 'It's still doctor. But I prefer Charlie.'

Helena inclined her head. 'Come in, Charlie. This is a surprise.' She held the door wide for Charlie to enter. 'Have a seat.'

For a moment, Charlie diced with the wicked thought of taking the armchair, but either her courage failed or her good manners prevailed and she made for the sofa.

'We don't see you in college very often,' Helena said, settling into her armchair and helping herself to one of the strong untipped cigarettes she used to smoke in tutorials, but only after six in the evening. She caught Charlie's raised eyebrows and said, 'I'm not permitted any longer to smoke in the company of undergraduates. So I take my pleasures when I may. Tell me, to what do I owe this visit, Charlie? Have you decided that a purely academic career is, after all, what you crave?'

She's playing with me. She knows about the Hopton case and she's enjoying herself. Charlie smiled. 'Too late for that, I think.'

'Such a pity. If only you'd believed in your abilities and stuck to philosophy, you could have taken a First, and all of this could have been yours.' Helena gestured magnanimously with both hands, indicating that the room, the college, Oxford itself had all been within her gift and Charlie's grasp.

'I wasn't that good a philosopher.'

'On the contrary, my dear. You had a very fine grasp of the complexities of moral philosophy. You could have made a lasting contribution. It was always my regret that you chose so ephemeral a field in which to work.'

Charlie had been determined not to let Helena get under her defences, but she could feel the niggles and barbs cutting into her. 'Helping people deal with their psychoses isn't exactly ephemeral. And I could never have achieved the enthusiasm for Greek philosophers that you bring to Zeno and Aristotle.' There was truth in what she said; Helena was a passionate teacher, with the articulacy and energy to pass her enthusiasm on to her pupils. But Charlie had come to Oxford for more than academic credentials and she wasn't about to be deflected by any steel-eyed bluestocking who wanted her for a scholar far more than Jesus had ever wanted her for a sunbeam. It dawned on Charlie that at least part of the reason for Helena's attitude was that Charlie had demonstrated the independence of mind to plough her own furrow, turning her back on what had been mapped out for her. 'You look remarkably well, by the way. I heard you'd been ill.'

Helena's wide mouth curved into a thin sickle smile, the deep lines in her fine skin spreading out like concentric ripples on a pond. 'I had a lump removed from my groin,' she said bluntly. 'Doubtless some of my colleagues will have recalled the comment made by Evelyn Waugh of Randolph Churchill when he had a similar experience.'

Charlie raised a questioning eyebrow. Helena had always enjoyed her little triumphs; even though Charlie knew the quotation, it cost nothing to pretend ignorance.

'"How extraordinarily talented of the surgeon to find the one part of Randolph that was not malignant and to remove it,"' Helena said with a grim smile.

'I'm glad it was nothing serious.'

She acknowledged the reply with another gracious nod. 'And you? I hear you're being tested in a quite different manner.'

Charlie turned away from the twin scalpels of her eyes and stared out over the river. 'It's not been easy. But I will get through it.'

'You will. You're tough, and you're talented. So why are you here, Charlie? I don't imagine you think the answers to your problems lie in the tenets of Antisthenes.'

Charlie smiled. 'I'll leave the Cynicism to you. The reason I'm here is that I need you to confirm something I've been told.'

'That sounds intriguing. I can't imagine the intersection of what I know and what you need to know.'

Charlie knew she had to proceed carefully. Helena Winter had always been as generous to an unsupported statement as a fox to a wounded chicken. 'Seventeen years ago, Corinna Newsam came to you with a moral dilemma. I need you to confirm what she told you that morning.'

Charlie had never seen Helena genuinely taken aback. It was a beautiful moment. 'I have no idea to what you're referring,' she said. It was a good attempt at her best hauteur, but it fell short.

'Let me jog your memory. I know how it is when we get older and things don't surface as readily as they once did.' Charlie enjoyed the brief tightening of the muscles round Helena's mouth. 'It was a memorable day here. The day

Jess Edwards died.' Helena did not look away; she held Charlie's steady gaze, a trickle of smoke rising unwavering from her hand. 'Corinna tells me she came to see you.'

'Suppose for a moment that the circumstance you describe took place. Why on earth should I disclose it to you? You have no standing here. We haven't spoken for years. I know nothing of your motives.' She raised her hand and inhaled deeply. 'But that is idle speculation. I have no recollection of any such event.'

Charlie shook her head. 'Call Corinna and ask her if you can trust me.' She dug into her pocket and produced her mobile. 'Here. Save yourself the bother of getting up. Use my phone.'

Helena ignored the offer, reaching instead for her own landline handset. She stubbed out her cigarette then keyed in a number from memory and waited. 'Corinna? It's Helena. I . . .' Obviously cut off by Corinna, her lips tightened in displeasure. 'She is indeed,' she said, then fell silent again. 'Very well. Come and see me tomorrow at quarter to nine.' She ended the call and gave Charlie a long, considering look. 'Whatever information I have is impotent. Nothing can come of it. Where there is no proof, there can be no purpose in dissemination. Do you understand me?'

'I'm not about to run off to the tabloids.' Charlie let her disapproval leak into her voice. 'If I was that sort of person, do you think for a moment that Corinna would have entrusted me with this?'

'Whatever "this" is,' Helena said tartly. 'I have no idea why Corinna feels the need to revisit this episode.'

'That's her business. What did she tell you?'

At last, Helena looked away, studying the hand that had held the cigarette. 'It was towards the end of the morning. The news of Jess's death had shaken everyone. It's always the same when an undergraduate dies. There's a profound sense of shock, but also an anger that so much promise will never be fulfilled. That's even stronger when it's someone like Jess who has obvious gifts over and above their intellectual ability. The details fly round the place like wildfire, so by mid-morning everyone knew that Jess had somehow fallen, hit her head and drowned. We also knew that this must have happened very early in the morning, since she was already dead when the rest of the rowers arrived for their morning practice. According to the other rowers, Jess had complained that her seat wasn't moving smoothly and she planned to go down to the boathouse ahead of practice to see if she could sort out the problem.'

'Was that common knowledge before the accident?' Charlie asked. Opening the subject out was often the best way to draw information from a reluctant witness.

'I couldn't say. I seem to remember the girls saying that Jess talked about it over dinner the previous evening. In theory, I suppose anyone could have overheard.' Helena reached for another cigarette but didn't light it straight away, preferring to roll it between her fingers. Her hands, roped with veins and marked with liver spots, revealed the passage of the years far more than her face or posture. With a sudden shock, Charlie realised Helena had become an old woman.

'Why did Corinna need to see you?' she asked.

Helena took her time lighting the cigarette. 'She needed

advice. She had seen something – or rather, someone – in the meadow that morning. Very early in the morning. And she was in a quandary as to what she should do about it.'

'Why was she in a quandary? She'd seen someone at the scene of a violent death. Surely the obvious thing to do would be to talk to the police?' Charlie kept any accusation out of her voice, making her question sound like a casual query.

'But it wasn't that simple. It was late November. When Corinna had entered the meadow by the side gate, it had still been dark. She was certain of her identification because she knew the person in question very well, but she was well aware that in a coroner's court or a criminal court, she could soon be made to look unreliable on the question of identification at a distance in poor lighting. Furthermore, the presence of an individual did not, in and of itself, point to any kind of involvement in Jess's death. Even if the person in question had met Jess at the boathouse, there was no reason to suppose anything sinister in that.'

'Even if the person in question benefited from Jess's death? And it's OK to use her name, Helena. We both know we're talking about Jay Stewart. That's who Corinna saw, and that's whose ambition was being thwarted by Jess Edwards' popularity. And, according to Corinna, victim of a dirty tricks campaign led by Jess.'

Helena gave Charlie a pained smile. 'Much as I love this college, it's hard for me to believe that someone would murder in order to become JCR President.'

'I'm with you on that. But I've spent time with a lot of

killers, and you'd be depressed beyond measure by the apparent triviality of most of their motives.'

'You may be right. But I did point out to Corinna that what she thought she had seen was open to several interpretations. And that as soon as she voiced any suspicion to the police, both the college and the person in question would become media fodder in the most unpleasant of ways. At a time when the college was desperately trying to raise endowment, it would have been a disaster. And a pointless one at that.'

It was, Charlie thought, breathtaking. Stifle any possibility of suspicion attaching to what might well have been a murder just to protect the reputation of a college, and its fund-raising programme. Only in Oxford. Well, maybe in Cambridge too. 'You don't think that if the police had been alerted to the possibility of foul play they might have found evidence?'

'My dear Charlie, our intention was not to suppress evidence. As I said to Corinna at the time, had there been the slightest suggestion of anything untoward about Jess's death, it would have been her duty to report what she had seen. But it was never suggested that Jess's death was anything other than an accident.'

'So far as you know,' Charlie said.

'I believe the police did keep the college fully informed of their thinking.'

Charlie shook her head wearily. That might be a comfortable thought for Helena to cling to, but she knew there was little chance of the police having shared vague suspicions with anyone outside their closed circle. 'In my experience, the police only tell what they want you to

know,' she said. 'Corinna's information might have transformed the nature of their inquiry.'

Helena tilted her head back and savoured the smoke. 'I
think it far more likely that it would merely have served to
tarnish the name of the college and of the person involved.'

'You still haven't said her name,' Charlie said.

'And I have every intention of continuing my discretion
on that point. Corinna may trust you, but I do not have
her certainty. For all I know, you may be recording this on
some clever electronic gadget. I have no desire to expose
myself to a slander suit.'

'You are something else, Dr Winter.'

'I'll take that as a compliment, Dr Flint.'

Charlie made a small derisive sound. 'I wouldn't. Is
there anything else that Corinna said that might be of
interest to someone who was taking a fresh look at Jess
Edwards' death?'

Helena gave Charlie a contemplative look, as if she were
weighing her in some internal balance. 'To be perfectly
frank, I was surprised that Corinna shared what she had
seen with anyone.'

'Because a secret can be kept by two people providing
one of them be dead?'

Helena's smile was wry. 'In a way. But more specifically,
because at that time, the undergraduate in question was
Corinna's protégée. Much as you had been a couple of years
before. Corinna always spoke highly of her and defended
her against any criticism. That she was prepared to say anything that was in any way potentially critical of her
favourite seemed to me to be highly surprising. That it was
something that rendered the girl so potentially vulnerable

was staggering. It was an indication to me of how seriously troubled Corinna was by what she'd seen.'

'Did you put that point to her?'

Helena gave Charlie a hard stare, her manner condescending. 'That would not have been appropriate.'

'Appropriate. Of course.' Charlie shook her head as she sat up, gathering herself together to rise and leave. 'One small thing. Why was Corinna coming into college so early in the morning?'

There was nothing kind in Helena's smile. 'She had ambition. She desperately wanted a fellowship. She refused to accept she was too much of an outsider, that there was too much stacked against her – marriage, motherhood, being Canadian, being Catholic. So she would come into college around six in the morning and do a couple of hours' work before rushing home to see her children off to school. She thought hard work would be enough to overcome her drawbacks.'

'Apparently it was,' Charlie said, getting to her feet. 'I mean, she is a fellow now.'

'We have men who are fellows now,' Helena said, using the word 'men' as if it were comparable to 'cats' or 'monkeys'.

'Thank you for talking to me,' Charlie said, moving towards the door. 'You know, I always thought you were a brilliant philosopher. I had so much respect for the quality of your mind.' This time Helena's smile was sincere, if surprised. 'We all make mistakes, I guess.' Charlie went on. 'You and Corinna, with your desperate desire to protect the college – it looks like you might have let a killer walk free to take more lives.' One hand on the door handle,

Charlie realised that somewhere in the past half hour she'd crossed a line. She'd decided Jay Stewart had a case to answer, and she was going to do her best to make her answer it. 'You should have stopped her then, if you really cared about the college.'

7

Finding the perfect ending for her previous chapter left Jay feeling stranded. Writing about her exploits as JCR President, the final terms at Oxford, the process of coming out once she had a glamorous London journalist girlfriend, the friendships and the contacts that would pave the way for her future seemed flat and uninteresting after the high adrenalin flush of love and death. The drama of her enforced separation from Louise, followed by her lover's suicide attempt, would make good copy, she knew. And she relished the chance finally to take her revenge on Louise's family of narrow-minded bigots. But that posed its own problems. And it wasn't what she wanted to think about now.

She'd heard some writers describe their process of memoir writing as starting at the beginning and continuing steadily to the end. But that hadn't been a formula that worked for her. She remembered how it had been with

Unrepentant. She'd written the high points first – the powerful memories, the dramatic set pieces that had changed the course of her early life. Then she'd gone back and sketched in the gaps. Finally, she'd filled in the background, like a graphic artist colouring in their drawings and giving Superman his scarlet cape. When she'd described it to her agent, he'd frowned. 'But don't you get fed up when you've cherry-picked the best bits? Isn't it boring to go back and fill in the gaps?'

Jay had thought about it, then said, 'I think it's more like what a jeweller does. You start with the stone. It's been cut and polished to make the most of what's there. Then the jeweller has to make a setting that shows it off to the best advantage. That's a real challenge, to make something sparkle even more than it would on its own.'

Jasper had laughed in delight. 'How very lyrical. Darling, you're wasted on memoir. I really must get you to write a romance.'

They'd both known how absurd a notion that was. Jay checked out the time on the computer screen. Almost four. How long did it take to have lunch and argue with your parents? She knew Magda would call before she set off from Oxford, so she had at least an hour to continue writing.

Given the theme that seemed to be gripping her today, the next section was obvious. No need to write much about Kathy – by the time the reader had reached this point, they'd know all they needed to know about her business partner. The geeky one, the practical mind behind doitnow.com. The crazy climber, the one who was safety first at work but put all her risks in the single basket of rock faces and perilous pitches. They'd been working together for three years at that point, climbing together for almost as long. They'd been planning the Skye trip for months. Winter climbing on the Black Cuillin, the most challenging and dramatic experience you could have on a mountain in the UK.

There's plenty of time to back out of the Inaccessible Pinnacle. Like most of the climbing in Skye, it's a long walk to get to where the view is secondary to the effort. The Black Cuillin ridge in the west of Skye is the only place in the country where the raw jaggedness of the rock comes close to standing shoulder to shoulder with the Alps and the Rockies. And the Inaccessible Pinnacle – the In Pinn to those in the in crowd who have climbed it – is the most serious summit of all.

Even the man who gave his name to the list of Scottish mountains over 3000ft, Sir Hugh Munro, never managed the In Pinn on Sgurr Dearg. Everybody agrees Sgurr Dearg is the hardest Munro to bag, because it's the only one that requires rock-climbing skills. You can't scramble your way up the In Pinn. You need to know what you're doing. And we did. We weren't novices or idiots.

We'd waited weeks for the right conditions, ready to abandon the office and our work commitments the minute we heard the ice conditions were right for winter climbing. Our rucksacks had been sitting in the office, packed, checked and double-checked. When we got the call from our contact in Glen Brittle, we headed for the airport. When you run a travel company called doit-now.com, you're well placed to pick up those last-minute flights! A quick hop to Glasgow, then a nail-biting seven hours on icy roads to Skye itself.

We'd decided to do the In Pinn on our second climbing day of the holiday. The first day was a warm-up, getting us accustomed to the effect of the snow and ice on the black basalt and gabbro that combine to make the Cuillin such a fantastic surface for rock climbing. We did a couple of slab faces and some chimneys, enough to limber us up for the main attraction. As usual, we climbed well together. Kathy and I never had to talk much when we were on the hill; we had an instinctive understanding of each other's needs. It always surprised me, how well we got on when we were climbing. In any other circumstances we didn't have much to say to each other unless it was to do with work.

We went to bed early that first night so we'd be at our best for the climb. Not for us the camaraderie and carousing of some of the others who were planning assaults on the ridge and Sgurr Alasdair in the morning. The weather forecast wasn't great so we wanted to be up and gone early. We'd already decided to set off while it was still dark. That's the trouble with winter climbing in the north – your days are so short and the best climbs often involve a long walk in and out again.

We parked beside the Glen Brittle mountain rescue post. We were excited about the day ahead of us; it never occurred to me that we might end up needing the services of that very mountain rescue team. We had headlamps on, and even under the thin crust of snow there was no possibility of missing the start of the footpath, a wide depression running along the side of sheep pens. We could hear the rushing water of the Allt Coire na Banachdich, and before long we reached the wooden bridge that crosses the stream, which was a black-and-white torrent in the dawn light.

I wished we'd been able to leave later, because it was still too dark to appreciate the grandeur of the Eas Mor waterfalls tumbling down into the gorge. I remembered the guidebook I'd bought the first time I visited Skye. 'On Skye,' it announced, 'it rains 323 days out of 365. Never mind. Think how lovely it makes the waterfalls.' Kathy wasn't impressed, not least because the occasional flurry of sleet was buffeting us in the face as we carried on up the rough path, past impressive buttresses and gullies that looked as challenging as anything I'd ever climbed. By the time it was fully light, we were surrounded by astonishing views – great crags, sensational shapes and contours, a jagged skyline, all streaked white with snow and glittering with ice.

When we first caught sight of the In Pinn it was a bit of a let-down. From that distance, it looks insignificant, a canine tooth a bit longer than the incisors and premolars around it. But as we scrambled and traversed, crossing bealachs – the Gaelic word for mountain pass – and scree slopes, the scale of what we were going to attempt gradually dawned on us. And it was daunting.

The pinnacle itself is an obelisk of gabbro, an imposing fin of rock that stretches 50 metres upwards from a small plateau just below the main summit of Sgurr Dearg. It doesn't sound much, but once you start the climb, there's a 1000-metre plummet to the valley floor on one side. If you can look at that without feeling vertigo, you've got a stronger stomach than most climbers.

Before we climbed, we ate a bar of chocolate and took long drinks from our water bottles. There's no water once you get up on to the Cuillin Ridge so you have to carry what you need with you. Taking a big drink before you start means you've got less weight to carry on your back. Kathy's face was alight with anticipation and excitement. I imagine I would have looked much the same.

I don't know how to explain the exhilaration of climbing to someone who has never done it. Nothing else in my life has ever felt quite the same. I was once in an Alpine climbing hut with a Scottish poet who said he thought it was similar to the excitement you feel when you've clicked with somebody you know is special and you realise tonight's the night you're going to sleep together for the first time. I didn't agree then and I don't agree now. Here's the difference. You don't enter into a partnership with a mountain. A climb is a challenge and it's about victory. I don't feel like that about love, or even sex.

Jay smiled to herself. Another little white lie to keep Magda happy. Of course love was a challenge. The moment she'd seen Magda as a woman rather than a child, she'd been determined to find a way to have her. So yes, it was like a climb. You assessed the obstacles, you figured out how to surmount or go round them, you planned your route and then you got on with it.

But the feeling of facing a climb – that was different

from waging a campaign of conquest against a woman. Maybe it was something to do with the absolute focus that climbing required. The blend of mind and body, both operating at their limits to make sure you ended up where you wanted to be. Maybe it was also something to do with the danger. Love had its dangers, but they were seldom fatal. Whereas a climb always contained the seeds of disaster. Jay remembered the words of the legendary Joe Simpson, the man who had crawled down a South American mountain with a broken leg and frostbite after being left for dead at the bottom of a crevasse: 'Everything is safe until it goes wrong.'

8

Walking back to her parents' house, Magda felt slightly bemused. She wasn't in the habit of opening up to virtual strangers. But there was something about Charlie Flint that invited confidences. Maybe that was why she was so good at her job. Or maybe it was a skill she had acquired because of her job. Chicken, or egg? Then it dawned slowly on Magda that since she'd fallen in love with Jay, Charlie was the first lesbian she'd spent any time with who wasn't already a friend of her lover's. And she'd seized that chance to talk about what was real, not the confection she'd created for public consumption. Although she didn't recognise it at that moment, Magda had just passed the milestone that marked the end of the first phase of being in love – the unfolding of the need for confidantes other than her lover.

As she approached the house, her spirits sank. Her father's bike had joined the others chained up in the lean-to by the back door. Henry was home. However awkward things had been with her mother, they were about to get a whole lot worse.

When Magda walked into the kitchen, Henry looked up from the plate of food he was eating and smiled. 'I wondered where you'd got to. Your mother said you'd gone for a walk, which seemed . . .' He searched for the word. Magda had heard the faint slur in his voice and knew he'd already had a couple of gins. 'Unlike you,' he said.

Both Corinna and Catherine looked wary. Magda crossed to her father and kissed his bald patch. 'I've been stuck in stuffy courtrooms all week,' she said. 'I just needed some fresh air.' She shrugged off her coat and sat down opposite him. Henry drained the glass of red wine in front of him and waved the empty glass at his wife. She pushed the bottle towards him and he helped himself to a brimming refill. As if she was seeing him for the first time after a long absence, Magda noticed with a shock how much he had aged. Her mother seemed timeless, but the years were trampling all over Henry. His lank gingery hair had greyed to the colour of scuffed ashes in an early-morning fireplace. The flesh of his face seemed to have melted away, leaving his cheeks hollow and his watery blue eyes more prominent. He'd always looked pink and scrubbed like one of the schoolboys he taught, but lately his cheeks had grown purplish red. He was only fifty-eight, but he looked like a wrecked old man. She didn't need medical training to know this was what drink had done to him. Once she had despised him for his lack of self-control; now she pitied him.

'At least the jury came up with the right verdict,' Henry said. 'Mind you, I suppose they'll be out on the streets again in no time. Bloody murderers, half of them get shorter sentences than bank robbers. The punishment should fit the crime.' Another swig of wine, a couple of mouthfuls of food, then he pushed his half-full plate away from him. 'You always give me too much.' Corinna said nothing, merely taking his plate and noisily scraping the remains into the bin.

'How was your Open Day?' Magda said, expecting a series of complaints.

She wasn't disappointed. Standards, apparently, were dropping like a stone. The quality of prospective pupils, the social class of prospective parents and the laziness of his colleagues all came under fire. 'Thank heavens I'll be retiring in a few years,' Henry concluded. He'd been counting the years to his retirement for as long as Magda could remember. Once, in her teens, she'd asked him why he stayed if he hated it so much. He'd looked at her, bleary with drink, and said, 'The pension, you stupid girl. The pension.' She'd understood enough to realise it was one of the most depressing things she'd ever heard.

'Will you retire at the same time as Dad?' Catherine asked Corinna. 'I bet you're making plans already.'

Corinna looked startled. 'I've a few years yet, Wheelie. I can't say I'd given it any thought. Of course, I can stay on past minimum retirement if I want. And unlike your father I still love the teaching. So I don't know.'

'Bloody college. It's always been more important than your family,' Henry muttered.

Well done, Wheelie. The last thing Magda wanted right

now was a retread of the familiar parental row that had echoed through her life. 'Dad,' she said quickly, 'I've got something to tell you. I wanted to wait till after the trial. Time for a fresh start, you know?'

Henry leaned back in his chair and beamed at her, his irritation with Corinna vanquished by the prospect of good news from his favourite child. 'That sounds promising. Fresh start. So, what is it? You've met someone? Some chap taken your mind off all the sadness? About time, my girl, you can't mourn for ever.'

Magda closed her eyes momentarily and prayed for courage. Catherine reached out under the table and patted her thigh. 'I have met someone, yes. But it's not a man.'

Henry squinted at her, as if he couldn't quite make sense of what she was saying. 'I don't understand. Not a man? What? Someone's offered you a job or something?'

'No, Dad. Not a job. I'm in love with someone. But it's not a man, it's a woman. I'm having a relationship with a woman.'

Henry looked confused, then appalled. 'You're a lesbian?' It was hard to imagine how he could have packed more disgust into three words.

'Yes,' Magda said.

He pushed his chair back and stood up, reeling away from the table, his head in his hands. 'How can that be? You were married to Philip. You've always had boyfriends. This is madness.' He whirled round and glowered at the three women. 'Someone has corrupted you. Taken advantage of your grief. Weaselled their way in when you were down.' His voice dropped, dark with anger. 'Who has done this to you? Who's seduced my daughter? Tell me, Magda.'

191

Magda jumped up, determined not to be faced down. 'I'm a grown woman, Dad. I'm not a child who can be sweet-talked into something she doesn't want to do. I'm in love and I'm not ashamed of it. And if you're interested in who my lover is, I'll tell you. It's Jay Macallan Stewart. You probably remember her as plain Jay Stewart.'

Henry stopped in his tracks, mouthing the name without any sound coming out. Then he turned to Corinna. 'Jay Stewart. Isn't that . . . didn't she . . . wasn't she one of your retinue? The silly hero-worshippers you lined up to babysit the kids?'

Corinna sighed. 'Jay was one of my students, yes. And yes, she did babysit the kids.'

Henry clutched at the lower half of his face. 'You left my children with a pervert.' Now his hands were like claws, waving in front of him as if he was looking for a target to rip apart. 'Now look what's happened.' He pointed at Corinna. 'This is all your fault.' Henry enunciated each word carefully and softly, his disdain obvious.

'Dad, calm down.' Catherine walked up to her father and put a calming hand on his shoulder. 'Jay's not a pervert, not like you make it sound. She was great with us when we were kids. She never did or even said anything remotely inappropriate.' Henry shrugged off her hand and stepped forward, pushing her aside. He was only feet away from Corinna, his hands balling into fists. Corinna stood her ground, and Magda understood that her mother was safe from physical attack. Henry was too much of a coward to risk hitting a woman as tough as his wife.

'Jay's a lesbian, not a paedophile,' Magda said, her jaw tight with anger. 'Just like me, actually. Get it straight,

Dad. She's not a Catholic priest, she doesn't prey on children. And even if this was about blame, which it isn't, it wouldn't be Mum's fault.'

'This is disgusting,' Henry said, his voice cracking. 'You disgust me. We brought you up with standards, with beliefs. And now this . . . this vile, vile thing.'

Catherine tried again to inject some calm into the moment. 'Dad, you're getting this all wrong. How can two people loving each other be vile?'

This time, Henry turned on her. 'How can you be so naïve, you stupid girl? If love was enough, then incest or paedophilia would be acceptable in the eyes of the world, and the church. Some things are just wrong. They're sins. They go against nature.' He spun back round and glared at Magda. 'That your sister can even ask that question . . . you've corrupted her as well.' He shrugged off Catherine's hand and slumped back in his chair, head in hands. 'I can't bear this.' He looked up at her blearily, his eyes bloodshot and damp. 'My beautiful girl. Tainted now.'

'Can we all stop being so melodramatic?' Catherine said plaintively. 'Let's just sit down and talk about this like adults.'

'Be quiet, Catherine,' Henry said savagely, his voice low and hard. 'Magda, I can't bear to look at you. I want you out of this house, now. And don't even think about coming back till you've repented of your evil. Get out, Magda.'

'This is wrong, Dad,' Catherine said. 'This is so wrong. We're family. You can't treat Magda like this.'

'I can and I will, because right is on my side,' Henry said, his face tight and mean with conviction.

'You make me sick, Henry,' Corinna said.

'You brought the sickness in,' he replied. 'Believe me, I know who to blame for this. Think yourself lucky I'm not throwing you out along with your sick daughter.'

'I've heard enough of this,' Magda said. 'If there's anybody sick in here, it's you. You're a drunk and a bigot and you'd love to be a bully if you only had the guts. Well, you won't bully me out of happiness.' She grabbed her coat and ran for the stairs.

Catherine moved to face her father. 'And I'm saying goodbye too. What Magda's doing, it's life-affirming. It's about love. I don't think you know what that means any more. You need help, Dad.' Without waiting for the abuse she knew would come, she followed her sister.

She caught up with Magda as she reached the car. She flung her arms round her sister and held her tight. Magda gave a shaky laugh, tears in her eyes. 'So how do you think it went, Wheelie?'

Catherine rubbed her back. 'Could have been worse, Maggot. Hard to see how, but I'm sure it could have been worse.'

9

It was amazing how vivid her memories were of that morning on Sgurr Dearg. Jay didn't even have to close her eyes to see the monochrome landscape of cloud and rock and snow and ice. Kathy's red jacket and fleece hat were a splash of outrageous colour in the landscape. What should have been a breathtaking panorama over peaks to the sea lochs to east and west was pared to the bone by the low cloud and the scattered bouts of sleety rain. But the view had never been the point of the trip.

We were quiet as we put on our harnesses and roped up in preparation for the climb. The rope is the symbol of the bond between climbing partners. Its practical purpose is to minimise the risk from dangers that the individual climber would struggle to handle alone. No matter how high your levels of skill, experience and physical ability, it's always psychologically easier to be attached to somebody else when you're struggling for the next handhold on a sheer slippery slab of rock.

The east route up the In Pinn was described by the Victorian climbers who first conquered it as a ridge less than a foot wide, 'with an overhanging and infinite drop on one side, and steeper and further on the other'. They weren't exaggerating. Technically, it's only a 'Moderate' climb in terms of the skills you need to be able to accomplish the ascent. But a glance to either side at any time during the ascent can make your bowels turn to water and your stomach flip. And in terms of the consequences if you get it wrong, it's totally unforgiving. Nobody knows that better than me.

When we set off, the clouds were heavy and the air was freezing, but the sleet had stopped and we felt confident we could manage the climb. And to begin with, that's exactly what we did. We set off up a short, steep but easy pitch, the perfect confidence builder for what was to come. And so we began the next pitch, a section of rock that rewarded slow and steady progress. We'd built up a rhythm with hands and feet, moving with confidence, trusting the rock and trusting each other. At the halfway point, we stopped briefly on a ledge. But there was no shelter from the biting wind so we set off again almost immediately. The first few moves were tricky and I had to get my ice axes out, but then the route appeared as obvious as a flight of stairs.

But what a flight of stairs! Imagine crawling up a fifty-foot set of uneven steps with a sheer drop on either side. Now think about doing it on ice. Now think about doing it on ice with someone throwing handfuls of stinging snow in your face. For by now, our worst fear had come to pass. It was snowing. Not just the odd flake, but a full-on fall. Great flakes that covered my eyes and filled my mouth and nose, hurled at me by the harsh wind. Kathy had taken over the lead at the midway point, and the snow that had come out of nowhere was like a curtain between us. She was only a few feet ahead of me yet I could barely see her.

At moments like this, there's not a climber in the world who doesn't know the fear. You try to force it from the front of your mind by concentrating on every move, making sure your hold is solid before you trust your weight to it. But the fear can't be denied. It hums through your veins alongside the adrenalin that keeps you going. That day, as I carried on towards the summit, all I could think was that I couldn't see, I couldn't hear, and as the wet and cold ate into me I was gradually becoming less capable of feeling my hands and feet. In no time at all, I felt like an automaton struggling to keep with the programme.

When the change came, it came without warning. The rope jerked so suddenly and so hard it nearly pulled me straight off the mountain. If I hadn't been wearing spiked crampons on my boots, I'd have been ripped straight off the icy surface to the valley below. As it was, I was yanked sideways so that the top half of my body was twisted across the ridge. The pain was instant and excruciating. My instinct was to grab the rope, to try to shift some of the weight that was pulling me on to the edge of the ridge so hard I could scarcely breathe. It took an agonisingly long time, but at last I managed to straighten myself enough to be able to catch my breath and try to work out what had happened.

The one thing that was clear as soon as I started thinking rather than reacting was that Kathy had come off the mountain. What I desperately needed to find out was what kind of state she was in. If she was conscious and relatively unhurt, it shouldn't be a problem. We both carried the equipment to make what's called a Prusik loop which can be used to help a climber get back up a rope. If I could hold on, she could get back up little by little.

If she wasn't able to climb, things would get more difficult. Using the same piece of equipment, the Prusik loop, the climber who's left on the mountain can attach the rope to a solid piece of rock and let that take the strain. If I could get out of the rope like that, I could try to hoist Kathy back on to the ridge. Or in the worst case, I could secure the rope and go for help.

I prayed the vertigo wouldn't get me and moved my head so I could look down the side of the In Pinn ridge. I needn't have worried. The snow was so thick by then that I could barely see the scarlet of Kathy's jacket. As far as I could make out, she was swinging in the wind, arms and legs dangling. 'Kathy!' I yelled at the top of my voice. 'Kathy!'

I was sure I heard a response, a low moan rising from my partner. My spirits rose like the sudden jagged peak on a hospital bedside monitor. She was conscious. We could get out of this. We were going to be all right. I called out again. And again.

Nothing.

Desperate, I shouted one more time, but there was no response except for the sound of the wind. It dawned on me that what I had heard was the weather, not Kathy. The realisation was like a blow. It looked as if Plan A was a non-starter. All I could think was that she must have hit her head in the fall. These days, I wouldn't dream of climbing without a helmet, but back then, like most of the young climbers I knew, I was convinced I was immortal. Neither of us had worn a helmet that day. Just one of many things I would go back and change if I could.

Plan B was dependent on there being an anchor point for the Prusik loop. If I was going to escape the terrible pressure of the rope, there had to be something else sturdy enough to take the strain. I knew the basalt and gabbro were strong enough. All I needed was a sturdy knob of rock or a little pinnacle that I could get a sling around. I lifted my head and studied the area around me.

Nothing.

I looked again. But there wasn't anything that remotely resembled the kind of promontory I needed. We'd passed plenty of suitable bits of rock on the way up, but it was our bad luck that this part of the climb consisted of the kind of planes and angles that didn't provide anything suitable to tie off the rope.

There was one last possibility. Climbing technology has provided us with an amazing range of gadgets and gizmos. Given the smallest crack or crevice, we can create an anchor using one of the nuts or hexes or cams that we all routinely carry. But all I had in easy reach were my ice axes. I didn't trust their grip with Kathy's weight. Somehow I was going to have to get at my back-pack.

That wasn't as easy as it sounds. My first attempt nearly ended in disaster. Even so slight a shift in my weight was enough to destabilise my position. I felt my balance alter and for one terrible moment I thought I was going to plummet down the mountain, taking Kathy with me. I realised I was going to have to do this infinitely slowly.

That would have been fine if we'd been climbing on a warm summer day with hours of daylight ahead of us. But we were in a blizzard on a February day in the Cuillin, and now that I wasn't moving, my body was starting to seize up. My fingers were chilled, and the cold was slowing my brain and my reactions. But I had to keep going. Time and light were slipping away now we were past noon and heading for darkness.

As I eased my backpack off my shoulders with agonising slowness, I remembered there might be another hope of rescue. There was a mobile phone in my back-pack. Not any old mobile, which would of course have had no signal back in those days in the remote heart of Skye. Thanks to Kathy's love of gadgetry, we both had satellite phones. I had grumbled about the extra weight in my pack, but she had insisted. Now, if the gods smiled on me and I could get a signal, I could simply call the mountain rescue to come and pluck us off this hateful chunk of rock.

Trying to free the backpack meant I was crushed against the rock, taking Kathy's full weight with my upper body strength. I was starting to feel drained as

well as frozen. And still the snow fell, coating my eyelashes and making ledges on my eyebrows, catching in
every breath I dragged into my chest. At last I got one
arm out of the pack and lifted my shoulder so it would
slide towards my other arm, then into my waiting hand.

I'd reckoned without the paralysing cold. I curled my
hand round to reach for the strap as my pack slid down
my arm. But somehow, my fingers didn't close on the
strap and it carried on sliding, its weight adding momentum. I heard my own voice echo inside my head
screaming, 'No,' as my pack hurtled into the void, tumbling through the snow and out of sight.

I sobbed for the first time then. Hope was vanishing
with the light. Yes, we'd left a climb plan with the hotel
reception, but they wouldn't sound the alert until we
didn't show up for dinner. By then, I would have been
lying on the spine of the In Pinn for six hours in a blizzard, supporting the weight of my climbing partner. I
didn't fancy my chances. But I didn't feel I had any
choice.

The wind, already strong, began to pick up. It felt like
a gale up there on the icy rock. And then a bad situation
got worse. The wind shifted its quarter from due north to
north east. Kathy's body, which had been sheltered by the
mass of Sgurr Dearg, was now in the path of the wind. It
began to swing, but not predictably like a pendulum.
That I could have predicted and made adjustments for.
This movement was unpredictable and jerky. I braced
myself, trying to dig my crampons further into the ice. It
was useless. After I'd been wrenched sideways a couple
of times, it became very clear to me that we were both

going to die. I couldn't hold position on the rock, not against the erratic tugging on the rope that the wind was creating. If I came off, there was nothing between us and the valley floor. Our bodies would smash to pulp on the rock below.

The wind whistled round us again and this time the effort of staying put twisted my leg under me. I could feel a tearing, then a searing pain in my left knee. My foot sprang free from the ice. I rammed it back again, almost passing out with the pain. I knew enough about my body to realise I'd torn the ligaments in my knee. I knew then I couldn't hold my position for long. I was done for.

Then I remembered I had a mini multi-tool in the inside pocket of my jacket. Tiny pliers, a nail file, a screwdriver and a two-inch penknife blade. Even as I thought the unthinkable, my heart recoiled in horror. Cutting the rope would condemn Kathy to death. But not cutting it would condemn both of us to death. No other climbers would be coming up here now, not this late in the day. There was no salvation. No rescue. Not any time soon.

I pulled my glove off with my teeth and pushed my frozen hand inside my jacket. My fingers tingled and burned as the residual heat from my body warmed them a little. I closed my hand round the knife and pulled it out. Holding it between my gloved hand and the rock, I managed to get the blade open. But still I dithered. I couldn't bring myself to do it.

Then another gust yanked me hard against the rock, smashing my face and chest against the icy gabbro. I had no choice. Any more of this and I would be over the edge too.

    I cut the rope.

Right on cue, the phone rang. Jay reached for it automatically. It was halfway to her ear before she realised she was crying.

10

Charlie could feel her heart beat, a fast steady thud beneath her ribs. Excitement vibrated through her like a low-level electrical charge. She remembered nothing of the drive from north Oxford across town to Iffley village. She'd always loved coming here as an undergraduate, walking up the towpath from Folly Bridge to the lock. The river was never empty; there were always boats: college eights putting their back into it; intrepid punters prepared to brave the big river; motor cruisers and day boats pottering back and forth. By contrast, the path was often quiet, leading to the incongruity of Iffley itself, a village within a city. Prosperous, quiet and self-contained, it seemed to have resisted the infection of university life. Although the houses were different in style, it reminded Charlie of the Lincolnshire village where her grandparents had lived. So whenever she'd needed an anchor during those sometimes tempestuous Oxford years, this was where she'd walked to.

Lisa's house stood in a quiet lane of substantial cottages a couple of streets away from the river. Charlie imagined it would be chilly and damp on one of Oxford's many foggy winter days, but as this afternoon petered out, some late shafts of sunlight had escaped the clouds and made everything charming. She drove slowly, checking the numbers till she found the right house. She recognised Lisa's sleek silver Audi sports car, but not the Toyota estate squeezed next to it in the tight driveway. It was another fifty yards before Charlie found somewhere to leave her own car without obstructing anyone else's access. She checked her watch. Twenty-five past three. She sat behind the wheel for another three minutes then walked back to the cottage, wondering what she would find there.

As she approached, she couldn't help admiring the house. She must have passed it a dozen times when she was an exploring undergraduate, but she had no recollection of it. There was nothing fancy about it – weathered red brick, tiled roof, white-painted woodwork – but its symmetry and proportions were pleasing to the eye. Above the neat pillared porch was a circular window, the rich colours of its stained glass apparent even in the sunshine. The cars were parked on a driveway of herringbone brick, and the small area in front of the house featured a miniature knot garden of clipped box. Everything was picture perfect. Charlie felt she was making the place look untidy simply by walking up to the front door.

She took a deep breath, trying to calm her agitation. She was as excited as a teenager at the prospect of seeing Lisa on her home turf. Charlie rang the bell and took a half-step back. Almost immediately, she heard footsteps approach and the door opened wide. Lisa grinned, Charlie's heart bounded and she stepped into open arms. 'It's great to see you,' she said.

Lisa's lips grazed her cheek and her warm breath tickled her ear as she said, 'Perfect timing. There's still a couple of people here but they're about to leave.' Then she let Charlie go and stepped back, inviting her in.

Even in this emotional state, Charlie's professional training took over. She couldn't help noting surroundings, letting them inform her judgement. The hallway was simply decorated. White walls and ceiling, parquet floor with the patina of age, four small abstract seascapes in heavy oils. Light from the stained-glass window splashed random colour, giving warmth. And at the heart of it, Lisa herself. Slim hips, wide shoulders, sleeveless top chosen to show the warm gold of her skin and the beautiful curves of clearly defined muscles, and a sassy gait that reminded Charlie of the catwalk. Lisa walked the walk that would attract people's gaze and talked the talk that would hold that attention on her.

Charlie followed her into a sitting room furnished with a trio of sofas in cream chintz, a scatter of low tables and an elaborate Art Nouveau fireplace. A William Morris fire screen sat in front of it. French windows gave on to a long grassy expanse that ended in a wall of shrubbery. A man and a woman occupied two of the sofas, papers spread around them. Their eyes were already fixed on the door, waiting for Lisa.

'Charlie, these are two of my colleagues. Tom and Linda. This is my friend Charlie,' Lisa said briskly. Everyone exchanged smiles and nods. 'So, that's it for today.

When you've had a chance to let the new material sink in, email me with your comments. Otherwise, I'll see you in Swindon on Tuesday.'

Tom and Linda gathered their papers together quickly and stood to leave. It was clear Lisa ran a tight operation. She waved Charlie to the vacant sofa as they were packing their things away. 'Coffee, tea? Juice? Water?' she said.

If she truly only had an hour of Lisa's time, Charlie wasn't going to waste a minute of it on the boiling of kettles. 'I'm fine, thanks.'

'I'll be right back.' Lisa was gently but firmly moving Tom and Linda out of the room, even though he was still trying to zip up his laptop bag.

When she returned almost immediately, Lisa settled on the sofa at right angles to Charlie, tucking her legs under her and leaning on its arm so she appeared to be completely absorbed by her visitor. To Charlie, so accustomed to reading the body language of others, it was a welcome moment. 'So,' Lisa said, turning it into three distinct syllables. 'An interesting day.' There was the trace of a tease in her voice, the undercurrent of something that went beyond social pleasantries.

Charlie smiled. She wanted to point out it was getting better all the time, but she was wary of sounding cheesy. Or predatory. 'Interesting company, too.'

'So tell me all about it.' Lisa propped her chin on her arm and gave Charlie the full headlight stare. 'I love listening to you.'

Charlie took Lisa through her encounter with the Newsams, keeping her narrative tight and to the point. She finished with a brief account of her meeting with Dr

Winter, then leaned back. 'It all turned out to be much more dramatic than I expected,' she said.

'No kidding. What an extraordinary tale,' Lisa said, her voice a low drawl. 'Your old tutor thinks Jay Macallan Stewart is a multiple murderer? I don't think I've heard anything that bizarre since Edwina Currie confessed to her affair with John Major.'

'I thought so too, at first. But then it turned out Jay was in Schollie's on the day of the murder. And Helena Winter confirmed what Corinna had told her about the morning Jess Edwards died. And it started to sound . . . I don't know. Almost plausible.'

Lisa laughed. 'That's a very big almost. What does Maria think about it?'

The mention of Maria was a jarring moment. Charlie had managed to put her partner to the back of her mind ever since she'd arranged to meet Lisa. It was uncomfortable to hear her name from Lisa. 'I haven't had a chance to talk to her yet.'

Lisa looked gratified. 'I'm flattered that you told me about it first,' she said. 'So what will you do now? Gently ease yourself out of the picture? I know you're an expert at working out what goes on in people's heads, but it sounds as if what Corinna Newsam needs is a proper detective.'

'I know. But I thought I might take a look at it, actually,' Charlie said, a little tentatively. 'It's kind of interesting. And if there is something there and I can pin it down . . .'

'I understand that it's tempting, Charlie. But even if you do uncover a miscarriage of justice, it's not going to redeem you in the eyes of the GMC,' Lisa said gently, her expression concerned. 'Or the readership of the *Daily Mail*.'

It was a shrewd comment, demonstrating how clearly she understood Charlie's motives.

'Maybe not. But it might make me feel better about myself.'

'You're sure it's not just an excuse to revisit your own history? To time-warp back to a place and time when you were happy? When you had untainted possibilities in front of you?'

Charlie pondered the idea for a moment. 'I don't think so,' she said. 'I don't dwell on the past. Besides, I still feel like I have possibilities of happiness. Sitting here with you, for example. That's a pretty good place and time for me.'

Lisa ran the tip of her tongue along the inside of her top lip. 'For me too. Even though we haven't known each other long, I do feel a connection between us.'

Charlie's heart leapt. There was no other way to describe that lurch in the chest. How could a few words provoke such a strong physical reaction? 'Some things you just can't ignore,' she said, clearing her throat when she heard how husky her voice had become. 'I really want to explore what's happening between us.'

'But there's no rush, Charlie. We're going to be friends for a long, long time. I'm convinced of it. I think our vulnerabilities and our strengths mesh so well.'

Charlie's mouth was dry. She wished she'd asked for a drink after all. 'You're right. Sometimes you just know. Right from the start.' She shifted so she was leaning on the arm of her sofa, her face closer to Lisa.

'But if you're busy chasing shadows for Corinna Newsam, you're not going to have much time for anything else,' Lisa drawled, her voice filled with regret.

Charlie wasn't dismayed. 'I'll make time.'

Lisa gave her a long, considering look. 'I think you'll be wasting your time.'

After the flirting, it felt like a slap in the face. Charlie's head jerked back. 'What?'

'Trying to prove Jay Stewart is a killer, I mean.' Lisa laughed. 'What did you think I meant, Charlie?'

Charlie didn't know what to say. Her emotions were ramping up then spiralling downwards. 'Why do you say I'll be wasting my time?'

Lisa shrugged. 'It just doesn't seem very likely.'

'Do you know her?' Charlie's professional wariness, hogtied thus far by her hormones, suddenly fought its way to the surface. Was it possible Lisa had another agenda here?

'Not really,' Lisa said. 'We were up at the same time. But of course I was at Univ, so we didn't really cross paths very often. I knew her in that vague way where you bump into people at the same parties from time to time. She was a bit notorious – the dyke who'd made it to JCR President – so she attracted more attention.'

'People knew she was a dyke? I thought she was closeted back then?'

Lisa chuckled. 'She might have thought nobody knew. But you know how it is, Charlie. The rumour mill in Oxford grinds very small. Nothing gets past it. I was still only going out with men back then, but I knew Jay Stewart was a lesbian.'

Charlie's heart bounded in her chest. Never mind what Lisa had said about Jay Stewart, 'I was still only going out with men back then,' she'd said. There was only one way to read that, and it refreshed Charlie's fantasies like spring water after a drought. The blood was beating in her temples, her mouth dry again. 'Sounds like your gaydar was well developed for someone who was only going out with men.'

Lisa leaned back on the sofa and stretched her arms above her head, fingers locked. Charlie was very conscious of how beautiful her arms and her breasts were. Lisa gave a mischievous smile. 'I guess I didn't realise it at the time, but even then I was good at spotting vulnerability.'

11

Her morning shower had left Charlie still dazed with lack of proper sleep. Maybe the breakfast coffee would help. She'd had two nights of restless shifting about under the covers, trying not to disturb Maria. There was too much turmoil in heart and head and the hardest part, ironically, was not being able to share it with Maria. Charlie had grown so accustomed to seven years of Maria taking the weight of her dilemmas and decisions, it was strange to be keeping something from her.

But at least she'd been able to talk to her about Corinna's bizarre request. She'd got home late on Saturday evening, still dazed from her encounter with Lisa. Her comment about vulnerability had marked the end of their conversation. Their hour was up, and Lisa's client's finger was on the doorbell. Charlie had swallowed her disappointment that this encounter hadn't moved their relationship further forward.

She'd been too quick off the mark on that score. As she followed her host into the hallway, Lisa had turned to face her, moving backwards towards the door. She'd stopped then and reached for Charlie's hand, pulling her into an embrace. Charlie felt an explosion of light and heat inside her. This wasn't a friendly farewell kiss. This was the sort of urgent clinch that was a precursor to something hot and sweaty. It had come from nowhere, and even as she surrendered to it, Charlie realised it couldn't go anywhere. Even as lips and tongues and hands explored, the clock was ticking.

The second ring on the doorbell startled them apart. Charlie was flushed and panting. Lisa, two spots of colour on her cheeks, gave her a twisted, flirtatious smile. 'To be continued,' she said.

And opened the door.

Charlie's departure had been a blur. She barely noticed the man who had arrived. She registered Lisa's casual farewell, wondering at so abrupt a shift from one state to another. Then she'd stumbled back to her car, not entirely convinced she was fit to drive. She'd sat for a while, trying to process what had just happened, attempting to divorce her emotional response from a dispassionate analysis of Lisa's behaviour. That turned out to be a waste of time too; her thoughts simply chased their own tails.

She wasn't quite sure where the time had gone between leaving Lisa's and arriving back home in Manchester close to midnight. Seven hours for a three-and-a-half-hour drive. She had a vague recollection of sitting in a coffee shop at a motorway services, but the rest was a blur. Telling Maria about the Newsams had been a welcome distraction when she'd finally fallen into bed.

Maria had been more interested in Corinna's story than Charlie had expected. 'It's fascinating,' she'd said, snuggling into Charlie's back. 'The way that "mother lioness protecting her cubs" thing clicks into place. Corinna clearly wasn't that bothered about Jay Stewart's murderous ways when it was other women's kids in the frame. But put her daughter anywhere near harm's way, and she's calling in the heavy artillery. What are you going to do?'

'I'm not entirely sure,' Charlie had prevaricated. 'One minute I think it's Corinna's paranoia, then I go about-face and think there's too much lurking in Jay's past to be coincidence. It's hard to get my head round the idea that this charismatic, successful businesswoman could be a serial killer.'

'You're going to do it, though. Aren't you?' There was a note of resignation in Maria's voice.

'You think I should?'

'I was thinking about it while you were gone. And while there's part of me wants you to steer clear of other people's battles, I've got to be honest with myself. I know you, Charlie. You need something to keep your mind from eating itself like a rat in a trap.' Maria put her arm on Charlie's thigh. It was a movement of consolation, not eroticism. 'We'll talk about it tomorrow.'

And they had talked about it. On and off, they'd talked about it most of the day, teasing every last drop of possibility from what Charlie knew. Because Maria was familiar with none of the players, Charlie had confidence in her judgement. Maria wasn't swayed by her history with Corinna, her sympathy for Magda, or her inclination to believe Lisa's estimation of Jay Stewart.

'The trouble is, you don't do well when you haven't got something to worry at like a dog with a bone,' Maria had said finally and firmly after dinner. Neither of them was paying much attention to the Sunday-night BBC costume drama; it had reached a quotient of silliness that neither could easily bear. The drama on the fringe of their own life was much more interesting.

'I've still got some teaching.'

'That's not what I mean. Your job's all about getting to the heart of the really difficult stuff. Challenge is what you thrive on. When that's not there, you don't know what to do with yourself. It's hard for someone who loves you, watching how difficult it is for you not to have a problem to wrestle with.'

Charlie snorted. 'I've had plenty of problems, thanks to Bill Hopton.'

'I don't mean that kind of problem. I know you've been trying to put together a defence for the GMC, but that's not the sort of challenge that keeps you on top form. It's more like you need a puzzle. A conundrum. Something to stretch your imagination. You've always needed that. That's why you did so well, working with the police on the profiling. That was high-stakes problem solving. You haven't had anything like that since you had to hand over your caseload. And it's bad for you, Charlie.'

'And you think raking around in the ashes of Jay Stewart's past is what I need to get my mind working properly?'

'I can't answer that for you. But I suppose the question is, why not?'

'For starters, I'm not a detective. I'm a psychiatrist. I don't know how to gather evidence and build a case.'

'Don't be silly. It's exactly what you do all the time. You spend your life gathering evidence on people's mental states then putting together conclusions based on what you've figured out.'

'It's not the same,' Charlie protested. 'I'm not a cop. I don't have access.'

Maria poked her in the ribs. 'You've been watching the cops for years. You've sat in on enough interviews. And nobody is better at blagging their way in where they're not supposed to be than you. Who always manages to get us into the executive lounge at the airport?'

Charlie giggled. 'Not always. Remember that intractable cow at Charles de Gaulle? I thought she was going to get us arrested.'

'Don't try and change the subject, Charlie. If Corinna's even vaguely on the money, then the stakes are certainly high enough. You're looking at righting a miscarriage of justice and putting a stop to someone who might see murder as the most efficient way of getting what she wants. And if she is right, and you prove it, then you get to set up camp on the moral high ground. It would make it hard for the GMC to come down against you if you're the hero of the hour.'

It was interesting, Charlie thought, that Maria's view on the publicly redemptive power of such a success was almost the exact opposite of Lisa's. It was hard to know whose judgement was more likely to be on the money. Charlie leaned her head on Maria's shoulder. 'This wouldn't be a get-out-of-jail-free card for Bill Hopton, sweetheart. That's not going to go away, however the thing with Jay turns out. I still can't escape knowing that if I'd pushed harder for him to be sectioned, four women would still be alive.'

Maria tutted. 'You know that's not true. You said yourself there was no basis for locking him up as the law stands. You'd have had to lie to have him committed. And you'd have had to persuade another doctor to lie too. And even if you'd been successful, he'd have been released in the long run. You know that. And then it would just have been four different women. So stop beating yourself up and focus on something where you can do some good. Either find evidence against Jay, or exonerate her.'

Stretching out on the sofa, Charlie laid her head in Maria's lap. 'You make a strong argument. But there is one other thing that makes me hesitate.'

'What's that?' Maria started fiddling with Charlie's hair, running her fingers through it, twisting locks into corkscrews and watching them spring straight again. It was a familiar routine that always relaxed Charlie.

She wriggled herself more comfortable. 'Lesbian solidarity. Am I being an Uncle Tom? Am I letting myself be used in what's essentially a homophobic witch hunt? Would Corinna have called on me if Jay had been a bloke?'

'Maybe. Well, probably not, if I'm honest. But if Jay had been a bloke, Corinna wouldn't have known anything about his past. So the question would never have arisen.'

Charlie smiled. Trust Maria – down-to-earth, practical Maria – to resolve at least one of the questions that had been torturing Charlie with a piece of logic that she should have had the sense to come up with herself.

'Besides,' Maria added, 'you're not obliged to share your conclusions with Corinna. You're not a private eye. She hasn't hired you. You can do whatever you think best with whatever you uncover. Tell Corinna or not. Tell Magda or not. Tell Jay or not, even.'

So Charlie had settled her argument with herself and decided to do what Corinna had asked. In spite of Lisa's conviction that Jay was no killer, Charlie would chase down whatever evidence might still be found and weigh it in the balance.

It had seemed a straightforward choice at bedtime, but by morning it had become a thorny problem again. Charlie stared into her coffee, frowning. It was all very well, setting herself up to investigate Jay. But where could she begin? What was she even looking for?

Maria flapped a hand in front of her. 'Hello? Anybody home?'

Charlie gave a weak smile. 'I don't know where to start,' she said.

Maria shrugged. 'I've always believed in starting at the beginning.'

'And in this case, the beginning would be . . .?'

'The first instance we know about. The rowing captain's death.'

'And where do I look?'

Maria spread butter on her toast, frowning. 'Oxford, obviously. This happened back before everything was online. You'll need to go and look at the newspaper archives. There must have been an inquest. Surely there'll be a record of that somewhere? And there must have been a police investigation. Maybe there's some old retired cop ready to spill the beans like you get in the best detective novels.'

Charlie laughed. 'I think you're more into this than I am.'

'You've got to admit, it's a hell of a tale. I expect full reports at every stage.'

Charlie felt a twinge of guilt. There would be some aspects of her activities that she wouldn't be reporting to Maria. Maybe chasing Jay's history would turn out to be an antidote to her feelings for Lisa. She'd tried to convince herself that her illicit emotions had simply expanded to fill the space available, but it wasn't working. 'I'll keep you posted,' she said. 'I've not got any teaching till Wednesday, so I can go back to Oxford today.'

'That makes sense,' Maria said. 'Will Corinna put you up?'

Charlie shook her head. 'I don't think that's a good idea. If Magda came out to Henry yesterday like she was planning to, he's not going to welcome another lesbian under his roof. I'll get Corinna to book me into a college guest room. Back to the Spartan cell of the undergraduate.'

Maria grinned. 'Nothing to distract you from the task in hand.'

Charlie had the grace to feel ashamed. 'Not in Schollie's, no,' she said.

Maria finished the last mouthful of toast and stood up. 'Take care,' she said, rounding the corner of the table and hugging Charlie. 'There might just be a killer out there.'

That wasn't the only risk, Charlie thought, her smile wan. Not by a long chalk.

12

The numbers on the clock morphed from 4:16 to 4:17. Jay shifted carefully, anxious to avoid waking Magda. They tended to sleep with legs intertwined, their upper bodies apart. It had quickly evolved as a position they were both comfortable with. There was comfort in the contact, but it wasn't easy to extricate herself when she woke in the early hours, knowing there was no prospect of further sleep. That was the pattern of her life, had been since Kathy's death and the nightmares that came with it. Night after night, Jay woke sweating, body clenched. The dream was always the same: the swirling snow, the freezing cold, the monochrome mountain. Then the imagined scream, a scream there had never been in life, a scream that severed Jay from sleep every night.

The nightmare had gone on for months before she'd finally accepted that she would be stuck with it until she sought help. There was one obvious person – a therapist she'd known since they were students. Jay had been amazed at her susceptibility to hypnosis. She'd always imagined strong-willed characters like her would find it hard to let go. But she slipped easily into the altered state and had little recollection of what had happened while she'd been under. That didn't matter. What mattered was that the bad dreams stopped. She could go to bed secure in the knowledge that whatever she dreamed wouldn't rise up and destroy her sleep.

But the period of nightmare nights had changed one thing for ever. Jay discovered that, like Margaret Thatcher, she could function perfectly well on less sleep than most people needed. Now, four or five hours was all it took to refresh her and set her up for another day. It was, she believed, one reason for her business success. While other people were still sleeping, she was already at her computer surfing the web, dealing with emails, making connections and playing with new ideas. Or writing.

She'd wondered whether revisiting that terrible day on Sgurr Dearg would bring the bad dreams roaring back. Wondered, not in an anxious, frightened way, but more in a clinical, 'How does this work?' kind of way. But nothing had surfaced in spite of her emotional reaction to writing about that moment when she'd cut the rope.

She'd been outwardly composed by the time Magda had returned from Oxford upset and angry. At Jay's suggestion, Catherine had joined them for dinner, a DVD and a bottle of wine. By the time her sister had left, Magda had calmed down and they'd gone to bed with all possible conflict dispelled. They'd made love with all the urgency of

221

reaffirmation, then Jay had slept as if a switch had been thrown in her brain.

Sunday had been a perfect day. Jay had gone out while Magda was still asleep and bought fresh pastries and newspapers. They'd lazed in bed reading and talking, eating and drinking coffee, Craig Armstrong's piano music in the background. When they'd finally dragged themselves out of bed, they'd walked along the river, ending up having an early dinner in an intimate little Italian restaurant near St James's Park. 'During the week it's packed with politicians and journalists,' Jay told Magda. 'But on Sundays, it's got a completely different atmosphere.' She sensed her inside knowledge of London was one of the things Magda found seductive about their time together. It seemed that Philip, for all his money and his generosity, had moved in quite limited tram tracks.

After dinner, they'd walked on through the evening streets to Magda's flat. They didn't often spend the night there, but tomorrow she would have to return to work, and Jay had suggested it would be less complicated if she set off from her own home. Exhausted by fresh air and exercise, Jay had fallen asleep more readily than she generally did in beds that were not her own.

But now she was wide awake, two and a half hours before Magda's alarm clock would sound. Inch by careful inch she withdrew the leg that was trapped between Magda's thighs. Magda groaned in her sleep and shifted on to her side, allowing Jay to slide free. She padded across the room, grabbing Magda's dressing gown from the back of the door and heading for the little room Philip had used as a study. There was, she knew, a computer there she could use, and a memory stick in her trouser pocket to transfer whatever she wrote back to her home machine.

While the machine booted up, Jay cast her mind back to where she had finished on Saturday, before the phone had rung and derailed her concentration. Sometimes, any excuse would do.

I have very little memory of how I got off the In Pinn. All I know is that it took a long time. The pain in my knee took my breath away every time I had to put any weight on my left leg. More than once, I thought I was about to join Kathy on the valley floor. It wasn't just because of the dead weight of my leg. And it wasn't because of the weather; ironically, that had eased a little, certainly enough for most serious climbers to feel confident of getting off the hill in perfect safety. No, it was because I was emotionally shattered. I had sent my business partner and closest ally to her death. It didn't matter that I had only done it so that one of the two of us would survive. I was distraught. Probably borderline hypothermic. And almost certainly in shock.

The whole thing had taken so long that the mountain rescue team had been alerted. Later, I found out that I'd been a couple of hundred feet below the summit of Sgurr Dearg when they'd come across me, dragging myself down the mountain with agonising slowness. They wrapped me in thermal blankets and in stumbling sentences I managed to tell them what had happened. One of the few things I remember is the look that two of them exchanged when I told them I'd had to cut the rope. The pity and sadness in their faces haunts me still.

223

I knew that, in the outside world, I was going to be condemned and reviled. But these men who understood the cruelty of the mountains had no anger in their hearts for me.

They formed a phalanx of support around me and got me off the mountain. If you ever have a chunk of money you feel like donating to charity but you're not sure who to give it to, please send it to the Glen Brittle Mountain Rescue. Those guys are amazing. To turn out without hesitation in the dark in a blizzard to help a stranger is a demonstration of the kind of courage we don't often see in the modern world. If not for them, I could have died that day.

At the time, though, it felt like a mixed blessing to be alive. Kathy's death was a terrible blow. The loss of her friendship, her business acumen, her company – all of that was hard to bear. But I had no peace to grieve. What had happened to us on the In Pinn was an instant media sensation. As the owners of one of Britain's leading dotcom companies, Kathy and I were accustomed to finding our names on the financial pages. We quite liked it – we were proud of what we'd achieved.

This was very different. Any climbing accident where someone perished because of a cut rope would have made a page lead in most of the papers for a day. But because of who we were and because of when it happened, this was a story that was all set for a long run. So I had to contend with the perpetual attentions of hungry journalists who couldn't quite decide if I was a tragic heroine or an evil villain.

As if that wasn't enough, I was in the thick of a major business deal. Really, Kathy and I shouldn't have sneaked away to the Cuillin when we did, because we were in the middle of the most crucial period of our entire professional life up to that point. What nobody except the parties to the deal had known when we went to Skye was that Kathy and I were in the midst of selling doitnow.com. I'd been having secret meetings with Joshua Pitt, the CEO of AMTAGEN, for weeks and the deal was on the point of completion when the weather had offered Kathy and me the perfect opportunity for the climb we'd always dreamed of. Now, with Kathy gone, for the sake of everyone who worked for us, I had to find a way to make the deal go forward. The problem was that Kathy owned half of doitnow.com, and though we both had wills leaving our halves of the company to each other, it takes time to process inheritances. The company lawyers had to persuade the executors of Kathy's will that selling her share of doitnow.com was in the best interests of the person she'd left her shares to. Even though that was the same person as the one who was trying to persuade them to sell the shares . . . There were times when I felt like I was Alice in Wonderland. I've never come under more pressure in my life.

What was worse than the pressure was not having time to grieve. I wanted to rage at the loss, to weep at the waste, to curse the moment's inattention that had cost Kathy her life. But I had to be civil to the press, to the lawyers and to the people who were trying to buy my company.

I sometimes feel I never got the chance to mourn Kathy properly.

Instead, I concentrated on preserving the jobs of all the people who worked for us. I truly believed that I would be giving them the chance to scale new heights as part of a much bigger corporation, a company that had real ambition for the digital future.

We completed the sale on 9 March 2000, three weeks after Kathy's death. And on 10 March the dotcom bubble burst.

A month after I had sold doitnow.com, AMTAGEN had lost 90 per cent of its value.

Jay ran a hand through her spiky bed hair. She was on thin ice here. She'd lost a business partner but at least she'd managed to hang on to her assets. Anyone who was interested enough to do a little research would soon find out she'd made £237 million from the sale of doitnow.com. There was no need to turn her readers off by rubbing their noses in it. Time, instead, for a little judicious tweaking of the truth.

By pure chance, Kathy and I had set up the sale of doitnow.com at the perfect moment. Thanks in part to her understanding of the dotcom world, I was a very rich woman.

I'd have given it all to have Kathy back.

'As if,' Jay said out loud, saving the file and transferring it to her memory stick before erasing it from Magda's machine. She pushed back from the desk and stretched luxuriously. If she woke Magda now, there would be time to make love before she left for the cancer ward. Jay smiled. Nothing like some early-morning work to waken those appetites.

13

Charlie had spent more hours than she cared to count inside libraries in Oxford. But she'd never crossed the threshold of the city library. Incongruously set down in the heart of the Westgate shopping centre, its seventies concrete and glass and steel were still more modern than most of the buildings where she'd studied. She didn't think the readers here suffered from tourists clambering up to take photographs through the windows, as happened regularly to students in the Radcliffe Camera. She didn't imagine she'd have to swear an oath before she could consult their stocks, either. Charlie still remembered being charmed by having to promise never to bring fire or flame into the Bodleian Library before they would give her a reader's ticket.

Within fifteen minutes, Charlie was set up with a microfiche reader and the relevant films from the local paper. She already knew the date of Jess Edwards' death and some preliminary research online had pinpointed the date of the inquest. She began the tedious business of scrolling through the pages, trying to ignore the man at the next reader who alternated between sniffing loudly and scratching various parts of his body. His languid turning of the knob on his machine convinced Charlie he was only there to pass the time in a warm place. But when she found the first story about Jess's death, she soon forgot any distraction. There it was in black and white. STAR STUDENT IN TRAGIC DROWNING, read the headline.

A student was found dead in the River Cherwell at St Scholastika's College early this morning.

Jess Edwards, a keen rower, was discovered in the water by the college boathouse by her fellow team members when they arrived for early-morning practice. Paramedics were unable to revive her at the scene and she was declared dead on arrival at the John Radcliffe Hospital.

According to one of the students who found her, she appeared to have sustained a head injury. Police said her death had all the hallmarks of a tragic accident.

Jess, 20, was a second-year geography student at St Scholastika's. She was captain of the college rowing eight and had already won a university Blue for the sport. She was a member of the Junior Common Room committee and was in the running to become student president of the college.

A friend said, 'The whole college is in mourning. Everybody loved Jess. It's a terrible shock.'

Charlie's mouth curled in a derisive sneer. That quote was such an obvious fabrication. If the reporter had spoken to any undergraduate from Schollie's, Charlie would dance naked down Westgate. What was even more annoying than the journalistic laziness was that the article told her nothing she didn't already know.

She scanned the next few days but there were no follow-up stories. St Scholastika's would have been buzzing with Jess's death, but the accidental death of a student wasn't that big a deal for the non-academic citizens of Oxford. In that respect, Charlie thought, the university was as solipsistic as a small child – the centre of its own universe, bemused that the rest of the world didn't see things in its terms.

Charlie removed the reel and loaded the one that covered the period of the inquest into Jess's death. When she found it, she was surprised to read STUDENT DEATH AVOIDABLE as the headline.

The drowning of a promising student could have been avoided by a simple safety measure, the Oxford coroner told an inquest yesterday.

Jess Edwards died in the River Cherwell after hitting her head on the edge of the boathouse jetty at St Scholastika's College last November. But if the college had installed a non-slip surface, the tragic accident might not have taken place.

Delivering a verdict of accidental death, Coroner David Stanton said, 'We cannot be certain what happened at the boathouse that morning but, based on the forensic evidence, it seems clear that Miss Edwards slipped and hit her head on the edge of the jetty as she fell into the water. We have heard evidence that this blow would almost certainly have rendered her unconscious, which in turn led to her drowning.

'While I attach no blame to St Scholastika's College, it seems clear that, had a non-slip surface been installed, this accident might never have occurred. I urge all colleges and rowing clubs to review the conditions of their jetties as a matter of urgency.'

After the inquest, Terry Franks, solicitor for the Edwards family, read out a statement on their behalf. 'We are satisfied with the verdict of the inquest. While we applaud the coroner's remarks, we do not blame anyone for what was a genuine accident.'

When asked to comment on the coroner's remarks, Wanda Henderson, the principal of St Scholastika's, said, 'Jess Edwards' death has been a blow for this college. We have already undertaken a full review of the safety of the boathouse area and have made significant improvements, including the application of non-slip materials to all external areas. We would like to extend our deepest sympathy to Jess's family.'

And that was that. Charlie was surprised by the reaction of the family. The natural impulse after the accidental death of a child is to want to find someone to blame. A lot of families in the Edwardses' position would be shouting about negligence and litigation, not quietly accepting that Schollie's wasn't responsible for their daughter's death. It indicated a remarkable maturity on the part of her parents. Or perhaps her mother was a Schollie's graduate herself, possessed of a powerful loyalty to the college that had nurtured her. Either way, it was no help to Charlie. Bitter resentment might have given her some leverage, even after all this time. Calm acceptance was the sane route, but for once, Charlie would have preferred the unbalanced response.

With a sigh, she turned off the reader and returned the films to the librarian. Charlie walked back through the pedestrian precinct towards Carfax, its medieval tower a reproach to the disposable shopfronts surrounding it. She'd hit a dead end already. What she needed to see was the inquest report, but a call to the coroner's office had made it plain that wasn't going to happen without authorisation from Jess Edwards' family. Having no official standing had introduced Charlie to a level of frustration that was entirely new to her.

She walked down Cornmarket and on up the Banbury Road towards Schollie's. She'd parked her car in a nearby side street, one of the first roads where city-centre parking restrictions didn't apply. As she walked, Charlie considered her limited options. She didn't want to admit she was already defeated, but she couldn't see how to make progress on Jess Edwards' death. Maybe she should just accept that this wasn't the death where she was going to implicate Jay. And if that was the case, there was little point in hanging around in Oxford. She'd hoped to find something that would keep her here long enough to see Lisa again. But she couldn't justify sticking around with no leads to follow.

Still, it wouldn't hurt just to drive past her house, to drop in on the off chance. It was almost lunchtime, after all. Even Lisa had to stop for food sometime.

Skirting the city centre, it didn't take too long to get to Iffley village. Cruising past Lisa's, Charlie was disappointed to see another car in the drive beside Lisa's Audi. Still, they might not be staying for long. Charlie found a parking spot that provided a view of Lisa's front door and her drive and settled down to wait.

While she waited, she considered her next course of action. Kathy Lipson's death on Skye was the obvious next place to look. There was plenty about that online, but she needed to get past the headlines and talk to someone who understood what had really happened. That probably meant a trip to Skye. This was starting to get expensive. Charlie wondered whether Corinna had considered that aspect of what she had asked Charlie to do.

On the other hand, taking money from Corinna, even if it was only expenses, would place her under an obligation. If Corinna was paying for the investigation, she was entitled to its product. And Charlie didn't want to lose control of whatever she uncovered. She didn't want to find herself in a position where she was blocked from sharing information with someone else because Corinna didn't want that. However much she had once admired Corinna, it didn't mean she completely trusted her now. On balance, Charlie decided she'd fund her redemption from her own pocket. Now she just had to figure out how to get her hands on the information that would allow her to redeem herself.

However hard she tried to develop a strategy for the next phase, Charlie kept coming back to Jess Edwards. The idea that Jay might have committed the perfect murder affronted Charlie. That she could do nothing about it affronted her still more.

The ringing of her phone startled her out of her reverie. Maria, the screen read. Feeling uncomfortable at taking a call from her partner while she was staking out the house of the woman she wanted for her lover, Charlie spoke. 'Hi,' she said, sounding as flat as she felt.

'Just finished my morning list and thought I'd give you a call. How's it going?' Maria, cheerful, upbeat. The one who had always kept her going.

'Dead-end street,' Charlie said. 'The newspaper reports don't say anything I didn't know already. The inquest report's been transferred to the county archives and I can't get to it unless I'm an interested party. Like, Jess's family.'

'Poor you,' Maria said. 'What about the police?'

'I haven't even bothered trying to talk to them. Nobody's going to remember who was in charge of an accidental death seventeen years ago. There was never anything suspicious about it officially, so it would barely have made an impact on anyone in CID.'

'No, no, that's not what I meant.'

'What, then?'

'Wouldn't the police be able to access an inquest report?'

'I suppose so. But that doesn't help me. I'm not the police.'

'God, Charlie.' Maria's tone was the verbal equivalent of eye-rolling. 'You may not *be* the police, but you know plenty.'

Charlie gave a little bark of laughter. 'Most of whom want to forget they ever heard my name right now.'

'I'm not thinking of the ones you've worked with, necessarily. What about Nick? He thinks the sun shines out of your backside. You know he does. He sent you a card when you got suspended, remember?'

Charlie groaned. 'You're right. Why didn't I think of Nick? Oh yes. Could it be because he's an ambitious young cop who's not going to take chances with his career just because I've turned into Don Quixote?'

'You don't know till you ask. Call him. He's just down the road. You could take him out to dinner and ask him.'

'Just down the road,' Charlie muttered. 'He's in London.'

'That's what I mean. It's just down the road. Or you could catch a train. It's better than coming home with your tail between your legs,' Maria said. 'What have you got to lose? If he says no, you're no worse off than you are now.'

She was right, and Charlie knew it. 'All right,' she sighed. 'I'll give him a call. How was your morning?' she added, suddenly remembering that Maria also had a professional life.

Maria chuckled. 'Nothing I need to share with you. But I have to go now and scrub up for my first afternoon appointment. I've got to hammer two titanium screws into a footballer's jaw. I think he must have spent his entire adolescence sucking sweets, the state of his teeth. I love you. Talk to me later, OK?'

'Will do.' Charlie ended the call just in time to notice Lisa's front door opening. She recognised the man who emerged carrying a laptop bag. Tom, the colleague who had been there when she'd arrived on Saturday. Lisa followed him on to the doorstep. She was wearing what looked like a Westernised version of the shalwar kameez – oversized collarless shirt and baggy pants gathered at the ankle, both in vivid turquoise. Her feet were bare, but she seemed not to notice the cold. Tom turned to Lisa and put his free arm round her shoulder. Lisa put her hands on his chest and leaned into him.

The kiss went far beyond what Charlie expected between a boss and her subordinate. True, it fell short of what she and Lisa had shared on the other side of the door, but it didn't look like something that had taken either of them by surprise. This looked like habit; it looked like a fragment of something more.

Charlie fought a sudden wave of nausea. The last thing she wanted right now was to be caught throwing up on the grass verge in plain sight of Lisa's house. The misery she felt was bad enough without adding a dose of humiliation. A small voice at the back of her head kept saying, 'You've had a lucky escape.' The trouble was, Charlie still didn't quite believe it.

This was not over.

14

Detective Sergeant Nick Nicolaides swapped the National guitar for his Martin D16 and checked the tuning. This was the first day off that hadn't been hijacked by the job for over two weeks and he was determined to lay down the backing guitar tracks for the new tune that had been teasing at the corner of his mind for days. He knew his colleagues were wary of him because he wasn't interested in football or fishing or boxing or pumping iron or any of the other pursuits that marked you out as a real man. It was OK to like music, provided that didn't go beyond having the right sounds in your car or on your MP3 player. But wanting to spend your spare time making music on your own or with a bunch of civilians – that was definitely on the weird side.

What they didn't know was that the music was what kept Nick sane, what locked him into a sense of himself. The music was the only remnant of the life he'd had before the life he had now. It was his bridge across a distance most of his colleagues would not believe.

It was a miracle that he had made it through his teens without a substantial police record. Someone less smart, less quick on their feet, less able to cover their tracks would have ended their adolescence in custody rather than in university.

But that was a secret history. And he planned to keep it that way. Nick had been fast-tracked ever since he'd joined the police. To begin with it had been because of his first class degree in psychology, but his aptitude had been demonstrated both at the National Police Academy and at the sharp end. He was a young man who was going places. And he never forgot that the reason it had all become possible was Dr Charlie Flint.

Nick had scraped into the psychology course at Manchester, his exam results the bottom of the barrel for a course in such high demand. The main reason for choosing to go to university at all had been to extend the range of his drug dealing and to postpone having to consider any kind of career that would interfere with making music, taking drugs and shagging girls who didn't have the brains to snag him. Within a few weeks, in spite of himself, he'd found he was actually interested in some aspects of the course he'd signed up for. The main reason for that had been Dr Charlie Flint.

She was the only member of the department he came across who was a psychiatrist rather than a psychologist. What she did was underpinned by medical training; almost as interesting as what she had to say was the fact that she could prescribe legal drugs. And she was young enough in the job that he reckoned she wouldn't know how to stand up to him. Halfway through the first term he'd gone to her with an offer he'd thought she couldn't refuse. She would write prescriptions for him for stuff he could sell on. In exchange, he would pay her. More importantly, he would not make her life a misery. When she'd asked him what he meant, he'd said, 'I'm not a man who's short on imagination. Trust me, you don't want to go there.'

'Try me,' she'd said, leaning back in her office chair, hands locked behind her head, the picture of insouciance.

'Well, for a start there's sexual harassment,' Nick had said. 'A woman of your age, it's not pretty to be accused of throwing yourself at a young student.' She laughed out loud. He was affronted. 'Don't think I won't do it.'

'Be my guest,' Charlie said. 'But before you do, let me say just one thing. Your choice of attack suggests to me that you need this course far more than you know.'

'What do you mean?' People usually caved in to whatever Nick demanded. He was a mixture of good looks and danger, a walking carrot-and-stick.

'You can't work it out? Well, you'll just have to go ahead and make a complete arse of yourself.' Charlie sat up straight, hands flat on the desk. 'And I expect you'll be doing it from the inside of a police cell. What you don't know about me, Nick, is that I work with the police. I have friends who will take great pleasure in dogging your every step and nicking you for everything from dropping litter upwards. And I will grass you up. Make no mistake about that. I had an idea you were trying to extend your little empire of fucked-upness to my students but I wasn't sure. Now I am. And I will not have it.'

'You're threatening me?' He was amused, but outraged too. Who the fuck did this chubby cow think she was? More to the point, how the fuck did she not get who he was, what he was?

Charlie shrugged. 'It's not a threat. It's a wake-up call. You are a very bright young man. The essay you gave me last week was clearly dashed off at the last minute. Probably fuelled by cocaine. You clearly hadn't done most of the reading. But it was still one of the best pieces of work I've ever seen from a student in his first term. The way I see it, you've got two options.' She held her hands apart as though she were literally weighing up his options. 'You can carry on the way you are. Build a criminal empire. Never sleep at night for fear of betrayal and jail, or worse. Or you can actually harness your potential. Do some work. Demonstrate how good you really are. Sleep at night.'

In some respects, it had been a pretty trite Damascene moment. What Charlie couldn't have known was how much pressure Nick had been under. From his family, from the dealers further up the chain, from the cops cracking down on dealing to kids too young to be out clubbing. So far, he'd kept his nose clean. But he understood what she was saying. That wouldn't continue. Eventually, he'd be fingered and there wouldn't be two options. 'And be like you?' was the only counter he could manage then. He knew even as he said it how weak it was.

'I will help you,' Charlie said. And she had. In three years, he'd turned his life around. By the time he did his final exams, he wasn't even using any more. He was studying and making music. There wasn't time for anything else.

He'd also worked out why Charlie had been so amused that he'd threatened her with an accusation of sexual harassment. Now, he blushed to think of the fuckwit he'd been back then.

So when the phone screen flashed her name in the middle of his first run-through of the new piece, he stopped finger-picking and grabbed the phone. 'Charlie,' he said.

'Hi, Nick. Is this a good time? Can you talk?'

'Day off,' he said. 'I was beginning to wonder what that felt like.'

'I'm sorry. I'll call you tomorrow if that's better?'

'No, Charlie. I'm always happy to talk to you. How are you coping? How's tricks?'

'Well, it's a bit complicated.'

'It's not Maria, is it? She's OK, right?'

'Yes, she's fine. It's just that . . . Well, I'm in the thick of something and I could use a bit of help. But I don't want to get into it on the phone. Can I buy you dinner?'

Nick checked the time. It was barely two o'clock. 'I can't do dinner,' he said. 'One of my mates has a studio booked, I promised I'd do some backing tracks for him. Are you in London now?'

'No. I'm in Oxford.'

'Look, I'm only ten minutes' walk from Paddington. Are you busy this afternoon? Can you jump on a train? You could be here by four. I don't have to go out till six. Would that work for you?'

Charlie thought the new flats in Paddington Basin covered both extremes. You either got a great view across

London rooftops or you got an unrivalled view of the Westway on stilts and its endless stream of traffic. As she waited for the lift, she made a bet with herself. A couple of minutes later, she congratulated herself on getting it right. Nick had not settled for a flash address at the expense of a lousy view. The vista from the wall of glass that occupied one side of his living room was breathtaking. The room itself was devoted to music. Guitars hung along one wall, a keyboard sat on a long desk beside a bank of computer peripherals, an array of mics and music stands occupied one corner. A squidgy leather sofa faced the view, the only concession to standard living-room furniture. 'It's very you,' Charlie said, looking around.

'You wouldn't have to be a psychologist to work out that music's very important to me,' Nick said, a sardonic twist to his mouth. 'I'll get the wine.'

Charlie watched him disappear into a narrow galley kitchen. He was looking good, she thought. When she'd first met him, he'd resembled the king of the alley cats – skinny, feral, vibrant and good-looking in the piratical style. He'd filled out a bit, built some muscle round his basic wiriness, learned how not to frighten the horses. His jeans were slung low on his narrow hips, his shirt unpressed, his hair shaggier than the last time they'd met. He did not look like an off-duty cop. That was one of his professional strengths. He returned with a bottle of chewy red wine and a couple of tumblers, giving her that familiar twinkling smile, brown eyes crinkling at the corners. 'You look well,' she said.

'It's an illusion. I need a holiday. I'm tired all the time.' He perched on the edge of a high wooden stool and poured wine, passing a glass to Charlie. 'Cheers.' He leaned forward to clink glasses and she got a whiff of his smell – a faint animal muskiness overlaying the citrus sharpness of shampoo.

'Too much work or too much play?'

He chuckled. 'Too much playing.' He jerked a thumb towards the guitars. 'The more shit I see in the job, the more I want to lose myself in the music. But never mind me.' He shook his head. 'Are they out of their minds, or what? Axing the best profiler and analyst in the game? I cannot believe what's happening to you.'

'You should. You've been in the game long enough.'

'So what can I do to help? That's why you're here, right? For my help?'

His eagerness made her feel cherished in a way that little had since Bill Hopton's second trial. 'I wish my professional problems were straightforward enough that you could help,' she said. 'But the reason I'm here is totally different.'

Nick's eyes turned wary. 'You came for the cop, not the friend?'

'I like to think they're both on my side,' Charlie said. 'Let me tell you what I've got myself into.' She outlined the task she'd accepted from Corinna succinctly, leaving nothing out except her discussion with Lisa Kent. The last thing she wanted was to introduce the subject of Lisa with someone as acute as Nick. 'Maria wants me to take this on,' she finished up. 'She thinks I need something challenging to keep me from going mad. But I don't have the skills or the access for this.'

Nick gave her a sceptical look. 'You've got the skills,' he

said. 'No question of that. I've never seen a better inter-viewer. But you're right, access is a problem.'

'Right. If I'm going to make any progress with Jess Edwards, I need that inquest report. I've got no authority to get sight of it. But you have.'

Nick shook his head and Charlie felt suddenly numb. She'd thought she could rely on Nick, but it seemed she'd been mistaken. It was a harsh blow. But when he spoke, it wasn't what she expected. 'You don't need the inquest report.'

'How else do I make progress?'

'If anything of any substance had come out in court, it would have made it into the paper. My guess is that this was written up as an accident from the get-go, that it barely rippled the surface of CID. There's not going to be anything in the police evidence and there's not going to be a copper walking around with this case engraved on his memory. The one person who might have something to say – and it's a big "might" – is the pathologist. Sometimes they notice things that don't end up in their final report because they're too insignificant. Or they're details that are unnecessary for the legal resolution of a case. The only thing you need from the inquest report is the name of the pathologist who did the PM.'

'So how do I get that?'

Nick smirked. 'You don't. I do. I'll call the county archives and blag it out of them.'

'You don't mind?'

'It'll make a nice change.' He looked away. 'I'm work-ing on trafficking kids in the sex industry right now. Anything that isn't that feels like a holiday. I'll do it first thing tomorrow. I need to make the call from work so they can call back and check my bona fides, otherwise I'd do it now. Will you still be in Oxford?'

Charlie's spirits sank. Oxford with no prospect of whiling away the hours with Lisa. Because she couldn't let that be an option now, however much it hurt to turn her back, not given what she'd seen earlier. She sighed. 'Yeah, I'll still be there.'

'OK. I'll call you as soon as I have what you need.' He leaned over and topped up her glass. 'You want to hear what I've been working on?'

Charlie couldn't help smiling, admiring his bounceback skills. 'Why not?' she said. It had to be better than listening to the arguments inside her head.

15

Others might fail her, but Nick hadn't let Charlie down. Just after ten, he texted her with all she needed to know. Dr Vikram (Vik) Patel. Still @ John Radcliffe Hosp. At least Dr Patel was local. She could try to talk to him today then get out of Oxford before the depression that was nibbling at her really took hold.

Listening to Nick's multitextured guitar compositions had been the last enjoyable element in her day. The train had been overheated and overcrowded, the Chinese take-away she'd picked up on her way back to her cheerless guest room at Schollie's had been greasy and bland, and Maria had been out at the cinema with a colleague so she couldn't even whinge to her. By the time they'd been able to talk, Charlie had been too tired to be bothered. The one thing she could point to with pride was that she hadn't gone near Lisa. Hadn't phoned her, texted her, emailed her or even checked her Facebook page.

In spite of her exhaustion, she'd slept fitfully. She'd almost fallen out of the narrow bed at one point, waking just before her body reached the tipping point. 'I can't even manage to lie in bed now,' she said aloud. 'Is it just me or is everything shit?' By any objective measure, she had to concede it was just her. Sometimes she wished she could acquire a taste for drugs. At least that would keep the world at a distance.

Breakfast had been an ordeal. Faces from her student days kept drifting past her or stopping to say hello. From kitchen staff to college fellows, it seemed she'd made more of an impact than she knew. Or maybe it was just that they all read the *Daily Mail* and it was notoriety jogging their memory rather than affection. Of course, they were all curious to know why she was there. Luckily Oxford's personnel and libraries always provided the easy answer of 'doing some research'. Even the disgraced could hide behind that excuse.

As she'd been leaving the dining hall, Corinna had walked out of the Senior Common Room opposite. A furtive glance to see how close any observers might be, then Corinna hurried across to her. 'How are you getting on?' she said. Her face looked strained, her eyes tired. Charlie imagined things had not been particularly pleasant in the Newsam household since Magda's Saturday revelations.

'It's not easy,' Charlie said. 'You'd have been better off hiring a private investigator.'

Corinna gave her a shrewd look. 'They wouldn't understand the way you do. And they wouldn't have anything at stake. I've got confidence in you, Charlie. I know you will do whatever you can to protect my daughter. Just keep me posted, eh? A quick phone call every day, that should do it, right?'

'I'm sorry, Corinna, but that's not going to happen,' Charlie said firmly. 'I don't do my best work when I feel like somebody's looking over my shoulder. Leave me to get on with things in my own way, and I'll talk to you when I have something to say.' The door of the SCR opened and two other fellows emerged. It signalled the end of their conversation and spared Charlie from getting into an argument.

'We'll talk soon,' Corinna said, frustration drawing her brows down.

'When I'm ready.' Charlie walked away, wondering again how she'd let herself be sucked into this.

By the time Nick's text arrived, she was prowling round the remains of the boathouse, checking out the scene of the alleged crime for herself. It had changed dramatically since Jess's death, replaced now by a more modern facility on the Isis. The wood was grey with untended age, the dilapidation far advanced. Charlie was surprised the college hadn't demolished it on the notorious grounds of health and safety. But enough remained for her to conjure up its image. The main change, apart from the state of disrepair, was that famous non-slip surface. It covered all the exposed wood of the decking, its bright green faded now to a dull mud colour, its edges nibbled at by the passage of time. Evidentially, this was a meaningless visit. But it made more vivid the hazy images of memory. Charlie could envisage the scene much more clearly now.

And then the text had arrived that gave her no more excuse to hang around Schollie's. Charlie took the Marston Ferry Road towards the John Radcliffe Hospital, trying out various strategies in her head as she drove. She had confidence in none of them. Only if Vik Patel had been living on Mars for the past year did she have any chance of getting him to talk to her.

Like most hospitals, the John Radcliffe did not advertise the location of its mortuary on the maps conveniently provided for patients and visitors. Charlie headed for the information desk and mustered her best smile. 'I'm looking for Dr Vikram Patel, the pathologist. I wonder if you could direct me to the autopsy suite?' By one of fortune's lucky oversights, nobody had asked her to surrender the Home Office ID card she had been given to allow her entry to police premises. She slid it in front of the woman on the information counter, who gave it a cursory glance. She pulled a map towards her and scribbled on it, then passed it to Charlie. 'You're here. You need to be here.' She pointed. 'There's the entrance, the lifts are down the hall.'

Charlie couldn't quite believe her luck. She'd expected a knock-back; at the very least, a call to Dr Patel to check whether she was expected. Perhaps it was because she'd taken the trouble to look like a medical professional, with her best suit and laptop bag slung over her shoulder. It almost made her feel she was on a roll.

The building that housed the mortuary was either pretty new or had recently been refurbished. It didn't have that slightly scuffed, entirely unloved feeling that Charlie associated with NHS premises. The walls were clean, the doors fit properly and the signs on the doors were all in the same font. She followed the directions and ended up in a tiny reception area with two chairs facing a desk that barely had room for the monitor and keyboard that formed a barrier between the public and the receptionist, a scrawny man in his early twenties dressed in pale blue surgical scrubs. Not for the first time, Charlie thought she had never encountered anyone whose appearance was improved by scrubs. Real life was never like *ER* in that respect.

The receptionist didn't look up when Charlie entered. His eyes were focused on the monitor, his freckled fingers flying over the keys. It took her a moment to realise that under the thatch of springy ginger hair, he had ear buds that were presumably pumping dictation directly into his brain. She moved closer and waved a hand at him.

He started and pushed back from the desk as if she'd physically hit him. 'Jeez,' he said, yanking the ear phones clear. 'You nearly gave me a heart attack.'

'Sorry,' Charlie said. 'I'm looking for Dr Patel. Vik Patel.'

The young man frowned. 'Is he expecting you? Only, he's doing an autopsy right now.'

Charlie made a rueful face. 'I know I should have phoned ahead. But I found myself in the area and I thought I'd take the chance.' She smiled. 'Any idea how much longer he's going to be?'

The young man looked surprised, as if nobody had ever asked such a question before. 'Can I ask who you are?' Charlie produced the ID again. This time, it was carefully scrutinised. Blank-faced, he said, 'What is it that you want to see Dr Patel about, Dr Flint?'

'I want to talk to Dr Patel about an old case,' she said. 'I won't take up much of his time.'

'I need to go and see what's possible,' he said. He glanced at her, frowning again, and closed down his computer before he left by a door in the back of the room. Charlie sat down on one of the visitor chairs, crossed her legs, and waited.

It took almost ten minutes for the young man to return. 'If you can hang on for quarter of an hour, Dr Patel will meet you.' He stared at her, as if committing her face to memory in case he needed to take part in an identity parade at some point down the line.

Charlie smiled. All this pleasantness was starting to hurt her face. 'Thank you. That'll be fine.'

In the end, it took almost twenty-five minutes for the door at the back of the room to open again. A short, squat Asian man in green scrubs appeared in the doorway and stared at Charlie. He ran a hand over thick black hair brushed straight back from his forehead in an impressive quiff and his mouth twitched. 'You're Dr Flint?' he said.

Charlie stood up. 'That's right. Dr Patel?'

'Call me Vik,' he said. 'Come through. We'll need to make this quick. I've got another autopsy before lunch.'

Charlie followed him into another unspoiled corridor. Halfway down, he wheeled left into a cubicle office. One internal wall was a long window that looked on to a pathology suite. A technician in a white overall and rubber boots was methodically cleaning surfaces. Patel tutted and pulled the blinds down. 'Have a seat,' he said, gesturing to a folding chair squeezed into a corner at the end of his desk. Neat piles of paper flanked a flashy laptop. A stainless steel

Thermos and a phone sat beside the computer. Charlie couldn't imagine a life that involved being constantly up to your elbows in human remains, but she did envy Vik Patel his obvious capacity for neatness.

He pushed black-rimmed glasses up his nose and gave Charlie a puzzled stare. Closer up, she could see a few strands of silver in his hair and fine lines in his tea-coloured skin. He was older than she'd thought at first. 'I'm bemused,' he said. 'You're a psychiatrist, right?'

That detail wasn't on her ID. They'd either recognised her name or quickly Googled her. But still Patel had decided to see her. That was probably a point in her favour. 'That's right,' Charlie said, on her guard nevertheless.

'By definition, you deal with the living. Me, I'm a pathologist. By definition, I deal with the dead. I'll be honest with you, Dr Flint. I'm struggling to find some common ground here.'

His accent wasn't local. He was a northerner, like her. Leeds or Bradford, she thought and wondered if she could use that as a bridge between them. Instead, she said, 'Call me Charlie.' Another of the charm-offensive smiles. 'I'm looking for some information, Vik. About an old case of yours.'

'How is an old case of mine a concern of yours?'

He wasn't making this easy. But then, why should he? 'In my line of work, people have a tendency to make confessions or allegations that aren't always truthful. But sometimes they are true and they force us to take another look at cases that may have been closed years before. I've got a situation where someone is making an allegation about a death that was written up as an accident. If they're right, then we could be looking at a murder investigation.'

Patel nodded impatiently. 'I get that, Charlie. I assumed it was something like that. What I'm not getting is why it's you sitting here, not a police officer. In my experience, they're the ones that hunt down murderers.' Again the hand smoothed his hair. It seemed to be a mechanism for reassuring himself, she thought. His hair was under control, so was the situation.

'There's no point in wasting police time until I know whether there's anything worth investigating, is there?' She'd worked this answer out over breakfast and hoped it would hold up under pressure.

'We don't want to waste police time, do we? And time's what you've got a lot of right now, isn't it, Charlie?' He wanted to be pleased with himself, so Charlie let herself look more dismayed than she felt.

'I wondered if you'd recognised my name,' she said. 'It's true that I'm not as busy as usual. It's given me the chance to look more closely at some of the files I'd had to put to one side.' She spread her hands, palms upward. A gesture of openness and trust. 'You know how it is. There's only so much time, and certain cases carry more weight.' A dart aimed straight for common ground.

Patel returned her smile. 'Tell me about it.' He glanced over his shoulder at the clock on the wall. 'I've got ten more minutes. I'm interested in what it is that is worth taking you away from building your defence against the GMC.'

Charlie gave a dry laugh. 'It's no big deal. I've been working with someone who claims she witnessed a murder. I get this kind of thing all the time, but when I checked out what she told me, I discovered there had been an unexpected death at the precise time and place she'd given me. That's more unusual than you'd think.'

'And this unexpected death was one I dealt with? Is that why you're here?'

'That's it in a nutshell, Vik. The inquest wrote it up as accidental death. The police said all the evidence was congruent with accidental death. But I wanted to ask you if there was anything at all ambiguous in what you saw on the table. Anything that gave you pause but wasn't enough to make the police change their tack.' Charlie shrugged. 'To be honest, Vik, I fully expect to walk out of here empty-handed.' It was a line calculated to make him want to prove her wrong.

'Thames Valley Police take me seriously,' he said, the hand running over the hair again. 'They don't ignore my concerns.'

'I'm sure they don't. But like you said, we've all got to prioritise.' He hadn't said that; she had. But she didn't think he'd argue with her.

'When was this case?'

'November 1993.'

Patel's eyes widened. 'And you expect me to remember the details of a case from seventeen years ago?' His voice rose in incredulity. 'Do you have any idea how many autopsies I perform every week?'

'You don't perform many on twenty-year-old women in peak physical condition,' Charlie said. 'Her name was Jess Edwards and she drowned in the Cherwell by the St Scholastika's boathouse.'

Watching the light dawn behind Patel's eyes was a beautiful thing. 'I do remember,' he said slowly. 'No detail, mind you. But I do remember the case.' He made tutting noises behind his teeth. 'November 1993. We were using computers by then. This should be on the server . . .' He picked up his phone, turning away from Charlie. 'Matthew? I need you to pull down a report for me from November 1993 . . . Jess Edwards . . . How soon?' He nodded. 'Thank you.'

He woke up the laptop. His calendar for the day filled the screen. He ran his finger down the list of appointments then turned back to Charlie. 'Can you come back this afternoon? Three thirty? Would that work for you?'

'That would be perfect.' Charlie stood up. 'I appreciate your time.'

Patel nodded. 'She was the same age as my daughter,' he said. 'Sometimes we have to go the extra mile.'

16

Waiting patiently had never been one of Charlie's skills. She had friends and colleagues who seized downtime like a gift from the gods but she'd always suffered a compulsion to fill those inevitable gaps in the action with something productive. So she left Vik Patel's office with great plans for going back to Schollie's to continue her online researches. But when she logged on to her laptop, the first thing on her screen was an email from Lisa.

If she tried to work online now, the message would taunt her till she opened it. And she didn't want to read anything Lisa had to say. Charlie knew herself well enough to understand that Lisa still had power over her. And she didn't want to be seduced by her words again. So she closed the laptop and stretched out on the bed to consider her options.

When she woke up, it was after two o'clock. Charlie couldn't believe she'd slept for almost three hours. She didn't do naps, and the way she felt now reminded her why. Groggy and thick-headed, she stripped and showered, desperately trying to get her brain back in gear. Vik Patel was no pushover; she couldn't afford to have a head full of cotton wool for this encounter.

Hair still damp, she hurried to her car, checking her phone for messages as she went. A text from Lisa. 'For Christ's sake,' Charlie muttered. When she'd been desperate for a crumb from Lisa's life, next to nothing had been forthcoming. Now she wanted to be left alone, Lisa seemed to be in pursuit. 'I'm going to ignore you,' she said as she got into the car. 'I don't need this.'

She made it to the hospital mortuary with five minutes to spare. But this time, the receptionist hustled her straight through to his boss's office. Patel jumped up when she walked in, a troubled look on his face. 'This is very disturbing,' he said, cutting straight to the point.

'You found something?' Charlie said, not bothering to hide her eagerness.

Patel sucked in a sharp breath. 'Oh yes,' he said. 'As soon as I looked at the file, I remembered. An anomaly. A very definite anomaly.' He waved Charlie to the corner seat and pointed to his desk. To her bewilderment, the space where his laptop had been was occupied by a chunky Lego model sitting on a sheet of paper. He sat down and patted a blocky rectangle sitting on the green base. 'Think of this as the boathouse and jetty at St Scholastika's College,' he said. 'And this sheet of paper is the river.'

Charlie nodded. It was a loose interpretation of the scene she'd visited that morning, but she could do imagination. 'OK.'

He produced a Lego figure that looked suspiciously like Princess Leia. 'This is Jess. She comes out of the boat-house . . .' He moved the stunted figure from the building towards the edge of the platform. 'She slips . . .' The feet go from under Princess Leia and her head hits the sharp edge. She falls on to the paper, face down. 'She's unconscious when she hits the water. She drowns. And there you have it. A perfect narrative of death.'

'What's the anomaly?' Charlie asked, excitement buzzing inside. 'What's the problem with this perfect narrative?'

'Imagine the skull hitting the edge of the jetty on a downward trajectory. The wound is wedge-shaped. So when I examined Jess Edwards' skull, I expected to see a wedge-shaped wound. And that's what I did see. Except that the wedge was upside down.' He picked up Princess Leia again. He walked her backwards from the boathouse to the edge of the jetty and pulled her feet out from under her again. This time, the back of her head hit the edge of the jetty but her body remained on the decking. 'For the wound to exhibit the shape I saw, she would have had to fall backwards on to the edge. So her body would have stayed on the jetty. And she wouldn't have drowned.'

Charlie thought about what he'd said, looking for the wriggle room. 'What if she'd still been conscious? Rolling about in pain? Could she not have gone over the edge then?' It wasn't that Charlie doubted Patel. She wanted to believe him, wanted to be convinced that Corinna hadn't sent her on a wild-goose chase. But she was trained to mistrust, to call into question, to test.

'Exactly what the policeman said. And I will tell you

what I said to him. It is my professional opinion that she could not have been conscious after that blow to the head. But here's the thing. It's notoriously difficult to be definitive about the effect of head wounds. There are recorded cases of people being shot in the head and walking round perfectly coherent afterwards. So in theory, what you suggest is right out there on the outside edge of what might be possible.'

Charlie released the breath she'd been holding. 'What did the policeman say?'

'He said there was no evidence to indicate this was anything other than a tragic accident. Nothing. No circumstantial, no forensics, no witnesses. If there was an explanation that covered it, he would take it. If an anomaly was the only way to explain it, he'd live with the anomaly.'

'You didn't say anything about this at the inquest,' Charlie said.

'No. Because anomalies do happen. And apart from that, there was nothing that raised the slightest question in anybody's mind. In those circumstances, you have to think of the impact on the family. There was no evidence to support a murder inquiry, and if I'd raised a doubt in their minds . . .' Patel ran a hand over his hair. 'All I would have done was to deny them closure. For ever. Because there could be no closure.'

'What if she was murdered?'

'You mean, what if your patient is telling the truth about witnessing a murder?'

'Yes.'

Patel looked troubled. 'Then there's a lot of pain coming up for a lot of people.'

'You included?'

He gave a sad smile. 'I won't be joining your club, Charlie. I'm not the one rocking the boat.' He stood up. 'Good luck getting anyone to take your crazy person seriously.'

Charlie was feeling pretty pleased with herself. Halfway round the barely moving car park that was the motorway encircling Birmingham, and she still hadn't opened Lisa's text or email. Just as she was congratulating herself on her strength of will, her phone rang. 'Blocked,' the screen read. Could be anyone from her lawyer to her mother, who liked to call from work when her boss was out of the office. Charlie decided to go for it. 'Hello?' she said cautiously, aiming for an accent not quite her own.

'Charlie?' From the sound of it, she'd succeeded in confusing Nick. 'Is that you?'

'Hi, Nick.'

'I just thought I'd give you a ring to see how it went with Dr Patel.'

Charlie told him. At the end, he gave a low whistle. 'An anomaly, eh? We like anomalies, don't we, Charlie?'

'What's this "we", Nick?'

A moment's silence, then he said, 'You're not fit to be let out on your own on this, Charlie. You need somebody that knows which way is up.'

'And that would be you?'

'It would.'

Charlie was touched, but she was also wary on Nick's account. Heaven forbid he should get dragged into her particular professional hell. 'You've got a job of your own already. Don't be greedy,' she said sternly, braking as the van in front juddered to a halt.

'This is like a stress-buster for me,' he said. 'I want to help, Charlie. You've never let me do anything for you, and that's not good. Friendship's supposed to be a two-way street. So let me help you with this.'

Charlie felt tears constrict her throat. She wasn't accustomed to people seeing her vulnerability, never mind acting on it. 'Whatever,' she said gruffly. 'I can't very well stop you, can I?'

'Good. Now, the way I see it, we're not going to get much further with the Jess Edwards case. Its main evidential value is that it establishes an MO – this is how she killed Jess Edwards, almost identical to the way Philip Carling was killed. And the two people banged up for his murder very definitely didn't kill Jess Edwards. So what you need to do now—'

'Nick?' Charlie interrupted. 'Is this some meaning of the word "help" that I'm unfamiliar with? The one where you just take over?' There was a laugh in her voice, but she hoped he picked up on her underlying seriousness.

'Sorry, Charlie. Just getting carried away in my own area of expertise. What were you thinking of doing next?'

'I want to find out as much as I can about Kathy Lipson's death. Apparently, in Scotland they have a thing called a Fatal Accident Inquiry instead of an inquest, and the reports are in the public domain. Online, even. How advanced is that?'

'Very impressive. Are you going to go to Skye and talk to the mountain rescue people?'

'Funnily enough, I thought I might do just that.' The

261

traffic started inching forward again and Charlie put the car in gear.

'Don't forget to ask about the phone,' he said.

'What about the phone?'

'If it was retrieved with Jay's backpack.'

'I don't even know that the backpack was retrieved,' Charlie pointed out.

'Something else to ask about, then.'

'Nick, with it being a satellite phone, would there be a record of the calls made to and from it?'

'Back in 2000? I suppose so, in theory.'

'Do you think there's any way you could get hold of it?'

'Probably not without a warrant. Even if I knew which company it was.'

'There can't have been many sat-phone companies around in 2000.'

'Yeah, and the chances of any still being around now in the same form are pretty low.' Nick sounded glum.

'They were so expensive back then, it would be really interesting to see who she thought it was worth spending money talking to.'

'You'll get no argument from me on that. I just think the chances of getting hold of that info are near to vanishing point.'

Seeing a space opening up, Charlie moved over to the outside lane. 'You're probably right. Thank God it's not the only shot in our locker. I also want to touch base with Magda, ideally when Jay's not around. She opened up to me so readily on Saturday, I think it would be useful to capitalise on that. Find out what she might know that she doesn't know she knows, if you see what I mean.'

'Totally. Good idea.'

'So, what was it you thought I should do next?'

Nick chuckled. 'I think you should talk to Paul Barker or Joanna Sanderson. If Corinna's right and they've been framed, they might have something to say worth listening to. You know how it is – the lawyers decide on a line of defence and anything that doesn't sit right with that gets put to one side.'

Charlie sighed. 'You're probably right. But they're in jail now and I've got no standing to get in to see them.'

'You could talk to the lawyer. Offer to help with the appeal. They'd jump at a free psychological assessment from you, Charlie.'

Charlie snorted incredulously. 'I'm in disgrace, Nick. I'm persona non grata. Nobody's going to want an assessment from me, free or otherwise.'

'Ah, bollocks to that, Charlie. You're going to be back in the driver's seat in no time. We both know they're going to find you're guilty of nothing more than honesty. You'll be queen of the castle again before you know it.'

She wished she could believe him. But the Bill Hopton case wasn't going to disappear from memories or headlines any time soon. And for as long as it lived in people's minds, she would have no role as an expert witness. 'Yeah, sure,' she said, subdued now.

'Talk to the lawyer, Charlie. Make the call when you get home. If you're accredited by the lawyer, you can get in to see them at short notice. What have you got to lose? Promise me you'll make the call.'

'All right, Nick. I'll make the call. And since you're so desperate to help, you can talk to your opposite numbers in Spain and find out what you can about Ulf Ingemarsson.'

It was Nick's turn to sigh. 'He's the one whose work on 24/7 she allegedly stole, right? How do I spell that?'

Charlie obliged. 'He died in Spain in 2004. If you can talk to the cops, that would be great. What I really want is a contact for Ingemarsson's girlfriend. She apparently knew all about his work. I'd be interested to hear what she has to say about Jay.'

'OK, boss. I'll get on to Spain, you get on to one of the defence solicitors. We'll talk again.'

And he was gone. So too was the traffic jam, dissolved as if by magic. Charlie put her foot down, feeling more uncomplicated delight than she had for a long time. Until Nick had weighed in on her side, she hadn't allowed herself to realise how isolated she'd been. Or how negative an impact that had been having on her. Now she had someone to bounce her ideas off and, more importantly, she had someone to take on the things she couldn't do.

By the time she got home, Charlie was more upbeat than she'd been in a while. It was far too late to get hold of lawyers; she would deal with that first thing in the morning. She had two hours' teaching in the morning at a sixth-form college, but the rest of her day was free to chase solicitors.

She pulled into the drive, glad to be done with the journey. The M6 was always hideous. Clotted with traffic, clogged with lorries and plagued with roadworks. Charlie, an inveterate driver, hated to admit it, but now they had free Wi-Fi and power points, she was definitely starting to prefer trains. She got out and stretched, then realised Maria's car wasn't already parked up by the garage. She checked her watch. It was after eight. When she'd called earlier to say she'd be back, Maria hadn't said anything about going out.

The house was dark and chilly. The heating had obviously been off since Maria had left in the morning. Charlie snapped the lights on as she went, ending up in the kitchen where there was no note on the table. Odd, she thought, pulling out her phone to call Maria. She noticed a text had come in earlier, presumably when she'd been talking to Nick. Going to early movie with girls from work. Home by nine. Xxx, Charlie read. It was unreasonable of her, but she felt pissed off. She'd wanted Maria to be home.

She knew even as she pressed the keys that what she was about to do was petulant and childish. But she didn't care. The text message from Lisa filled the screen. Stomach suddenly hurting, Charlie read it. Sent u email, gues u didnt get. Hope ur OK. Want 2 c u b4 u go bk. Any time aftr 3. Pse? Hope ur gd. Xxx. For Lisa, it was effusive. It was, Charlie thought, the first time Lisa had been the one doing the asking. The second anomaly of the day, and even more welcome than the first.

And it made the email impossible to resist any longer. Charlie ran upstairs to the box room over the garage that had become her home office. She woke the computer and went straight to her email program. There, nestled among the twenty-seven emails that had arrived since Monday afternoon, was the message from Lisa.

Hi

Hope you are going well and not too cluttered by the
burden Corinna has tried to place on your shoulders. I
wish we'd had longer to spend together on Saturday. I
feel neither of us really got the chance to say the
things we wanted to. But still, I suspect it was more
pleasant for both of us than the other calls on our time.
I've been dealing with poor Tom, who is struggling with
his wife's terminal cancer. He's very emotional,
understandably. He's confusing me with a mother
figure which is not his wisest move.

Are you back in Oxford? I thought I saw you in the
car. Come and see me if you are. On the one hand, I
want you not to waste your time on this crazy chimera
Corinna has set breathing flame. On the other, I quite
like the thought of you having a reason to come to
Oxford. It's hard on both of us when we get so few
chances to talk properly.

Thinking of you.

Lisa

Charlie leapt on the mention of Tom and his grief.
Immediately she replayed the scene in her head. Could
she have been mistaken? Had her mind created what she
feared in what had been an emotional but sexually innocent embrace? It wasn't impossible. Charlie herself had
been in a disturbed frame of mind, her incontinent emotions already churned up. And here was the innocuous
explanation, offered before it had even been sought. She
almost laughed aloud, cursing herself for a fool who'd
been ready to believe the worst instead of keeping an open

mind. Years of professional training tossed aside just because she was suffering the adolescent torments of longing for someone she thought was out of her reach. 'You're a fuckwit, Charlie Flint,' she said, hitting the 'reply' button with a flourish. 'But it's never too late to make amends.'

17

Magda ran through the rain, ducking into the scaled-down Sainsbury's round the corner from her flat. She'd come home ready to fix herself dinner and been shocked by how low her supplies had fallen. She'd been spending so much time at Jay's, she hadn't noticed how she'd been eating into her kitchen cupboard staples whenever she was in the flat. Tonight, Jay was in Bologna, probably eating a sensational meal in an intimate family-run trattoria, and she didn't even have a bag of dried pasta and a jar of sauce to pour over it.

With only half her mind on shopping, Magda filled her basket and stood in line. Here was yet another difference between her past life and her present one. When she'd been living with Philip, she'd savoured his occasional absences on business. They'd been an opportunity to do the things she never seemed to manage when he was around: a long candlelit soak in the bath with a gin and tonic; late-night book shopping on the Charing Cross Road; renting a DVD to watch with a couple of the oncology nurses whose company always cheered her up; or just taking a good novel to bed with a bottle of San Pellegrino and a packet of chocolate digestives.

But when Jay left town there was never any cause for rejoicing. The flat seemed empty in a way it never had before. Magda felt restless, unable to settle to anything. Maybe it was because she never felt guilty indulging in whatever took her fancy when Jay was around. Either Jay would join her, or she'd do her own thing without the faintest flicker of reproach. So there was nothing she could do when Jay was gone that she couldn't do when she was around.

Except miss her, of course.

By the time she'd paid for her basket of food, the rain had eased. Even so, she was glad to reach the shelter of her lobby. She shook her hair like a wet dog as she headed for the lifts. Before she could put down one of her carrier bags to press the bell, a man appeared at her side, poking a finger at the button.

He was a stranger, which wasn't particularly unusual. The block was large enough and her hours sufficiently irregular for Magda to be unfamiliar with most of her neighbours. The man followed her in and as she turned to face the doors, she gave him a covert glance. Yes, definitely nobody she'd seen before. Only a few centimetres taller than her, a bristle of light brown stubble surrounding his bald patch, soft features and eyes the colour of boiled gooseberries. He was wearing one of those overcoats she always thought of as the preserve of public school men –

camel-coloured with a brown velveteen collar, slightly nipped in at the waist – and carrying an umbrella and briefcase. He didn't look much older than her, but he was dressed at least a generation older.

'It's Magda, isn't it?' he said as soon as the doors closed and they were alone in the small metal compartment. His voice matched his overcoat – plummy, posh and very smooth.

Startled, Magda half-turned and stepped back simultaneously. 'I'm sorry? Do I know you?'

'I was on my way to call on you when you appeared just now.' It was as if she hadn't spoken to him in her best 'keep your distance' tone. 'I have something for you. I was a friend of Phil, you see.'

Not if you called him Phil, Magda thought. Philip had hated being called by anything other than his given name.

As if reading her mind, the man gave a little self-deprecating shrug. 'Well, not so much a friend. More a business associate.' He thrust a hand inside his overcoat and rummaged in an inside pocket. For a mad moment she thought he was reaching for a gun. Too many late nights watching film noir, she told herself as he produced an innocuous business card. 'This is me.' He seemed not to notice that Magda didn't have a free hand to accept it with.

The doors opened and Magda wasted no time leaving the lift and heading for her front door. She put down the bags of shopping and turned to face the man. He was a few feet from her, holding his card out. She took it and read, *Nigel Fisher Boyd. Fisher Boyd Investments*. A mobile number and a URL but no physical address. 'I've never heard of you,' she said.

'I appreciate that,' Fisher Boyd said. 'But as I said, I do have something for you. And I'd rather not conduct business out here in the hallway.'

'And I don't invite strangers into my flat.'

'Very sensible. Why don't you put your shopping inside and meet me downstairs? I noticed an agreeable little wine bar just down the street. We might go there for a drink?'

Magda looked at his proposition from all sides and couldn't see anything wrong with it. 'Fine,' she said at last. 'I'll see you downstairs.' They both stood for a moment staring at each other. Then he got it.

He wagged a finger at her. 'Very sensible.' He backed away, then wheeled round and marched back to the lift. Magda watched him disappear behind the brushed steel doors before she let herself in.

The strange encounter had unsettled her. Of course she wanted to know what Nigel Fisher Boyd had for her that couldn't be handed over on her own doorstep. But she was aware that her recent notoriety made her interesting to the sort of criminals who saw crime victims as potential prey. And he had called her late husband 'Phil'. She wished for Jay's presence; not because she couldn't handle this alone but because it was always nice to have back-up.

Magda left her bags on the kitchen counter next to Fisher Boyd's card. If anything did happen to her, at least she'd left a clue behind.

Ten minutes later, she was sitting at a corner table in a wine bar she'd never visited before in spite of its proximity to her home. She'd never been tempted inside; it always appeared rather dim and sad, its occupants an odd assortment who looked as if they didn't fit in anywhere else so they'd fetched up there like driftwood. Fisher Boyd returned to the table with a bottle of Sancerre and a dubious look on his face. 'Not sure this is quite chilled enough,' he said, pouring two glasses and sipping it. He swilled it round his mouth, puffing out his cheeks, pursing his lips then swallowing ostentatiously. 'It'll do, I suppose.'

Magda tasted the wine. It seemed fine to her. 'How did you know my husband?' she said.

Fisher Boyd took off his overcoat and folded it carefully over the back of a chair. Magda hated those sharp chalk-stripe suits with the double vents and slanted pockets that she only ever saw on the backs of the kind of men that Philip described as 'necessary evils' in the world he moved in. Because of his company's specialised role as confidential printers, he had to work with a wide range of people involved in making and taking money. 'From borderline spivs to the grandees of private banking,' he'd once said, adding, 'And sometimes the extremes are closer than you might think.' She was pretty sure which end of the spectrum Nigel Fisher Boyd tended towards.

'Some of my clients need very high-quality confidential printing. Share certificates, bonds, that sort of thing. That's how we met.'

It was plausible. But nothing that couldn't be cobbled together from reading the trial reports. 'So if you've got something for me, why has it taken you this long to bring it to me?'

Fisher Boyd gave her a pitying look. 'It seemed sensible to wait until after the trial. So there could be no possibility of you perjuring yourself.'

'Perjuring myself?' Outrage battled bewilderment and

won. 'How dare you suggest I would lie in the witness box!'

He flashed a quick, sharp-toothed smile. 'Precisely as I feared. You're much too honest a person not to have told the truth, the whole truth and nothing but the truth in court. And that would have been awkward for all of us.'

'I don't like the sound of this. What's all this about?' Magda gripped the stem of her glass tightly, feeling out of her depth.

Fisher Boyd snapped open his briefcase and took out a slim leather folder the size of a hardback novel. He pushed it across to her. 'Go on, open it,' he said when she just sat there looking at it with foreboding.

Magda opened the flap and looked inside. There were a few sheets of heavy linen paper but she couldn't see what was written on them. She pulled them clear and stared at the fine engraving, uncomprehending. The figure of €200,000 jumped out at her. There were four of them, each with the same amount embossed on them. 'I don't understand,' she said.

'They're bearer bonds,' he said. 'Whoever holds them owns them. They're not registered in anyone's name. It's like having the money in your hand without the inconvenience of walking round with a suitcase full of fifty-pound notes.'

'Why are you showing these to me? Where have they come from?'

'Didn't Phil tell you about them?' He looked faintly amused.

'No. I have no idea where this money has come from.

His estate's been settled. Everything's accounted for. There's no missing eight hundred thousand euros.' She slipped the bonds back in the wallet and closed the flap as if that would somehow make it all go away.

Fisher Boyd shook his head, his mouth a tight, twisted line. 'Just as well I'm not a thief, then. I could have pocketed the lot and you'd have been none the wiser. Luckily for you, I don't believe in cheating my clients.'

'Look, you're going to have to explain this to me,' Magda said. 'I don't understand any of this.'

'It's quite simple. The motive that Paul Barker and Joanna Sanderson had for killing Phil was insider trading, right?'

'Yes. He was going to report them to the police and the FSA. They were finished. They'd go to jail.'

Fisher Boyd flashed his scary smile again. 'Well done, my dear. And how do you suppose Phil worked out what they were up to?'

'He found out they were spending far too much money and he discovered they were insider trading.'

'And how did he know what to look for?'

Magda frowned. 'I don't know. He just knew how the financial world worked, I suppose.'

Fisher Boyd's expression was pitying. 'He knew because he was doing it himself. This' – he tapped the wallet – 'is the laundered proceeds.' He raised his glass in a toast to the wallet, draining it and refilling it from the sweating bottle.

Magda felt her chest constrict with shock. What this man was saying was so at odds with her view of Philip that she couldn't make sense of it. 'Philip wouldn't do that,' she said.

'My dear, he not only would, he did. Why else would I be handing you a small fortune in bearer bonds?'

'But why would he inform on Paul and Joanna if he was doing the same thing?'

He shrugged. 'I wondered that too. My only conclusion was that they were doing it so badly that he was afraid they'd be unmasked and his own little house of cards would be pulled down with them. At least this way he was in control of things. He was prepared for the investigation.' He patted the wallet. 'And the proof of the pudding is in here. The investigators didn't find a trace of what he'd been up to.'

'I can't take this in,' Magda said.

'I know. It's a lot of money to fall into your lap,' he said, misunderstanding.

'I can't believe Philip did this.'

'He was trying to take care of you. As a good husband should.'

It was as if they were speaking different languages. Magda had never wanted Jay by her side more than she did right then. Jay was solid ground. And Magda needed something in her life to be solid ground. Her parents had failed her, and now it seemed her husband had done the same. 'I don't know what to do with this,' she said.

Still at cross-purposes, Fisher Boyd responded briskly. 'You'll need to deal with a private bank. Much easier than trying to get someone at your local branch to understand what this is, never mind what to do with it. I'll give you some covering documentation about it being a life insurance payout to keep you straight with the taxman. Perfect way to clean it up.'

'That doesn't seem very honest. I thought you said you weren't a crook? That sounds pretty crooked to me.'

A flicker of annoyance crossed Fisher Boyd's face. 'I said I wasn't a thief. I provide a service. I don't ask why my clients need this service, and I don't cheat them. Frankly, that's more than one can say for an awful lot of people in this business.'

'I can't make sense of any of this,' Magda said.

'Just think of it as a nice little nest egg,' Fisher Boyd said. He drank some more wine, smacking his lips at its dryness. 'You're a very lucky lady.' He reached for his coat and stood up. 'I'll send you that bogus insurance stuff in the post. You've nothing to worry about, I've done this sort of thing before and nobody's ever batted an eyelid.' He slipped into his coat with a flash of scarlet lining then picked up his umbrella and briefcase. 'Should you ever need my services, don't hesitate to call.' He tipped an imaginary hat to her. 'A pleasure to meet you.'

Dazed, Magda barely noticed him leave. She sat for a long time staring at the leather wallet. Part of her wanted to tear the bonds into small pieces and flush them down the toilet. But that wouldn't erase the memory of their existence. That wouldn't diminish the betrayal. Destroying them couldn't restore the image she'd always held of Philip as an honest, decent man.

And then there were the precepts dinned into her as a child. 'Waste not, want not.' 'There are poor children who would be grateful for what you take for granted.' She could hear her mother's voice in the back of her mind saying, 'Just think of the good you could do with it, honey.'

Magda picked up the wallet and thrust it into her hand-bag. For now, at least, she would hang on to it. She pushed her wine glass away and got up to leave. She was halfway to the door before the barmaid called her back. 'You need to settle up,' the woman said. 'A bottle of Sancerre.' Somehow, Magda wasn't entirely surprised.

With a wry smile, she paid for the wine. It was good to be reminded there was no such thing as a free lunch.

18

Unlike most cops, Nick Nicolaides never minded days when he was due to give evidence in court. Most of his colleagues liked activity. Sitting around for hours waiting to be called to the witness stand drove them mad with boredom. Nick had never had any problem with occupying his mind. Music in his ears, a book in his hand, and he was happy. The iPhone had been a glorious addition to his life. He could compose music, he could surf the web, he could read, he could play games. If he felt like it, he could even download files from the office and catch up on his report reading.

Or, like today, he could pursue his own investigations without anybody looking over his shoulder and wondering why in God's name he was Googling Swedish newspapers when he was supposed to be smashing an international child-trafficking ring. Because here, today, all he was supposed to do was wait till he was called into court and then respond to questions he already knew the answers to.

After he'd spoken to Charlie, Nick had put Jay Macallan Stewart to the back of his mind and concentrated on the operation his team were working on. But when he fell into bed, exhausted by a day of comparing CCTV images against their databank of known traffickers and pimps, his mind had drifted back to their earlier conversation. He'd gone to sleep thinking about what Charlie had told him and what information they needed to gather. And in the morning, staring at his reflection in the mirror as he shaved, he'd realised he was looking at the Ulf Ingemarsson case from the wrong end of the telescope.

'Alibi,' he muttered. That was the place to start. The only problem was how to nail down what Jay Macallan Stewart was doing during a particular week in 2004. Nobody could be expected to remember what they were doing six years ago.

'But their staff might.' He rinsed his face in the basin and gave himself a confident wink. Now all he had to do was figure out an approach.

Meanwhile, he could use the waiting time to see what he could find out about Ulf Ingemarsson. The translate function Google offered sometimes provoked more hilarity than clarity, but it was good enough to cope with press articles. The initial news stories – 'Swedish man murdered in Spain' – gave the usual spin of outrage. Bloodthirsty foreign brigands, incompetent foreign police, the risks of Abroad to decent Swedes. Behind the headlines, a story of a man holidaying in an isolated mountain villa, confronting burglars. A scuffle, a knife. A corpse lying on the floor for days, until the next visit from the cleaning company.

Then the counter-attack. Ingemarsson's girlfriend, a primary school teacher called Liv Aronsson, claimed this had been no ordinary burglary. As well as the obvious valuables, the thieves had stolen Ingemarsson's papers, which she insisted were meaningless and worthless to anyone other than a handful of web developers. She talked about his plans for an individually tailored travel guide system and revealed that he had been in talks with a British software developer, but the discussions had broken down over the issue of how the profits should be split. Her story was covered briefly in a couple of newspapers and one news magazine wrote a longer feature. Then the story died for a while.

When Jay Macallan Stewart launched 24/7, Liv Aronsson's story surfaced again on a couple of Swedish internet sites. Nothing was said to link Ingemarsson directly with 24/7, but it was there between the lines for anyone savvy enough. Again, the Spanish police were criticised for their refusal to consider this was more than a simple burglary, and Aronsson hinted that she believed her partner might have been killed for his idea.

Definitely worth talking to, Nick thought. He emailed the journalist who had written the article, asking for contact details for Aronsson. It's possible there may be a connection between Ulf Ingemarsson's death and a cold case I am investigating, he wrote. It seems that Liv Aronsson may have some helpful information. Either it would work or it wouldn't. In the UK, journalists didn't generally want to hand information over to the police. Maybe it would be easier in Sweden.

Now he'd read the Swedish coverage, Nick was even less keen to call the Spanish police. He didn't suppose there was much difference between them and his own colleagues when it came to being slagged off in the press, especially the foreign press. Lazy journalism was a great shield to hide behind when you knew you hadn't covered yourselves in glory. He'd have been very surprised if the Spanish cops were too dim to understand the significance of the stolen papers. And they would have been under pressure from their foreign ministry to solve the murder of a Swede. Bad for business, apart from anything else. If the cops had failed, he reckoned it wouldn't have been for lack of trying. And they wouldn't be thrilled by some Brit sticking his nose in and suggesting they weren't up to the job.

The option was taken from him by the arrival of the court usher, calling him to the witness box. To his surprise, Nick's testimony was over and done with by the time the court rose for lunch. Nobody would be expecting him back at base till late afternoon. If Jay was out of her office, he could make some useful progress without anyone noticing. He felt no guilt about sneaking off; in any given week, he did hours of unpaid overtime. Doing a little work on his own account was hardly stealing time from his employer.

Nick pulled up Twitter on his phone and typed 'Jay Macallan Stewart' into the search box. And there, posted two hours before, was a tweet from the woman herself: At prosciutto tasting, Bologna. Will post best on 24/7 site l8r. If she'd been in Bologna two hours ago, she wasn't going to be in her office off the Brompton Road in the time it would take him to get there. As the thought struck him, he fired off a text passing on the information to Charlie. She'd wanted to talk to Magda without Jay being around. This could be her perfect opportunity.

The 24/7 offices occupied the upper floors of a double-fronted brick building. The entrance was a discreet doorway next to the designer handbag shop on the ground floor. Nick had read somewhere that the average woman spends £4000 in her lifetime on handbags. Looking in the shop window as he waited for someone to answer the intercom, it was easy to see how.

His photo ID held up to the security camera was enough to have him buzzed in. The stairwell was clean and fresh, the carpet recently vacuumed and the walls bright with glamorous photographs of European cities. The reception office was just as smart – decent furniture, a proper coffee machine and plenty of space. Nick was impressed. He'd been behind the scenes of too many businesses that didn't seem to care about the working environment of their staff. The Metropolitan Police could learn something from Jay Stewart, he thought.

The woman behind the desk fit the room. She was beautifully groomed without fussiness. Nick put her at a good-looking thirty-something. Her immaculate white shirt amazed him. He could never manage to look that perfect, not even when he sent his shirts to the ironing service. He gave her his best smile, holding his ID up beside his face. 'Detective Sergeant Nick Nicolaides,' he said.

She smiled, but Nick could see she was anxious. That didn't mean anything. Most innocent people were unnerved by the presence of a policeman they hadn't actually summoned. 'Hi,' she said. 'I'm Lauren Archer. Is there a problem? How can I help you?'

Conscious that he was looming over her, Nick perched on the edge of a table set against the wall. 'It's OK, I've not come to arrest anyone, I promise you. This is a bit of a long shot,' he said, giving her a wry smile that invited complicity. 'We're investigating a cold case.'

Lauren nodded, still looking uncertain. 'Yes?'

'It goes back to 2004 but we've got fresh evidence analysis that has pointed us to a new suspect,' Nick lied fluently. 'The problem is, the guy we're looking at is claiming he has an alibi.'

Lauren frowned. 'How can that have anything to do with us? 24/7 wasn't even up and running then.'

'No, but as I understand it, the business was in the development stages. We understand that Ms Macallan Stewart wasn't working alone?'

Lauren smiled. 'That's right. Anne, her PA, has been with her since doitnow.com.' She frowned again. 'But what's that got to do with your case?'

Nick sighed. 'It's all a little bit complicated. We can't be precise about when the crime occurred. It could have taken place any time in the course of a particular week. And the man in question claims he spent that week doing work experience with Ms Macallan Stewart's company. That he was actually shadowing her for most of the time.'

Lauren's eyebrows shot up. 'That doesn't sound like Jay,' she said. 'She hates people looking over her shoulder.'

'You see? Already you're being helpful. I wonder – do you think Anne would have a record of what Jay was actually doing on the week in question? An old diary or something?'

'Hang on a minute, I'll get her to come through.' Lauren picked up the phone. 'Anne? I've got a police officer here, he's got a query relating to Jay's schedule . . . No, not this week. A while back. Can you come through?' She replaced the phone. This time her smile was wholehearted, the look of a woman who has passed the baton to the next person in the team.

A door behind Nick opened and a deep voice said, 'I'm Anne Perkins. And you are?'

Nick stood up straight and introduced himself again, submitting his ID for scrutiny. Anne Perkins could have been any age between forty and sixty. Her thick salt and pepper hair was cut and styled in fashionable disarray, her glasses were on the cutting edge of chic and she wore a tight-fitting cap-sleeved T-shirt and cropped cargo pants that revealed tanned limbs and toned muscles. She looked like someone who cycled to work, Nick thought. And without getting out of breath. 'Thank you, Sergeant,' she said, handing back his ID. 'How can I help you?'

Nick repeated his story. Anne Perkins listened carefully, her head cocked to one side, a line of concentration between her brows. 'Your man's a liar,' she said. 'We have given people internships and work experience opportunities in the past, but never at the level of shadowing our chief executive. We'd never take that degree of risk in terms of corporate confidentiality.' She half-turned, as if her saying her piece should mark the end of the matter.

'Thank you,' Nick said. 'Please don't take this the wrong way, but I can't just accept the uncorroborated word of one person on a matter like this.' He gave an apologetic shrug. 'Rules of evidence, and all that. I'm sure you appreciate my problem.'

She looked shocked. Nick imagined she wasn't accustomed to her position being contradicted. He hoped he hadn't overplayed his hand. 'I thought our legal system thrived on the word of one person against another?' she said coolly.

'We prefer it when we don't have to trust to the intelligence of a jury,' he said, playing to her sense of superiority. 'Maybe if I could confirm that with Jay herself?'

Anne shook her head. 'She's not in today.'

'Could I call her?'

'That would be tricky. She's got a very full programme.'

Interestingly defensive of the boss, Nick noted. He nodded sympathetically. 'She's obviously a very busy lady. What about if you've got a diary for 2004 that I could look at? Problem solved. And I'm out of here, never to be seen again.'

Anne Perkins raised one eyebrow. '2004? Give me a minute. Lauren, show the nice policeman how the coffee machine works.'

Lauren gave him an anguished smile as they were left alone. 'Would you like a coffee?'

'That would be too much of a commitment. I'm not planning on being here that long.' He perched on the edge of the desk again. 'Have you worked here for long?'

'Five years now,' Lauren said. 'Since 24/7 launched.'

'Must be a good place to work if you've stayed here that long.'

Lauren grinned. 'We get great travel perks. And I love to

travel. Plus Jay's a good boss. She demands a lot from her staff, but she gives a lot in return. Have you been a policeman for long?'

Nick pulled a face. 'Too long. We don't get travel perks. So what's she like, Jay? I imagine she must be pretty ruthless, being such a success in business.'

'She knows what she wants and she's very good at getting it.' Lauren stopped abruptly, as if realising she was giving too much away to the nice policeman. 'But if you really want to know what she's like, you should read her memoir, *Unrepentant*. She had a pretty difficult childhood. Getting over that and making such a success of her life, that's inspiring, you know?'

Before Nick could respond, Anne Perkins returned carrying a slim notebook computer. 'I think this is what you need,' she said, putting the machine on the side table and flipping it open. Her fingers flashed over the keys and an application opened up on the screen. Nick came closer and saw it was a calendar for 2004. 'What were the dates you were interested in?'

'May ninth to May sixteenth,' he said.

She stopped abruptly, fingers poised over the keys. She turned her head to look directly at him. 'I've looked up those dates before,' she said. 'It was a long time ago, but I remember it well. It's not often you get asked about the same dates for two different reasons by two different police forces.'

Startled, Nick managed to maintain his composure. 'We do work closely with our colleagues in Europe,' he said.

'So this is about that Swedish software developer who got killed? What was his name? Ulf something or other?'

Anne had moved from defensive to wary now. 'Surely they haven't finally got someone?'

Nick shrugged. 'I can't comment. I just need to be sure whether this man was shadowing Jay that week.'

'Really?' She sounded sceptical. 'I'll tell you what I told the Spaniards. No way was it possible for Jay to have been in northern Spain that week.'

'I never said—'

'Of course you didn't. You're just a foot soldier investigating an unnamed suspect in an unidentified crime.' She turned back to the computer and navigated to the relevant dates. This was obviously the real thing, not something faked up at the last minute to keep him happy. Seconds later he was looking at seven rectangular boxes. At the top was the day and date; down the side, 'JMS', 'AP' and 'VF'. Each day, including the weekends, was filled with details of appointments.

'Who's VF?' Nick asked as he tried to take in Jay's movements.

'Vinny Fitzgerald,' Anne said. 'He's our systems guy. Very talented man. He's in charge of making the site work. Jay discovered him when she was setting up doitnow.com. And he wasn't anywhere near Spain that week either.' She tapped the screen, which revealed VF had been running a training course in Bracknell. Then she pointed to Jay's schedule. 'As you can see, nothing here about a work experience person. And obviously nobody was shadowing Jay that week. Sunday and Monday she was in Brussels, Tuesday and Wednesday in Marseilles, Thursday and Friday in Biarritz. Lots of appointments with potential contributors. And a schedule of things to visit and places to eat

287

and drink. Jay doesn't like company when she's travelling for work. There's no way your suspect was shadowing her that week.'

'I can see that,' Nick said. 'Any chance you could give me a print-out, make it easier for me to convince my boss?'

Anne chewed her lip for a moment. 'I don't see why not. There's nothing commercially sensitive about it. No privacy issues that I can see.' She straightened up, clearly having come to a decision. 'Yes, I can do that. You're sure you can't give me a name for your suspect?'

It was an odd way to phrase it and for a moment Nick wondered if he'd been rumbled. 'Why do you ask?' he said.

'I just wondered why on earth he chose us for his alibi.' She picked up the notebook and tapped in the print commands. 'There must be hundreds of big companies where he could pretend he'd just slipped through the bureaucratic net without a record. It occurred to me that he might have a connection to 24/7 or to Jay.'

Nick gave her an anguished look. 'I'm not supposed to reveal that,' he said. 'People are entitled to their privacy until they're arrested. I'm afraid it'll just have to remain a mystery.'

Anne chuckled. 'Just as well Jay's not here, then. There's nothing she hates more than a mystery.'

Nick smiled. 'Me and her both,' he said. 'Me and her both.' Then he turned his most feral smile on her. 'One interesting thing, though. You've got a lot of time that week that isn't blocked out. I don't suppose you were in Spain?'

She looked as if he'd slapped her. 'I think it's time you left, Sergeant.' She crossed to the printer and handed him the printed page from the diary.

Nick gave her a long, considering look. 'You've been very helpful. Maybe we'll talk again.'

'I doubt that very much.' Her voice was ice, her eyes watchful. 'I can't imagine why there would be any need for that.'

Right then, neither could Nick. But there was some undercurrent in Anne Perkins' reaction to his casual comment that made him wonder.

19

When it came to the psychology of individual differ-ence, Charlie thought the group of A-level students she was teaching were bloody lucky to have her. Instead of a dry academic discussion about gathering empirical evidence on mental and behavioural disturbance and deviance, they were getting despatches from the front line of psychiatry. And, thank heavens, they were smart enough to appreciate it. Her two hours of teaching had turned out to be less of a chore than she'd feared. All the same, she was glad to escape the clamour of teenage girls and recover the peace of her car.

When she turned her phone back on, she picked up the text from Nick, offering her the chance to talk to Magda without Jay eavesdropping. No point in calling now, though. Magda would be at work, her mind on her patients. Charlie made a mental note to remember to con-tact Magda later.

Meanwhile, she had other work to do. None of the media reports of the trial had mentioned the names of the defence solicitors, only the barristers who had represented Barker and Sanderson in court. The barristers would be on to their next cases, their disappointed clients forgotten; the solicitors were still involved and only they could get her into prison to interview Philip Carling's supposed killers. She drove home, planning her strategy.

Charlie settled down at the computer with the phone and a mug of coffee. She had the names of the barristers but not the chambers where they worked. Google gave her the information she needed in a matter of moments; all she had to decide now was which one to go for. Sanderson was probably the junior partner in whatever had gone on, so she might be more willing to spill the beans. But Barker might respond better to a woman. 'Eeny meeny miny mo,' she said. 'So much for the scientific method.'

A young male voice answered the phone at the first chambers she called. 'Friary Court Chambers,' he said, brisk and businesslike.

Charlie tried to match him on both counts. 'Hi, I wonder if you can help me? I'm trying to track down the solicitor for Joanne Sanderson. Your Mr Cordier represented her last week at the Bailey? I'm trying to find out who the instructing solicitor was.'

'Who am I speaking to, please?'

Just what she didn't want to get into. 'This is Dr Flint. I'm a psychiatrist. I'm supposed to set up an interview with Sanderson, but for some reason I don't have the solicitor's name. I don't have to tell you how it goes sometimes.' She sighed.

'Tell me about it,' he said. 'Bear with me a minute.'

She could hear keys being clattered at the other end. 'No problem.'

'OK. It was Miss Pilger from Pennant Taylor who gave us the Sanderson brief.'

'Perfect.' Charlie held it together long enough to thank him and put the phone down. Then she jumped to her feet and did a little dance round the room, swivelling hips and yipping with delight. Finally, something had broken her way. Pauline Pilger was one of the first solicitors who had hired Charlie as an expert witness and over the years, the women had worked together a dozen times or more. There were a handful of lawyers Charlie knew she could count on right now and Pauline was pretty close to the top of the list. More than that, she was a passionate fighter for her clients, refusing to give up even in the teeth of absurdly overwhelming odds.

She pulled up Pauline's direct line and called it. She answered almost immediately. 'Charlie?' Pauline sounded surprised, but in a good way.

'That's right. How are things?'

'Good. I'm not going to ask you the same, I don't expect you're having a ball right now.'

'I've been worse. Listen, is this a good time to talk?'

'Let me call you back in ten minutes. I need to get this bit of dictation finished, then I can concentrate properly. OK?'

Ten minutes had never gone so slowly. When the phone finally rang, Charlie was drumming her fingers on the desk like a freeform jazz pianist. 'Pauline? Thanks for getting back to me.'

'Charlie, it's always a pleasure. I hate the way they're trying to make you a tabloid scapegoat. You did your job, you did the right thing.'

Charlie sighed. 'I know, Pauline. But those dead women weigh on my heart, you know?'

A long pause. Charlie knew Pauline carried her own weights. Impossible not to as a criminal defence lawyer. 'I know,' Pauline said at last. 'I take it this isn't just a social call?'

'I'm afraid not. I'm warning you now that this is going to sound bizarre. But bear with me, please.'

'Fire away. I could use a little bizarre. Right now things are very bland round here. I tell you, Charlie, the Human Rights Act is a two-edged sword. We've made it work for us, but every bloody client I see these days starts off with a rant about how their human rights have been violated. I'm getting tired of explaining that the police's refusal to let you smoke in the back of a police car does not come under the heading of cruel and unusual punishment. So hit me with bizarrerie.'

'It's about your client, Joanna Sanderson.'

'Currently banged up in Holloway awaiting sentence for murder. I'm guessing life with a recommended tariff of ten. What about her?'

'Magda Newsam's mother is my former tutor. And strange though it may seem, she's convinced your client is not guilty. Neither Joanna nor Paul Barker. She thinks they've been fitted up.'

'Wait . . . let me get this straight. The widow's mother thinks my client's innocent?'

'Of murder, anyway. She knows nothing about the

293

insider trading. But she believes the wrong people ended up in court and she's asked me to take a look at the case to see if there's any way of unpicking what's happened.'

'You think I didn't do my job?' Pauline said. 'Hell, I agree with the Newsam mother, I think my client is innocent of murder. But the circumstantial was against her, especially since she and the boyfriend had the kind of motive that juries who watch bloody *Midsomer Murders* understand.'

'I don't think for a minute you dropped the ball.' Charlie was conciliatory, but she was also convinced. 'I just want to talk to Joanna so I can go back to Corinna Newsam and say, Sorry, there's no loose threads to pull at here.'

'Jo won't tell you anything you don't already know,' Pauline insisted. 'But I may as well tell you there was one line of defence we didn't run because we thought it would alienate the jury. As it turns out, we might as well have gone all out.'

Charlie liked the sound of that. In her experience, when lawyers tried to act like psychologists, mistakes got made. It wouldn't be the first time that game-playing in court ended up as the first brick in the wall of an appeal. 'What was that?' she said.

'How much do you know about the case?'

'I've read all the media coverage.'

'OK. So you know all this started when a back-up hard drive turned up with copies of letters that didn't appear anywhere else on any of Philip Carling's computers?'

'Yes. Magda found it in her parents' house, where they'd been staying the night before the wedding.'

'Well, my client and her partner are adamant that Philip Carling would never have written those letters shopping them for the very good reason that he was the one who instigated the whole insider trading scam.'

'You're kidding. The bridegroom, Mr Pure-as-the-driven-snow? He was at it?' This was the most surprising thing Charlie had heard so far. It turned the evidence of the letters on their head.

'So my client claims. He'd been doing it for a while when Joanna noticed he seemed to be spending a lot more money than he was earning. Her first thought was that he was ripping them off. Taking more out of the company than he was entitled to. So her and Paul fronted him up. He realised the only way out of a very difficult situation was to come clean about what he was really up to. And he showed them how to set up systems to get away with it.'

'Jesus,' Charlie said. 'That blows the motive out of the water, doesn't it?'

'Just a bit.'

'I don't get why you didn't want to run with it.'

'Juries don't like it when you blame the dead without any evidence. There were two major problems. Philip Carling was good. There's no trace of dodgy money in his accounts. There's the odd irregularity – selling a painting for thirty thousand that he allegedly picked up for a hundred quid in a junk shop, that sort of thing. And he claimed to be a high-stakes poker player. He must have been a helluva good one to rake in the kind of winnings he was declaring and banking. But nothing you could point to and say, That's his insider trading profits.'

'That does make it harder. But still . . .' Charlie tailed off, trying not to sound too reproachful.

'Then there was the nail in the coffin. Who supposedly discovered the letters? The grieving widow. Have you seen her? Drop-dead gorgeous, Charlie. Every man in the court was drooling, believe me. Plus she's a doctor who treats kids with cancer. Robbed of her husband on her wedding night. It's hard to imagine someone with more appeal to a jury than Magdalene Newsam. So if we try to suggest the letters were planted to frame our client, it follows that we're suggesting the Virgin Magda has a finger in the pie. And that was a no-brainer.'

'I can see your problem. Not to mention that your clients weren't covering their tracks as well as Carling had been. I mean, there's no suggestion that they were fitted up over the insider trading, is there?'

'No, even I can't get that one to fly. But I don't think they killed Philip Carling. Barker might have, with his back up against the wall. But they alibi each other. Unshakeable. I did point out to Joanna that she wasn't doing herself any favours if she was lying about being with Barker while he was off killing Carling, but she was adamant. They were together, and they didn't kill Carling. Of course, the other problem is there are no other obvious suspects. He didn't live the sort of life where you make enemies who kill you on your wedding day. So if my girl and her bloke didn't do it, who did? The other wedding guests are all covered – overlapping alibis, nobody walking around in wet clothes. Does your old tutor have any bright ideas about who really killed him?'

'She has an idea,' Charlie said. 'I wouldn't call it bright

and there's nothing you'd call evidence to back it up. But it's suggestive.'

'You want to share it with me?'

Charlie laughed. 'You'd send round the men with the nice white coat that buttons up the back. No, I don't want to share it at this stage. It's too off the wall, even for you.'

'That's so unfair. I showed you mine and you won't show me yours.'

'I promise you, as soon as I have anything concrete, I will share. But for now, it's best if I keep it to myself. So, can I see your client? I could do you a nice psychiatric report for the appeal.'

'That's something I will bear in mind. But I'm going to have to knock you back, Charlie. Joanna's not doing well. Not well enough to expose her to a fishing expedition. She'd say anything right now if she thought there was even the faintest chance of it getting her out of there. She'd pick the Pope out of a line-up.'

'Probably with some justification.' Charlie tried not to show her disappointment. She was torn between the desire to interview a genuine witness and her understanding of the state that Pauline was describing. She knew she would only cause Joanna more grief if she appeared to offer any kind of hope. And while there were times when she didn't mind lying in a good cause, damaging someone who was already vulnerable wasn't one of them. 'It's OK, Pauline. What you've given me already, it's probably all she's got. I still can't get over the idea that Carling was the one who set the whole racket up. That's wild.'

'Maybe he double-crossed somebody. You get into those murky waters, who knows what sort of pond life you'll stir up. Listen, you keep me posted on this, you hear? My girl shouldn't be behind bars.'

'I hear you,' Charlie said. They spent a few more minutes catching up on their personal lives, but Charlie's heart wasn't in it and she was glad to end the call. 'That changes everything,' she said. She couldn't quite see what the new picture was, but the kaleidoscope had definitely turned.

20

The Marconi business lounge at Bologna Airport was pretty basic as executive lounges went. Beer, soft drinks or coffee and a limited range of prepackaged snacks; it was an insult to the palate after the glorious food and drink Jay had enjoyed on her two-day visit to the city. But she wasn't here to eat or drink. She was stuck here because her flight had a three-hour delay. That was the downside of her insistence on still doing some of the frontline work that was mostly done by stringers and reliable local informants, but it was a small price to pay for keeping in touch with the reality of travel as it was for most people. Well, the reality gilded with little luxuries like executive lounges. Because there was always some work to be getting on with. Jay had never believed in wasting the serendipitous parcels of time that professional travel regularly dropped into her lap.

She'd used the first hour to make notes of the high

points of her trip – restaurants, bars, shops, museums, galleries, but also the oddities and unusual possibilities that made 24/7's offering unique. Jay read through her summary and checked against her calendar to make sure she'd missed nothing. Then she took advantage of the business lounge's Wi-Fi to upload her top five prosciutto recommendations to the 24/7 website. Most of the site visitors would never have the chance to taste them, never mind buy them, but now they could sit around dinner tables and hold forth as if they were experts. This was the side of 24/7 that Jay didn't feel proud of. The information and experiences she'd made available had been responsible for a measurable increase in pretentiousness round a certain class of dinner table. She hoped she could get through life without being punished for it. God help her if her just desserts ever came to call.

With work out of the way, she still had the best part of two hours before they would be boarding her flight. She hoped Magda checked the live arrivals website before she left for the airport. She'd told her not to bother coming out to Gatwick to meet her, but Magda had been particularly insistent. It would wear off, Jay knew, but for now this devotion warmed her.

To take her mind off home, she decided to knock out some more of the book. Jasper had called her on Monday to tell her he'd squeezed another twenty grand out of her publisher on condition she could offer an early delivery date. The money was no big deal, but the eagerness it represented was a positive indication of how much they wanted her book. For that vote of confidence, she didn't mind dragging herself back into the past and reshaping it into the sort of narrative that would fly off the supermarket shelves.

She'd have to write about the time she'd spent travelling after she'd sold doitnow.com. Throw in a generous dollop of grief and regret over Kathy, but make it read like forward movement towards the idea that became 24/7. But not tonight. It was too dispiriting to write about travel in an airport. Airports were, in Jay's view, the antithesis of travelling. They were the necessary evil of transit.

The trouble with travel is that, no matter how far you go, you wake up with yourself. The time I spent moving around, getting as far from the beaten track as I could, was the incubation period for my next business, but it was also a futile attempt to escape from the pain of losing Kathy. Only when I realised I was going to have to confront that and then move past it was I able to escape my restlessness and start thinking positively about what I was going to do with the rest of my life.

Everyone dreams of getting rich. Coming from my background, I never thought it would be more than a dream. We all think that if we had enough money, we could give up work and have a wonderful life of swimming pools and beautiful meals washed down with vintage wines on terraces overlooking spectacular views. I can remember once when I was a student thinking that being truly rich meant not having to finish the bottle of wine. Because there would always be more.

Maybe some people manage contentment like that. I'm not sure, though. I've read enough stories about people who have won the lottery and ended up with messed-up, miserable lives to think I'm right when I say we all need purpose in our lives beyond the empty pursuit of pleasure. Some rich people find that purpose in philanthropy — setting up charitable foundations and working with them to make other people's lives better. And that has its place. I've given away enough of my money to know there's genuine fulfilment in that.

But for me, the true fulfilment comes from work. From creating something where nothing existed. From generating jobs, contributing to the economy and helping other people to make their own lives better. I suppose it's not surprising, when you consider my childhood. I saw at first hand and close range the results of fecklessness and idleness. The waste of talent and spirit, when the most stimulating thought is where the next spliff or fix is coming from. I'd nearly been sucked into that world myself. I could have squandered my abilities in the hazy New Age dreaminess I saw all around me.

It's true that I might have reacted against it in my own time and become the diametric opposite. But I was catapulted into that diametric opposite whether I liked it or not. The new set of lessons I learned were duty before pleasure, sacrifice before love, self-righteousness before compassion. All of these drastically different values were thrust upon me.

So I made a double rejection. I went for a pick-and-mix philosophy that let me choose the best elements of both sets of values. Work that created possibilities. Duty that embraced delight. And, at the heart of all I did, love.

I'd never been happier than when we'd been getting

doitnow.com off the ground, making a success story out of my crazy late-night idea. The buzz of making the business work, figuring out the finances and talking people into seeing the world my way – all of that had inspired me. Once we were successful, I still took a lot of pleasure from the business. I enjoyed basking in the glory, I won't deny it. But I wasn't sorry when the time came to sell. I was ready for a fresh challenge. I had the bare bones of an idea I thought we could make into something people would like as much as doitnow.com.

Kathy's death changed all that. My idea had been something we were going to do together, the way we had with doitnow.com. Without her, my heart wasn't in it. In all the miles I travelled, among all the people I talked, ate, drank, slept and played with, I didn't meet a single person who inspired me to share my next project. I slowly came to realise that, this time, my challenge was to do it alone.

One of the things I had realised during my travels is that most travel guides are 'one size fits all'. Your only real choice is deciding whether you're a Lonely Planet type of person, or a Rough Guide, or a Frommer's. It's a cookie-cutter way of arranging travel, and it's one that's hopelessly out of date now we have the ability to deliver what people need directly to their email inbox. It's also no way to cater to a market where the needs of travellers are so varied. I wanted to create something that helped people make the most of their trips, whether they were experienced, seasoned travellers or newbies making their first tentative forays out into the wider world. Their needs are different, but I thought one company could serve them all.

And so 24/7 was conceived.

Just like babies, businesses take a while from conception to birth. And just like babies, a lot of them miscarry on the way. And some are stillborn. The internet age has opened up amazing new horizons for many people. But it's also given false hope to a lot of people. Ideas are ten a penny. Good ideas are more rare than that. But finding someone who can turn a good idea into a profitable reality is more like a one-in-a-million shot.

I'd done it once, so I was confident I could do it again. I returned to London and settled into the house I'd bought two years before and hardly lived in. I enlisted Vinny Fitzgerald, who had worked on the IT end of doit-now.com alongside Kathy, and Anne Perkins, my devoted former PA, to help me put 24/7 together.

While Vinny began work on constructing the software package that would allow us to tailor the guides as individually as I wanted, I started researching how we would actually assemble the body of knowledge that would make our guides so special and how we would generate subscribers. I soon became aware that I wasn't the only person with a similar idea. When the word went out that I was looking at travel guides, those people flocked to me because I had a proven track record in online business.

Mostly they came with half-baked, half-formed notions with nothing solid to back them up. It always amazes me that so many people think it's enough just to have an idea, without doing any work to underpin it. I was appalled and astonished at the number of people who turned up with nothing more concrete than a sense of entitlement. Just because they'd had an idea. It's the difference between being a good pub raconteur and a bestselling novelist. That difference is hard work.

Of course, some of the people who beat a path to our door were very far from a waste of time. We ended up buying the work of an Italian entrepreneur who had been working on a similar idea. He had some great marketing ideas, but no software expertise. Without someone like us, he'd never have got his project off the ground and he knew it. He was happy to turn his work into hard cash, and we were happy we'd ended up with something that would save us a lot of time in the long run.

We were also in talks with a Swedish software developer who had been working on a package that would cover similar ground to the software suite Vinny was engineering for us.

Careful now, Jay told herself. Ulf Ingemarsson's death was still an unsolved murder. Caution should be her watchword. Liv Aronsson was a mad bitch who would fall on the slightest ambiguity like a terrier on a rat. She was still hawking her case round lawyers in Stockholm and London, trying to find one who thought there was any point in bringing a case against Jay. She'd failed so far because she always insisted that they pursue a claim against Jay for unlawful killing as well as theft. But one of these days, some slick bastard in a fancy suit might persuade her to solo on the theft accusation. And then it could get messy.

Vinny had warned her that a forensic software architect might be able to isolate elements of code that had come from Ingemarsson's work. Luckily, lawyers didn't have

Vinny's insight into the intricacies of programming code. But even so, if Aronsson did manage to demonstrate that some of their code had been written by Ingemarsson, she couldn't prove they'd stolen it. Because of course, they hadn't. They had a paper trail of payments made to various programmers, any one of whom could have introduced that code into the finished program. 24/7 was vulnerable only to the accusation that they'd been conned, the innocent victims of someone else's theft.

And besides, after all the unsuccessful lawsuits over the Harry Potter books and *The Da Vinci Code*, the public were deeply sceptical about the idea of plagiarism in any field of creative activity. They got excited for about five minutes, then they sat back sipping their Pinot Grigio and talking vaguely about Zeitgeist and ideas floating around in the ether. Still, there was no point in making it easier for Aronsson.

To our horror, he was murdered in a burglary at his holiday villa in Spain before we could reach an agreement on how we could work together. So his work died with him. The tragic waste of another life reawakened the pain I had felt when Kathy died, and for a few weeks I found it hard to concentrate on work. I wanted to run away again, but this time I had responsibilities to other people. So I stayed.

Jay read what she'd written. Nothing there that Aronsson could use, she thought. And a good place to end a chapter. She reckoned she'd given them enough grief and pain on Kathy's account. Nobody could accuse her of being heartless, not on the basis of this. And of course, with the up-to-the-minute ending, where Jay could wax lyrical about her new life and new love with Magda, she'd be demonstrating even more of her warm and emotional side. She'd never really written much about her personal life, nor talked about it in interviews. So this was the best possible climax to a book that was all about overcoming adversity. See, readers? Work hard, do the right thing and you too will end up rich and beloved.

If only it had been that easy.

21

When she got home from work, Magda almost expected there would be no leather wallet sitting on the dining table. That it would all have been a dream, like a bad soap opera. But it was still exactly where she'd left it. She hung up her coat then sat down at the table. Opened the wallet and there were the four bearer bonds. More money than she'd ever dreamed of holding in her hands. It should have been exciting but instead it was puzzling and frightening.

More than anything, she wanted to talk to Jay about it. But that prospect was even further away now. Magda planned to drive down to Gatwick to pick Jay up, but before she'd left work, she'd checked the airport website and discovered the Bologna flight had been hit by a three-hour delay. No point in heading straight there, so she'd come home to grab a sandwich and a coffee first. Now at least she could take the bonds with her to Jay's tonight, to prove to her lover she wasn't dreaming.

She went through to the kitchen and started assembling a sandwich with the remains of a roast chicken, some black olives and half a Little Gem lettuce. But her mind wasn't on food. All day, she'd found herself drifting off in the middle of conversations with patients and parents, her mind worrying at the notion of Philip as a crook. It wasn't how she wanted to remember him. Knowing this about him undermined everything she believed about the man she had been happy to marry. She'd thought he had integrity. She'd believed he'd worked to earn what he'd achieved. But she'd been wrong. He was a cheat and a liar. Worse, he was willing to betray his friends to protect himself. If she'd been so wrong about Philip, how could she trust her judgement again? She shivered, the knife sliding off the chicken and catching the side of her finger.

Blood oozed from the fine cut and Magda swore, reaching for the kitchen roll and pressing a sheet tight against the wound. She closed her eyes and leaned back against the table, feeling sick and pathetic. After Saturday, she couldn't even pour her heart out to her mother. It was all too hard and too horrible.

As if on cue, the phone rang. Expecting Jay, Magda jerked into full awareness and grabbed it. 'Hello?' Even to her own ears, her voice sounded desperate.

'Magda? It's Charlie Flint.'

'Charlie?' For a moment, Magda was nonplussed. Then everything fell into place. 'Of course, how lovely to hear from you.'

Charlie chuckled. 'You don't sound like it's lovely. Is this a bad time?'

'No, it is lovely,' she insisted. 'I just cut my finger, right before the phone rang. I was a bit discombobulated. How are you?'

'I'm good. More to the point, how are you? I just wanted to touch base. I know you were apprehensive about telling your dad about you and Jay. I thought I'd give you a ring, check you were OK.'

Magda felt herself choke up at Charlie's consideration. What was that thing they said about the kindness of strangers? Well, Charlie wasn't exactly a stranger, but she wasn't exactly a friend either. She was simply someone who was easy to talk to. 'Thanks,' Magda said. 'It was pretty grisly. Dad and I had a terrible row. He was so hostile, so cold. It ended up with me walking out and Wheelie coming with me.' She forced out a wry laugh. 'It was pretty harsh. A real "never darken these doors" moment. I think his only regret was that it wasn't snowing.'

'I'm sorry it was so shit.'

'It's not like I was expecting anything else.' Magda sniffed. 'He's just an unreconstructed old bigot.' She tucked the phone into her neck and opened the drawer beneath the cutlery, her version of what her mother called 'the all drawer'. She raked through, looking for an Elastoplast while she listened to Charlie.

'Well, you've got it out of the way now. That's one less person you're going to have to come out to. And most people are not like him.'

Magda sighed. 'At least he's honest about his feelings, Charlie. I don't know what's worse – facing that kind of abuse directly, or dealing with the sneaky, behind-your-back stuff that you can't fight because you never see it head on. Just catch it out of the corner of your eye, if you get my drift.'

'I'm not quite sure I do.'

She found the tin with the plasters and yanked the top off. 'We used to have a pretty busy social life, me and Philip.' She sighed again. 'Maybe it was my way of not having to spend too much time alone with him. I don't know. Everything is cast in a different light now I've finally got to grips with my sexuality. Anyway, we had lots of friends. Couples mostly, but some singles. And some of the women I thought had become proper friends. We did stuff together – shopping, cinema outings, meals. You know?'

'I know,' Charlie said. 'Nothing special, just the fabric of friendships that develop over the years.'

'Exactly. And they were really kind to me after Philip died. At least one of them spoke to me every day on the phone, they came round with flowers and wine. They were totally there for me. Anyway, once Jay and I became an item, obviously I told them. I didn't want to lie to them. They were my friends. And they were all apparently cool with it. Only one of them said anything remotely nega-tive, and she was just concerned that I'd jumped into something too soon after Philip's death.' Magda stripped the backing paper off the plaster and wrapped it round the cut, which had stopped bleeding. Uncertain how to express the tenuousness of what had happened, she ground to a halt.

But Charlie understood very well. 'And then they drifted away, am I right? They stopped calling or texting or commenting on your status on Facebook.'

'Bang on. And when I left a message, they just never got back to me. At first, I thought they were maybe being tactful. You know? Giving us the chance to spend time together without people butting in every five minutes. Then I realised it was because they didn't know how to connect with me.' She paused again, trying to figure out how to say what she meant. And appreciated the way Charlie didn't feel the need to fill every silence. 'I'm not saying they're homophobic. I don't think they hate people because they're gay. It's more that they think we don't have anything to say to each other any more. Like I suddenly stopped being interested in going to the movies or shopping for a new pair of jeans.' Another sigh. 'And it's been hard, because you can't actually confront a blank. So that's what I mean about it almost being easier to deal with the way Dad was.'

'Makes perfect sense to me,' Charlie said. 'You've had a complicated year. And right at the heart of it is losing Philip. And that's a massive loss.'

'Yeah. And that's sort of got lost in everything else.' Magda walked through to the living room and stretched out on the sofa. 'People think because I'm with Jay now that I've somehow forgotten Philip. And that's rubbish.'

'Of course it is. I don't want to intrude – I don't know what your rationale was for marrying Philip – but I imagine you really cared for him.'

Magda smiled, a sad reminiscent look in her eyes. 'I loved him. The same way I love Patrick and Andrew. He reminded me of my brothers in so many ways. He was very kind, and the sex thing, that was OK. You know? Nothing sensational, but not repulsive or anything. I've thought a lot about this and I'm not proud of myself. The bottom line is I married him because he asked me, Charlie. Because he asked me and I knew it was the easy option. Easy for me, and also what everyone wanted me to do. That's pathetic, isn't it?'

'It's not pathetic. I've known a lot of people who have married for much worse reasons. I didn't imagine for a moment that you'd done it lightly. Or that you had any intention other than to make it work. Bad luck for you that you hadn't worked out why you liked the girls so much.'

Magda could hear the sympathetic laughter in Charlie's voice. In spite of herself, she was laughing too. 'No, really,' she said. 'I kept telling myself it was just a sign of how immature I was, that I was still having teenage crushes.'

'At least you finally picked up the clue phone. But that doesn't mean you stopped grieving for the person you lost.'

Magda didn't know what to say. Yesterday that would have been true, unequivocally. But today, nothing to do with Philip was quite that simple. 'I was grieving for the person I thought he was,' she said at last. 'The trouble is, I'm still learning things about him. And they're not all likeable.'

'I'm sorry,' Charlie said. 'That doesn't sound good. I can see how it would be confusing, on top of everything else you've been going through.'

'To tell you the truth, I'm still trying to make sense of something I just found out. Something . . . It's hard to say this without sounding like a drama queen, but it's true. Something that's changed my whole picture of him.'

A pause, then Charlie spoke gently. 'That sounds pretty shocking. I mean, it's been a while now since Philip died. I'd have thought anything that was going to come to light would have already.'

'You'd think so,' Magda said heavily. She so wanted to tell someone, but she still wasn't sure that Charlie was the person. 'And you'd think I'd have known the real character of the man I chose to marry. Apparently not, though.'

'It's no reflection on you,' Charlie said. 'We all want to think the best of people we care about. Nobody ever wants to believe their friend or their partner or their kid is capable of the really shameful stuff. When we love people, we can tie ourselves in all sorts of knots to find an explanation for their behaviour.'

It was hard to resist the warmth of Charlie's voice as well as the sense of what she said. Magda knew she was accustomed professionally to holding people's secrets. And she hadn't turned a hair when Magda had told her the truth about when she'd met Jay. Almost without realising she'd made the decision, Magda decided to talk. 'He was a cheat and a liar and a traitor to his friends. And I don't understand why.'

She could hear Charlie's intake of breath. But the hard words didn't shock Charlie into silence. 'Those are big words, Magda.'

'Believe me, Charlie, this is a big thing. What would you say if a complete stranger handed you an envelope with eight hundred thousand euros? Then told you it came from the proceeds of illegal insider trading?'

'Eight hundred thousand euros? In cash? Someone gave you eight hundred thousand euros in cash?'

'Not actual cash. Bearer bonds, they're called. Apparently they're the equivalent of cash. Untraceable, anonymous. But yes. This total spiv was waiting for me when I got home last night and he handed them over to me. I was shaken to the core. I mean, what would you have done, Charlie?'

'I suppose the first thing I'd want to know was what it had to do with me. To make sure the guy had the right person.'

'Oh, he had the right person all right. It's my money. It's mine because it belonged to my dead husband. Un-attributable, it's true. But freshly laundered. And mine.'

'It sounds like something out of a movie. How come you're only hearing about this now?'

'The spivvy guy – Nigel Fisher Boyd, his name is – said he'd hung on to it till now because he didn't want to put me in an awkward position at the trial. Because here's what really gets me, Charlie. Philip made all this money – all this and more – doing exactly what he was planning to shop Joanna and Paul for. That's what makes no sense to me.'

'I'm still trying to get my head round the idea of having that much money put in your hands when you're not expecting it.'

Magda jumped to her feet again and began to pace in agitation. 'Tell me about it. It completely freaked me out, and Jay's away on a trip so I couldn't even talk to her about it.'

'Poor you. It's no fun, having to deal with something like that by yourself.'

'Why would Philip expose himself to a police investiga-tion by shopping Joanna and Paul? Why take the chance?'

Charlie made a wordless sound that seemed to indicate puzzled agreement. 'On the face of it, it's taking a hell of a risk. He must have been very confident of having covered his own tracks to set the cops on his business partners.'

'Maybe he thought the authorities wouldn't look too closely at him if he was the supposedly shocked whistle-blower,' Magda said, unable to keep the bitterness from her voice.

'There must have been some pressing reason. Something that made the risk worth taking. What if they were being a bit careless, throwing the money around, leaving a paper trail? And Philip thought he needed to close them down to protect himself. And you too, I suppose. Maybe he'd even decided to clean up his act since you were getting married. What if that's what it was about? Get everything above board, ready for a fresh start?'

Magda considered the idea for a moment then dismissed it. 'Nice thought, but it doesn't make me feel any better about what he planned to do to Joanna and Paul. They were supposed to be his best pals. I could never do that to my friends. Could you?'

'I'd like to think not. But none of us knows what we're capable of till we're confronted by it. Don't judge him too harshly, Magda. You can't ask him what he did and why he did it. There's no point in torturing yourself imagining what was going on when you can never know.'

Magda sighed. She could see the sense in what Charlie was saying, but she was a long way from accepting it. 'I don't know where I'm going to end up with this, Charlie.

And then there's the money. What am I going to do about that?'

'It's your money. Philip wanted you to have it.'

'But it's dirty money. It's tainted. I don't want it.'

'Give it away, then. Do something good with it. Take your time and think about it. Choose a charity that does work you believe in. And make the gift in Philip's name, if that feels right. I know you're shocked, you despise what he did. But don't let that destroy your good memories. Hold on to the things you know were good about him. He was that man too, you know.'

Magda felt tears pricking her eyes and sniffed hard. 'You're right,' she croaked.

'It's always best to take your time. Don't make any decisions in a hurry.'

Magda managed a cracked laugh through the tears. 'I let myself fall for Jay pretty quickly. And that's turned out OK.'

For a moment, there was silence and she wondered if they'd been cut off. But at last, Charlie said, 'And she'll help you come to terms with this, I'm sure.'

'Thanks for listening, Charlie. It's really helped to get it off my chest before Jay gets back from Bologna. Sometimes it feels like all I've done is bring her problem after problem.'

'That's what partners are for.'

Magda smiled. 'That's what she says. But she's much better at handling her own shit rather than bringing it all home to me. I feel guilty sometimes.'

'Well, any time you want another set of ears, you can give me a call.'

'Thanks. I appreciate you listening. And what you had to say. I'd better go, though. I've got to pick Jay up at Gatwick.'

Magda returned to the kitchen, in spite of the tears more cheered than she'd thought possible half an hour before. Hooking up with Charlie Flint had been an unexpected bonus. She remembered something Charlie had said the other day and realised how right she'd been. Her mother had indeed had great taste in babysitters.

22

One of the reasons Charlie had fallen in love with science in her teens was her need to find answers. It wasn't enough for her to learn textbooks by rote; she wanted the why and the wherefore. So she was never going to be satisfied by a text from Nick saying he'd drawn a blank on Jay Stewart's sat-phone. 'There's got to be a way,' Charlie muttered to herself. She stared at the computer screen, frowning at 24/7's home page.

Then it dawned on her. Ranged around the main content of the page were sponsored links to 24/7's partner sites. Bargain flight companies. Hotel booking sites. Car rental. And cheap international phone calls. She clicked through to doitnow.com and found similar links to their associate companies. 'They would have had a deal,' Charlie said. 'Of course they would.'

But that was only the first part of the answer. Knowing who 24/7's phone partner was in 2010 wasn't much help when it came to finding out who the preferred satellite phone company of doitnow.com had been ten years earlier. She could try calling doitnow.com, but she didn't rate her chances of finding anyone who'd been out of school at the turn of the millennium, never mind working for the company and paying attention to details like sat-phone deals.

She was pretty sure that what she needed didn't exist. When you wanted to know what the *Daily Mirror* looked like in 1900, never mind 2000, you could go and look at an archive copy. But all those early websites with their mad colour contrasts and ugly fonts had disappeared without trace. Hadn't they? Expecting nothing, Charlie Googled 'website archive' and was amazed to discover a site dedicated to preserving the digital equivalent of back numbers. Admittedly, it only went back as far as 2004, but it was impressive.

What was even more impressive was that they had doitnow.com's home page from August 2004. There was a link to a regular mobile phone company. And to her astonishment and delight, right down at the bottom left-hand corner of the page was a tiny sponsored ad. 'Going where they don't even have railway signals? You need a sat-phone. We supply the world's news organisations. Rent a holiday sat-phone from us.' Of course, when she tried to click on the site, she discovered it was deactivated. But at least this was a starting point.

She called Nick, forgetting he'd be at work. His phone went to voicemail. 'Nick, it's Charlie. Doitnow.com had a sat-phone partnership with Stratosphone back in 2004. Maybe they gave the boss a freebie? Worth checking, don't you think?' Donkey work, it was true, but he had offered to help. He couldn't start complaining now.

Next on Charlie's list was sorting out a trip to Skye. She'd been amazed to discover you couldn't fly to the island. It seemed counter-intuitive. You could fly to any Greek island that had enough level ground to squeeze a runway on, but you couldn't fly to one of the UK's tourist magnets. It was a five-hour drive or more from Glasgow, itself three and a half hours from Manchester. And she had a teaching session on Monday that she couldn't afford to miss. Getting back on Sunday would take most of the day, so it made sense to leave at the crack of dawn on Friday. To her surprise, Maria had announced over breakfast that she wanted to come along. 'I've always wanted to go to Skye,' she'd said. 'And I expect there really aren't very many midges around so early in the season. What do you say? You're not going to be sleuthing all the time, are you? We'll be able to see a bit of the place?'

'I expect so. And you can always go off on your own if I find a hot scent to sniff at. But what about your patients?'

Maria spread her toast and gave Charlie a wicked little smile. 'I'm always so bloody dutiful,' she said. 'Just for once, I feel like playing truant. Besides, I only ever book morning appointments on a Friday. It won't be the end of the world if I miss an afternoon's admin. I'll get Sharla to call my patients this morning. It won't kill them to rebook. There's nothing urgent, as far as I recall. What do you say? Shall I come? Shall we have a bit of fun?'

It had been hard to resist Maria's enthusiasm, even

though a tiny corner of Charlie's mind had been playing with the dangerous notion of inviting Lisa to come to Skye with her. Much more sensible to go with Maria, she told herself. With a wry smile, she logged on to doit-now.com and set about arranging a short break on the Isle of Skye at even shorter notice.

That done, there was nothing to distract her from communicating with Lisa. She'd sent a quick text yesterday, just to say she'd had to go back to Manchester and had been too busy to see Lisa before she left. Charlie didn't know what was worse – going cold turkey on communication with Lisa or diving in at the deep end. For now, she was giving up giving up and getting back into the groove of weighing every word.

Hi, Lisa

Sorry I didn't get back to you yesterday. The day just ran away from me. I don't have to tell you how that goes.

I wish there had been the opportunity for us to spend more time together when I was in Oxford. As it turned out, there were more calls on my time than I anticipated. But I hope I'll have good reason for coming back to Oxford very soon. It's clear there are things we have to discuss, and I can't wait to see you again. I'm sorry I have brought complication to your life, but I can't help thinking that the complication carries the seed of something very positive.

In the meantime, I am off to the Isle of Skye, where Kathy Lipson died in the notorious 'cutting the rope' incident back in 2000. Maria's coming too, apparently she's always had a hankering to visit. We're staying at the same hotel where Jay and Kathy were based. Not that any of the staff will still be there. I expect there will be a Lithuanian receptionist, Polish barman and a Romanian breakfast waitress, like everywhere rural these days. The locals escape as soon as they can to cities with anonymous nightlife and better wages. Thank heavens for the Eastern Europeans or our leisure culture would collapse. I expect the mountain rescue team will still have most of the same guys, though.

Let me know if there are any days that are better for you next week. I can do any day except Wednesday.

Love, Charlie

She read it through twice, changed a couple of words, then sent it, knowing she would be checking her inbox every twenty minutes for the rest of the day. But to her surprise, when she came back from the kitchen with a fresh cup of coffee, the new mail icon was flashing on her desktop. One click brought her mail box up, but the fresh message wasn't from Lisa. She couldn't help the pang of disappointment, only slightly tempered by the realisation it was from Nick.

With a sigh, Charlie opened it.

Charlie: Swedes are amazing. I got a number for Ulf Ingemarsson's gf, Liv Aronsson, from a journalist! Can you believe it? No warrant or threats necessary, he just handed it over. School's out 3.30 local time, so 2.30 here. This is a mobile, so any time after that I

guess. I think she might talk more to you than to a
cop.

Not so disappointing after all. Charlie glanced at the
clock. Three hours to kill. It was strange. When she'd had
a job, she'd always craved time to herself to read, to catch
up with Radio 4 podcasts, to go swimming or just to lie on
the sofa listening to music. Now she had the time, it hung
heavy on her hands. She struggled to keep her mind occupied, and when her mind was at a loose end, either Lisa
crept out of the corners and invaded her space or else she
brooded endlessly and fruitlessly about her upcoming trials
and tribulations. It was a toss-up which activity was the
more pointless. Sometimes it seemed all she could think of
was Lisa – her eyes, her smile, her playful humour, her
emotional intelligence. There was something irresistible
about her, some attraction so powerful it bled the bright-
ness from Charlie's image of Maria. This wasn't what she
wanted, but it was growing no easier to resist.

'Get over yourself, Charlie,' she said, abruptly switching
to Google. She wanted to see whether she could track
down the record of the Fatal Accident Inquiry relating to
Kathy Lipson's death. The more she could uncover before
she went to Skye, the easier it would be.

The FAI report made riveting reading. There was a list of
witnesses, a précis of all their evidence, a description of the
background and circumstances of the incident as well as
the cause of death – injuries to the head and internal
organs as a result of a fall from Sgurr Dearg mountain on
the Isle of Skye. The only critical note sounded in the

324

Sheriff's conclusion was the suggestion that climbers should make sure their routes were within their capabilities and experience. By the time she'd finished reading and making notes about what she might ask the mountain rescue witnesses, it was almost three o'clock. Liv Aronsson should be free of small children by now, she reckoned.

Charlie plugged the phone into her digital recorder then dialled the number, still without a clear idea of how she was going to play it. She'd let Ms Aronsson take the lead and see where that got them. The phone rang out several times before a breathless voice answered. 'Tja?'

'Is that Liv Aronsson?' Charlie said.

A short pause, then the voice said, 'This is Liv. Who are you?'

'My name is Charlie Flint. Dr Charlie Flint. I wondered if I might speak to you about Ulf Ingemarsson.' Charlie was conscious of speaking distinctly and more slowly than usual while trying not to sound condescending.

'Are you a journalist?' Her English was clear, her accent imposing a sing-song rhythm.

'No. I'm a psychiatrist.' She checked that the recorder was working, then wondered if she should be recording herself in what was, at the very least, a deceptive role.

'A shrink?'

Charlie winced at the Americanism she hated. 'Kind of.'

'Why does a shrink want to talk about Ulf?'

'Your English is very good.'

'Ulf and I lived in California for a year when he was doing his masters degree. I am a little rusty, but I think I do OK. So, I ask you again. Why does a shrink want to talk about Ulf?'

'It's a bit complicated,' Charlie said. 'Is this a good time to talk?'

'Where are you calling from? Are you here in Stockholm?'

'No, I'm in England. I can phone you later if that's better for you.'

A long moment, then Liv said, 'This is good for me. But I don't understand why a shrink is interested in my dead boyfriend after all this time.'

'As well as being a therapist, I work with the police,' Charlie said, trying to come up with an explanation that was clear and didn't contain too many lies.

'The police in Spain? That seems strange to me.'

'No, not in Spain. Here in England.'

Liv Aronsson sniffed. 'So. I understand even less. Why are the police in England interested in a murder in Spain?'

'The starting point for this inquiry was not the murder but the theft that took place at the same time,' Charlie said. 'In the course of another investigation, the police were told that Ulf Ingemarsson's work had ended up in the hands of a British company. If this is true and we can find out how it came to be, then we might be able to help the Spanish police to solve the murder of your partner.'

'Well, of course it's true,' Liv snapped. 'I have said this from the beginning. This was not a Spanish burglar stealing from a holiday villa. This was an organised crime, for the benefit of his rival.'

'When you say "his rival" do you have anyone specific in mind?'

'Of course I do. The woman who has made herself rich on Ulf's work. Jay Macallan Stewart.'

It was what she'd hoped for, but hearing the words was the moment she always worked for in her patient interviews. It was never enough to assume that what you thought you were going to hear was what had been said. 'What makes you so definite about this?'

'Ulf had this idea about three years before he died. He thought it should be possible to make guides that fitted with what people were interested in. He was a geek, he had the skills to write the software that would make this idea work. But what he didn't have was the knowledge of how to sell it. And how to get the information to put on the site. And I knew nothing about this also. I am an elementary school teacher, I know seven-year-old children, that's all.'

'Not the most transferable skill when it comes to an online business.'

Liv gave a dry laugh. 'No, not at all. So, he knew he was going to have to find a partner who knew the other end of the business. He did some research and he found Jay Macallan Stewart. She had been away from commerce since she sold her first web business for a lot of money. But he thought she understood the travel business. More important, he thought she understood people's dreams and desires.'

Charlie thought that had been a very shrewd judgement for a geek. The more she found out about Jay, the more convinced she became that she had never met anyone with a clearer vision of her dreams and desires. Being able to translate that outwards empathetically was a rare talent. And one that was never in the armoury of a psychopathic killer. However, it wouldn't be the first time that such a person had been able to mask their reality. Ted

Bundy was the classic example. But there had been others. 'He made contact with her, then?'

'He sent her an email. And she responded within a day or two.'

'Did he make contact with any other potential business partners?'

'No. I said he should speak to various people. To see who gave him the best offer. But he said he didn't want to get caught up in all that. Stressful shit, he called it. He wanted to find someone he could work with, that he trusted. That was the most important thing to him.' Liv sighed. 'He trusted the wrong one, as it turns out.'

'So what happened next?'

'They exchanged a few emails. It seemed like they might have a fit. So she came over here to Stockholm to meet Ulf. She was here for three or four days. She brought a software guy with her, somebody she had worked with before, I don't remember his name. We had dinner with them. I didn't like her, I'll be honest. Sometimes with little kids, they've not learned to cover what's really going on inside them and you get a glimpse of something a bit wild. A bit feral, is that the word?'

'That's the word, yes.'

'I thought she was like that. At one point Ulf started to sound a little cool about the whole idea, saying he wanted time to think his way through it. And there was this flash in her eyes, just a moment then gone. And I thought, I would not want to be your enemy.'

Charlie contemplated this dramatic statement and wondered how much it had been shaped by hindsight. 'What happened after that?' she asked, her tone mild.

'After she went back to the UK, she sent a proposal to Ulf. But he didn't think it was a fair agreement. They spoke on the phone a couple of times, and in the end he said he didn't think they would be working together.'

'I guess that was a disappointment for him.'

'More for her, I think. To get where Ulf was would have taken her years of software development and testing. But he could more easily find a partner who knew about online business. Anyway, he decided he would go away for a couple of weeks. We'd been there before and he knew he would have no distraction, so he could refine the program. The next thing, he was dead.'

'I can't imagine how hard that must have been for you,' Charlie said. 'Had you spoken to him while he was in Spain?'

'Just when he arrived, to let me know he was safe. But I told you, he didn't want any distraction, so he was planning to have his phone turned off. When he was in the middle of something, he was totally into it. But she knew where he was going. I heard him telling her on the phone before he left. She was interested in places off the beaten track, he said. Always looking for new places to send people.' Her voice was bitter. Charlie heard the unmistakable sound of a cigarette being lit. 'It's hard, talking about all this again.'

'I know. And I appreciate you being so frank with me. Did you tell the Spanish police about Jay Stewart?'

'Of course I did. I'm not stupid and I'm not afraid of her. As soon as they said there were no papers and no laptop, I knew this wasn't an ordinary burglar. Why would a burglar take notebooks and papers? The only person interested in that stuff is someone in the software business.'

'What did the police say?'

'They stuck to it being a simple burglary gone wrong. They weren't interested in anything more than that. And of course they didn't catch any burglar among their usual suspects. They thought I was a stupid hysterical girl. That's what the lawyer said. And I had no kind of evidence, so in the end I came home and tried to tell the police here what had happened. But they didn't want to get caught in the middle so they just played hide and seek with me. The trouble is, nobody in the police understands the process. When 24/7 launched less than a year after Ulf was killed I knew they must have his codes. They couldn't have developed this sophisticated software so much like Ulf's in less than a year.'

It was suggestive, Charlie thought. But hardly conclusive. 'Unless Jay Stewart was already working on a similar idea with her software guy.'

'If they were that far down the line, why would they need Ulf in the first place?' Liv said triumphantly.

'Maybe they wanted to buy him out because they didn't want the competition,' Charlie suggested.

'That's not how it was. He told me the software guy was really impressed with his work. No, what happened here is that Jay Stewart stole Ulf's work. I'm not accusing her of murder.' A harsh bark of laughter. 'I'm not so stupid. But I think she ordered the theft. And it all went wrong. So she is responsible, even if she didn't mean it to happen. I want her to pay for that.'

'But you've not been able to sue her?'

A long silence broken by a heavy exhale. 'My problem is I have no hard evidence. I have a little bit of Ulf's early work on the project on his old laptop. But nothing of the later work. If I had complete code, we could maybe force her to let some independent experts compare. But that's not possible. So, do you think the English police can prove anything?' It seemed finally to have sunk in that Charlie was offering a lifeline.

'I don't know. It's my job to assess the credibility of the witness.'

'You mean to figure out if he's lying? You're like a human lie detector?'

Charlie chuckled. 'In a way.'

'Then the person you need to speak to is Jay Macallan Stewart. Ask her to her face if she is responsible for my man's death. And you'll see it in her eyes. The feral person behind her smooth outside.'

'Unfortunately, they don't let me do that. Tell me, Liv. Did you ever try to establish whether Jay Stewart had been in the area when Ulf was killed?'

This time, when she spoke Charlie could hear grief instead of the earlier anger. 'I printed some photos of her from the web. I took them round hotels and bars and restaurants and car-rental agencies. But it's a tourist area. Nobody looks twice at their customers. They just run their credit cards and pretend to look at their passports. Also, I don't bet that she did it herself.'

'So the only evidence is the program?'

'It's not much, is it? But it's about Ulf and his work. It's about him getting credit for leaving his mark on how we live.'

That struck Charlie as the most telling thing Liv Aronsson had said. It restored the human dimension to what had happened to Ulf Ingemarsson. 'I'll do what I can,' she said.

'I am not going to hold my breath,' Liv said, not unkindly. 'But if you can find something you can punish Jay Macallan Stewart for, be sure you send me a ticket.'

23

Magda's intention to tell Jay about her encounter with Nigel Fisher Boyd had been thwarted by her lover's inability to stay awake. She'd looked tired in spite of her obvious pleasure at seeing Magda and they'd barely cleared the precincts of the airport when Jay's eyelids had fluttered and she'd slumped in her seat. Their relationship was new enough for Magda to find this endearing. 'She trusts me enough to sleep while I drive,' she told herself. It didn't cross her mind that nobody could survive the amount or the type of travel Jay had done over the past few years without learning to sleep when you were tired, no matter where you were.

When Magda pulled into the underground garage, Jay unwound, stretching and yawning as cats do. 'Nice driving,' she said in a sleepy drawl. 'Sorry I wasn't company for you. But I did tell you not to bother.'

'It wasn't a bother. I wanted to see you. Being in the car

with you asleep is better than being home alone.' Magda leaned over and kissed Jay. 'Besides, now you've had a nap, you'll be restored and refreshed.'

Jay laughed. 'Ah, the insatiable appetites of the young.' She grabbed her bag from the back of the car and followed Magda upstairs. 'I hope you don't have to be up too early in the morning.'

After that, there hadn't been a suitable moment to bring up her strange encounter in the wine bar. And in the morning, Jay had already been at the computer when Magda got up. She'd stopped work for long enough to share a pot of coffee and some toast, but it was clear her mind was still on work.

By the time Magda returned from the hospital, the bearer bonds were burning a hole in her mind, never mind her bag. She hung up her coat and went in search of Jay, who was sweating in the sauna she'd had installed in the basement garage. There was nothing for it but to strip off and join her. Jay looked pleased to see her, rolling on to her stomach on the higher bench the better to watch her settle lower down where the heat wasn't quite so fierce. 'You're like a salamander,' Magda said. 'I can't take the heat like you can.'

'It's just a matter of getting used to it. Give it time, you'll be fighting me for space up here. Have you had a good day?'

'The usual sort of thing.' Magda sighed. 'I had to tell a woman her seven-year-old isn't going to make it to another Christmas. That took the gloss off my day.'

Jay ruffled Magda's hair, already damp with sweat. 'That's just one of the reasons why I prefer doing what I do. The worst news I have to deal with is that the best brasserie in Deauville has closed down.'

'Yeah, but you don't get those magic moments where you tell someone that their treatment has worked. That's a kick that money can't buy.' Magda arched her back, stretching her spine, feeling some of the day's tensions leach away. She shifted her position so she was at right angles to Jay, able to see her face. Studying her lover's face still captivated her. She wanted to memorise every line and angle, every expression, every detail. 'I missed you when you were away. I always do, it's like there's a space in my day where you should be.'

Jay chuckled. 'That'll wear off soon enough. You'll be counting the days till my next trip and your next chance to do whatever it is you're not doing now we're together.'

'I don't think it will. I always felt entirely self-sufficient. I never bothered when Philip was away. Or any of my other boyfriends. But with you, it's an active absence. Something happens, I want to tell you. I hear some stupid story on the news and I want to rant to you about it.'

'That's very sweet,' Jay said, her voice husky. 'I don't think anyone's ever said anything like that to me before. My lovers in the past have tended to confess that they quite enjoyed having their space when I was out of town. I must admit though, when I was gone this time, there were moments I really wanted to share with you too. And that's not like me. I've always believed that line about travelling fastest when you travel alone.'

'Travelling fast, you can miss a lot.'

'That was always a chance I was willing to take,' Jay

said with a rueful half-smile. 'Throw some water on the coals, would you?'

Magda reached for the wooden ladle in the water bucket and scattered some drops of water on the coals. The steam that clouded up from the brazier took her breath away, making it hard to breathe for a moment. *You take my breath away.* When she could get some air back into her lungs, she said, 'I had a strange encounter on Tuesday evening.'

'Don't tell me your father came up to London to horse-whip me.'

Magda groaned. 'Don't. You can be very sick and scary sometimes.'

'OK, so it wasn't Henry on the warpath. What else could it have been? Another dyke came on to you?'

Magda reached up and shoved Jay's shoulder. 'As if. No, it was a man. And before you get all outraged, there was nothing remotely sexual in the encounter.'

'I'm glad to hear it. But before you go on, let me say that just because you are with me, it doesn't mean you can't enjoy it when someone flirts with you. I don't have a problem with other people wanting what I have.'

'Oh.' Magda dragged it over four disappointed syllables. 'Aren't you going to be jealous and badly behaved?' She tutted. 'Honestly, you're just so well adjusted.'

'I'll be cool about it. Until they step over the line. And then I'll remove their spleen. Through the nose. With a crochet hook.' Jay looked momentarily stern, then the giggles tripped in. 'Sorry,' she spluttered. 'Tell me about your strange encounter.'

'I popped out to Sainsbury's and when I got back, this

bloke I'd never seen before was waiting for me. Nigel Fisher Boyd.'

Jay made a face indicating she'd never heard the name.

'He's something to do with financial services. He didn't go into detail and I didn't ask. He seemed a bit creepy to me, a bit spivvy, you know? He claimed he was a friend of Philip's but I knew he was lying because he called him Phil and he hated that.'

'What did he want? Was he trying to get you to invest in some scheme?'

Magda laughed. 'You sound like a bulldog. No, he wasn't trying to get me to part with my money. Quite the opposite. He was there because he had something belonging to Philip that he wanted to pass on to me.'

Jay pushed herself up on her elbows. Magda couldn't help admiring the line of her shoulders, the fullness of her breasts. Trickles of sweat ran salt down her body and she longed to lick them. 'Sounds intriguing.' She frowned. 'If a little overdue.'

Magda sighed. 'Well, it turns out there was a good reason for that. He gave me eight hundred thousand euros in bearer bonds, Jay.'

'What?' Jay's face froze in an expression of absolute incredulity. Magda had never seen her look so shocked.

'I know. I was completely freaked out too. I've never even seen a bearer bond. The only reason I'd ever heard of them was Patrick went through a phase of watching *Die Hard* every night and that's what Alan Rickman's crew are supposed to be stealing. But that's what these are, supposedly.'

'But why?'

Just thinking about this aspect of her story made Magda feel tearful. 'This Nigel Fisher Boyd said it was Philip's profits from insider trading.'

Jay's eyes widened further. 'Insider trading? *Philip* was insider trading?'

'According to Fisher Boyd, yes. It's incredible. I thought I knew Philip. But the Philip I knew wasn't a crook. And I wondered for a moment if it was some kind of twisted practical joke. But eight hundred thousand euros isn't the kind of money you use to fuck with somebody's head. And then I thought of what you did and I started to freak out.'

Jay sat up and lowered herself on to the bench beside Magda. 'Christ Almighty,' she said. 'We could have totally fucked ourselves. I went through all Philip's stuff, business and personal, with a fine-tooth comb and I didn't see a trace of anything dodgy. It wasn't hard to figure out the paper trail with Joanna and Paul once I had an idea what I was looking for. But I thought Philip was clean. I'd never have written those letters if I'd thought . . .' She covered her face with her hands. 'God, we've had a lucky escape,' she said, letting out a long breath.

'We're in the clear now, though, aren't we? It's not like you made up the fact that Joanna and Paul were insider trading. All you did was bring it to the attention of the authorities.'

'But it's only a motive if Philip was clean,' Jay protested. 'If he was as bad as them, why on earth would he shop them?' Jay smacked the side of her fist down on the bench. 'Fuck.'

Magda thought back to her conversation with Charlie.

Some instinct told her this wasn't the time to tell Jay she'd confided in someone else. 'You could argue that maybe they were being careless and threatening to bring the whole edifice tumbling down. And Philip was trying to shut them down on his terms.'

'It's a line we could use if it ever comes to it,' Jay said. 'But we were so sure that Joanna and Paul had killed him. You remember? That's the only reason I went trawling through all the financial stuff in the first place. I was looking for a reason why they would want rid of him. I went hunting for motive, and when I saw what they'd been doing, it seemed so obvious. Without that, I'd never have taken the risk of faking the letters to make the motive obvious to the police.' Jay shook her head. 'But if he was doing it too, there's no way he would have been threatening their activities. So their motive disappears. Why would they have wanted to kill him?'

Magda was perplexed, not least because she hadn't worked that out for herself. She was supposed to be smart. Was this what love did to you? Turned your brain to incompetent mush? 'I don't know. Maybe they wanted his share of the business.'

'Then they should have killed him before the wedding, because afterwards, there's no question of his share going anywhere else except to you.' Jay ran her hands through her hair in agitation. 'Christ, Magda. This is a nightmare.'

'I don't see how it changes anything. They killed him, Jay. That's the bottom line. They did slip away from the party at the crucial time. I saw them, just yards away from where Philip died.'

'But that's not what you told the court, is it? You didn't

tell the exact truth about where you saw them because you had to lie about where you were. You were with me, not in your mother's office.'

'But nobody knows that. The defence never tried to cast any doubt on my story. It's history now, Jay.'

Jay looked a million miles from convinced. 'It's not over. There's sentencing, there's appeal. If what Philip was up to comes out, they're not the ones with the motive any more, Magda. That would be you and me.'

Magda was taken aback by Jay's agitation. If she'd thought about it in advance, she'd have expected it to freak her out. Instead, her bedside manner kicked in and she reacted as if she was dealing with a parent faced with a terrible diagnosis. Magda put her arm round Jay's shoulders, shocked by the tension she could feel in her muscles. 'But we're OK. I'm your alibi.'

'Which makes me your alibi.' Jay gave a bleak laugh. 'And you don't think some people might wonder about that? We end up together after a secret tryst at your wedding?'

'It wasn't like that,' Magda protested. 'And you know it.'

'We know that, but the world might not see it like that. We have a secret meeting, your husband is murdered, leaving you a very rich widow. And I step in and sweep you off your feet.'

'That's crazy. It's not like you need the money, for God's sake. You're worth millions more than me.'

Jay wiped her face with the back of her hand. 'For some people there's no such word as "enough". Trust me, Magda, it wouldn't be hard to make us look very bad indeed if this ever came out.'

'Well, it's not going to come out, is it? Even if – and it's a huge if – anybody finds out what Philip was up to, they're not going to find out you forged the letters.'

Jay leaned into her lover. 'I suppose not,' she said wearily. 'But there is one thing you've not taken into consideration.'

'What's that?'

'Without a motive, it's hard to picture Joanna and Paul killing Philip. And if they didn't kill him . . . who did, Magda? Who did?'

Part Three

1

It was the first night Jay could remember that they'd slept together without making love. The conversation begun in the sauna had chased its own tail for the rest of the evening, always coming back to the terrible point where they had to confront their decision to point the police in the direction of the people they were convinced had killed Philip. They kept revisiting the afternoon when they'd lain in bed and talked through the failure of the police to make any headway in solving Philip's murder.

Jay, who knew her Agatha Christie, had spoken then of the ordeal by innocence, the taint that would always cling to Magda if nobody was brought to book for the crime. 'Even though everyone who knows you and knows the situation wouldn't think for a moment you could have killed Philip. But that doesn't matter to the pumpkins out

345

there. As soon as we come out, before you know it, there'll be a Facebook lynch mob, "I bet I can find a million people who believe Magda Newsam is an evil man-hating lesbian who murdered her husband for the money."'

And it wasn't as if they'd made anything up. The insider trading was real enough. Jay had just made it obvious. Even now, she couldn't avoid feeling proud of how well she'd handled the situation. It was a great feeling, to sort out so big a thing for someone you loved. Now she just had to pray that it stayed sorted the way they'd arranged it. Otherwise they could end up changing places with Paul Barker and Joanna Sanderson. That would be the night-mare scenario – her and Magda taking the fall. That simply couldn't be allowed to happen, and she'd do whatever it took to make sure it never did.

Worst-case scenario, there was always the Costa Rica option.

With all this on their minds, she thought it was a mira-cle they'd slept at all. But Magda had exhaustion on her side. And even Jay had managed to fall asleep in the cold-est, darkest part of the night.

She'd had meetings for most of the day, her mind occu-pied with 24/7's latest expansion plans. The only disruption in the smooth flow had been Anne recounting an odd encounter with some cop who'd come to the office wanting to know whether they'd had some cold-case suspect as an intern. 'It was while we were still in the development stages, so obviously we didn't have any work placements running then,' she'd said. 'And you were travelling all week, so it was even less likely.'

'When was this?'

'May 2004,' Anne said, already turning over to the next page in their agenda for the morning. She gave Jay a look freighted with meaning. 'The week Ulf Ingemarsson died.'

Jay resisted a shudder. She remembered May 2004. What the hell was going on? Inquiries from strange detectives about her movements around the time Ingemarsson was murdered might not be quite as innocent as they appeared. As if she didn't have enough on her mind. No, in May 2004, she certainly wasn't wiping the arse of some graduate intern. 'Definitely not,' she said.

'Odd, though,' Anne said absently, scribbling some notes in the margin. 'After he'd gone, I remembered how I had to look out your travel receipts for that nice Spanish detective who came over after the girlfriend started kicking off. I knew exactly where you'd been and when, but he said he needed proof.'

Of course she'd known exactly where Jay had been. Anne's devotion was legendary. The lengths to which she would go to ensure smooth running for Jay's professional life knew no limits. Jay suspected that Anne was in love with her but that she preferred the attachment to be unrequited. You could never discover someone's feet of clay if you didn't actually push the relationship to intimacy, after all. It was an arrangement that suited both of them. But sometimes, like today, Jay wondered if she really knew everything Anne did in her service. She had a sneaky suspicion there were things she would be better off not knowing.

It was a relief to get away from the office and walk back through the quieter side streets of Knightsbridge. She never allowed the office to follow her on her walks; she'd mastered the art of letting her mind roam free. It always amazed her how London changed so quickly. You could go from the bustle and throb of a main artery to empty residential streets in a couple of minutes. Her own house felt like an oasis, the triple glazing keeping the city's rattle and hum at bay. But there were plenty of escapes from the bustle if you knew where to look. She remembered her first encounter with the London the tourists don't see.

After she and Louise had been split apart like a log under an axe, Jay had let herself be picked up at a gay night in one of the Oxford clubs by a good-looking butch in bike leathers. Susanne was a graphic artist who lived in north London and came to Oxford to visit her sister. They both knew there was nothing between them but fun, and there had been no hard feelings when Jay had abandoned Susanne at the party where she'd met Ella Marcus. Ella was the fashion editor of the kind of women's magazine that featured clothes no normal woman would ever wear. She was glamorous, prosperous and she liked Jay's mix of intellectual sophistication and cultural naïveté. She enlivened Jay's final year at Oxford and initiated her into the kind of life it was possible to live in the capital. Theatre, galleries, art house cinema and an absolute commitment to the cutting edge. Once the mass market got its hands on something, it was over for Ella and her crew.

It had been fun while it lasted. Jay escaped with her heart and her pride intact, and the delicious knowledge that their relationship had scandalised some and annoyed others. They'd stayed in touch – Ella had been one of the first journalists to get behind doitnow.com and, later, 24/7.

Jay was still thinking about Ella when she got home. It

was more enjoyable than the other things on her mind. She needed to maintain the distraction, but Magda was working late. Since she was in a romantic mood, she decided it might be time to navigate the treacherous shoals of what she could tell the world about how she and Magda had connected after so long. This would be tricky. Things she didn't want Magda to know; things she definitely couldn't afford for the world to know; and things that needed to be spun like spider silk to keep the rest of the world happy.

For a moment, she felt a flutter of annoyance. This was supposed to be her story, but even here she couldn't be honest. The truth was, the truth was impossible to share with anyone else. But maybe for now she could write the real story of what happened between the two of them on Magda's wedding day. Nobody else would have to see it, not even Magda. Jay could edit it afterwards. It might even be easier to do it that way. In black and white, she would recognise the things she must not say.

My first job at the conference that Saturday afternoon was to deliver a seminar on viral marketing. I'd be lying if I said I had enjoyed myself. Afterwards, trying to cool down on that stifling July afternoon, I walked back along the river, breathing in the same heavy scent of lilies that had perfumed those heady summer nights when I was a baby dyke. But before I could sink too far into the slough of memory, the grumble of car engines pulled me back into the present. I looked up the bank and watched a trail of cars led by a white Rolls-Royce drive past the Sackville Building and down to the meadow. Someone had mentioned earlier there was a wedding in college that afternoon. I couldn't have been less interested.

I carried on along the riverside to the end of the path, where steps cut into the steep grassy bank led back up towards the Sackville Building. I was about halfway up when the wedding party started to spill out of the narrow pathway from the meadow. The bride and groom led the way. He was the tall husky type, dark hair so freshly barbered I could see a thin white line between his tan and his hairline. Although it didn't look as if there were much spare flesh under his morning suit, he had the cheerful, chubby face of a pre-adolescent schoolboy, all turned-up nose, chin round as a plum and cheeks like a latex puppet. He resembled a Bunter whose postal order has finally arrived.

The bride could not have been a greater contrast. Tall, with most of her height in long shapely legs, she wore a sleeveless knee-length sheath of ivory slubbed silk revealing arms evenly tanned the same golden colour as her legs. The Cossack-style toque on her head was of the same material, toning perfectly with a swatch of honey blonde hair. I have always been a sucker for blondes with long legs. But this afternoon it was far, far more than a momentary stab of lust that knocked the feet from under me. Literally.

I knelt by the steps, ravished and ravaged. The instant I recognised the bride, some self-defence mechanism kicked in, telling me, 'It's not her, it's not her! You're hallucinating; you're kidding yourself. You can't recognise someone after sixteen years. She was only twelve the last time you saw her. This woman only looks like she could be her. Don't be stupid, get a grip!' I tried to convince myself and forced myself upright. I got as far as staggering up another step before the revelation that clinched it.

A couple of yards behind the bride were her parents. I might have made a mistake over Maggot Newsam sixteen years on, but I could never have been wrong about Corinna and Henry. Henry looked like an exaggerated version of his younger self, an exemplar of the wreckage drink makes of a person. But Corinna was timeless. Unmistakable, from the shellacked hair to the unfashionable shoes.

I stood there watching the wedding guests pass, a whirling kaleidoscope of memories blurring my vision. Snatches of music from Crowded House, Corinna's favourite band, kept fading in and out of my head like a badly tuned radio station. Dazed, I eventually managed to walk calmly up the remaining steps. One or two of the conference attendees sitting under the shade of the cedars looked at me oddly, but I did not know any of them, so I did not care.

I carried on past the Sackville Building to the punt station. Patsy Dillard, the conference organiser's wife, waved as I approached. 'Jay, we've got the cushions and the pole, but we didn't realise the punts are locked up,' she called. 'Can you go to the lodge and get the key for the padlock?'

'Of course. I'd be happy to.'

'Are you all right?' Patsy demanded when I came back with the key for the heavy padlock that fastens the anchor chain of the punt to the dock. 'You look as if you've seen a ghost.'

I forced a smile. 'It's a long time since I graduated from this place, Patsy. It's wall to wall ghosts for me. I can barely see today for the shadows of yesterday.' I took the key back, but the lodge was empty so I left it lying on the counter where the porter was sure to see it as soon as he returned. It's funny, I remember all the details so vividly, even the small unimportant stuff.

Since I was near Magnusson Hall, I decided to slip inside and revisit the Junior Common Room. This had been the domain where I reigned as president of the JCR. The room was surprisingly little changed since the days when I presided over meetings there. Certainly the smell was still the same: stale cigarette smoke and alcohol overlaid with the synthetic lemon of furniture polish and a whiff of chlorine bleach wafting in from the neighbouring toilets. The dartboard was still there, though by then they had run to a spotlight. The table football still lurked in a gloomy corner by the bar, where they had replaced the wooden hatch that served in my day with a metal grille. Bizarrely, the chairs looked exactly as decrepit and uncomfortable as they always did; it was hard to believe they were the same ones, but equally hard to work out where the Domestic Bursar might have managed to acquire a roomful of doppelgangers, or indeed why she might have wanted to.

More importantly, the French windows were still there, leading out on to the long lawn shaded by a pair of cedars. That day they were wide open, providing a short cut for the wedding guests from the marquee to the toilets. I watched for a few minutes, eyes roving over the peacock colours of the guests. But the face I was searching for was nowhere to be seen. Oh well, I thought. Busy bride.

I turned away and walked back towards the front entrance of Magnusson Hall, making a detour to the ladies' toilets. Nothing much had changed there either. Everything was still institutional cream paint and white porcelain. Even the rape crisis line sticker was still there. Improbably, it looked identical to the one that had been there fifteen years earlier, its adhesive specially formulated to make it impossible for the cleaning staff to scrape it off.

Inside the cubicle, I sat for a few minutes, relishing the cool of the cistern against my back, feeling it lower the heat of my body by a degree or two. The sound of the next-door cubicle closing disturbed my relaxation, and a quick glance at my watch reminded me I didn't have much time before my panel on growing an online economy. I flushed the toilet and let myself out, turning on the tap to splash face and hands with refreshingly cold water.

As the other cubicle door opened, I raised my head and looked in the mirror. Beside my dripping face, the ivory silk and golden skin of Magda Newsam appeared like the mirage of an oasis. Our eyes connected in the mirror, inevitably. I watched Magda's expression change from indifference to shock. Her mouth opened as her face flushed.

I wiped the back of my hand over my mouth and said, 'Hello, Maggot.'

Magda shook her head in disbelief. 'Jay?' she said in the tone of childhood wonder, eyes still locked on mine, mouth moving hesitantly towards a smile.

I grabbed a paper towel without looking and sketchily wiped my face, keeping my eyes on Magda. I couldn't get enough of how lovely she'd become. Magda had been a gawky but interesting child, never called beautiful. She is now, and I saw that clearly, no doubt about it. Some strange twist of genetics had taken the unpromising raw material of her moderately attractive but very different-looking parents and turned it into planes and curves that photographers would fight over. I found it hard to credit that this beautiful face was smiling so radiantly at me.

'It is you, isn't it?' Magda yelped, her voice rising through an octave with excitement.

'Who else would it be with this face on?' I turned to meet the grin head on.

Magda took a step towards me, then stopped. 'I can't believe it,' she breathed. I imagined I felt the disturbance of the air on my skin.

'Why not?'

'It's like seeing a ghost. Some manifestation of my subconscious mind,' she said softly, her voice rich with music that had always been there, but which was now the controlled modulation of an adult, not the artless piping of a child.

'A dream?' I said, trying for sardonic and failing.

'Come true. You just disappeared out of our lives. One day, you were always there, then suddenly, you were gone. No warning. Just gone. No explanation, no goodbye.'

Magda wasn't the only one with vivid recall of the sudden exile. 'It wasn't my choice, Maggot,' I said softly.

'My God, nobody's called me Maggot for years,' Magda exclaimed, laughter bubbling under. 'Not even

Wheelie. But what are you doing here? Is this a surprise for me? Did Ma invite you?'

Not bloody likely, I thought but didn't say. 'I'm here for a conference,' I told Magda. 'I had no idea about . . . all this,' I added, my voice cracking unexpectedly. Without conscious thought, we'd both moved a step forward. There were less than a dozen inches between us. I could smell something sharp and spicy on Magda's skin, like lime and cinnamon. I could even see the dilated pupils of her eyes. My stomach hurt.

'Jesus, Jay,' Magda said, her voice bewildered and tense. 'I wish to God you'd come back before this.'

'Me too,' I croaked. I wondered if my face mirrored Magda's mixture of awe, confusion, fear and wonder. 'Better late than never?' I asked. It felt like a plea, a prayer, a supplication.

'I got married this afternoon.' It sounded like a confession.

'Sorry. I should have offered my congratulations.'

'Oh Christ, what have I done?' Magda's voice was low and angry.

Suddenly, I felt afraid. The emotions dancing around us were too powerful, like live cables snaking across the floor, sparking and threatening. I took a step backwards. I did not want to walk that way again. I could see something opening before my feet and it looked more like a pit than a path. The last time, I'd sworn it would be the last time. 'Good luck, Maggot. It was good to see you,' I said, pulling down the shutters behind my eyes.

'Wait,' Magda cried. 'You can't just go. I've only just found you again.'

'It's your wedding day, Magda. There's a marquee full of people waiting for you.' *Don't make me feel this, Magda. Please,* was what I thought.

'Meet me later,' Magda said urgently, her hand reaching out and gripping my wrist. 'Meet me later, Jay. Please? Just so we can catch up? Swap addresses?'

'I'm not sure that's a good idea,' I said, dry-mouthed at the touch of her. I'd never felt the way I was feeling right then, never anything so instant, so terrifying.

Magda grinned, an open, unselfconscious beam of generous mirth. 'Of course it's not a good idea,' she said. 'But I'm the bride. You're supposed to humour me.'

I was hooked. 'Give me a time and a place.'

Magda frowned, as if calculating something. 'Nine o'clock? The far end of the meadow? You know the old boathouse? It's virtually fallen down now, but if you go round the blind side, no one can see you.'

So saying, she let me know that she understood that any meeting involving me was something no one should see. That was fine by me. The last thing I wanted was a confrontation with the mother of the bride. 'I'll be there,' I said, wondering even as I spoke whether I'd taken leave of my senses.

'Promise?'

'I promise.'

Magda's smile lit her up like a beacon. 'Till then,' she said, moving round me, still holding my wrist. Then her mouth was on mine.

It wasn't the sort of kiss a new bride should give anyone except her husband.

> And then Magda was gone, just as suddenly as I had
> been excised from her life all those years before.

Writing it brought it all back in its immediacy. Jay could feel the shivery suddenness of it all, the bewildering baffle of emotions she didn't expect to experience in a ladies' toilet in Schollie's, of all places. And Magda's reaction. Still it blew her away to remember the look on Magda's face as all the pieces of her personal jigsaw finally fell into place. It was the kind of moment that happens in movies and musicals, not in real life. Or so she'd thought.

Until it had happened to her.

It had been a beginning. Standing by the sink in the ladies' toilets, Jay felt like she'd been sandbagged. But that was just the start. There were still miles to go before she would sleep.

2

Driving to from Glasgow to Skye on a sunny day was one of the more visually spectacular experiences of Charlie's life. Mountains and water, conifers and bracken, tiny communities dotted randomly on the landscape and – the icing on the cake – driving over the bridge across the Atlantic to the island itself. It was all picture-book perfect. The sort of experience that made the most hardened urbanite long for the simple life. Charlie understood herself well enough to know that she'd go crazy in a week, but for the duration of the long glamorous drive it was possible to enjoy the fantasy. It didn't hurt that she had Maria there to share the driving. But enjoying her partner's company didn't stop the perpetual consciousness that there was another woman absorbing her attention. What was it Lisa had said in her last email? *Perhaps the clear island air will help you clear your heart. You can't move forward until you know what's past and what's coming with you on the journey. Sometimes things are only attractive* *because we know in our hearts we can't have them. I want you to be sure about all the possible consequences of your choices, Charlie. Some things there's no going back from.*

As usual, Lisa's words left Charlie with more questions than answers. Was it all a game, or was it a series of tests designed to help Charlie draw out the right answers from inside herself? Whatever was going on, she needed to stop dithering. It was beyond unfair to Maria, who didn't even know her future was in the balance. Charlie had no instinct for cruelty and she was uncomfortable with what Lisa called the possible consequences of her choices. But Lisa was like a fever in her blood. The trouble was, Charlie didn't know whether she wanted to resist or to succumb.

They stopped to eat in Fort William, Maria leaving Charlie to finish her meal alone so she could have a quick walk round the town. She came back as excited as a small child. 'It's so different,' she said. 'Why have we never come to the proper Highlands before?'

'We went skiing at Aviemore one year,' Charlie said.

'That's not proper, though. Skiing, you could be anywhere as long as the snow's half-decent. But this place is lovely. We need to do this sort of thing more often.'

'What? Spend two days driving on crappy roads to have one day on a Scottish island interrogating mountain men?' Charlie wasn't quite sure whether she was pretending to be curmudgeonly or if her grumpiness was genuine. Maria was right, though. There was something special about moving through this landscape, even if the reason for their trip was unusual.

'You're loving it,' Maria said. 'And it's your turn to drive. Once you're behind the wheel, you'll be too busy enjoying the challenge to complain about the crappy roads. Come on, let's go.'

Charlie thought it would be hard to beat the grandeur of the Great Glen, the hump-backed whale of Ben Nevis on their right as they drove up the lochside. But when she saw the Skye Bridge, she had to recalibrate her scale of breathtaking. Sleek, elegant and somehow organic, it had the wow factor. Beyond, the dark ridge of the Cuillins was outlined.

'How could you drive through all of this knowing you were going to kill someone?' Maria said. 'I mean, it's knockout, isn't it? It makes me feel insignificant. How can you experience all this and feel that your concerns are important enough to kill for?'

Charlie sighed. 'Not everybody has that reaction. Some people see the landscape almost as a challenge. "You might be big and you might be here long after I'm gone, but I'm going to make my mark too, just you watch".'

'Why couldn't she just kill her someplace ugly? Make it look like a mugging?'

'Because she's clever enough to know that the police are not stupid. Smart guys like Nick are trained to tell the difference between a real mugging and a fake one. If Jay had formed the intention of killing Kathy Lipson, it was a clever move to bring her to a place where there's so much lethal potential. People die on the Scottish mountains every year. Some of them from inexperience, arrogance and stupidity. But for some of them, it's just bad luck. Either way, you're dealing with a system that's predisposed to see accident rather than design.'

Maria nodded. 'So you're saying that Jay took advantage

of the psychological environment as well as the physical one?'

'It looks that way.'

'It's a bit chancy, isn't it? I mean, a lot of things had to come together for it to work. The weather conditions, Kathy agreeing to such a potentially dangerous climb, there not being anybody else around.'

Charlie slowed as they crossed the Atlantic. 'We're actually driving over a finger of an ocean now. How amazing is that?' They were both silent for as long as it took them to reach land again. 'It wasn't as chancy as you might think,' she said. 'I managed to track down the Fatal Accident Inquiry online. There was a list of witnesses, the mountain rescue guys, so I was able to track a couple of them down. The Scottish court records system is amazing. Open access to all sorts of stuff—'

'Never mind that,' Maria interrupted. 'What do you mean, it wasn't chancy?'

'Her father gave evidence at the inquiry, and he talked about how experienced she was. She'd climbed in the Alps, in the Rockies, in the Andes. She'd done ice climbing before, and she'd always talked about doing the winter traverse of the Cuillins. So if Jay wanted to set her up, it was handed to her on a plate. If anything, Jay was the less experienced climber in winter conditions. Where she nearly got seriously unlucky was in getting hurt herself.'

'If she really did get hurt,' Maria said. 'She didn't break anything, did she?'

'No, she tore the ligaments in her knee.'

Maria snorted. 'It's easy to make out that a soft tissue injury's a lot worse than it really is.'

Charlie grinned. 'You're starting to sound like Corinna.'

'Well, the more you tell me about these so-called accidental deaths, the more unlikely they sound.'

'But there's no proof. It's all very suggestive, but there's nothing I can take to the cops and say, "Look, here's incontrovertible evidence that somebody committed murder." And without that, it's just a slander action waiting to happen.' Her voice trailed off as she tried to make sense of the sat-nav. 'I think I have to go left here,' she said.

Maria took the printed instructions out of the glove box. 'Yes. Then after four miles you turn right and the hotel's on the left.' She looked across the empty landscape of machair and rock. 'I'm starting to understand why she could expect to be undisturbed up there. The only things with a pulse are the sheep.'

'Yeah. Apparently some of the routes up here get busy, but only in the summer months. In the winter it's not hard to be alone in the Cuillins.'

'See, that's why I like walking, not climbing,' Maria said. 'Less opportunity to get shoved off a precipice if you get bored with me.'

Charlie forced a laugh. 'As if.'

'As if you'd shove me, or as if you'd get bored?'

'Both,' Charlie said firmly. And it was true. That was the worst of it. She wasn't bored with Maria. Just then she saw a signboard for the hotel. 'There it is,' she said. 'Glenbrittle Lodge Hotel.'

They turned off the single-track road towards a low stone building that sprawled across the flat bottom of a glen flanked on both sides by slopes of grey scree. Its slate roof and broad gables gleamed in the late afternoon light.

'It's amazing how many shades of grey and green there are,' Charlie said as they approached.

'Almost as many as there are shades of teeth,' Maria said. 'You'd be amazed at the colour chart for crowns and veneers.'

By the time they made it to their room, they were both charmed by the hotel. As they'd drawn up alongside the half-dozen cars already there, a young man in work boots, a kilt and a ghillie shirt had emerged and insisted on carrying their bags into a wood-panelled reception area where a log fire crackled and hissed in a deep stone fireplace. A decanter and glasses sat on the check-in desk, and before they could protest, they each had a whisky in hand. 'This started life as a hunting lodge,' the young man said, his accent revealing that wherever he was a local, it wasn't here. 'We kept the traditional feel as much as possible. We're pretty quiet this weekend, so we've upgraded you to the Sligachan suite. It's got a view right up the glen towards the Cuillin. I think you'll like it.'

He was right. Maria surveyed the bedroom with its kingsize four-poster and subdued tartan fabrics while Charlie checked out the marble and painted porcelain of the bathroom. 'Wow,' Maria said, crossing to the window and checking out the view. 'This is lovely, Charlie.' She swung round as Charlie came back into the room. 'Come here.' She opened her arms and Charlie stepped into her embrace, losing herself momentarily in familiarity, wishing this oddly tender moment could expand to push out any other thoughts or feelings. Maria nuzzled her ear. 'When was the last time we did something this romantic?' she whispered.

Charlie chuckled. 'What? Tried to nail a serial killer? I can't think.'

Maria laughed, pushing her away. 'Kill the moment, why don't you? So, what's the plan for this evening?'

'It would be good to see if any of the staff were around ten years ago. I was hoping for an aged retainer. Maybe the barman will be more of a relic. But right now, I want a bath and a nap before dinner.' She twitched one corner of her mouth in a half-smile. 'You could join me if you wanted?'

Maria didn't need asking twice. And if Charlie's mind slipped sideways a couple of times in what followed, she didn't think Maria noticed. There were worse sins, and she hadn't committed them yet, after all.

It was almost eight before they made their way down to the restaurant, another panelled room with beautifully laid tables gleaming with silver and crystal. Only two tables were occupied and the waiter seated them on the other side of the room so they had a sense of privacy. The mood between them was relaxed and intimate. Charlie felt less tense than she had for weeks. She picked up the menu and made her choices quickly. Then she looked around properly for the first time, shifting slightly so she could check out the other tables while Maria was still frowning over the possibilities.

It was as well that Charlie didn't have a mouthful of food or drink or she would have choked. At first, she couldn't believe her eyes. But there was no mistake. Across the room, two women were leaning across their table towards each other, talking animatedly in low voices.

The younger woman, an unexcitingly pretty blonde in a multicoloured silky shirt, was a stranger. But sitting opposite her, apparently oblivious to anyone or anything else, was Lisa Kent.

If she'd just taken a punch to the head, Charlie couldn't have been more dazed. What the fuck was going on? Lisa knew her plans. But she'd said nothing to indicate that she would be here. Yet here she was, flirting with another woman in the very restaurant where she knew Charlie and Maria would be at dinner. It beggared belief. Suddenly realising that Maria was speaking, Charlie pulled attention back to her own table. 'Sorry?'

'I said, do you think they're batting for our team,' Maria said, inclining her head towards Lisa and her dinner date.

'If not, they should be,' Charlie said mechanically. 'What are you having? Have you decided?'

Afterwards, Charlie would remember nothing of what she'd eaten or drunk, except that quite a lot of red wine was part of the deal. Judging by Maria's rave reviews, the food had been exceptional, and she must have managed to keep up her end of the conversation. But all she could think about was Lisa on the other side of the room and what her presence might mean. Was Lisa crazy? Was she trying to create some monstrous confrontation? Or worse, some bizarre girlfriend-swapping encounter group? Or could it possibly be that she was as stricken with Charlie as Charlie was with her? She hadn't allowed herself to think that way before, but it was feasible. Wasn't it? But if Lisa was drawn so powerfully to Charlie, why had she brought someone else with her? Was she trying to make Charlie jealous? If so, she'd succeeded.

The other women left the restaurant before Charlie and Maria, nodding a polite greeting in passing as one does to fellow guests in a small hotel. 'They seem friendly,' Maria said. 'Maybe they'll be in the bar afterwards.'

'I'm not sure I want another drink,' Charlie said.

'I thought the point of us being here was for you to interrogate any passing islander?' Maria's voice was teasing. 'Or have you rediscovered a better reason for whisking your beloved off to romantic hotels?'

The idea of making love with Maria while Lisa was in the same building was impossible, Charlie realised. 'I think you've had the best of me,' she said. 'And you're right, of course. I shouldn't forget why we're here.' She drained her wine. 'Come on then, let's go and see if the bar staff were out of nappies when Jay and Kathy were here.'

The bar was a cosy room at the far end of the hall. Lisa and the other woman were sitting near the door, as far from the bar as possible. As they walked in, Lisa turned the full blaze of her eyes on Maria. 'Hi,' she said. 'Can I persuade you to join us for a drink? It seems silly to sit on opposite sides of the room.'

Before Charlie could refuse, Maria had already accepted the invitation. 'Thanks. I'm Maria, by the way, and this is Charlie.'

Lisa gave Charlie a welcoming smile, inclining her head. 'I'm Lisa. And this is Nadia.'

Nadia waggled her fingers at them. 'This is cool,' she said.

'Let me go and get some drinks,' Charlie muttered. 'What can I get you?'

'We're both drinking red wine.'

'I might as well get a bottle, then,' Charlie said, heading for the bar. There was nobody in sight, but a notice next to a bell push instructed her to press for service. She couldn't decide whether bewilderment or fear had the upper hand. Before anyone could respond to the bell, Lisa appeared at her side.

'I told Maria I'd help you choose,' she said.

'Are you fucking her?' It was out before Charlie could stop herself. Low and harsh, bitter and brutal.

'I could ask you the same question,' Lisa said. 'And it would be just as meaningless. We both know sex can mean everything or nothing. And we both know whatever is happening between us, it's about a lot more than sex. Smile, Charlie, Maria can probably read your body language at a hundred yards.'

Just then, the young man from reception arrived behind the bar. He grinned and said, 'Tonight I am the jack of all. What can I get you ladies?'

'We'd like a bottle of red. A Shiraz or something similar,' Charlie said.

'We like something fruity and chewy,' Lisa said with as much innuendo as a seventies comedian.

The barman blushed. 'I'll see what I can do,' he said, disappearing again.

'Why are you here?' Charlie said. 'And why are you pretending you've no idea who I am?'

Lisa smiled, her eyes sparkling with amusement. 'Relax, Charlie. You already played the incognito trick on me, remember? I thought it might be fun to turn the tables. And I wanted to see you. Is that so bad of me?'

Charlie felt herself softening. If Lisa's feelings were

anything like her own, it made perfect sense. She could imagine doing the same thing. 'No,' she said. 'I just wish you'd given me some warning.'

'That would have taken all the fun out of it.'

'It's not a game, Lisa. Maria's here. How do you think she's going to feel down the line if I leave her for you and she remembers this weekend? She's going to feel humiliated.'

Serious now, Lisa nodded. 'You're right. I'm sorry. But I couldn't help myself. I know this is going to sound a little strange. But you know what I really wanted?'

'No, I don't. Because what is happening to me now is so out of my experience.' Charlie forced a smile in Maria's direction.

'I wanted to see what you're like when you're not with me,' Lisa said. 'I wanted to see the sides of you that I would never see otherwise. If I'm going to be with someone I want to make an informed decision.'

Charlie's reply was sabotaged by the reappearance of the barman with a bottle of Wolf Blass Shiraz. 'That'll do fine,' Charlie said. 'Charge it to my room.'

He reached for a corkscrew and set about the bottle. 'So I wanted to see you with Maria and I wanted to see how you chased your crazy chimera,' Lisa said.

'By "crazy chimera", are you referring to yourself or to Jay?'

'Oh, Charlie,' Lisa said reproachfully. 'Jay, of course. I wanted to try to understand why it's got such a grip on you.'

'Because I think Corinna's right.' Charlie shook her head at the barman. 'Just pour, I'm sure it's fine.'

'You see, that's what I don't get,' Lisa said. 'Why are you investing so much of yourself in this? It's going nowhere, but it's obsessing you and it's not where you should be focusing your energy.'

'What should I be focusing on?' Charlie said, responding to the flirtatiousness in Lisa's voice.

'Something that has the potential to go somewhere, of course.' Lisa smiled. 'I could offer some suggestions?'

Charlie could feel a blush climbing her neck. 'How can you be so sure it's going nowhere?'

Lisa's smile grew mischievous. 'Because you'd have told me if you were getting somewhere. You couldn't help it. You want to impress me, so you'd have told me.' She picked up the first two glasses and started to turn away.

'Not necessarily,' Charlie said. 'I think you're forgetting how wedded I am to the notion of confidentiality. I'm a medical doctor, it's an article of faith for me. And I've worked with the police enough to understand the importance of holding information close.'

'I still think you'd tell me,' Lisa said as Charlie signed for the wine and picked up the other glasses.

'Maybe you don't know me quite as well as you think you do, then.' And with a smile, Charlie walked past Lisa and headed for Maria.

3

Plugging back into that shocking surge of emotion had unleashed a flood of words. Producing this memoir had hardly been a struggle for Jay, but now she was writing with the brakes off, she was unstoppable. Of course, most of it would end up on the cutting-room floor, but there was something liberating about letting it spill. Just so long as it never made it out into the wild. She'd have to be careful with this. She was saving it directly to a memory stick rather than the hard drive; the memory stick itself would have to go into the safe-deposit box that was so secret it didn't even feature in her will. When she died, the contents would stay in limbo for ever.

Jay stood up and put herself through the sequence of stretches her osteopath had devised for her. The legacy of that terrible day on Skye had to be combated both emotionally and physically. Hence the osteopathy and the hypnotherapy. Luckily she had enough on her hypnotherapist to protect anything unguarded that might come out of her mouth while she was in an altered state. There was nothing quite like Mutually Assured Destruction to keep the power in a relationship balanced, whether it was personal or professional.

She rubbed some almond oil into her hands, enjoying the aromas of the essential oils of rosemary and black pepper she'd infused it with. She thought back to that afternoon in Oxford and how the minutes had dragged. Recalled the irresistible urge to share this extraordinary experience in spite of herself. As if she'd had a premonition of what might happen. Of what had happened.

Ten minutes before nine, I slipped down the back stairs of the Sackville Building and into the night garden. There was no one in sight. The conference attendees were drinking in the Lady Hortensia Sinclair Room or sitting out on the front lawn. The looming bulk of Magnusson Hall cut the wedding off from view. I moved into the shadows and flitted down the narrow avenue of plane trees that led to the meadow. Just before I emerged, I stopped and checked it out. There were a few dozen cars parked on the far side of the grass but they all seemed to be empty.

I stepped clear of the shadows and walked down the river bank to the dilapidated remains of the boathouse where Jess Edwards had met her end. More memories from the distant past surfaced, every bit as complicated as my memories of the Newsam family. After Jess's death, the college decided to set up a fund for a new, larger boathouse. Now, the Edwards boathouse graces the main stretch of the Isis alongside the older, richer colleges. Left empty, the old boathouse has mouldered to the point where it's caving in on itself like a decayed tooth. That night, I could see that the roof beam sagged hopelessly, the windows were long broken and the side walls bowed like the hull of a galleon. The collapsing structure hunched behind a paling fence that would have taken a determined squatter all of five minutes to penetrate.

I skirted the boathouse and found a small clearing a few yards wide between the fence and the spiked berberis hedge that marked the end of St Scholastika's domain. I'd brought a light wrap with me in the forlorn hope that the night might turn chilly, and I spread it over the ground. Not because it was damp, but because a bride shouldn't have grass stains on her dress. I leaned against a tree and waited, wondering if she would have changed her mind. Somewhere down the river, ducks splashed and cackled. I heard the heavy beat of a heron's wings, then the last wittering cries of the birds.

I didn't hear Magda approach, but she was right on time. In the beginnings of twilight, everything about her was heightened, as if someone had adjusted the contrast control of a TV. She'd changed into her going-away outfit, a simple dress of midnight blue silk with a full skirt. She'd taken off her hat and unpinned her hair, and it cascaded over her shoulders in gleaming waves the colour of pound coins whose initial brassiness has been blunted in the hand. The fading of bright sunshine brightened the blue light of her eyes and deepened the matt gold of her skin. Magda took a couple of steps towards me and smiled. 'You came,' she said quietly.

I shrugged away from the tree. 'It would be hard to break a promise made to you.'

'I think I've made a seriously bad mistake,' Magda said, taking another couple of steps forward.

It wasn't what I wanted to hear. I swallowed the lump that had lodged in my throat. 'I'll go, then.'

Magda shook her head and put a hand on my arm. Where the flesh touched felt like the burn of ice. 'Not about meeting you. About marrying Philip.'

Our eyes stared hungrily at each other. At that moment, the words didn't matter. Magda could have recited 'Mary Had a Little Lamb' and it would have mattered as much or as little. All I was aware of was her touch, her face, her scent. Something was exploding inside my head and I couldn't make sense of anything except Magda's closeness. Knowing it was the most dangerous thing I'd ever done, I leaned into her and kissed her.

I thought we were never going to be able to stop. When we finally broke free, we were both trembling, our breathing ragged and noisy. 'Oh dear,' Magda gasped.

'I didn't mean . . .' I stuttered. 'I didn't mean that to happen.'

Magda touched my cheek with her fingertips, making my skin tingle. 'You'd have had to leave the country to prevent it.'

'Come and sit down,' I said, my voice thick and rough, like I'd never heard it before. 'We need to talk, Magda.'

We sat carefully on the wrap, side by side, my arm round her shoulders, hers round my waist. 'This didn't just come out of nowhere,' Magda said.

'It did for me.'

I could sense her smile. With her free hand, Magda fiddled in the evening bag slung across her body. She came up with a packet of Gitanes and a lighter then fumbled a cigarette out. She offered it to me but I shook my head. She gave a little shrug and lit it. The familiar aromatic smell hit me like a time machine. I hadn't smoked French cigarettes for ten years, but the taste was as familiar as my morning blend of coffee beans.

'Smoking's bad for you.' I was only half-teasing. Already I didn't want bad things to happen to Magda.

'I save them for special occasions. You remember these?' she asked. There was no need for a reply. 'You had no idea, did you? I worshipped the ground you walked on. When you and Mum went to the pub, I used to struggle to stay awake till you got home so I could sneak halfway down the stairs just to listen to your voice. I used to try and persuade Dad to take Mum out for the evening, so you would come and babysit. You were my first major crush.'

I took a deep breath, inhaling the second-hand tobacco taste. 'You're right. I had no idea. Eight years is a huge gulf at that age. I'm sorry, Maggot, I never noticed. I thought we just got on really well.'

'Which we did, of course. But I was crazy about you. If I was meeting Mum at Schollie's, I'd always try to get there early and hope that I'd see you. Then, suddenly, you were gone. One day you were part of the family, the next day you were anathema.'

'What did she tell you?' I really wanted to know.

'Patrick said you'd come to the door and Mum had told you a lie to make you go away.' Unconsciously,

Magda had slipped straight into the dialect of childhood. 'I asked Mum what was going on and she said that she didn't want you in her home. She said she'd found something out about you and it meant you couldn't come to the house any more. I asked what you'd done that was so terrible, and she got all bad-tempered and said I'd just have to take her word for it.'

'And you never found out what it was I was supposed to have done?'

Magda chuckled. 'Not in so many words. But I read an interview with you a few years ago in a magazine where you talked about being gay. And that answered the question for me, really. Knowing Mum's views on "homosexuality".' She dropped her voice and stretched the word out syllable by syllable.

'And that's why you've married? Because Corinna hates gays?'

Magda hung her head. 'Sort of. It's what I do, Jay. I keep everybody happy. After you, I had crushes on other women, but lots of my friends did too. It wasn't exactly totally weird. But I had all that oppressive Catholic conditioning dumped on me. And then there were the parents. I've always had a really good relationship with Mum, and Dad's OK if you catch him before the fourth gin. But they're really anti-gay. Dad especially. He genuinely believes it's a mortal sin. So I never had the nerve to do anything about all these crushes I had.' She sighed. 'I just couldn't imagine the conversation.'

I understood. Better than she knew. I could never have had that conversation with my stepfather. Unlike Henry Newsam, he would have had no hesitation in trying to beat it out of me. And my mother wouldn't have stood in his way. Not when it came to following the word of God. 'And so now you've got married.'

Magda nodded, leaning into me. 'Philip's been asking me for ever. His baby brother was in med school with me, and we've sort of been going out for the last three years. We've only just started living together, but we've been an item, kind of. He's a nice man, Jay. He's kind. And he's undemanding. He's also as crazy about his work as I am about mine.'

'Which is?'

Magda gave a quick, puzzled frown. My stomach cramped. 'This is all new to me,' I said gently. 'I know nothing about the last fifteen years of your life, Magda.'

'Of course. Why should you? Philip's a partner in a specialist printing business. They produce a lot of finan-cial instruments and confidential corporate stuff. And I'm a junior registrar in paediatric oncology. I work mostly with children who have been diagnosed with leukaemia.' She pulled a face. 'Another good reason for not experimenting with my sexuality. Hospitals run on rumour, and consultants don't like the combination of queers and kids.'

'Never been tempted?' I asked. I'll be honest, I was having trouble getting my head round the picture Magda was painting of an emotionally starved life.

Magda nuzzled my cheek. 'Of course I've been tempted,' she said. 'But I wimped out. You can sublimate a hell of a lot of sexual energy in the business of learning to become a doctor, you know. All that adrenalin, and the total exhaustion in between. It was just easier to go with the flow. Besides, it never seemed to be the right time and the right place with the right person. Until today.'

'It's your wedding day, Maggot,' I forced myself to remind her.

Magda sighed, a deep, empty sound that seemed to move her even closer to me. She flicked the end of her cigarette into the river. It was so still I could hear the hiss of the dying ember above the pounding of my blood. Then Magda looked up at me. There was still enough light to reveal her eyes glistening with tears. 'So why is it that I'd rather be here with you than over there with my husband?'

I closed my eyes. I didn't want to see Magda any longer. I couldn't handle the contradictory emotions tumbling inside me. 'Cold feet. That's all it is.'

'You know that's not true,' she protested. 'You feel it too. I know you do. You can't pretend you don't.'

'It's too late,' I said, my voice cracking under the strain. 'It's too late.'

Suddenly she was on her knees between my legs, hands gripping my shoulders. 'Don't say that,' she wailed, frustration mapped across her face. 'It can't be. I won't let it be. I've only just found you, Jay, I can't let you go.' She was almost sobbing, hair falling over us both like a curtain closing out the world.

I put my arms out to steady Magda. But she fell into me, pushing me back, body to body, the heat of our summer madness between us. 'Magda,' I protested. But it was a weak protest. My body was giving out a different message. We clung desperately to each other, like children before they discover inhibition.

'We've got to do something, Jay,' Magda moaned.

'You have to go back,' I said, gently rolling over and disengaging myself from Magda's grasp. It wasn't what I wanted. But what I wanted was probably not survivable. 'This is not the end, I promise you. But you have to go back now. You can't change the fact that you married Philip this afternoon. If he's the nice man you say he is, he doesn't deserve to be humiliated. Go back now, and call me when you can. Any time, day or night.' I groped in my pocket for the business card I'd put there earlier. The one with my private mobile number. I pressed it to my lips and handed it to Magda. 'Sealed with a kiss.'

Magda looked twelve again, about to burst into tears. But she took the card and tucked it into her bag. I checked my watch. It was just after twenty past nine. 'You've got to go, Magda. People'll be wondering where you are. Philip'll be wondering where you are.'

Magda nodded. 'You're right. Walk back with me?'

I smiled, but it was bittersweet. I thought I was done with hiding who I was and who I loved. But apparently not. 'Not all the way back. For your sake, not mine.'

'I know.'

We started back across the meadow, carefully not touching. There was no innocent contact possible between us. That much was clear. As we reached the shelter of the avenue, Magda gripped my wrist again, as she had earlier by the washbasins. 'This isn't a game, Jay. I mean this.'

'So do I. I never thought I'd fall in love like this again.'

Magda smiled. 'You said the L-word first.'

I truly hadn't meant to. And I'd regretted it the moment it passed my lips. Not because I didn't mean it but because I did. Still, love might well be a hostage to fortune, but I didn't think Magda was the person to use it against me. I returned her smile. 'One of us had to.'

'Right,' Magda said, suddenly sombre. 'One of us had to. Jay, this is scary. I feel out of control. Like we've started some chain reaction and I don't know where it'll end.'

'I know it's scary,' I said, stroking Magda's arm with my free hand. 'But I won't abandon you this time. I promise.'

Her breath exploded in relief. 'I've loved you for years, Jay.'

I moved closer, till my lips brushed her hair. 'I understand. I won't abandon you,' I sighed softly.

Magda released my wrist and without any further words, we walked up the twilight avenue to the gardens by the Sackville Building and into the shadows at the rear of Magnusson Hall. 'Chin up, Maggot,' I said, coming to a halt.

Magda looked over her shoulder as she rounded the corner of the building, her face ghostly in the cast of light from the porter's lodge, her smile a promise. Then she was gone, leaving me feeling dizzy and light-headed, wondering what I'd got myself into and how I was going to resolve it without Corinna assuming I was using her daughter to exact a long-delayed vengeance.

I turned away and walked into Magnusson Hall. This

time, instead of going down to the JCR, I walked up to the first floor and followed the corridor down to the Mary Cockcroft Room, named after the college's first principal back in the 1920s and used for meetings and seminars. The Cockcroft was directly above the JCR, but only about half the size. Although it was almost dark, there was still light enough coming from the wedding party on the lawn for me to see that the room was in total disarray. Some sort of major refurbishment was clearly under way, with builders' and painters' bits and pieces scattered throughout. A couple of the windows were even out of their frames, the gaps covered with tarpaulins. Luckily, work on the deep pentagonal bay was either completed or had not yet begun, so I picked my way through the obstacles and crossed to the window.

Though there must have been nearly a hundred people milling around between the lawn and the marquee, I spotted Magda instantly, a measure of how tight we'd been drawn together. She was mingling expertly, a few words here, a laugh there, then subtly moving on to the next knot of friends or swirl of dancers pausing in their swooping polka to talk to the bride. As I watched, I felt dazed by her beauty and the change in circumstance that had brought it under my hand. It was almost more than I could credit.

Before she could start the next paragraph, Jay heard the distant sound of the front door closing. 'I'm home,' Magda called up the stairs. Probably just as well, Jay thought, saving the file and retrieving the memory stick. She slid it into her pocket and stepped away from the desk.

'I'll be right there, hon,' she shouted back, switching off the light as she left the office. It was a good place to stop, while things were still scary in a good way. Before they became terrifying for real.

4

Saturday

When Charlie woke, the light was too bright. Her head felt thick and heavy, her stomach uneasy. 'We're going to miss breakfast if you don't get out of your pit,' Maria said cheerily, one hand still on the curtain as she stared out at the view. She was wrapped in a bath towel, her hair a damp unruly mop. 'It's a gorgeous day.'

'Unh,' Charlie grunted. If she didn't move, it might be all right.

'I did think you probably should have passed on that last round,' Maria said, absolutely no sympathy in her face or her voice. 'But you seemed determined to drink your own body weight in Shiraz. It's not like you, Charlie. You generally know when to stop.'

'Yeah, well. We were having such fun,' she said tonelessly.

'Yes. They're good company, Lisa and Nadia.'

'Oh yes. Good company.' If you enjoyed spending your evening on tenterhooks, wondering whether the sky was about to fall on your head. Wondering whether she was revealing her true feelings every time she looked at Lisa. Wondering if Lisa was going to reveal her true identity, instead of hiding behind 'I'm a trainer. I help people develop a variety of people skills.' That Maria had not skewered such vagueness with her usual practicality still had Charlie reeling. It was a powerful reminder of Lisa's charisma.

Maria plonked herself down next to Charlie. 'Come on, babe. Time to get up. Look at me, showered already. I can't wait for breakfast. After that wonderful meal last night, it should be something really special. According to the room service menu, they have award-winning sausages and black pudding from Lewis.'

Charlie's stomach lurched at the very thought of black pudding from anywhere. 'I'll get in the shower,' she mumbled. Anything to escape Maria's relentless good cheer. She rolled out of bed, knowing it was fifty/fifty whether she was going to hold on to the contents of her guts. She made it to the shower, where things improved dramatically. They usually did, in Charlie's experience of hangovers. By the time she'd finished, the prospect of breakfast had grown markedly less unsettling.

The prospect of seeing Lisa, however, was as disturbing as ever. Hiding her feelings while scrutinising Lisa's every glance or remark for significance was exhausting. 'We should have ordered room service breakfast,' she grumbled as she dressed.

'That's what you said last night. God knows why,

because you never want room service in a hotel. You always complain that it's never hot enough and they never get the order right.'

Seven years of negotiating Charlie's prejudices and preferences meant Maria was right, of course. 'I was a bit pissed. I suppose I fancied a lie-in,' Charlie said.

'Not much point when you have the mountain rescue guys coming at ten. While you're with them, I thought I might take a drive, see a bit of the island. Is that OK with you?'

Anything that took Maria out of the ambit of Lisa and Nadia was a major plus in Charlie's book. 'Fine.' She turned on the hairdrier, effectively ending the conversation.

To her relief, the dining room was empty when they walked in. Their table from the night before was the only one still set for breakfast. 'Looks like Lisa and Nadia had an early start,' Maria said. 'That's a pity. I was thinking about asking them if they fancied linking up this morning.'

Charlie hid her relief behind the breakfast menu, deciding to try her luck with the award-winning sausages and some scrambled eggs washed down with enough coffee to jump start her synapses. She tried not to think about the acid in Maria's freshly squeezed orange juice or the noise generated by her muesli crunch. Their meal was drawing to a close when Charlie's reprieve ended.

Lisa and Nadia drifted into the dining room. 'Morning,' Lisa said. 'You're very dutiful, getting up for breakfast. We were lazy and had it in bed.' She looked remarkably pleased with herself. Charlie was gratified to see Nadia was looking less thrilled with life. She had the faint pout of a woman who thinks she's not getting enough attention.

'I like my breakfast piping hot,' Charlie said. 'Always worth getting out of bed for.'

'What are your plans for today?' Lisa asked.

'Charlie's got some people to see this morning, so I'm going to go for a drive. What about you? You're welcome to join me, if you want.'

'That's very tempting,' Lisa said. 'Is this work then, Charlie?'

'I'm interviewing a couple of the mountain rescue team.' She'd managed to keep that out of the conversation the night before, she was pretty sure. Nadia looked as if she was about to pass out with boredom.

'Really? They have some sort of unique insight into abnormal psychology?'

'You'd be amazed,' Charlie said. 'They do have to deal with people in extreme situations. It can be very revelatory.'

'I suppose you have to manufacture things to keep yourself interested while you're waiting to find out your fate,' Lisa said with a sad smile. 'I know we didn't mention it last night, Charlie, but I am familiar with your situation.'

Nadia perked up. 'What are you on about? What's Charlie's situation?'

'I'm temporarily suspended from practising. I have a disciplinary hearing coming up,' Charlie said, wondering momentarily if this was Lisa's way of showing support. If it was, it backfired immediately.

Nadia's mouth opened and she covered it with her

hand. 'Oh my God,' she said. 'I recognise you now. I thought you looked familiar. You're the one who got that bloke off who went on to murder all those other women. God. How do you live with something like that?'

'Charlie has nothing to reproach herself with,' Maria said, abruptly standing up. 'There's nothing clever or good about helping the prosecution convict an innocent man.'

'He wasn't very innocent, though, was he? He killed four women. And that's just what we know about,' Nadia said.

'He did not commit the first murder he was charged with,' Maria said. 'That's what everybody seems to forget.'

Nadia shrugged. 'But nobody else has been arrested, have they?'

'For heaven's sake, Nadia. We should stop talking about this,' Lisa said, visibly dismayed at the turn of the conversation. 'Thanks for your kind offer, Maria, but we're planning on making a full day of it. We're going up to Dunvegan Castle.'

'I'm sure you'll have a lovely time,' Maria said, her voice cool now. 'Charlie, you need to keep an eye on the time, your guys will be here soon.'

Charlie seized the chance to escape the room. 'I need to get my stuff. Thanks for reminding me. See you girls later.' And she was off, walking briskly out the door and trotting upstairs. She closed the bedroom door behind her with a sense of relief, squeezing her eyelids tight together to keep tears at bay. She felt like her emotions had been hurled into a washing machine on the spin cycle. It had been hard enough when she'd thought her feelings for Lisa were not reciprocated. But now that it seemed something significant was coming back at her, it was harder and harder to deal with the situation. The point where she was going to have to make a decision was growing closer. And whichever way she jumped, Charlie knew her present sense of being in hell would be a day at the seaside by comparison.

The two men sitting in the bar could hardly have looked less alike. One was short and wiry, folded into the chair like a jack-in-the-box waiting for the lid to lift. His wavy hair was black, his beard slightly ginger in the sunlight flooding into the bar. He had the raw-boned look of the Gaelic Celt, blue eyes dark and darting under a ridge of black brows. The other was much bigger, a Viking of a man with broad shoulders and chest. His red-blond hair was tied back in a ponytail, his thick beard a shade darker. His long legs sprawled carelessly at angles to each other. With their weathered skin and hundred-yard stares, they could have been any age from thirty to fifty. Charlie had no doubt that these were the men she was due to meet.

The small dark one jumped to his feet as she approached. The other, more languid, just leaned forward. 'Dr Flint?' the small one said, sticking his hand out to shake.

Charlie took it. 'That's right. You're Calum Macleod?'

He shook his head. 'No, I'm Eric Peterson. Everybody thinks I'm the local, but he is.' Now he'd spoken more than two words, it was evident that he came from much further south. Cumbria, at a guess. He jerked his head towards the other man. 'He's Calum.'

Calum nodded. 'Pleased to meet you,' he said, the soft sibilance of the islands evident.

Charlie ordered the Cokes they wanted and more coffee for herself then sat down. They went through the usual ritual of small talk, then after the drinks arrived with a plate of home-made shortbread, she took out her recorder. 'I hope you don't mind,' she said as they attacked the sugar-dusted biscuits. 'My memory isn't what it used to be.'

'You and me both,' Eric said. 'My wife says it's the drink, but I say it's because I've hit my head too often climbing. She says I've always been soft in the head. No respect, these local girls. You don't bring them up obedient enough, Calum.' He grinned, clearly used to being the cheerful life and soul of the party. Calum said nothing, settling for a delicate sip of his Coke to wash down the biscuit.

'So, I want to talk to you about what happened on Friday, 18 February 2000. Am I right in thinking you both remember that day?'

'I remember every rescue,' Eric said eagerly. 'I love to climb, but there's an extra rush that you get from going out there in extreme conditions, knowing somebody's life could depend on how well you do your job. I don't want to sound big-headed about it, but we do save lives out there, and that's a buzz like nothing else.'

Calum cleared his throat. 'You always remember when the mountain takes a life,' he said, his voice a soft, deep rumble.

'Well, yeah. Of course. It doesn't always have a happy ending. But we still got somebody off that day. And the lass that died' – the shrug of one shoulder – 'well, she was dead before we were called out. Nothing we could have done about that. These mountains, they're not to be taken lightly, you know.'

'When did you get the call-out? Do you remember?'

Eric looked at Calum, who nodded. 'I'm a teacher,' he said. Charlie struggled to get her head round that one. 'It was after the bell went. So, four o'clock. It's never good that late in the winter. You know it's going to be dark before you get on the hill.'

'Do you remember where the call came from? Was it the hotel here? Or the emergency services?'

'I never took the call. I just got a page.'

Eric bounced in his seat. 'I never took the call either. That was Gordon Macdonald. He was the on-call person for the team back then.'

'Is he still around? Could I talk to him, maybe?'

'He's dead,' Calum said. 'Car accident on the A82. Head on into a supermarket delivery lorry. Hellish.'

'Oh. I'm sorry to hear that,' Charlie said.

'But I remember Gordon talking about the call-out, later that night when we were all in the bar. He said it was peculiar. When we get a call, it's nearly always one of three sources.' Eric counted them out on his fingers. 'One: the emergency services get a call from the climber's mobile. Two: one of the other people in their party worries when they don't make a rendezvous. Three: the hotel or guest house or pub where they've left a climb plan and an ETA. But he said the call-out was wrong. It was a woman. She said she was calling from the hotel, here.' He waved his arm to encompass the bar. 'But we know all the staff here, and it wasn't anybody Gordon knew. She said she'd had a call that two of their guests were in difficulty on the In Pinn – that's the Inaccessible Pinnacle on the summit of Sgurr Dearg,' he added helpfully.

'She knows that,' Calum said. 'Gordon was uneasy about the call. So he phoned back. Only nobody put their hand up to phoning us. But right enough, they had a couple of guests who'd set off for the In Pinn that morning. So Gordon thought we should take a look.'

Eric picked up the story. 'It was a shit night. Really cold, snowing on and off. There was a wind coming off the north east like a knife. Not a night when we could call out the chopper. But we know the ground, so we made good time. It's not easy, looking for a couple of climbers on a mountainside in the dark and the snow. But the route up the mountain's reasonably obvious so we reckoned we were in with a shout if they were still on the hill. You'd be amazed how often we get called out for people that are sitting in some pub somewhere nursing a malt because they couldn't be bothered to get back to where they said they'd be.'

'We came up on the lassie a couple of hundred feet down from the main summit of Sgurr Dearg. She was in a bad way.'

'That's right. Shock, hypothermia setting in, and dragging one leg behind her like a useless lump of meat,' Eric said. 'We got the thermal wrap round her smartish, because obviously we needed to find out where her climbing partner was. We'd gone out for two women, but we'd only found the one. She was in a helluva state, but she told us right off. She'd had to cut the rope.' Even Eric shut up as he contemplated that.

'We all understood,' Calum said. 'It's something you think about. If you don't climb, you can't understand.'

'The way she explained it, it made sense,' Eric added. 'She didn't have any choice. Cut the rope or you both die.

Cut the rope and one of you has a chance. To tell you the truth, we all felt for her. We knew she'd get stick, but there was nothing else she could have done. Not and lived.'

'Were you surprised that they were up there in those weather conditions?' Charlie asked.

Eric's face twisted into an expression of concentration. 'Not really. The forecast hadn't been that bad. The weather definitely closed in much worse than we expected that afternoon. And what you have to remember is that if you love to climb in snow and ice, there is nothing in the UK to match the Cuillin ridge in winter. Nothing. It's the biggest challenge in British winter climbing. The nearest you can get to the Alps.'

'So you didn't think it was selfish? Out of order, going up in weather like that, knowing that if anything went wrong it was putting you guys at risk?' she persisted.

'If you think like that, all climbing's selfish,' Calum said. 'I wouldn't quarrel with their choice that day.'

'They got unlucky,' Eric said. Out came the fingers again. 'One, the weather turned against them. Two, the lass Kathy, she slipped on the narrowest bit of a narrow ridge. Three, she hit her head so she couldn't help herself. Four, the other lass couldn't find an anchor for the rope. And five, the other lass dropped her backpack with all her gear on board so she had no equipment to get them out of the mess they'd gotten into. They were – forgive my French – fucked every which way. I tell you, we all pray we never have a day like that on the hill.'

'So you knew even then there was no point in looking for Kathy Lipson that night?'

Calum gave her an incredulous look. 'We knew she'd

gone the best part of three thousand feet down a mountain. What do you think?'

'Our priority was getting the other lass off the hill and to hospital. You look to the living before you think about the dead,' Eric said. 'But we knew we'd be out there at first light. You don't want civilians stumbling across a body. Believe me, you don't want to think about what somebody looks like after a fall like that.'

He was right. Charlie absolutely didn't want to think about it. 'You said that Jay Stewart had dropped her backpack. Do you know how that happened?'

'She was spread-eagled across a ridge in the middle of a blizzard supporting another woman's entire body weight. The pack slipped through her fingers as she was trying to get access to her gear. Like Eric said, bad luck. Sometimes when one thing goes wrong, everything goes wrong.' Calum stared gloomily into his Coke, then knocked it back. 'Like dominoes.'

They all sat locked in glum silence for a long moment, then Eric looked around expectantly. 'You think they'd bring us some more biscuits if we asked?'

Charlie went off in search of more biscuits. She wasn't finished yet and if shortbread was what it took, she'd make sure they got it. When she returned, Calum was on his feet, examining an old map of the island that was framed on the wall. 'They're bringing some more,' she said. 'Did you ever find Jay's pack?'

'We found it before we found the body,' Eric said. 'It burst when it hit the ground. There were cams and hexes and nuts scattered all round, a split water canteen, all the usual stuff.'

'What about her phone?'

Calum turned back. 'It was near the backpack. Busted to smithereens. It looked like it had come flying out on the way down.'

'That's right,' Eric said, excited at having his memory jogged. 'She said it had been in a side pocket on its own.' He caught Charlie's look. 'What? You thought we wouldn't ask about a phone? We're not new to this, you know. Out here, it's a bit like the Wild West. The cops can't be everywhere so we've got to weigh in and do what we can to help. So we ask questions if there's anything needs explaining. And Gordon was still trying to make sense of the funny phone call. He wondered if she'd maybe called a pal or something. But she said no, she'd lost the phone before she could use it. So we were none the wiser.'

She could have been lying, Charlie thought. Maybe she did make a phone call. But if you're hanging off a mountain with your business partner on the end of a rope, who are you going to call? 999 was the obvious answer. Charlie couldn't imagine calling anyone else. Even if you couldn't do that with a sat-phone, which she didn't know anything about, surely there was an operator you could contact? And a sat-phone operator wouldn't need to pretend to be calling from a hotel on Skye. Nothing made sense, and all Charlie's instincts told her that when nothing made sense, something was going on that shouldn't be.

'I know this is maybe going to sound like a strange question. But apart from the phone call, was there anything about what happened that day that seemed unusual to you?'

Eric frowned and munched another biscuit while he

thought about it. Calum chewed on a fingernail. 'No,' Eric said at last. 'They were just really, really unlucky.'

'Except one thing was lucky,' Calum said.

'What do you mean?' Eric said. 'It was a perfect storm. All the crap came at them together. I don't see how you can say they got lucky.'

'I didn't say that. I said one thing was lucky.'

Charlie decided it was time to step in. 'What was that, Calum?'

'It was lucky the knife wasn't in the backpack, wasn't it?'

5

Sunday

Sunday morning was infinitely better than the one before. Thanks to some deft footwork, Charlie had avoided Lisa until last thing in the evening. Maria had returned to the hotel at lunchtime, bubbling with delight at the beauty of the landscape. Meanwhile, Charlie had managed to book a table for dinner at another hotel whose restaurant was said to be in the top twenty in Scotland. After lunch, they went for a walk up Glen Brittle, following in the footsteps of Jay and Kathy ten years before. Even though they barely climbed a few hundred feet, they had a sense of the challenge and the grandeur of the Cuillin ridge. 'I can see how people want to come back again and again,' Maria said. 'Places like this, they get under your skin.'

'We'll come back another time,' Charlie promised. 'When all this is behind us and I'm practising again. We'll rent a cottage and walk in the mountains and eat fabulous meals and sleep like babies.'

Maria laughed. 'And they say romance is dead. I was thinking we could make mad passionate love in front of a roaring fire.'

Charlie put an arm round her and hugged her. 'That too.' She wished she could have spoken without ambivalence, but until she could resolve her feelings for the two women in her life, Charlie would have to resign herself to that.

When they got back to their hotel room, Charlie sprawled on the chaise longue and revealed her plans for the evening. 'It's quite near so we don't have to set off for an hour or so.'

'We could go down to the bar for a drink.'

Again, that ambivalence. Charlie longed to see Lisa, but the stress of being in the same room with her and Maria was impossible to negotiate with equanimity. The bar for a drink was the last thing she wanted, with the prospect of Lisa and Nadia returning at any minute. 'No, I'll be driving and I want to save myself for some really good wine with the meal. Besides . . .' Charlie stretched to reach her backpack. 'For some reason, I've been avoiding this. But I think I've got to the point where I have to deal with it.' She pulled a book from her bag and waggled it at Maria. '*Unrepentant*, by Jay Macallan Stewart.'

Maria pulled off her sweater and began to undo her trousers. 'I know why you've been avoiding it,' she said.

'Why? And by the way, I meant it. I need to read, Maria. And you're distracting me.'

Maria poked her tongue out at Charlie. 'This is not for

your benefit. If you're going to read, I'm going to soak my weary muscles in the bath. The reason you've not buckled down to Jay's book is very simple.'

'I thought I was the psychiatrist round here? What's the reason?'

Maria slipped out of her trousers. 'You're scared you'll like her.'

'You think?'

'I do. Because if she charms you with her misery memoir, you're going to struggle to carry out Corinna's mission to split up her and Magda. You know it's true.'

Charlie, who hadn't really considered why she was finding lots of excuses not to read Jay's book, couldn't fault Maria's reasoning. It was reassuring to be known so well. 'You could be right,' she said.

By the time Maria emerged from the bathroom, Charlie was midway through Jay's early years, notable for the quantity of drugs that seemed to have flowed through the bodies of her mother and a succession of hopeless boyfriends. It was a disturbing narrative of a downward spiral seen through the uncomprehending eyes of a child. Jay's mother Jenna had started off as a nice middle-class girl who had been carried away by the spirit of the sixties. The Isle of Wight festival in 1968 had changed the path of her life, swinging her out of the gravitational field of Home Counties suburbia into the orbit of musicians, artists and writers.

It had probably been quite cool to begin with, Charlie thought. But the drugs became more important to Jenna than anything else, and gradually, the quality of her company diminished. The rock stars and published poets and exhibited artists had moved onwards and upwards and she'd fluttered downwards. By the time Jay had been born in 1974, Jenna had been living in a squat and working on a stall in the fledgling Camden Market.

They'd moved from place to place, from city to country and back again. From the few photos, it was clear that Jenna had been a beauty, even ravaged by the drugs. Jay's childhood milestones had been the succession of different men and different places to live. She'd never been enrolled in school but nobody ever came looking for her because Jenna had never registered her birth. Jay recounted one conversation she'd overheard in which the latest boyfriend had been berating Jenna because she didn't get child benefit like the other mothers in the caravan of travellers they were with at that point. 'That's a small price to pay for freedom,' Jenna had said. 'My child can float free in the world. She has no shackles to the state.'

Because nothing was ever constant, because drugs are unpredictable, because Jenna would do almost anything for the next fix, Jay saw more than any child should. She knew about going to bed hungry. She knew about watching her mother being beaten by men. She knew about women being forced into sexual activity they had not consented to. And somehow, in the middle of all that, she taught herself to read. She learned not just how to survive but also how to protect herself. She knew kids who were sexually abused. She watched the predators single them out. And somehow, Jay learned how not to be the one who was chosen.

Charlie found it all too credible. There were moments

where her professional experience kicked in and she understood that Jay was ascribing to herself judgements that could only have been made in hindsight. Like claiming to have recognised at the age of only seven that what she had was not freedom but a prison of ignorance.

I spied on other children. Sometimes it was easier than others. We lived for a while in a caravan on the edge of a wood somewhere in Somerset. Jenna's boyfriend was called Barry and he worked sometimes in the pub in a village nearby. I followed him one evening when he was walking through the wood to work so I learned the way to the village. Because the wood came right up to the edge of the houses, spying was easy.

Their lives were obviously very different from mine. They wore the same clothes every day to go to school. I couldn't understand that. Sometimes I wore the same clothes for a few days at a time, but not every single day. And other kids called me names for it.

Whenever these children came home, someone gave them a drink and something nice to eat. They didn't have to scavenge or settle for whatever they could find. And they looked like they just took it for granted, as if there was no question about that being how it should be.

They got to sit and watch TV by themselves, which meant they got to choose what they wanted to see. Sometimes there were two or more rooms with TVs in. I was used to having to put up with whatever Jenna and the boyfriend wanted to watch. And sometimes their choices were incomprehensible to me. Especially the porn, which none of the kids I spied on ever watched.

I should remind readers that, back in the seventies, porn was a very different experience. For a start, adults had pubic hair. You never really saw an erect penis either. There was a lot of soft focus, terrible muzak and acting that even I recognised was desperately bad. Compared to what you can see on terrestrial TV now, never mind the internet, it was pretty innocuous. Still, I probably shouldn't have been watching it.

It was fascinating stuff, Charlie thought. Literally fascinating. You couldn't stop reading because you wanted to know where Jay was going to take you. She had the knack of pinning her extraordinary experiences to the stuff of ordinary life. There were enough of these tangents to make the reader feel that this peculiar life could almost have happened to them. The counterpoint to that was the way she constantly contrasted her life with mainstream middle-class experience. It had the flavour of Craig Raine's famous poem about the Martian writing a letter home. The reader clearly understood that Jay had spent a lot of her early life trying to make sense of things that had no correspondence in her own world.

'How is it?' Maria had asked.

'I'm not sure whether I like her, but it's impossible not to admire her. The squalor and chaos of her early years make you want to weep for her. She didn't just survive, she's built a life that would have been unimaginable to her as a child. I can't wait to get on to the transformation.'

'You mean when she went to Oxford?' Maria said, throwing her towel over a chair and strutting naked across the room to put on fresh clothes.

'No. That's where it ends. I'm talking about before that. Her mother went from hapless junkie hippie to born-again Christian. And not just any old Christian. She plunged head first into one of the more repressive sects of evangelicals. Clearly someone who was hopelessly addicted to addiction. Heroin or Jesus, didn't seem to matter much.'

'Woo-hoo. That must have been some transition. If you want, I'll do the lion's share of the drive tomorrow, then you can carry on reading.'

'I could read it aloud if you like,' Charlie offered, marking her place with a hotel postcard and putting the book away. Maria did an impression of Munch's *The Scream*. 'OK, I was only joking. You can have Joan Osborne and Patty Griffin all the way to Fort William.'

The restaurant had lived up to its online reviews. They both chose a stew of local seafood to start with and exclaimed over its richness and the depth of its flavours. Venison followed with spiced beetroot and lemon thyme mash. When she tasted the meat, Charlie actually groaned aloud. They finished with cheese and Maria kept making small moaning noises as she savoured each morsel. 'I wish I was still hungry so I could eat it all over again,' Charlie said.

They'd planned to go straight to their room when they returned to the hotel but that was when Charlie's luck ran out again. As they walked in the door, Lisa emerged from the ladies' toilets. A radiant smile lit up her face. 'How lovely to see you both. We thought we'd missed you. We're in the bar. Come and have a drink?'

Charlie said, 'No, thanks,' as Maria said, 'That sounds nice.' They looked at each other and laughed.

'Seven years and we're still two minds with but a single thought,' Maria joked.

'I'm really tired,' Charlie said. 'I just want to go horizontal. Sorry.'

'That's OK,' Maria said. 'I want a brandy, though. Why don't you go on up and I'll get myself a drink and join you?'

Charlie, with visions of Lisa snagging Maria and drawing her into late-night conversation, said, 'It's OK, I'll wait for you, we can go up together.'

'I'll keep you company while Maria's getting served,' Lisa said quickly.

'What about Nadia? Won't she be wondering where you are?'

'I'll tell her,' Maria said over her shoulder as she headed for the bar.

'You look delicious this evening,' Lisa said. 'Good enough to eat.'

'Don't,' Charlie sighed. 'I feel like I'm on a rollercoaster. I can't cope with having both of you under one roof.'

'I'm sorry. I thought you might enjoy the frisson of knowing I was near.' Lisa looked contrite. 'I see now I misjudged things. But I'm not sorry that I've had the chance to see you.'

Charlie gave her a beseeching look. 'Please. I can't do this now.'

Lisa gave Charlie a sad-eyed look, the kind of up-and-under that Princess Diana always used to such effect. 'I understand. Believe me, I know how hard it is to resist.' She flashed a smile. 'So how did your pursuit of the mountain rescue team go? Did you manage to uncover new evidence that eluded the police and the coroner all those years ago?'

Charlie made a wry face. 'Much safer ground. Actually, they don't have coroners in Scotland. And as it happens, I did find out one or two things that seem suggestive.'

'Really?' Lisa said, with the appearance of genuine interest. 'You found the smoking gun?'

'If I was Sherlock Holmes and you were Watson, I would say something like, "There was the curious incident of the phone call to the rescue services from the hotel." And you would say, "What about the phone call to the rescue services from the hotel?" and I would say, "There was no phone call to the rescue services from the hotel."'

Now Lisa looked bemused. 'I'm sorry, you've lost me.'

'There was something odd about the phone call that set off the rescue alert for Jay and Kathy. The source wasn't what it purported to be.'

Lisa's mouth quirked in dismissal. 'What's that supposed to mean?'

'I don't know. Then there's the convenient matter of the knife.'

'Do you have to be so cryptic?'

Charlie laughed. 'Yes, I do have to be so cryptic because it's fun. But then, you know that. You are the queen of cryptic. The knife is significant because when Jay dropped her backpack, she lost every single piece of equipment that might be useful, including her sat-phone. All except her knife, which luckily was in her jacket pocket.'

Lisa laughed and wagged a finger at Charlie. 'Talk about grasping at straws. All sorts of people carry a Swiss Army knife or something similar in their pocket when they go out walking. It's hardly suspicious.'

'I never said it was suspicious. I said it was suggestive. It's what you would do if you were planning to stage an accident.'

Lisa shook her head indulgently. 'I'm beginning to wonder if playing detective has loosened you from your moorings.'

Charlie gave a sad little smile. 'You were the one who did that, Lisa.'

Lisa put a hand on her arm. 'And you know that's not a one-way street, Charlie. You know that.' Her voice was soft and seductive and in spite of her determination to stay cool, Charlie's flesh tingled. What saved her was the sight of Maria emerging from the bar with a crystal brandy bowl in her hand. Lisa let her hand fall away without any fuss and stepped back.

'I told Nadia you were just coming,' Maria said, slipping her free arm through Charlie's and steering her towards the lift. 'Good night, Lisa.'

As the lift doors closed, Maria giggled. 'Nadia's got a face like thunder. She's not keen on being left sitting alone in a busy bar, not when she thinks she's the trophy girl-friend.'

'She really thinks that?' Charlie couldn't stifle a laugh.

'I reckon so. Oh, what it is to be young and full of illusions. She'd better watch her step, that one.'

'Nadia? Why?'

'That Lisa. She's not somebody you'd want to mess with.'

Clever Maria, Charlie thought. Maybe we should do a

job swap. 'Well, chances are we'll never have to see them again.'

And so the evening had ended. They'd fallen into bed, still too full for anything but sleep. Waking with a clear head, the prospect of finishing Jay's book ahead of her, Charlie finally began to see how things might be made to come together.

6

They were on the road by ten. As if to make the leaving easier, the weather had changed. Mist and rain covered the landscape in a grey veil, turning the Cuillins into a vague looming presence in the distance. 'Nick's in court tomorrow. I think I should go down to London and talk to him,' Charlie said gloomily as they crossed the ocean back to the mainland. 'We need to make a decision about how much further we can pursue this. And what we do with our pitiful findings. Not a lot, I suspect.'

'It's not all been wasted,' Maria said. 'You've re-established contact with Corinna and Magda. And we've had a glorious weekend in Skye.' She took a hand off the wheel to pat Charlie's thigh. 'And it's taken your mind off the other shit. This has been the first time in a while when you seem to have let go of what's hanging over you.'

'Maybe I should start offering it as an alternative therapy,' Charlie said drily. 'Immerse yourself in a wild-goose chase. Perfect for taking your mind off what's oppressing you. Now, put your foot down and drive. I'm going to immerse myself even deeper.' She pulled *Unrepentant* from her jacket pocket and found her place.

Afterwards, when I asked my mother why we'd gone to see Blair Andreson in the big tent at Sunderland, the only possible answer was the one she always gave: because God called us. That's probably as far from the truth as it's possible to get.

By the time the American evangelist Blair Andreson launched his 1984 crusade to the UK, our lives had dipped to an all-time low. We were living in a squalid caravan encampment on the outskirts of one of the big towns in Teesside. I'm not even sure which one. The police and the local residents waged a constant war of attrition against us. I can't say I blame them. I'd probably do the same myself. We were not a romantic New Age camp of people who believed in beautiful things. We were scum. My mother was selling sex to keep herself in drugs. I was running wild with a bunch of other kids, stealing food and money whenever I got the chance.

We went to the conversion service at Andreson's big top with a couple of other women from the site. I suspect our intentions were criminal. They must have seen a way to make money out of the service, picking pockets or stealing collection plates. I don't know for sure because nobody confided in me. It was a cool afternoon in July but the tent was packed, the air heavy with the smell of too many bodies crammed together. My mother and I were sitting towards the back of the steeply banked seats, letting Andreson's hysterical rhetoric wash over us. At least, I thought that was what was going on. I was completely unmoved by the oratory. I'd far rather have had a lamb kebab than be washed in the blood of the lamb.

But something happened to my mother that afternoon. All she would ever say was that she was touched by the hand of God. I wanted to know what it had felt like. Whether it was a sudden, blinding revelation or a gradual, creeping realisation that there was a very different path open to her. But she would never go into detail. 'Filled with the spirit' was another of her meaningless phrases that was meant to make clear to me what had happened to her.

From where I was sitting it was more like demonic possession. When Andreson called upon people to come forward to be received by God, my mother stood up like an automaton and walked to the stage like she was sleepwalking. I assumed it was part of a scam, so I just sat there. Waiting for it to be over.

She looked very frail up there beside Andreson, who had the bristly pink sheen of a prize pig. She knelt before him and he placed his hands on her head, giving her a full measure of the mumbo jumbo. Then she was led away by two of his acolytes, taken off through the curtains at the back of the stage. At that point, I was just bored. I was barely ten years old and watching a bunch of weirdos being born again was not my idea of a good time.

After what felt like half a lifetime, we all had to pray together, then we got to sing a rousing hymn, something about God walking beside us on the hard road of life.

And then it was time to leave. An army of clean-cut young men in suits lined the exits with buckets for our donations. I was impressed with the amount of money they were scamming. Whatever Jenna and her pals had in mind, they'd picked a target that had plenty to go round. And weren't they supposed to be all about sharing in Christ's bounty, after all?

I hung around outside the tent but after the audience had emptied out, I didn't know where to go. In the end, I went up to one of the lads with the collecting buckets. 'My mum went up to the stage,' I said. 'And she hasn't come out.'

He nodded, as if this wasn't an unusual occurrence. 'Coming to the Lord can be an overwhelming experience,' he said, trying to sound important and portentous. 'If you think about it, being born the first time is a pretty traumatic happening. The second time isn't any less momentous.'

Even at ten, I wanted to slap him. 'But where's my mum?' I said instead.

'Come with me,' he said, leading me round the back of the main tent to a smaller enclosure. Inside, small knots of people were kneeling together. Blair Andreson was moving from group to group, laying his hands on whoever was at the heart of the group. After the bright lights and noise of the circus tent, this place felt very peaceful and cocooned. It took me a few moments to spot my mother, but at last I saw her in the far corner, being tended to by three other women. I had no idea what she was up to. Most of our scams were simple and quick. I didn't know what was going on here or why it was taking so long.

I started weaving my way towards Jenna, but I'd hardly taken a step when Blair Andreson himself blocked my path. 'Now, who do we have here?' he said in the deep rich voice that seemed to fill whatever space he occupied.

'You've got my mum over there,' I said. 'I want to go to her.'

'Your mom's having a pretty intense encounter with her Heavenly Father right now,' he said, taking a firm grip of my shoulder and steering me towards the entrance. 'Howsabout I get somebody to get you something to eat, then when your mom's done here, we'll come get you?'

It wasn't a suggestion. I thought about running for it but there was nowhere to run to. I didn't know where the other women from the camp had got to and I had no idea how to find my way back. So I pretended to be meek and mild and let one of the young men take me to another tent that was set up like a buffet. There were long tables of sandwiches and salads. And piles of muffins, which I had never seen before. I'd seen other kids tuck into home baking before — fairy cakes and butterfly buns — but never anything on this scale. So it wasn't much of a hardship, waiting there among the born again. I will give them credit for leaving me alone and not trying to cram Jesus down my throat along with the grub.

Eventually, somebody came for me and took me back to the tent. Jenna looked dazed, like she sometimes did when she'd smoked heroin, but when I appeared, she smiled and pulled me to her. I was surprised. She wasn't usually that demonstrative. 'Something wonderful's happened, Jennifer,' she said, stroking my hair, which was probably a mass of greasy rats' tails. 'I've accepted Jesus into my life.'

If you've ever seen *The Invasion of the Body Snatchers*, you'll have an idea of how I felt right then. I just wanted to get Jenna away from there and back into our scrappy shitty life where at least I knew what was what. 'When are we going home?' I asked her.

She smiled then, one of those radiant, peaceful smiles you get from people with a poor connection to reality. 'We're going to live in a new home, Jennifer,' she said. 'In a proper house. We're part of the Christian family now.'

And that was how I learned my life was being turned inside out.

Charlie looked up from the book. 'I tell you, she knows how to keep you reading. She gives you enough to latch on to but not so much detail that you get bogged down. And I suspect she uses a trick that comes up a lot with psychopathic personalities. And politicians. Not that I'm suggesting there's anything in common between those two groups.'

'What's that?' Maria turned down the volume on the CD player.

'Managing to give the appearance of candour without actually revealing anything she doesn't want you to know.'

'We all do that, don't we? We always want to give a good impression of ourselves.'

'Yes, but with most of us, it's not a consciously constructed process. And it ends up being a bit hit and miss. Sometimes we end up saying or doing something that can give away rather more than we intended. But with this narrative, it's all perfectly calibrated. The charm never slips. Every bad thing Jay has a hand in is somehow transformed into a scenario where she is the heroic victim.'

'Isn't that a contradiction in terms? Heroic victim?'

'Not the way Jay writes it. And she's far from alone in that. I've come across a lot of them over the years.'

'You think she's a psychopath?'

'I'm not sure. But I do think she has some degree of personality dysfunction. It's not surprising, given her early life. And what I sense is about to unfold now.' Charlie turned back to the book and read on. Jay and her mother were taken to live with a couple attached to the Andreson crusade, the inappropriately named Blythes. Mrs Blythe took Jenna back to the camp the next day to fetch their belongings. Jay was shocked by how little they brought back. Most of her clothes and books had been abandoned. Apparently they were 'inappropriate'.

Life became a tight little tunnel of school, church, Bible study and bed. The Blythes, it turned out, were members of a Pentecostal sect so restrictive and narrow that they made Andreson's evangelicals look positively liberal. Jay was like a caged animal at first, raging against the constraints and fighting against every curb on her freedom. But it was useless. The more she struggled, the tighter the rules became. And Jenna was no help. She'd found her new drug of choice and she couldn't get enough. The threat that ultimately brought Jay to heel was that she would be sent away to a Christian boarding school where she would be forbidden to have contact with her mother. Jay was tough, but the prospect of losing the only constant in her life was too much. So she buckled down, hating her life with a rage whose fires were never banked down.

The thought I clung to was that it couldn't last for long. Nothing in my life ever had. Men came and went, friends came and went, the rooms where I fell asleep changed so often I seldom knew my address. Jenna would get bored, or someone would come along with better drugs or a better pitch and it would be all change again. So I believed all I had to do was wait it out.

It never occurred to me that it could get worse. We'd been with the Blythes about eight months when a new man joined our prayer circle. Picture an ascetic saint in a medieval Italian painting and you'll get a sense of Howard Calder. Only Howard made those holy hermits look like party animals. Pleasure was an invention of the Devil, Howard believed. We were put on earth to dedicate our lives to the greater glory of God. Living among the ungodly was the Lord's way of testing us. I thought he was a royal pain in the arse from the first.

But Jenna didn't. Like any addict, she was after the pure stuff. And Howard Calder was definitely pure. I didn't cotton on to what was happening at first. My experience of Jenna and courtship was that it generally took a few hours plus some drugs and alcohol. From first shag to him being a fixture was often only a matter of days. So it didn't register that Howard coming round and being polite to my mother was the trailer for the main feature — marriage. When she told me they were getting wed, I didn't believe her at first. When it dawned on me that it was for real, I didn't know whether to laugh or cry.

I had thought nothing could be more joyless than the Blythes' house. That was before I saw inside Howard's two-up and two-down terrace in Roker. It was like walking into a black-and-white film — no colour anywhere. White walls, beige carpets, beige three-piece suite, white kitchen, white bathroom. Nothing on the walls except Bible texts. I swear the most visually exciting moment was when he turned on the gas fire and flames of blue and red and yellow licked at the discoloured ceramic element. 'This will be your new home,' he announced. 'You will address me as Mr Calder. I'm not your father and I won't have people thinking I am.'

'Bugger that,' I said.

I'd never been hit so hard in my life. He punched the side of my head so fast and so brutally that I bit my tongue. I stood there, dazed, my ears ringing and my mouth filling with blood. I'd been smacked before, I'd been in plenty of fights and ended up on the wrong end of bigger kids. But I'd never been assaulted by an adult with such ferocity. And Jenna let him do it without a word.

'That child has the Devil in her,' he said. 'She needs to be brought to the Lord.'

And my mother, by now in complete thrall to Jesus and his Heavenly Father, agreed. My mother, who had had the occasional violent man in her life, but who had never tolerated anyone who even threatened to raise a hand to me. My mother, who even in her most drug-addled state had told me I had the right to be my own person, stood back and let this fascist bully punch me in the head.

I'm a quick learner. I decided I wasn't going to give Howard Calder the excuse to do that to me again. I had better self-preservation skills at ten than most people acquire after a lifetime. And I was still, against all odds, convinced that one day Jenna was going to wake up and go 'What the *fuck*?' and spirit the pair of us out of there. So I did what I was told. I went to church and didn't laugh at their preposterous pronouncements. I did Bible study till my eyes smarted. I learned to pray and sing their stupid bloody happy-clappy songs.

My secret refuge was the fiction section of the public library. I was pretty safe there, because the members of the Bethany Pentecostal Church of Jesus Christ the Saviour thought the reading of fiction was like opening the door and inviting the Devil in for tea. There was an alcove at the far end of the fiction shelves with a couple of chairs. I'd sneak down there for half an hour after school and read. The irony was that by the time I went to secondary school I wasn't even reading fiction any more.

Because I had had so little formal schooling and such an off-kilter experience of life, I was curious about how people lived. So I gravitated to history and sociology, to philosophy and politics. I've always been interested in how things worked and to me there was no real difference between stripping down a VW Beetle engine and figuring out the order of battle at Waterloo. These days it was all forbidden knowledge – all the more appealing because it was an act of defiance.

As the weeks and the months and the years passed, I could not make sense of my mother's behaviour. Why were we still here? Why was her life revolving round this vile man? What did she do all day? There was only so much time you could devote to cleaning and cooking and washing and ironing. She said she was studying the Bible, but part of me was still sure that this was all part of some complicated scam that was going to leave us sitting pretty for the rest of our lives. I just couldn't see what it was. I fantasised that she was going to kill her husband with some undetectable poison and that we would then get our hands on his secret millions and go and live in Florida.

It didn't happen. My life remained screwed down tighter than a coffin lid. But just when I thought it couldn't get any worse, my mother dropped a bombshell.

Charlie snapped the book shut. 'Phew,' she said. 'Another cliffhanger. I've read thrillers with fewer twists than this.'

'Why are you stopping?'

'Because it's nearly Fort William and we need to eat. I'll drive after that, if you like.'

Maria laughed. 'What? And be on tenterhooks all the way to Glasgow? No, that would be cruel. Besides, I'm enjoying it. You can have the boring bit on the motorway. So are you liking her yet?'

'Let me put it this way. I'm conscious of being manipulated. But if I'd come to this with no preconceptions, I think I'd like her a lot. I do hope Magda hasn't read this.' Charlie shook her head. 'If she has, Corinna's going to need a hammer and chisel to separate them.'

7

Once she got stuck in again after lunch, Charlie reckoned it had been fair to describe what faced Jay as a bombshell. Her sixteenth birthday fast approaching, Jay had finally accepted her life was not an extended scam. This was how it was and it was up to her if it was going to change. So she'd started to carve out an escape route. In spite of having had no formal education until she was ten, she'd made a success of school. She was bright, she picked things up quickly and she had a good memory. Her teachers encouraged her, so in spite of the complete indifference of Jenna and her husband, Jay was doing well. There were hints she should be thinking of Oxbridge in a year or two.

Jay knew better than to talk about this at home. She kept her head down and produced school reports that even Howard Calder couldn't find fault with. There were other things she knew better than to talk about, at home and at school. Once she'd made her escape, it would be different.

But for now, she'd batten down the hatches about those feelings, just as she rammed everything else well below the surface.

And then one night, it all went to hell in a handcart.

I was in my bedroom, doing my maths homework, when Jenna came in. She didn't knock. Neither of them ever did. Well, why would they? There was nothing I was allowed to do that shouldn't be seen by either of them. I was supposed to be modest, to dress and undress either in the bathroom or under the bedclothes, for example. I, of course, always had to knock before entering a room where they were. Even if I was only coming to eat my tea with them in the living room. Just one of the many petty rules that hedged my life round and allowed my stepfather to exert his authority.

So, there was my mother, standing over me and looking nervous. I was surprised because usually her husband was the only one who ever made her nervous. 'Howard and I have been praying with the congregation for guidance about you.'

'About me? Why? What am I supposed to have done?'

'About your future. And we've decided, once you turn sixteen, we'll be arranging for you to meet a suitable young man and get married.'

I couldn't take it in at first. I felt like I'd fallen through a wormhole in time and landed in a Victorian novel. 'I'm not getting married,' I said. 'And certainly not to somebody Howard thinks is suitable.'

'You're my daughter and you'll do what you're told,' Jenna said. 'I know you didn't have the benefit of a

Christian upbringing from the start, but we can make up for that.'

'I'm going to university,' I howled. 'I've got plans.'

That was when my stepfather appeared in the doorway. 'There'll be no university for you,' he said. 'What use is a university education to a wife and mother? You'll be married in the church and devote your life to God and your family.'

'You can't make me,' I shouted.

'I think you'll find we can,' he said. 'Come your birthday, you won't have to go to school. We'll keep you here at home till you see sense. I'm amazed at you, Jennifer. You talk about loving your mother and yet here you are, setting out your stall to break her heart.'

'I'm too young to get married.'

'Nothing of the sort,' he said. 'You'll do as you're told. You'll either do it the easy way or the hard way. But you'll do it.'

'You can't force me. I'll shout my head off at the wedding service, you won't get away with it.'

His smile was evil. 'Pastor Green understands the importance of women being brought under discipline. You'll find dissent cuts no ice with him. Come now, Jenna. Best if we leave Jennifer alone to digest the good news.'

I watched them go, speechless for once. I didn't know what the hell to do. I'd been surviving them having all the power only because I knew there would come a point where I would be able to walk away and make my own life. But I wanted the life I chose. I wanted my A-levels and my university place. I'd spent too long living on the fringes with Jenna to have any romantic notions about running away from home. I knew that if I did that, Oxbridge would never happen. I'd be one more messed-up street kid. Nothing I dreamed of would ever happen. My life would just be a different shade of shit.

There wasn't even anyone I could talk to. I didn't really have friends because I wasn't allowed to do anything except church things. And the other teenagers in the church made me want to slit my throat.

The only thing I could hang on to was that I still had almost three months to go till my birthday. It was a tactical error on my stepfather's part. In his shoes, I'd have waited till the morning after my sixteenth birthday. I'd have stopped me going to school and locked me in the cellar till I saw sense.

I sometimes wonder if I learned my business ruthlessness from him.

Charlie gave a low whistle. 'Listen to this,' she said, reading the last couple of paragraphs to Maria. 'She doesn't pull her punches, does she? I think that's one of the standout sentences in the book so far. It's more honest than almost anything else. We can't help ourselves. Even when we're on the alert, the truth slips through.'

'You think that's a clue to murder?' Maria said, incredulous.

'Not on its own, no. Obviously. But it's indicative of her response to being challenged and put in a corner. Not only is she thinking of her escape route. She's considering how much better she'd have delivered the threat in the first place. That's someone who relishes working out how to get her own way. And who does not let the world put her in a box.' Charlie turned the page. 'Well, let me rephrase that. This is someone who only lets the world put her in a box so she can have some peace and quiet to figure out how to fuck the lot of them over.'

'You don't like her now, do you?' Maria teased.

'Not one bit,' Charlie said. 'But I think she's fascinating. And I can't put this down.'

Things were pretty strained at home after Jenna's big announcement. I mostly stayed in my room when I wasn't at school. I refused to go to church, which meant I got locked in my room. I can't say I was bothered. I knew there was no point in trying to change my stepfather's mind, but I had a faint hope that a small corner of my mother's heart and mind might have escaped the brainwashing.

That faint hope grew stronger as the week went by. Jenna's mind was definitely not quite as single track as usual. She burned the breakfast toast on Wednesday and forgot the cabbage for the gammon-and-mash dinner on Thursday. A couple of times I walked in on her standing in the kitchen staring out at nothing when normally she'd be washing dishes or wiping worktops. I had to speak to her more than once to get her attention. She was miles away. I couldn't help believing she was having second thoughts about my stepfather's plans for me.

I needed to talk to her, I decided. But not in the house or anywhere connected to the church. I wanted it to be somewhere that might even remind her of our old life together. Sure, she'd mostly ignored me, but it had been a benign neglect. Or so it seemed to me then. I racked my brains and then it came to me.

One of the few things Jenna had stood up to her husband about was food shopping. She was one of the first people I knew who stood out against the onward march of the supermarkets, refusing to buy her fresh food from them. Her husband complained that she was extravagant, that it was cheaper to go to the local ASDA than to drive up to Grainger Market in Newcastle once a week. But my mother was adamant. So on Fridays, he had to take the bus to his job at the local council offices and my mother took the car to the big city.

I remembered markets from my early childhood. Jenna had worked on markets and she'd loved wandering round as a customer too. I liked them because they were easy to steal food from. If I could find a way to talk to her there, maybe the atmosphere would waken her independence from its long sleep.

I never had any money, which complicated things. So on Thursday night, I forced myself to stay awake then crept downstairs. There was a collecting box for the church in the kitchen. My stepfather emptied his loose change into it every night when he came home. I prised open the bottom with a knife and painstakingly counted out enough money for my fares, plus a bit over for emergencies.

Next morning, I left at the usual time but instead of going to school, I caught a bus into Sunderland then took the Metro into Newcastle. Luckily it was cold, so I was wearing my winter coat which covered up my telltale school uniform. It was scary, because I'd only ever been to Newcastle a few times for church things. But it was also exciting to emerge from the Metro in Central

Station. The place was bustling with people, all looking like they knew where they were going.

I looked round at the station staff and picked a middle-aged woman who looked like most of the lines on her face had come from laughing. It turned out Grainger Market was only a few minutes' walk from the station. I checked my watch. Jenna would barely have set off from Roker by now. I reckoned it would be at least half an hour before she got there. Plenty of time to check out the market, to see where the best place would be to be sure of catching her.

It was a bit bewildering when I got there — lots of different entrances, and a huge number of stalls selling a vast range of stuff. Everything from knicker elastic to lambs' sweetbreads. There was nowhere I could really set up an observation point, so I decided just to walk around, keeping my eyes peeled for her.

Almost an hour went by without any luck, and by then I was bursting for the loo. When I came out, I glanced around to see if I could spot her. And I nearly fell through the floor. There was no doubt in my mind, even though I hadn't seen Jenna in make-up for six years. Sitting at a café table, wearing lipstick and eyeshadow and mascara and blusher was my mother. Her hair was loose around her shoulders instead of done up in a chignon like usual. She was smoking a cigarette. And she was with a man who was very definitely not Howard bloody Calder.

He looked a bit like Morrissey, only broad and muscled where Morrissey was willowy. At first I thought that was why he looked familiar. I edged along the outside wall and crossed to a second-hand bookstall, where I was more or less concealed behind a rack of romances. Their heads were close together; they were talking and laughing like people who know each other well.

Then he threw his head back to laugh and I saw the snake tattoo that curled from behind his ear down his neck and into the V of his open shirt collar. And I remembered him. He was Dutch. Rinks, that was his name. I used to call him Ice. At eight or so I thought I was hilarious. We'd lived with him on a boat in Norfolk for a summer season, then he'd gone back to Holland. He'd paid more attention to me than most of Jenna's men. When he came home with a quarter of dope, he'd always have a bar of chocolate or a comic for me.

So, fine. I'd slotted this man into my memory. But what on earth was Jenna doing with him in Grainger Market when she was supposed to be shopping for her husband's dinners for the week? And then I remembered how she'd been distracted the last couple of days. Like her mind had derailed from the tram tracks the church had laid down for her. Were the two things connected?

I wondered if I should confront her, threaten to tell her husband about the make-up and the assignation if she didn't change her mind about the marriage. But I didn't want to be the kind of person who would use emotional blackmail against my mother. I wanted her to support me because she wanted to support me, because it was the right thing to do. Maybe it would be better to say nothing, to hope that she would carry on seeing Rinks and finally come to her senses. She might leave Howard Calder for Rinks and take me with her. And then everything would be all right.

You think like that at fifteen.

So I carried on watching them. They drank their coffee then spent an hour shopping for meat and fish and fruit and vegetables. Rinks carried the heavy bags and I followed them back to the Eldon Square car park. They put the shopping in the car then they walked back down by the Earl Grey monument. Rinks had his arm round Jenna's shoulder, and she leaned into him. They went into Waterstone's and I watched through the window as they browsed the shelves. By the cookery books, he kissed her. Lightly, not a proper snog. But on the lips all the same. It was like watching someone come back to life, seeing the way my mother lit up with him.

I followed them down the hill towards the station then they went into a pub. Obviously I couldn't follow them in. I was only fifteen, so I would have been illegal. I thought people would know just by looking at me. More importantly, I didn't have much money and I didn't know how much a soft drink would cost in a pub. Only that it was probably more than I had. I thought it probably wasn't like a sweetshop where you could go in and ask what they had for 35p.

It was like a thriller, Charlie thought again. Twists and turns and suspense. She glanced out of the window and was relieved to see they were still in empty Highland scenery. Maria could drive to Glasgow at thirty miles an hour for all she cared. She wanted to know the ending.

The next section dealt with Jay taking on the role of spy in her mother's life. Within a few days of the Grainger Market encounter, Jenna was slipping away from the house every morning after the coast was clear and driving off with Rinks. Jay was convinced they were going to be spotted by a fellow member of the church, but they seemed to lead a charmed existence.

Then one evening a couple of weeks later, Jenna announced over dinner that she had signed up to take part in a charity project to refurbish the homes of a group of old people in a block of flats in the town. Howard had clearly not wanted her to do it, but she'd held her ground, talking about the need for practical Christian charity as well as spirituality. It had been hard to argue against.

Jay had turned up at the charity project the next day during her school lunch hour and wasn't in the least surprised to find Rinks was the project leader. She pretended she had no idea who he was and her mother didn't introduce them. She'd hugged her secret knowledge to herself and tried to work out what she could do to make it work to her advantage.

Being Jay, she got there eventually. But before she could put her plan into action, she was overtaken by events. Charlie didn't think that had happened very often.

I'd finally plucked up the courage to tell Jenna and Rinks that I knew what was going on. I wanted to encourage them to get back together properly, for Jenna to leave her husband and set up home with Rinks and me. It was my route to salvation and I knew I couldn't wait indefinitely. My birthday was getting closer and I didn't want to take any chances.

I knew the project was getting close to the end, so I chose a Friday. That way, we could get ourselves organised while my stepfather was at work. We could pack up and be gone before he got home. Then we'd have the weekend to get sorted out and I could be back at school on Monday as if nothing had happened.

I know it sounds very simplistic, looking back at it now. But I had no understanding of the complexities of adult relationships. How could I? I'd never had the chance to see how most people connected. As far as I was concerned, it was obvious what had to happen.

I turned up at the project on the Friday morning but there was nobody around. All the volunteers were gone and the flats were locked up. I managed to find the warden and to my dismay he told me all the work had been finished the day before, a week ahead of schedule. Most of the residents would be back by the end of next week, all but three who had decided they wanted to go into residential care. He just kept talking at me as if I should be interested. All I was interested in was that my plan had just fallen to bits.

'What about Rinks?' I asked.

'The Dutch lad? He's very pleased with himself because he's got a week off now before his next project, down in York. He said he was going back to Holland to see his folks.'

Suddenly, I felt excited. They must have decided to go off together after all. Jenna would be back at the house, packing her bags and waiting for me to get home from school so the three of us could leave for Holland. The fact that they'd made the decision for themselves rather than me having to persuade them was even better.

I hurried home, imagining my new life. We'd have a

tall canal house. Or live on a boat, like we had in Norfolk. I would cycle to school and see real Van Gogh paintings. I was practically skipping down the street. We'd be a happy family in Holland and I'd never see Howard bloody Calder again.

I couldn't have been more wrong. The person I would never see again was my mother.

'Oh my God,' Charlie said, letting out her breath with a whoosh. 'I didn't see that coming. I mean, I sort of knew that her mother walked out on her and the stepfather, but the way she tells it – my God, you really feel it like a punch in the guts.'

'What happened?'

'The mother hooked up with an old boyfriend from the days before she found Jesus. And they took off, leaving Jay behind. She says she never saw her mother again.'

'Is that it? The end of the book? The mother walks out, never to be seen again?'

Charlie flicked forward. 'Not quite. There's a short afterword. Like when you get those little précis things at the end of movies. You know. "Jimmy Brown moved to Buffalo and opened a tattoo parlour. Jane Brown gave up her work with disabled parakeets and married an albino rabbi."'

'You have a very bizarre imagination,' Maria said. 'So what happened to them all?'

Charlie turned the page. 'You want me to read it out to you?'

'Yeah, it's not like *I'm* going to read it.'

'"Jenna Calder left her husband and child with a single

suitcase whose contents included a framed photograph of her daughter, aged six. In spite of police missing person inquiries, nobody has heard from her or seen her since.

'"Rinks van Leer returned from Amsterdam after a week's holiday to run a renovation project in York. He claimed to have no idea where Jenna was. He has gone on to run major projects in Central America and sub-Saharan Africa.

'"Howard Calder burned the clothes and possessions Jenna left behind and refused to speak her name. He still lives in the family home in Roker. He has never divorced or remarried.

'"Jay Stewart was taken in by her history teacher and his wife. She lived with them while she sat her A-levels and her Oxford entrance exam. She matriculated at St Scholastika's College, Oxford in Michaelmas Term 1992." And that's it. After all that rollercoaster of emotion, all that pain and struggle, it ends with the mother walking away. No wonder Jay's got issues,' Charlie said.

'It's a pretty blunt ending.'

'I think that's deliberate. She's trying to reflect how stark it felt to her. She's skipping home, thinking that after all this shit, she's about to see a turnaround. And that's what she does get. It's just the opposite of the one she was expecting.'

Maria slowed down as they approached a roundabout. 'Glasgow coming up,' she said. 'Do you want to take over? I'm feeling pretty tired now, if I'm honest.'

'Sure. Pull over the next place we can get a cup of coffee.'

'So, given what you've read, are you more or less

inclined to think Jay Stewart could be a cold-blooded killer?'

Charlie chuckled. 'I wish it was that easy. What I do think is that this was a key event in shaping her future behaviour. Chances are, she'll do pretty much whatever it takes to avoid putting herself in a position where someone else has the power to undermine what she wants. In business, in love, in friendship. But the other side of the coin is her need. Her early years were divided between chaos and regimentation. The one constant was her mother. Even though she was a pretty crap mother, Jay knew she could trust her to be there. And she still needs somewhere to put that trust. Right now, I suspect she's putting it on Magda.'

'So coming between her and Magda would be a seriously bad thing to do?'

Charlie nodded. 'Trouble is, I think that's exactly what I'm going to have to do.'

8

Monday

Jay breezed through the office in the best of tempers. She stopped by her PA's desk and delivered her best Monday-morning smile. 'Anne, I need you to find me a company that will pack up Magda's personal stuff from her flat,' she said.

'Congratulations,' Anne said with a wry smile. 'Good to see you haven't lost your silver-tongued winning ways.'

'Thank you. Sooner the better. And can you chase up Tromsø for me? We were caught on the hop with that northern lights documentary last year. I hear it's going to be repeated in a couple of weeks, I don't want us scrabbling at the last minute again.' Jay stopped by the coffee machine and fixed herself a skinny latte. She turned and spoke loud enough to attract the attention of the half-dozen people in. 'Monday meeting at noon, I've booked the back room at Chung's.'

Jay carried on into her office and closed the door behind her, a signal that she wasn't available for non-urgent communication. She settled behind her desk and leaned back in her chair, feet up on the wastepaper bin. She was feeling very pleased with herself. Magda had finally agreed that it was time they acted on their decision to move in together. Jay's house was more than big enough for both of them, so the logical thing was to rent out Magda's flat. It meant a longer commute than her present short walk, but apparently that was a price she was ready to pay.

The thought of Henry's apoplectic reaction was enough to bring a sly smile. Sooner or later, there would have to be a family truce within the Newsams' camp. But she didn't mind the idea of Corinna and Henry suffering a bit of heartburn along the way.

She woke the computer from its hibernation but before she could check her messages, her iPhone rang. Recognising the number, she gave a short, sharp sigh, but answered it anyway. 'Hello,' she said.

'Greetings. Still in love?' The voice was ironic.

'Even if I wasn't, you know how it is. It wouldn't make any difference. What can I do for you?'

'It's what I can do for you.'

Jay experienced a familiar sinking feeling. 'I've told you. You don't owe me anything.'

'I know that. But I like to help the people I care about when I can. I thought I should tell you that you're being . . . what's the best word here? Investigated?'

'I don't know what you mean. Who's investigating me? And why?' In spite of herself, Jay wanted answers.

'Ultimately, Corinna Newsam. She's got somebody digging into your past. Looking, I believe, for dirt.'

Jay couldn't quite believe it. 'Corinna's what? Hired a private eye?'

'No, she's strictly amateur hour. She's another one of Corinna's former pupils. A psychiatrist. Dr Charlotte Flint. Charlie to her friends.' The voice was amused now, enjoying a private joke that Jay didn't understand.

'I remember Charlie Flint. She was in the news last year. She was involved in that serial killer case. What on earth is she doing working for Corinna? And how do you know this?'

'Not everyone is immune to my charms, Jay. Would you like to know where she spent the weekend?'

Jay straightened up in her chair. 'This isn't a game. Just tell me what you know, never mind dangling stuff in front of me. What the hell's going on here?'

A soft gurgle of laughter. 'Calm down, Jay. I'll tell you what you want to know. Charlie Flint spent the weekend on the Isle of Skye. She interviewed two guys from the mountain rescue. She's also been looking at a couple of other incidents in your past. Jess Edwards, and Ulf Ingemarsson. Oh, and the husband.'

'Tell me this is your idea of a joke,' Jay said, her voice dark with anger.

'Don't shoot the messenger, dear heart. I'm not the one who thinks you're a serial killer. That's your beloved's mother. And all because she saw somebody who looked like you in the meadow on the morning Jess Edwards died.'

Jay's chest constricted. After all these years, her banishment suddenly made a terrible kind of sense. 'Corinna was in the meadow?'

'Apparently. Who knew?'

'I don't understand. She saw someone in the meadow that she thought was me and she said nothing?'

'Amazing, isn't it? I imagine she thought she was too closely linked with you in people's minds to give you up.'

'Or she cared too much about Schollie's.'

'Well, if she did, she's stopped caring now. Corinna's determined to bring you down.'

Jay couldn't believe what she was hearing. The fear that had squatted for years in the back of her mind was becoming a reality. Nothing was more calculated to destroy the comfort and happiness of her new life. And that was something she couldn't allow to happen. 'How the hell has this happened? Jesus!'

'It's OK. Be calm.'

'Calm? How can I be calm?'

'Because there's nothing to find, is there? These deaths were all investigated at the time. If there was any evidence of you being involved with a murder, the police would have been all over you. There's nothing to find, so there's nothing to worry about.'

Jay clenched her fist, her nails biting into her palm. The urge to violence was as strong as it had ever been. How had she let things come to this? 'So why are you calling me? If there's nothing to worry about, nothing to find, why are you winding me up with this?' Her words emerged in staccato choppiness, as if she was biting them off one by one.

'Because I thought you should know. I didn't want you to be blindsided. She's coming after you, Jay. It's better to be forewarned, don't you think?'

'So now I'm forewarned.' Jay rubbed her forehead so hard her fingers left red streaks on her skin. 'Thank you.'

'You know you're always welcome. I'm looking out for you, Jay. Always looking out for you. Always have been.' The voice was soft and seductive. 'But you know that. Right?'

'Right.' She could feel a headache starting at the base of her skull. Not for the first time, she wished she could wind back the years and undo one single evening. 'And I appreciate it,' she said in a monotone.

'Good. Let's meet up soon.'

'Let's. I'm sorry, I have to go, I have a staff meeting to prepare.'

'Good to talk to you. As always.'

'And you.' Jay terminated the call and sat staring unseeing at her computer screen. Of course there was nothing to find. How could there be, after all this time?

But all the same . . .

Charlie found Nick sitting outside the courtroom where the case he was involved in was being heard. Dressed for court, he was smarter than she'd ever seen him. A well-fitting black suit, a pale blue shirt, a dark blue tie and well-polished shoes were an ensemble she'd never have imagined he owned, never mind one that he'd actually wear. He'd shaved and his hair, if not actually neat, had been brushed. He gave her a wan smile. 'Hey, Charlie.'

'How was the weekend?' she asked, parking herself beside him.

'Work, work and then some more work on the side. We had a strong tip but it needed a stake-out. So that was my weekend flushed down the toilet. I was hoping to sit in on a session last night in Kilburn, but I didn't get home till gone midnight.' He sighed. 'Still, it's money in the bank when it comes to building a case against these scumbags. What about you?'

'We went to Skye.'

'Speed bonny boat, and all that?'

'Not any more, there's a bridge. There's also some very helpful mountain rescue guys.' Charlie told him what she'd learned from Eric and Calum. 'So, the knife being in her pocket was apparently fortunate but not remarkable,' she concluded.

'That was a waste of time then,' Nick sighed.

'Not entirely. There's the question of the phone call to the emergency services. The caller was a woman who said she was phoning from the hotel because Jay and Kathy hadn't come back. But nobody from the hotel had made the call. It's not a big place, Nick. They don't have huge numbers of staff running round the place. Especially in February, I imagine. It's odd, that's all.'

'But odd isn't enough to make a case. Oh, by the way, I meant to tell you. I had a bit of luck with Stratosphone. They got taken over by MXP Communications in 2005, and it just so happens that we've got warrants out with MXP on this trafficking case. I had a word with the officer who's been dealing with them, asked her if she'd put in a word for me. Obviously, I didn't tell her what it was about, just said it was a tangential thing, might come to something or not. Anyway, she's making some inquiries with MXP for us.'

'That's great. Thanks for coming through on that, Nick.

But the funny phone call isn't the only thing I've managed to find out. I called Magda the other night, when Jay was out of town. I wanted to see what she might tell me. And you'll never believe what just landed in her lap.'

'Try me.'

'Eight hundred thousand euros. In untraceable bearer bonds.'

'Fuck,' he said. 'I mean, what the fuck?'

Charlie brought him up to speed, enjoying his astonishment. 'So it turns out Philip was an even bigger crook than either of his colleagues,' she said.

Nick frowned. 'But that doesn't make sense. Why would he grass them up if he was at it too? Why risk an investigation that might screw him even more than them?'

'I wondered about that too. On the face of it, it makes no sense. But maybe he thought they were being careless, exposing them all to unnecessary risks, and this was how he wanted to put a stop to it. Of course, that would be a pretty dangerous strategy. However . . .' She paused and sighed. 'On the train coming down this morning, I had a thought. The letters are the motive for the murder, right?'

'That's right. Without the threat of Philip shopping them, Barker and Sanderson had no reason to kill him. They were his mates, the company was successful, they were all on board the gravy train.'

'So what if Philip didn't write the letters?'

A long pause while Nick worked his way through the implications of that. 'But who else would have had access to the information?'

'Magda, obviously. She was the one who "discovered"

the back-up drive. We've no way of knowing how long she had it before she handed it over to the police.'

'But she's got no motive for fitting up Barker and Sanderson,' Nick protested.

Charlie pulled a face. 'Well, she has and she hasn't. I'll come back to that. But here's the thing. I don't think Magda understands a balance sheet or a financial statement well enough to unravel complex stuff like insider trading. But I think her girlfriend does. I think Jay went through all Philip's financial data, looking for something she could use to frame Barker and Sanderson.'

Nick stretched his legs out and crossed them at the ankles, then folded his arms across his chest. 'I know I'm being really dim here, but why would she do that? From what I've been able to find out, until those letters turned up, the local boys were struggling to find motive or opportunity, never mind any forensics. Why not leave it as an unsolved? Why take a flyer on trying to fit somebody up?'

'Because Magda saw them leave the wedding party at around the right time. In her head at least they were prime suspects for having killed Philip. And Jay's in love with Magda. She wants to bind Magda to her more tightly. She wants to impress her. What better way to do that than deliver her husband's killers to justice? Especially if she's the one who really killed him. No better way of getting herself off the hook for ever.'

Nick threw his head back and laughed in delight. 'That is so beautiful,' he said. 'You have an evil, devious twisted mind. That is so sick. But it fits with what we know about Jay. Indirect, cunning and untraceable.'

'That's the trouble. The "untraceable" bit.' Charlie sounded as glum as she felt. 'All this poking about and we haven't got anything remotely solid. Nothing that would induce your colleagues to open an investigation of any of those old cases. I hate to say it, but I think we've got to admit defeat.'

Nick scratched his head. 'It irritates the shit out of me to admit it, but I think you're right.'

Charlie slumped, head in hands. 'This is just like Bill Hopton all over again. I feel like such a failure, Nick.'

'You're not a failure, Charlie. I don't see what anybody else could have done in the circumstances.' Nick put his arm round her shoulders. 'You're going to be exonerated, you know. You'll be back doing what you do best.'

Charlie made a noise like a half-choked snort. 'Instead of pretending to be some half-arsed detective?' She butted her head against his chest. 'Stop trying to make me feel better. It's a waste of time.'

'I don't suppose you'd entertain an alternative explanation?'

'I'd love one. Why? Do you have one?'

Nick took a deep breath and let it out noisily. 'Well . . . It's all a bit "what if?" And seriously lacking in motive or evidence. But then, we've got bugger all on Jay, so we might as well have bugger all on other suspects, right?'

Charlie eased out from his arm and twisted round to face him. 'What are you talking about?'

'When I get stuck on a case, I try to figure out another way of looking at the evidence. When I was sitting on my stake-out, I started playing around with some other ideas. Take Jess Edwards' murder, for example. What's the one thing we do know about that? We know Corinna was in the meadow.' He stopped, expectantly.

After a long pause, Charlie said, 'You're suggesting Corinna might have killed Jess?'

'Why not? She put herself at the scene of the crime – if there was a crime – which is a good way of diverting suspicion.'

'But what possible motive could she have had?'

Nick shrugged. 'I've no idea. But I bet we could come up with a handful if we sat down and brainstormed it.'

'It's very thin,' Charlie complained.

'So's the case against Jay,' Nick said wearily.

'What about the other murders?'

He pulled a face. 'Well, I wondered about her PA, Anne Perkins. They've worked together a long time, and Anne was very defensive of Jay. And very quick to produce the alibi evidence. Which, incidentally, meant I also got sight of her diary for the week. It looks like she was working alone most of the time. Nobody to vouch for her.'

Charlie chuckled. 'And on that basis, you think she slipped off to Spain, murdered Ulf Ingemarsson and brought his work back to Jay like a dog with a newspaper? Jeez, Nick, this Anne Perkins must have made some impression on you.'

Nick gave a self-deprecating grin. 'Hey, I know it's a stretch, but Jay does seem to provoke strong reactions. For everybody who thinks she's somebody you wouldn't want your daughter to marry, there's someone with big loyalty to her. She's worked at close quarters with Vinny Fitzgerald and Anne Perkins for the best part of a decade. People don't stick around in that kind of job unless they're devoted to each other.'

Charlie shook her head, unwilling to believe him. 'And Philip?'

'Maybe it was Sanderson and Barker after all. I generally like the instincts of juries, Charlie.'

'And all these killers just happen to cluster around Jay Stewart?' She shook her head again. 'Far too many coincidences, Nick. You're playing devil's advocate here. You don't really believe all that. But I might be able to use your ideas to throw a bit of sand in Corinna's eyes.' She stood up. 'I need to go and see her now. Tell her there's nothing I can do for her.'

'I'm sorry,' Nick said. 'Really. And you're right. I was just trying to cheer you up with my crazy notions. For what it's worth, I think Corinna might be right. There's too much stacked against Jay Macallan Stewart to write off as bad luck. A bloke who lost four wives in incidents like these would be sitting in an interview room. But nobody suspected her at the time, which means nobody looked for the evidence to tie her in.'

'Don't,' Charlie said, bitterness in her voice. 'Don't go there, Nick.'

'Why? What have I said?'

'It's what you didn't say. It's the implication. We can't get her for the crimes in the past. If we want to nail her, we have to wait till she does it again.' Her voice shook and tears spilled from her eyes. 'Can't you see? It's just an interesting variation on Bill bloody Hopton.'

9

Charlie sat on the same hard chair she'd occupied twenty years before. Back then, she'd been waiting for her first tutorial with Corinna Newsam. Now she was waiting for some other undergraduate to finish her business so Charlie could find a way to divert Corinna from a disastrous course. For the duration of the train journey from London to Oxford, she'd been trying to figure out what to say.

This was one occasion when the truth wasn't an option. It didn't matter that Charlie actually agreed with Corinna. In fact, that was the most dangerous position for her to adopt in any conversation with her former tutor. While Charlie couldn't quite believe that Corinna was capable of killing Jay, there were some things you couldn't take a chance on. Either Charlie had to present Corinna with enough evidence to go to the police – which she didn't have – or else she had to make the case for Jay's inno-cence. Since there wasn't enough evidence, Charlie had no choice. She would have to protect Jay. And that meant lies.

By the time Corinna had finished teaching, Charlie was as rehearsed as she was ever going to be. She took the chair opposite her former tutor, noticing that Corinna seemed to have lost weight in the nine days since she'd seen her last. Fear for your child would do that to a woman, Charlie thought.

There was no time wasted in small talk. Corinna came straight to the point. 'You've news for me?'

Charlie nodded. 'I've covered a lot of ground in the last week. Talked to a lot of people and found out a lot of things. It's been an interesting experience.'

'I'm sure it has. I suspect you have a gift for finding the interesting, Charlie. But have you managed to find enough evidence to convince Magda?' Corinna leaned forward in her seat, hands clasped tight in her lap. The last person Charlie had seen that tightly wound was a paedophile priest waiting for the heavens to fall on his head.

'All the evidence I have points firmly in one direction. You're not going to like this, Corinna. Jay Macallan Stewart is not a serial killer.'

Corinna touched one side of her face, as though she wasn't convinced she could trust her hearing. 'You're mistaken,' she said. 'You can't have checked properly. Death follows her around like a pet dog. It defies logic to suggest that every time someone stands between Jay Stewart and what she wants, they simply happen to die.' Her voice was firm, her attitude the one that Charlie remembered from her student days – the teacher who had a solid grasp of her subject, who would welcome argument but seldom concede her point. Charlie knew her only recourse was coherent and substantial argument.

'I know,' she said. 'But that's how it is. Sometimes the world runs counter-intuitive. Look, I'm not asking you just to take my word for it. For a start, I've not been working alone. A friend of mine who is a detective with the Met has been helping me with information that it's hard for a civilian to access. He's also got the skills I lack. He's been able to suggest how I should proceed when I've not known what to do for the best.'

'Very enterprising of you,' Corinna said crisply. 'And I do appreciate it. I was right in thinking you were the person for the job. The sort of woman who has resources.'

'And I'm also a scientist. That means I believe what the evidence tells me even when it runs against my theory of what was the case. Let me run through the deaths you told me about. First, Jess Edwards. Now, you say you saw Jay in the meadow very early on the morning of Jess's death. You were convinced at the time, even though it was still dark and she was some distance away.' Corinna made to speak but Charlie held up her hand. 'Please, Corinna, let me finish.' *Let me lie to you and see if I can get you to fall for it.* 'I tracked down Jay's girlfriend at the time, Louise Proctor.'

'How did you manage that? The alumnae office has no current records for her. She severed all her ties with the college after she left. And no wonder. A vulnerable girl preyed on by Jay Stewart, preyed on to the extent that she tried to kill herself.'

Charlie was pretty sure that hadn't been quite the way it was, but she was on pretty shaky ground since she knew next to nothing about Jay's early love life. 'That's the advantage of having a policeman in your corner. Law-abiding people aren't that hard to trace when you have access to official records. So, I spoke to Louise. She doesn't have any loyalty towards Jay. As you suggest, she holds Jay responsible for one of the more miserable episodes of her life. So there's no reason why she should lie for her. Agreed?'

Corinna dipped her chin in a grudging nod. 'I suppose not.'

'According to Louise, on the morning Jess died, Jay was in bed with her until after seven o'clock. By that time, the rowers were down at the boathouse and Jess's body had been discovered.'

'That's impossible. How can she be sure? How can she remember one morning in particular so clearly?'

Charlie assembled her thoughts. This was not the time to be talking about anomalies. 'Because it was the morning Jess Edwards died. And because they'd been lying awake since just after six. Jay was raging about Jess and the JCR election. When she went down to breakfast and found out about Jess, Louise remembers thinking how awful it was that Jay had been so mean about Jess right when the poor girl was drowning. So she has an alibi.'

Corinna looked disgusted. 'How truly ironic,' she said.

'What do you mean?'

Her lip curled in contempt. 'If Jay had produced that as an alibi at the time, nobody would have believed it. They'd all have said Louise was lying for her out of love. But now Louise has every reason to hate her. And only now she comes out with it.' Corinna shook her head. 'I have to take your word for it, but it's hard to believe I was wrong. I know what I saw.'

'I don't want to seem patronising, Corinna, but eyewitness reports are notoriously inaccurate. And there's a perfectly respectable psychological mechanism behind it. Our brains look for patterns. We seek resemblances. So we overlay what we actually see with what we expect to see based on visual clues. And as time goes by, we reinforce the memory with more details that come not from what we saw but from what our brain tells us we must have seen. You saw a figure who for some reason reminded you of Jay. You saw them in an area where you might reasonably expect to see Jay herself. And your brain filled in the gaps.' Charlie spread her arms wide and shrugged. 'We all do it all the time. You've nothing to reproach yourself with.'

'I still believe my own eyes.' The stubborn set of Corinna's jaw didn't bode well for the success of Charlie's plan. But there was nothing to do but press on.

'Fine. But you have to ask yourself who Magda's going to accept – you with a figure glimpsed through the dark, or Jay with her perfect alibi. At this point, Magda has no reason to distrust Jay. But you? She knows you're violently opposed to her and Jay being together.'

Corinna's look was venomous. 'What else did you find out?' she demanded.

'I checked out the Fatal Accident Inquiry into Kathy Lipson's death. There's no question that Jay cut the rope when Kathy fell off the rock pinnacle they were climbing. But there's also nothing to contradict her version of events. Kathy was the driving force behind the trip to Skye. She'd apparently always wanted to do winter climbing in the Cuillins and you only get a couple of chances every winter.

446

You have to grab it when you can. And sometimes the weather closes in on you, as it did on them.'

'She could have pushed her off and made it look like an accident.'

Charlie nodded. 'She could have. But there's no witnesses. And nothing in the physical evidence to contradict Jay's version. I spoke to two of the mountain rescue guys who brought her off the mountain. They were sorry for her. They understood the stigma she's suffered after cutting the rope. But they also totally supported what she did. It's right to cut the rope when you have the stark choice. You're both going to die unless you cut the rope, in which case one of you might live. It's hard to argue with that, Corinna.'

Corinna glared at her. 'Has she got to you? Is this some kind of lesbian solidarity?'

Charlie felt the blush of anger spread up her neck. 'That is incredibly insulting. I've just spent nine days and a chunk of change trying to prove your crazy theory. Not because I owe you a thing, but because I like your daughter and I think she needs somebody in her corner. But if you think I would cover up evidence of murder just for the sake of sisterhood, you are so far off the scale of sanity that I could probably call a colleague right now and have you sectioned.' She picked up her bag and gathered her coat around her, preparing to leave.

'Wait,' Corinna said urgently. 'Please. I'm sorry, Charlie. I'm truly sorry.' Her voice cracked and she cleared her throat. 'You see how this business has thrown me off kilter?' She stood up abruptly and went to a tall mahogany cabinet. She opened it and took out a bottle of red wine. 'I do know you better than that, Charlie. Forgive me. I'm just so bitterly disappointed. Take a drink with me?'

Charlie sat back in the chair, but shook her head. She wanted nothing to blunt her edge for this conversation. She waited while Corinna poured herself a modest glass of wine. 'I looked at Ulf Ingemarsson's murder too. And while it's true that Jay was out of the country when it happened, my friend the detective has seen her schedule for that week. There's no room for a side trip to Spain,' she said earnestly. 'Even if she'd driven through the night, she couldn't have got to Ingemarsson's villa and back to where she was supposed to be next morning.' Another lie, but Charlie was on a roll now. Whatever her suspicions, she had no proof against Jay. The woman was entitled to the presumption of innocence; more importantly, she was entitled not to be the victim of Corinna's notion of justice.

'She could have hired someone,' Corinna said defiantly.

Charlie groaned. 'Sure, she could have hired someone. People in her line of work come across hitmen all the time.' Her voice was heavy with sarcasm. 'Would you know where to start looking for a hired killer? I've been working in the field of abnormal psychology for more than a dozen years. I spend my days with killers and rapists and paedophiles and I have no idea how to find a hitman. It's not like you can Google it.'

'She might have commissioned burglary and got murder,' Corinna insisted.

'Same argument. Where is she going to find herself a burglar for hire? Would you know where to start? It's not like you can ask one of your magistrate pals to recommend a good one, is it? And here's another thing. Speaking purely as a psychiatrist, with all I know about Jay Stewart, I cannot see her putting herself at someone else's mercy. Once you commission a crime, you're vulnerable for ever. It's just not her personality type. She likes being in control too much.'

Corinna drained her glass and put it down. 'You make a good case,' she said, voice and eyes dull. 'You always knew how to frame an argument. I'd hoped you were going to be marshalling that sharp intellect on the other side of the question.' She sighed and stood up, walking over to the window and staring down at the college garden where Magda's wedding reception had taken place. 'It's funny,' she said. 'That day started so perfectly. I'd worried about Magda. She'd always been so focused on her job, I thought she was missing out on love and friendship and the possibility of the kind of life I've been privileged to enjoy.'

Charlie bit her tongue, thinking of the inescapable Catholic misery of being married to Henry; of juggling the demands of four children, a big house and a constant stream of students with their intellectual challenges; of those six a.m. shifts at her college desk trying to achieve the publications that would make it impossible for the college not to offer her a fellowship; of the succession of bright young undergraduates who were needy enough to be grateful to Corinna for friendship and biddable enough to be cheap and reliable babysitters. And she was glad beyond words that Magda had a different prospect ahead of her.

'But then Philip came along,' Corinna continued. 'What I liked about him was something you don't find a lot in young men. He was kind. He wasn't pushy or aggressive.

You could see he was ambitious, but not ruthless. We figured he'd take good care of our girl. That morning, I felt like everything had fallen into place. Magda marrying a good man, the wedding here at my own college.'

Charlie was finding Corinna's melodramatic monologue hard to take. 'But by nightfall, it had all gone to shit,' she said drily.

Corinna winced at the language. 'It was a tragedy,' she said, turning back to the room. 'If Philip had lived, you can't tell me Magda wouldn't be happily married at this moment. We wouldn't have had any of this lesbian nonsense, never mind having to worry about our daughter living with a killer.'

'Excuse me? "Lesbian nonsense"? Are you deliberately trying to be offensive?' Charlie shook her head and reached for the spare glass Corinna had brought for her. She poured herself some wine and took a deep draught. This time, she let her anger flow. 'Your daughter's a lesbian, Corinna. It's not some adolescent phase. If Philip had lived, the marriage would have collapsed when Magda couldn't go on resisting her true nature. Either that or she'd have endured a life half-lived for the sake of respectability and not upsetting you and Henry. Whatever way it had gone, she'd have been bloody miserable. So spare me the fairy-tale romance. Magda's a dyke. Get over it.'

'You don't know that,' Corinna said. 'I've come across a few cases over the years where women have gone back to men after years of lesbian affairs. What is it you call them? Has-bians? Was-bians?'

'Lobotomised,' Charlie said acidly. Seeing Corinna's expression, she added wearily, 'That was a joke, Corinna.

I'm finding this all a bit hard to stomach. I haven't had a conversation like this in a dozen years. It's all a bit weird to find myself talking to someone who makes the *Daily Mail* look tolerant. Especially since you're the one who's been asking me favours.'

'It's hard to abandon a lifetime of principles,' Corinna said.

'One woman's principles are another woman's bigotry, Corinna. Even if you manage to prise Magda out of Jay's arms, she's not going to have a Damascene conversion back to heterosexuality.' Charlie gave a wicked grin. 'I think she's finally discovered fun.'

'I'd like to be able to cross that bridge when we come to it,' Corinna said, making her way back to her chair and refilling her glass. 'So. Was Philip's murder as much of a dead end as the other cases?'

One more lie. 'As far as Jay is concerned, yes. I can't tell you who her alibi is, but I've spoken to the person who was with her that evening and I am convinced that at the time Philip was murdered, she was in another part of the college altogether.'

'Why can't you tell me who she was with?'

'Because I promised not to reveal this person's identity. I could lie to you and say it was a business meeting, that it had to do with commercial confidentiality. But I'm not going to do that. The person Jay was with has good reasons for wanting their meeting to remain secret, and I agreed to honour that.'

Corinna's lip curled in disdain. 'Some married woman, no doubt.'

'Why do you care? Believe me, Jay's alibi for Philip's

murder is rock solid. I'll be completely candid with you, Corinna. When we talked about this last week, I came round to your way of thinking. I was more than halfway to being convinced that Jay really was a murderer. But I've had to accept that we were both wrong. What's happened around her has genuinely been coincidence. You made a mistake the morning Jess Edwards died, and it's tainted your opinion of everything that's occurred around Jay ever since. I know it's hard to unpick all those assumptions, but you have to accept that your brain tricked you into a misapprehension. The honest truth is that she didn't deserve to be shown the door all those years ago. And she doesn't deserve it now.' Charlie suddenly realised she was getting carried away with herself. She'd almost fallen for her own assumed sincerity. It was hard not to despise herself for her ability to persuade against what she herself believed had happened.

Corinna stared at her, glassy-eyed. 'I was so sure,' she said. 'And then everything else made sense.'

'I understand,' Charlie said gently. 'But if you take away that first certainty, you can see there's no real reason to hold Jay responsible for any of those other deaths.'

'I've got some thinking to do,' Corinna said, her voice heavy and slow. 'It's hard to hold on to my mental image of Jay as this evil psychopath in the teeth of what you're telling me. But I suppose, for Magda's sake, I should be grateful that she's not what I took her for.'

'You should,' Charlie said, getting to her feet. 'And you need to build some bridges there. Magda clearly values her place in your family. Don't punish her for being who she is.'

Charlie walked back through college, her depression building with every step. She'd saved Corinna from taking some drastic and destructive step, but it had taken its toll on her. She'd had to argue against what she had come to believe, all because Jay Stewart had been smart enough to commit a series of perfect murders. Charlie remembered hearing a radio presenter once asking a crime writer if she knew of anyone having committed a perfect murder. The writer had said, 'The perfect murder is the one nobody suspects *is* a murder.' Jay hadn't quite managed that every time, but she'd managed to vary her methods enough to keep herself out of the frame.

What Charlie had said to Nick had been right. They would have to wait for the next death before they could have any chance of making Jay pay for her crimes. It was a profoundly depressing thought. She wished there was another explanation for the chain of deaths that circled Jay Stewart, but any other theory would have to embrace an eye-popping amount of coincidence.

Charlie walked out into the north Oxford street, heading towards the University Parks with the force of a habit that hadn't been exercised for seventeen years. The spring afternoon had a distinct chill, the sky as grey as her mood. She had no eyes for the dramatic displays of spring bulbs. All she could see was that she'd reached the end of the road. What had started as a distraction had ended up magnifying the doubt and disappointment that had plagued her since Bill Hopton's second murder trial. She'd take a walk through the park then catch a bus to the station. There was still plenty of time to get back to Manchester.

Enough time for her to make one last detour, a little

voice in the back of her head suggested. She wouldn't be back in Oxford any time soon. How could it hurt? 'It could hurt a million ways,' she said out loud, earning an indulgent smile from a passing student.

She cut through the Parks and emerged opposite Keble College, taking a left down towards the Broad. She could cut down Queen's Lane to the High and easily catch a bus to Iffley. To Charlie, like some renegade banker, a million just wasn't enough.

10

This time, Charlie decided she wasn't going to call ahead and give Lisa the chance to prepare herself. If she was busy, so be it. Charlie would walk away, and this time maybe she could manage to make it for good. But the last proper thing that Lisa had said to her was that Charlie's feelings were not a one-way street. Charlie couldn't leave it at that. She realised that the time was approaching when she would have to choose between the life she had with Maria and the possibility of a future with Lisa, but she wanted to be sure it was a real choice. She needed to be clear that if she chose Lisa, there was a genuine offer of a relationship there.

But equally, Charlie knew it would be dishonest to stay with Maria if the only reason she was there was that there was nothing better on offer. Maria deserved so much more than that. If she was brutally honest with herself, Charlie had to admit that her feelings for Lisa had undermined their relationship. Pursuing Jay Stewart had provided her with the perfect excuse for spending time with Lisa and indulging her emotions. But as that investigation drew to a close, so too did the time for vacillation. The first decision was whether to stay with Maria; the second, whether to pursue a relationship with Lisa.

Sometimes Charlie wished she was more like the psychopaths she dealt with professionally. It must in some sense be a relief not to be possessed of insight into one's inner life.

Only Lisa's car was in the drive. Charlie walked up the path and physically gathered herself together, squaring her shoulders and straightening her spine. She reached for the bell and paused for a few seconds. It wasn't too late. She could still turn and walk away, walk back to a life that really should be sufficient for anybody.

But Charlie had to know. Charlie always had to know. And in this matter, not knowing wasn't just a matter of curiosity unsatisfied. This time, not knowing would torture her. It would take on a life of its own in her imagination. Every time she and Maria bickered, she would wonder how things would have been different with Lisa. Inevitably it would assume a gloss that would destroy their relationship. The promise not explored would always be the tantalising prospect of true happiness and fulfilment. Damned if she did, damned if she didn't.

Charlie pressed the bell.

It took Lisa a while to answer. Charlie had almost given up, assuming Lisa had gone somewhere on foot or by taxi. But at last, the door swung open and there she was. She was wearing another shalwar kameez, this time in deep fuchsia. She looked annoyed, but when she saw it was Charlie the frown disappeared and she produced the full-on smile. 'Charlie,' she exclaimed. 'What a delicious surprise. But you should have called, I could have postponed my next meeting.' She glanced at her watch. 'We've only got twenty minutes to ourselves. Come in, come in.'

Charlie was taken aback by the effusiveness of the welcome. Under the full glare of Lisa's charisma, she had no defence. 'I think we've got unfinished business,' she said, following Lisa down the hall to the sitting room. A single floor lamp turned the afternoon gloom to intimacy. There was a smell of spice in the air: cinnamon, nutmeg, allspice. Charlie wanted to lie down and make the world go away.

Lisa settled on one of the sofas, legs tucked under so she looked like a startling blossom on the cream fabric. 'Come and sit beside me,' she said, patting the sofa next to her. 'Take your coat off.'

Charlie obeyed, sitting beside Lisa but not quite touching. 'I didn't want to leave things between us the way they were,' she said.

'Of course not,' Lisa said. 'It's important that we recognise the power of the connection between us. We may not be able to do anything about it, but we'll always know there is that deep bond that draws us together.'

'I was wondering whether that's enough to get it out of our path and move forward,' Charlie said, her throat dry. She couldn't help wishing they could get past the abstractions to physical abandon.

Lisa shifted so that she was leaning into Charlie. Charlie was conscious of every point where their bodies touched. 'It's so tempting, isn't it? Just to fall into each other, to lose

457

ourselves and forget everything else? There's nothing I'd like more than for us to be lovers, Charlie. But this isn't the right time. It's too combustible. You need to be past Maria before you can open yourself to me. And me? Well, I'm still trying to free my spirit of the deep past. I won't give you the second best I can spend on the likes of Nadia. I wouldn't insult you.'

Charlie gave a wry smile. 'I've got a pretty thick skin, Lisa. I could live with an insult like that.'

Lisa didn't echo the smile. 'See, Charlie, I think that's precisely where you're wrong. I think you couldn't live with the insult. I think it would eat away at you and in the end it would poison everything between us. I've seen it happen to other people and I don't want it to happen to us. This isn't the time, Charlie. You need to be patient.'

It was an answer, though not the one she'd wanted to hear. Somehow, Charlie understood that whatever decision she made concerning Maria, there would always be a reason why Lisa wouldn't be able to commit. She drew away from her. 'In that case, better we don't touch at all.'

'Don't be offended. Be the opposite of offended. Be proud that we have enough care for each other not to fall into something tawdry.'

'So what was your appearance at the weekend really about? Was I supposed to compare and contrast? Was that meant to be some kind of watershed?'

Lisa stretched her arms above her head, a move that emphasised the beauty of her breasts. 'I told you,' she said. 'I wanted to see the Charlie who emerges when you're not with me. When you're with Maria. It was purely selfish and I'm sorry if it put you off your stride.'

'I did what I went there to do,' Charlie said. 'It just didn't work out quite the way I thought it would.'

Lisa smiled sadly. 'Poor Charlie. I told you this was a waste of time. Jay might have the killer instinct in business, but not when it comes to people.'

'You sound like you know her well,' Charlie said. 'I thought you said your paths had barely crossed when you were undergraduates?'

Lisa gave her an assessing look. 'That's right. But I've always been good at taking the measure of people. You of all people should know that. I knew you were special the moment I first heard you speak, after all. But Jay? I saw enough of her back then to understand the sort of woman she was. And I've heard nothing since to change my mind.'

'Well, on the face of it, it looks as if you were right. There's no evidence that would make the police look at Jay for more than a nanosecond.'

'I told you so. But you had to chase the chimera yourself.' She pouted. 'But then, that's one of the things I admire in you. Take nothing on trust.'

'I'd be a pretty crap psychiatrist if I took everyone at face value. But I didn't say Jay hadn't killed those people. I said there was no evidence that would stand up in court.' Somehow, realising there was no future for a relationship with Lisa had loosened Charlie's tongue where her investigation was concerned. If there was no point in talking about their relationship, she had to find something else to fill the space. 'That's the worst outcome for me. I'm fairly convinced Jay killed those people, but I have to live with the knowledge that she's not going to be brought to justice.

And now I have a quandary. The only chance of making her pay the price for her actions is to wait till she kills someone else. On the other hand, if I warn her that any deaths in her immediate vicinity will be scrutinised minutely to see if there's any trace of her hand in them, if she's got any sense she won't kill again. And there will never be any prospect of her paying the price for her actions. So I have to weigh the possibility of justice against the possibility of saving a life.'

Lisa's eyebrows rose. 'No contest, I would have thought. She might not take kindly to the accusation, but at least you'll have cleared your conscience. Justice isn't such a big deal, Charlie. It's a pretty moveable feast, in my estimation. Let the dead bury their dead, and let's all move forward.'

'I wish it was that easy,' Charlie said. 'Did you ever read her book? *Unrepentant*?'

'I did. I thought it made very interesting reading. Such a violent dissonance at the heart of her childhood – that would make you wary of trusting anyone. She reveals much more vulnerability than she realises, I believe. Her overreaching in business is a compensation for her inability to defend herself in childhood and adolescence against the forces ranged opposite her. Wouldn't you say?' Lisa smiled. 'You are the professional analyst, after all.'

'I don't know that I would have put it quite like that. I think she's all about constructing defences. But you're the vulnerability expert.'

Lisa inclined her head, acknowledging Charlie's riposte. 'Jenna is the key, isn't she? A woman of extremes. Total libertinism then total repression. It makes me wonder what on earth was going on in the mother's background for those two outer limits to be the attractive options. What exactly was she rebelling against or pulling towards?'

'And yet Jenna is quite a shadowy figure in some respects. What Jay gives us is very much the child's-eye view of a parent. The child is oblivious to a lot of what's going on because it's over her head. As we're reading, we don't notice because it's such a pacy narrative. But thinking about it, I feel like I've been shortchanged on Jenna.'

Lisa compressed her lips briefly. 'Maybe that's deliberate. Maybe Jay's afraid she'll give away too much about herself if she reveals Jenna more fully. I don't have to tell you how often it all comes back to the mother.'

The sensation inside Charlie's brain was almost physical. Lisa's words dislodged something in her head, like the stone that shifts and precipitates the avalanche. '"Nobody has heard from her or seen her since." That's what the book says.'

'A terrible, ultimate abandonment,' Lisa said. 'Some people think it's OK to leave your children by the time they're adolescents and can fend for themselves. But in many ways, that's their most vulnerable period.'

'It wasn't such a terrible abandonment for Jay. More of a result, really. She didn't get married off to some happy clappy. She got to go to Oxford and get away from the stifling repression of life in the Bethany Pentecostal Church of Christ the Saviour. Her mother disappearing was the making of her,' Charlie said slowly, looking from all angles at the thought that had hit her, seeing if it really made the sense she thought it did.

'I'm not certain I would put it like that,' Lisa said, looking at Charlie as if she wasn't quite sure of her any more. 'I think Jay overcame a terrible trauma remarkably well.'

Charlie got to her feet just as the doorbell rang. 'I need to go to Roker,' she said.

Lisa looked startled. 'Where?'

'Where Jay came from. I need to check out what happened to her mother.'

'We know what happened to her mother. She ran off with the Dutch boyfriend.'

'Who denied having run off with her.' Charlie started to head for the door.

'Wait,' Lisa said. 'What are you saying?'

'I need to check out what happened to her mother,' Charlie repeated, sounding dazed. 'There's somebody at your door,' she added as the bell rang again.

Lisa jumped off the sofa and caught up with her in the hallway. She put a hand on Charlie's arm. 'I thought you'd given up this crazy quest?'

Charlie turned and smiled. 'Not while there's still something to chase down.' Gently she picked Lisa's hand off her arm. 'Somebody else for you, Lisa,' she said, aware of the ambiguity and happy with it.

There was a new energy in Charlie's step as she strode back to the bus stop. According to the timetable, she only had ten minutes to wait for a bus that would take her close to the train station. She'd be back in Manchester this evening and in the morning she could make straight for the North East. Maybe she could short-circuit the trawl through local newspaper archives with a little help from Nick.

She pulled out her phone and called his mobile. It went

straight to voicemail, as she'd half-expected. 'Hi, Nick. It's Charlie,' she said. 'I've just been talking to Lisa Kent, she's a pal of mine who used to know Jay a bit. And she said something about Jay's mother that just set something off in my head. What if Jess Edwards wasn't the first? What if she started even earlier? What if Jenna was her first victim? I know it sounds crazy, and this is going to cut me off – Oh, bugger,' Charlie said as the voicemail ended. She called back immediately. 'Me again. 1990, Jenna Calder was her married name. She was reported as a missing person. Roker in Sunderland. I'm going up there first thing in the morning to see what I can dig up. It would be brilliant if you could get one of the local boys to open the file to me. Call me in the morning, I'll explain better. Thanks, Nick.' This time she beat the beep. Then remembered she still had a more immediate message for Nick. For the third time she called his number. 'Me again. Just to tell you I think I persuaded Corinna that Jay's innocent. At least planted enough doubt to stop her doing something stupid. I'm going back to Manc now. I promise to leave you alone.'

Charlie put her phone away. She wondered what she would find at Roker. It seemed an unlikely location for redemption.

11

The morning phone call had taken the gloss off Jay's day, but by the end of the afternoon, she'd almost recovered herself. The prospect of seeing Magda generally had that effect on her. But her feelings were more complicated than usual. Clearly she couldn't ignore Corinna's investigation of her history. Inevitably, that meant Magda would be confronted with awkward details from the past. Theoretically Jay could wait till she was forced to defend herself, but reaction was never as powerful as revelation. Better that what Magda heard first was Jay's version rather than Corinna's. But she wanted to pick her moment. A romantic setting, good food and wine, nothing to get up for in the morning. That was the way to do it.

But the luxury of choice was stripped from her just as she was preparing to leave the office. Her private phone chimed a text message alert. Expecting it to be Magda, Jay picked the phone up eagerly. Instead, it was the last name she wanted to see on the screen. Beneath that dreaded name, the opening words of the text: Charlie Flint's not giving up. Tomorrow she's going . . . Impatient, Jay summoned the full message: Tomorrow she's going to Roker. And we both know what's there to be found, don't we? Time to take care of business?

Jay stared at the screen as if the power of her gaze could transform the words into something innocuous. It was too late now for careful plans. It would have to be tonight. There would be no champagne to celebrate the booking of the removal team, no cheerful negotiation of wardrobe space and bookshelf allocation. No matter how carefully Jay constructed the version of her life she was going to deliver to Magda, it was going to alter their relationship profoundly. If she didn't hit the right note, tomorrow morning could easily find her cancelling the removal team Anne had just organised. The truth, certainly. But not the whole truth and nothing but the truth. That would be terminal.

Jay pressed the intercom and spoke to her PA. 'Anne, I need dinner delivered to the house. Get me my usual deli order, with extra artichoke hearts and a baguette instead of ciabattas. I'm leaving now but I need to walk, so any time after six is fine.' Magda wouldn't be home before seven; having dinner delivered would free Jay to plan what she was going to say.

She took the long way home, making a detour down to the river so she could let the rhythm of the water calm her anxiety. The low grey sky and congested air seemed to flatten the surface, giving the river a reptilian appearance, its deep hypnotic swells the forward motion of a giant slow-worm. It seemed inevitable, inexorable yet strangely relaxing. By the time she arrived home, Jay's restless agitation had passed, leaving her determined that the evening would unfold in her choice of direction.

Back home, she leaned on the balcony with a glass of red wine till the delivery arrived. Then she carefully arranged the food on the granite breakfast bar, making the array of meat, cheese and vegetables as attractive as possible. It was the kind of task Jay enjoyed; to an observer, it appeared she was giving it her full care and attention, but in truth, it left enough of her mind clear to untangle the thorniest of problems. Once she was satisfied with the look of the collation, she lay face down on the floor and did a series of McKenzie stretches to keep her lower back supple and free from pain. Too much tension, she knew from experience, would exact its price in pain later unless she took steps to prevent it. The last thing she wanted was for Magda to start thinking she'd hooked up with an old crock.

It was just after seven when Magda returned. 'Please tell me there's a bottle open,' she groaned as she walked into the kitchen.

'Open, aerated and at the perfect temperature,' Jay said, pouring her a glass. Magda hugged her from behind, nuzzling her neck, then reached round her for the wine.

'Perfect,' she said, taking a sip. 'And what a glorious spread. All I've had since breakfast is a slice of an eight-year-old's birthday cake.' She stretched for the olives. 'Mmm. You are the woman of my dreams.' She nibbled a black olive and jumped on to the stool next to Jay. 'How was your day?'

'This is the best part of it,' Jay said, passing Magda a

plate. She went to the fridge for a bowl of salad leaves then tossed them in olive oil from a bottle that had cost more than vintage champagne.

'The salad or me?' Magda teased.

Jay took a baby beetroot leaf from the bowl and savoured it, frowning. 'Definitely the salad.'

Magda laughed. 'You do have good taste.'

'Anne booked the removal firm for next Tuesday,' Jay said, sitting down again and piling food on her plate. 'They'll pack clothes, books, CDs, toiletries, all the personal stuff basically. Anything you don't want left for tenants, like good glassware or art, sort it out before then and they'll bring that too.'

Magda leaned over and kissed Jay's ear. 'You make everything so easy.'

'Money makes everything so easy,' Jay said wryly. 'There's not much in the practical realm that can't be sorted with the application of a wedge of cash.'

'It's not that simple,' Magda said. 'Thanks to Philip, I can afford all sorts of things – and I hope you're going to give me the bill for this, by the way – but what you do is the organising, which is the really hard bit.'

'Thanks. But arranging things for you makes me happy. Truly.' She stroked Magda's hair, letting her fingers stray down to the tender skin beneath her ear. Magda shivered with pleasure. 'Now eat. You need to keep your strength up.'

Magda giggled. 'No kidding.' For a while they concentrated on eating, their conversation focused on the delights of their food; the intensity of a sundried tomato, the subtlety of a grilled artichoke heart, the nuttiness of a prosciutto and the pungency of a cheese. For both women, the sharing of food had quickly taken a place at the heart of their life together. Each had an appetite for the sensual pleasure of good food; both would rather go without than eat rubbish. 'I'll happily eat food that's inexpensive,' Jay had once told an interviewer. 'But I won't eat food that's cheap. It ends up costing a lot more than money.'

Finally Magda polished off the last sliver of chargrilled red pepper and sighed. 'That was bliss. Let me sort out the leftovers and the dishwasher, you go and relax. Monday night, *University Challenge*, right?'

Another excuse to delay, Jay thought. And then there would be something else, she was sure. Before she knew it, it would be too late to begin tonight. And if Charlie Flint managed to find what nobody else ever had in Roker, it would be too late for ever. 'I need to talk to you,' she said, ignoring Magda's attempts to shoo her away from the clearing up.

Magda stopped scraping leftover salad into the bin and gave Jay a worried look. 'What's wrong?'

'Let's finish in here, then we'll sit down.'

'That sounds ominous,' Magda said.

Jay knew a push when she heard it, but she wasn't about to yield. They'd do this her way. 'We'll be done here in no time,' she said, loading dirty crockery into the dishwasher. People sometimes wondered why a woman as wealthy as she was did her own kitchen chores. For Jay, it was a tiny trade-off in return for the privacy she retained. She couldn't imagine having the conversation she was about to have with her lover if there was another living soul under her roof.

They cleared up in record time and Jay sat back down at the breakfast bar, this time gesturing to Magda to sit opposite. 'This is a hard thing for me to talk to you about,' Jay said, folding her hands together and meeting Magda's worried eyes.

'There's nothing you can't tell me,' Magda said, her words more certain than her voice.

If only. Jay spoke softly, her voice sorrowful, her face serious. 'I think I've found out why your mother banished me all those years ago. And why she is so hostile to the idea of us being together. And it's nothing to do with me being gay.'

Surprise widened Magda's eyes and straightened her back. 'What do you mean? What else could it be?'

Jay gave a twisted smile, her eyebrows steepled in apology. 'This is not a joke, OK? This is really what she thinks.' She waited. Magda frowned in puzzlement. 'Your mother thinks I'm a murderer.'

Magda's mouth fell open in incredulity. 'A murderer?'

'Better still, she thinks I've done it more than once. She thinks I'm kind of a serial killer.' Jay smiled and shrugged, spreading her hands in a gesture of baffled innocence.

Magda stuttered and spluttered, finally managing to get coherent words out. 'A serial killer? You? This is crazy. Why are you saying this? How can you think that?'

'I'm not the problem here, sweetheart. Corinna's the one who's got the crazy notions, not me.'

Magda shook her head as if to dislodge something unpleasant. She ran her hands over her face and through her hair. 'I've never heard anything so . . . so . . . so ridiculous. Where has this come from, this mad, stupid idea?'

Jay sighed. 'Let me try and tell it from the beginning.'

'You think that'll make any more sense of it? Jay, I feel like I've fallen down a rabbit hole and everything's gone *Alice in Wonderland*.'

'It's not exactly been easy for me either. I'm the one who's supposed to be the psychopathic multiple murderer, after all.'

'Of course, I'm sorry, it's just so mad. I'm listening, I'm listening.' Magda shook her head, disbelieving.

Jay poured them both some more wine. 'This all goes back to when I was running for JCR President. My main opponent was a rower called Jess Edwards. Just before the election, she had an accident. Early in the morning, she was at the boathouse on her own. She hit her head on the jetty and fell in the water and drowned. It was an accident, pure and simple. There was an inquest, accidental death. It never occurred to me that anyone would think anything different.' Jay rubbed her forehead with her fingertips. 'What I never knew at the time was that Corinna saw someone in the meadow around the time Jess died. In the dark and the morning mist, she thought it was me.' She gave a dry laugh that was more like a cough. 'She thought I'd killed Jess Edwards so I would get to be JCR President.'

Magda's face was screwed up in an expression of bewildered incredulity. 'She thought you're the kind of person who could kill somebody? And for something so pathetic?'

'That's the hard part to believe. That it was so easy for her to think so badly of me.' Jay bit her lip and looked downcast.

'That's the hard part? Jay, I'm struggling to find the easy part here. You're saying my mother thought you'd killed somebody. But she didn't say anything about it? She didn't call the police? Surely . . . I mean, why would you think that and not do anything about it?'

'It's insane, isn't it? But you've got to remember this was seventeen years ago, and I'm only just hearing about it for the first time. So all I've got to go on is what I've been told. Which isn't much. I don't know why she didn't go to the police, but what she did instead was cut me out of her life. And by extension, your life.'

'I can't believe I'm hearing this. The whole thing is completely mad. It's like a parallel universe. You say this is the first you've heard about this. Who told you? Did Corinna accuse you? Or what?'

Jay shook her head wearily. 'No. I wish she had. To tell you the truth, I wish she'd gone to the police.' She spoke with a vehemence it would be hard to doubt. 'Then this could all have been cleared up years ago. Whoever she saw, it wasn't me. She punished me for a crime I didn't commit.'

'So if it wasn't Corinna, who did tell you?'

'I had a phone call today from someone I used to know. This old friend knows a psychiatrist called Charlie Flint.'

'Charlie Flint? She was at my mother's house last Saturday. Remember? I told you about her. She's a dyke, she was really kind to me.'

Jay gave a mirthless smile. It took all the warmth from her face, turning it into a dangerous, sardonic mask. 'Exactly. She was really kind to you because she's the person your mother has asked to investigate me.'

Magda clamped her hands to the side of her head and pressed her fingers into her scalp. 'This just gets worse.

You're saying Charlie was kind to me because she's spying on us?'

'Not us. Me. According to my source, your mother wants to split us up. So she's set Charlie the task of digging into my past and proving I'm a serial killer. So when she reveals the awful truth, you'll run a mile.'

Magda laughed, an off-kilter sound that had nothing to do with joy. 'So who the fuck are you supposed to have killed? Apart from this rower?'

Jay ticked them off on her fingers. 'First, Jess. Then Kathy. My former business partner. I told you about that.'

'The climbing accident? But you had no choice. That wasn't murder. You told me, the judge said you did the only thing you could to save yourself. No way was it murder.'

'I know. But Charlie Flint spent the weekend on Skye, apparently trying to prove otherwise.' Jay drank some wine and shuddered. 'It's horrible, the idea that I could kill Kathy deliberately. She was my friend, for God's sake. I know we didn't always see eye to eye in business, but you don't throw someone off a bloody mountain for that.' She made a derisive sound. 'Besides, it's not exactly a reliable way of killing someone. People sometimes live to tell the tale when they come off a mountain. If I was the killing kind, I'd like to think I've got the brains to pick a better way of doing it.' She rubbed her eyes with one hand, as if brushing a tear away. 'Kathy. Unbelievable.'

'That's horrible,' Magda said, reaching out for Jay's free hand and squeezing it tight.

'And then there's Ulf Ingemarsson,' Jay said. 'At least he was actually murdered. Though not by me, obviously.'

'Who's that? I've never heard of him. Or her.'

'Ulf Ingemarsson was a Swedish programmer who had an idea very similar to 24/7. Back before we launched, we talked to him about licensing the software he was developing. It would have worked well with what we had in mind. But we couldn't agree terms. A bit later, he was murdered in the course of a burglary in the Spanish villa where he was on holiday. That's what the Spanish police say.' As anger seeped into her voice, Jay's narrative gained momentum. 'They couldn't pinpoint the exact day he died, but my diary was crammed with appointments all that week. Like I said, this was back before we launched and I was desperately trying to get all my ducks in a row. I didn't have time to nip off to some mountain village in Spain and knock off the so-called opposition. Who wasn't actually opposition because he didn't have the business nous or the travel contacts to make it work.' Jay threw up her hands in exasperation.

Magda frowned. 'So how did you get dragged in? If the police said it was a burglary?'

'Ingemarsson had a girlfriend who's developed an obsession about 24/7. She thinks either I killed him or I had him killed for his programs. Because Kathy was the IT brain behind doitnow.com and she wasn't around any more. So obviously I was going to have to steal the expertise,' she said sarcastically. 'Like Vinny Fitz couldn't write code or something. Bloody ridiculous. So the girlfriend keeps trying to get a prosecution or a civil case off the ground against me, but she's never got past the first hurdle. It's a nonsense from start to finish.'

'I don't understand. How would my mother get this crazy stuff into her head?'

Jay took another bottle of red from the wine store and opened it as she spoke. 'None of this is secret. On the face of it, it looks as if people who come between me and what I want have a nasty habit of dying. Of course, that doesn't take into account all the people who have thwarted me and lived to tell the tale.' Her smile was crooked, her eyes narrowed. 'I didn't kill anybody, Magda, but there have been rumours. Especially about Kathy and Ulf Ingemarsson. Dig deep enough on the internet and you'll always find conspiracy theories about all sorts of shit. Given that she already believed I'd killed Jess, I guess Corinna felt motivated to do the digging.'

Magda groaned. 'I can't believe this is my mother we're talking about. If she's got an issue with my lover, I'm the person she should be talking to, not some virtual stranger. I don't understand what's going on here.'

Jay drank some wine and closed her eyes. 'I imagine she's scared for you.' She opened her eyes and fixed Magda with a stare. 'Because there's one more death she's trying to pin on me.'

She saw dread dawn on Magda's face. 'Oh no. No. That would be . . .' She looked as if she would burst into tears. 'Not Philip. Tell me she doesn't think you killed Philip.'

Jay nodded. 'I'm afraid so. Ironic, isn't it? He was almost certainly killed when we were together. You're my alibi. Though it wouldn't carry much weight these days, not now you're sleeping with me. Thank God the court believed Paul and Joanna were guilty. Otherwise your bloody, bloody mother would probably be down the police station demanding they arrest me.' The sudden overspill of bitterness caught Jay by surprise. She'd managed to keep

474

the lid nailed down on her rage thus far, but it was threatening to break free now. And she couldn't afford that. Exposing Magda to the full flood of her fulminating fury would only scare her. Maybe even make her wonder whether there was a kernel of truth in what her mother was suggesting.

Magda jumped to her feet. 'I'm going to call her right now. She's got to put a stop to this. It's outrageous. It's slander, for fuck's sake.'

Quick on her feet, Jay intercepted her, grabbing her wrists in a hold that was strong but not rough. 'No,' she said softly. 'No, Magda. It'll just make things worse. I'm not trying to start a war between you and your family.'

'She's the one starting a war. I'm not having this, Jay. I won't have somebody sneaking around trying to smear your reputation.' Magda tried to pull free, but Jay held firm.

'Please, Magda. Leave it. What I told you, it wasn't intended to make you take sides. I know you love me. It's because I trust you that I was able to tell you all this.' She released one wrist and pulled Magda close. She could feel their hearts beating in counterpoint. Her body earthed the tension in Magda; she could feel her body soften. 'The only reason I've told you is so you know the truth. Corinna's going to find nothing against me because there's nothing to find because I didn't murder anybody.'

'But, Jay—'

'Ssh. She'll let it lie if she's got any sense.' Jay smooched half a dozen tiny kisses against Magda's mouth. Reassurance. 'But if she doesn't . . . well, you already know the truth. It's not going to come as a shock to you.'

Better to feel betrayed by Corinna than me. 'I know this has been a horrible shock for you. But we're OK, you and me. Charlie Flint can look where she likes, talk to whoever she fancies talking to. But she can't hurt us.'

'But what if . . .' Magda leaned into Jay, who released her other wrist. They stood tight together, arms wrapped around each other, heat to heat.

'What if nothing. I told you, there's nothing to find.'

Magda pulled back so she could look into Jay's face. 'There was nothing to find against Joanna and Paul either. Till you made something.'

It was a terrible, chilling moment. Until that point, it hadn't actually occurred to Jay that Corinna Newsam might be as ruthless as she was. Jay could feel her face freeze. For a moment, she could think of nothing to say. 'Corinna wouldn't do that,' she said at last. 'She wouldn't know where to start.'

Magda's eyes were wide with fear. 'She wouldn't, you're right. But Charlie Flint might.'

12

Tuesday

By the time Charlie set off that morning, only a little of her optimism had been knocked out of her. To her surprise, when she'd returned the night before, Maria had been less than enthusiastic about her trip to the North East. 'I think you should wait a day or two,' she'd said when Charlie had fallen into bed beside her. 'Look at you. You're exhausted. All that driving at the weekend and today you've been to London and Oxford. There's no rush, Charlie. Whatever happened in Roker happened twenty years ago. A couple of days is not going to make any difference.'

'I know that, but I don't want to lose momentum,' Charlie said, snuggling up to Maria, taking comfort in the familiar curves and angles of her body.

'If taking a two-day break means you lose momentum, it doesn't say much for your enthusiasm,' Maria said drily.

'Besides, there's always the risk that Corinna's going to sleep on it and decide she's not as convinced as she thought she was. If she confronts Magda and Jay finds out what's been going on, she might head up to the North East herself to make sure I don't find anything she doesn't want found.'

Maria jerked away from her and pushed herself upright, horror on her face. 'She'd come after you?'

'That's not what I said. And it's not what I meant.' The last thing she needed was Maria choosing now to become over-protective. Charlie rolled her eyes. 'I just meant she'd make sure there was nothing to be found. That's all.'

'This is the woman that you and Nick think is a killer. According to you, she kills people who get in her way. And getting in her way is exactly what you're doing. Christ, Charlie, how can you even think about going up there if there's the slightest chance of her coming after you?'

'She's not going to be coming after me, Maria. For a start, too many people know that I've been looking into the deaths in her past. Only a complete fool would think they could bump me off and not be at the heart of a massive and highly focused investigation. And Jay Stewart is nobody's fool.' Charlie put her arm around Maria and gave her a squeeze. 'You worry too much.'

'No,' Maria said, cross now. 'I don't worry too much. I don't worry nearly enough about you. If there's even a chance of Jay Stewart turning up in the North East, I don't want you going there. Death seems to follow her around. Even if she's not coming after you, knowing my luck you'd get swept away by a tsunami or something.'

'You don't get tsunamis in Tyne and Wear,' Charlie said, laughing at the thought. 'Nothing bad is going to happen, I promise.'

'You're determined, aren't you? There's nothing I can say that will make you change your mind?'

Charlie shook her head. 'I'm afraid not. I've got this under my skin. I need to follow it through to the end.'

'So why not wait till the weekend and I can go with you? Jay's not going to come after you if there's someone else around, is she?'

Charlie felt a surge of warmth towards Maria. Right now, the thought of being done with her to make way for Lisa was incomprehensible. If she could stay away from Lisa, if she could refuse to feed the appetite for her, she could get past this, Charlie was convinced. Maria would never know. She'd never have to comprehend the world of hurt Charlie had considered visiting on her. 'You're very sweet,' she said. 'And I love you for it. But I can't wait till the weekend. I don't know yet who I'm going to need to talk to, but chances are there will be places I need to go that won't be open at the weekend. Local paper offices, for example. Look, I'll be fine. You know me, babe. I don't take stupid risks.' She rubbed her head against Maria's chest.

'That's what I always thought,' Maria said. 'But when I hear you talk like this, I'm not so sure.' She stroked Charlie's hair. 'I love you. I don't want anything bad to happen to you.'

'And it won't. You think if it was that dangerous Nick would let me go? He knows what I'm planning and he hasn't tried to stop me.' Well, it was mostly true.

And so Maria had given in. But it had taken the edge off Charlie's pleasure with her brainwave. She was just past York when Nick called. 'Morning, Charlie,' he said cheerily. 'Got your message last night. You sure you don't want to wait till I've got a day off so I can come with you?'

'Nice of you to ask, Nick. But I don't think Corinna's going to rush into confronting Jay. So there's no reason to be worried, as I keep telling Maria. Besides, I'm already on the road.'

Nick chuckled. 'I wasn't thinking of Jay pursuing you like an avenging Fury. I just thought the local lads might be more helpful if you had a man with a warrant card with you.'

'You're probably right. But I'm just crossing the t's and dotting the i's.' Charlie pulled over into the middle lane where the driving was a little less hazardous. Even with hands-free, it wasn't straightforward to multitask when the conversation required concentration. 'I don't really expect to find any fresh evidence in a twenty-year-old missing persons case. All it was – I was talking about Jay with a friend of mine, Lisa Kent. She's a therapist – she runs NV, the self-help seminar company.'

'I've heard of them, yes.'

'Well, she used to know Jay years ago, when they were both undergraduates. Anyway, she said something about Jay's issues all going back to her mother. Nothing revelatory – if I'd thought about it, I'd have said exactly the same thing, it's basic. But in the context of what I'd been thinking about, it just clicked and I thought, "Of course. And if she is a killer, it's entirely possible her supposedly missing mother was the first victim." So I thought I'd take a look.'

'So do many of your clients kick off by murdering their mothers?'

It was Charlie's turn for the dark chuckle. 'I think it happens a lot more than we know about. Anyway, did you manage to find someone for me to talk to?'

'Like you said, it was twenty years ago. But that has an upside as well as the obvious downside that there's not likely to be any senior officers still serving.' He paused expectantly.

Charlie obliged. 'What's the upside?'

'It's been so long, there's not likely to be anything sensitive in there. And since you are an accredited Home Office expert witness—'

'You can't say that. I'm suspended,' Charlie protested.

'Damn, I knew there was something I forgot. It's OK, Charlie, they couldn't give a shit, not over case papers from 1990. If anybody calls you on it, tell them I've got the memory retention of a goldfish. Look, you'll be fine. It's not like you don't know how to behave in a cop shop.'

'So they're expecting me?'

'That's right. Because it's such an old case, the paperwork isn't held at the local office or at HQ. They've got a dedicated storage facility near force headquarters at Ponteland. I'll text you the address and the directions. The woman who runs it is a retired sergeant. Hester Langhope is her name. She wants you to give her an hour's notice. I'll text you her number as well.'

'Thanks, Nick. I owe you a big drink.'

'You do. By the way, how did it go with Corinna?'

'I took an executive decision to bullshit her. I told her there was no evidence because Jay hadn't done anything.'

There was a long pause, then Nick said, 'It's just as well you don't do this for a living. I don't think private investigators are meant to make it up as they go along. I thought we'd decided that she probably had done all of them? We just didn't have enough evidence?'

'We did. But "not proven" isn't a good verdict to deliver to someone who's already said she'd rather take the law into her own hands than sit quietly while her daughter shacks up with a woman she considers the lesbian equivalent of Hannibal Lecter. So until I get anything approaching solid evidence, the sane thing is to keep lying to Corinna.' Charlie slowed to let a white van cut in front of her as the three lanes narrowed to two.

'And you're comfortable with Magda Newsam under Jay's roof?'

'You sound like Corinna. I don't think Magda's at risk. It sounds like they're besotted with each other. Besides, Jay doesn't do crimes of passion. Her murders are strictly functional. They're about getting what she wants. And right now, she's got that. Come on, Nick, you allegedly did a degree in psychology, you should be as sure of this as I am.'

'I suppose,' he said. 'OK. I'm texting you that stuff now. Call me when you've done your digging.'

Charlie quickly understood how Hester Langhope had ended up spending her retirement running the evidence and records-storage facility for Northumbria Police. Within minutes of meeting her, it was obvious that she married terrifying efficiency with the sort of personal warmth that makes people want to sit down and unburden themselves of their woes. Not that she looked motherly. She was tall and rangy with the kind of haircut and make-up that require minimal commitment in the morning. Her jeans were clean and pressed, her Northumbria Police polo shirt spotless and her trainers gleamed in the fluorescent light. Though she was clearly in her late fifties, Langhope still moved like an athlete.

When Charlie arrived, Langhope was at the front counter to greet her. After inspecting her ID, she led Charlie into the bowels of a warehouse crammed with shelving jammed with file boxes. As they walked, Langhope asked about Charlie's journey, with every appearance of genuine interest. She led the way to a bare office at the far side of the warehouse. It contained a table, two chairs, a file box. Langhope opened the box and presented Charlie with the lid. For a moment she was baffled, till she realised that taped to the inside was a log of who had inspected it. 'You'll need to sign for it,' Langhope said. 'You'll see the history of reviews. After the investigation was mothballed, it had an annual review for the first five years. Then every two years for the next six. Now it's every five years. You'll see the last one was 2008.' She tapped it with her biro. 'NFA. No further action.'

'I'm not really expecting to find anything,' Charlie said.

'DS Nicolaides said you're looking for possible victims of a serial offender?'

'That's right. Jenna Stewart fits the profile. I want to see if there are any possible intersections. It's a long shot.'

Langhope smiled. 'But sometimes they're the ones that pay off. I'll leave you to it. I'm sorry, but I have to lock you in for security reasons.' She pointed to a button on the wall by the door. 'If you need anything – coffee, toilet, to go outside for a smoke – just press the bell and someone will come and fetch you.'

Charlie was impressed. Most of the evidence stores she had been in took the view that if you were in the building, you were trustworthy. Experience had shown how empty that confidence had too often been. But nobody was going to walk out the door with Hester Langhope's treasures. Not unless they'd signed for them first. With a sigh, Charlie withdrew the stack of papers that filled the box and set to work.

What it boiled down to was this. Everything had seemed normal in the Calder household on the morning of Friday, 11 October 1990. Howard Calder had left to catch the bus to work as usual at five past eight. Jay – or Jennifer, as she had been then – had dawdled over breakfast, complaining of toothache. Her mother had called the dentist at half past eight, arranging an emergency appointment for twenty past nine. Jenna had written a note for her daughter to hand in at school to account for her lateness, then given her bus fare to make sure she arrived at the dentist on time. That was the last Jay saw of her mother. After the dental appointment, Jay had returned home because she felt dizzy and sick. The house was empty, but she thought nothing of it because her mother had been working as a volunteer with a project doing up a block of old people's flats nearby. She'd gone to bed and slept the day away.

When Howard Calder returned from work, he was surprised to find only Jay at home. Jenna had never failed to be back from her volunteer work in time to prepare the family's evening meal. He and Jay waited till six, then Howard walked over to the restoration project. He found the building locked up and deserted. It took him the best part of an hour to track down the warden of the flats, who told him the work was now complete. Only a handful of volunteers had been there that day, putting the finishing touches to a couple of the flats. He recognised Jenna from Howard's description, but had no recollection of seeing her that day. She'd been working last on flat 4C, and he thought that had been finished the day before.

Howard returned home, but Jenna still hadn't turned up or phoned. He decided to call the police to report her missing. Charlie imagined the officer taking the call. Another wife who'd had enough of a husband who couldn't believe she'd have the cheek to walk out on him. The officer had suggested Howard should check to see if any of his wife's personal items were missing. At that point, it hadn't even occurred to Howard that Jenna might have left him.

It didn't take him long to work out what was missing. A small suitcase, some underwear and a couple of blouses, toothbrush and toiletries, her passport, birth certificate and a framed photograph of Jay, aged six. All you'd need to walk away from a life and start over, Charlie thought. It was amazing how little you could get away with.

The police weren't very interested, and Charlie couldn't blame them. But Howard was persistent. He tracked down the other volunteers at the project and learned that his wife had been friendly with the project manager, a Dutchman called Rinks van Leer. Van Leer had returned to Holland but was due to begin a new restoration scheme in

York a week later. Howard went to York, expecting to find Jenna, but she wasn't there and van Leer denied that she had left Roker with him.

So Howard had gone back to the police. This time, they took a little more notice. It was unusual for a woman to abandon a child, even a sixteen-year-old, without a word and without any obvious boyfriend to go to. But their inquiries soon hit a brick wall. They spoke to their counterparts in Holland but there was no evidence that Jenna had ever been there and she'd certainly not been with van Leer, who had been staying with friends in Leyden for most of the week. None of the other volunteers admitted to having seen Jenna on the Friday she'd disappeared. Charlie had the distinct impression that Jenna Calder would soon have drifted off the police radar had it not been for Howard's weekly visits to the station demanding an update. He was adamant that while she might have gone away willingly, she must have been murdered because nothing else could explain her silence. After a year of this, the file noted tersely, 'Mr Calder was advised that the case was no longer a priority and that if there were any developments he would be contacted.' The case reviews had been thorough but routine. There were no developments.

The file also noted tersely that Calder's stepdaughter had moved out two weeks after her mother's departure to lodge with a teacher from her school. It noted Jay's belief that her mother had run away with a boyfriend because her stepfather was 'an oppressive bastard'. She believed her mother's silence arose from a determination not to give Calder the slightest clue as to her whereabouts. An officer had noted, 'Jennifer seems reconciled to the idea.

She does not blame her mother and claims she would have done the same thing in her shoes.'

Charlie sat back, digesting what she'd read. From a police perspective, there was nothing suspicious about Jenna Calder's disappearance. Women and men walked out on their families all the time without warning. Books had been written about the impact of a parent or a partner cutting themselves adrift from their previous lives. Charlie had interviewed people on both sides of the divide – the abandoned and the abandoners – and she felt deep sympathy for both groups. It happened more often than most people liked to believe possible. So it wasn't surprising that it had been regarded as a relatively insignificant missing persons case.

But if you looked at it from the perspective of someone investigating Jay Stewart's past for possible murder victims, the case took on a different appearance. Because the one thing that leapt out from the pile of pages was that the version of that Friday morning that appeared in *Unrepentant* was very different from the one contained in the police records. According to what Charlie had read, Jay had gone to the flats to confront her mother and Rinks. But the building had been locked up and the caretaker had told her the work was finished. She'd gone home, convinced she and her mother would be leaving Roker behind for a new life with Rinks. But she hadn't found Jenna and she'd never seen her again.

Charlie recognised that Jay might have tweaked reality for a more dramatic narrative, though in this instance, it didn't seem to have improved the quality of the story. Relating the visit to the dentist might have slowed the pace, however. And of course, the great advantage of the version in the memoir was that it gave Jay a more dynamic role. Rather than going to the dentist and coming home, where her mother never returned, it inserted her into the narrative, taking her to the very site of her illicit meetings with Rinks.

The crucial point remained that Jay had no alibi for the day her mother disappeared. She'd gone to the dentist, but she hadn't carried on to school. She claimed she'd been in bed all day following her visit to the dentist, but there was no corroboration. Come to that, there was no evidence that she'd actually been to the dentist at all since nobody had thought to check. If you discounted Jay's evidence to the police or to her readership, there was no reason to believe that Jenna had ever left the house.

'Get a grip,' Charlie said aloud as she replaced the paperwork in the box. Even if Jay had killed her mother in the family home, it was beyond belief that a sixteen-year-old could have disposed of the body without a trace before Howard Calder got home from work. Charlie knew from her own experience of dealing with killers that getting rid of a corpse is far from simple, especially in a country as densely populated as the UK. Unless Charlie could come up with another scenario, Jay remained off the hook.

She rang the bell and waited for Hester Langhope to release her. There was only one other person who might have some insight to offer. But Charlie didn't hold out much hope of Howard Calder shedding light on the mysterious disappearance of his wife. If he'd had anything to say, he'd have said it years before to the police. But at least she had an address, thanks to the police files.

As she drove back down the A1 towards Roker, Charlie called Nick. 'Not quite a waste of time,' she told him. 'There's a discrepancy between what she says in her book and the police statement.' She outlined the problem. 'But it's academic, really. Because either way Jay doesn't have an alibi from about ten in the morning till five in the afternoon.'

Nick was straight on to the problem. 'So where's the body? She was a kid. She wouldn't have the strength or the knowledge to get rid of it.'

'My conclusion exactly. But since I'm up here, I might as well pay Howard Calder a visit. You never know, he might have the mythical piece of knowledge whose significance he's never understood.'

Nick laughed. 'You've been reading too many bad novels.'

'Guilty as charged. I know it's a long shot, but any news from the phone company?'

'No joy so far. I'll let you know as soon as I hear anything. Good luck with Howard.'

As she passed the Angel of the North, its massive aircraft wings spread in benediction, Charlie thought it was more than luck she needed.

13

There was nothing prepossessing about the house where Jay Stewart had spent her adolescence. It sat in the middle of a long terraced street of dirty red brick, neither the best nor the worst on view. The black door and white paintwork were grubby, a combination of city grime and tiny grains of sand carried on the wind from the nearby beach. The curtains seemed to droop, as if all the spirit had gone from them, and the light that showed behind the fanlight above the door was the discouraging pale yellow of a bulb whose wattage was too low for the space it had to illuminate. If this was how it had been twenty years ago, Charlie wasn't surprised that Jay had chosen to get out as soon as she could.

She rang the doorbell, which gave a loud angry buzz. As she waited, she looked around. Four o'clock on a cold Tuesday afternoon, and not a soul stirring. No kids playing football in the road, no youths hanging around on a street corner smoking, no knots of pensioners gossiping. No sense at all of the lives being lived behind those doors. It didn't feel like a community, which surprised her. Maybe it was just because she didn't know the area, didn't know how to read the signs.

The door opened behind her and she spun round. The man framed by the door looked irritated, thick grey eyebrows drawn down over deep-set eyes magnified by his steel-rimmed glasses. He seemed to be an assembly of sharp angles – thin face, nose like a blade, skinny shoulders, bony hands – all compressed in a tight, narrow space. He had a full head of grey hair, cropped so close at the sides that Charlie could see the greyish pink flesh of his scalp. His skin was pale and lined, the contours those of a face that seldom smiled. 'Are you the woman from the council?' he demanded, his voice still strong and overbearing.

Charlie smiled. No point in beating about the bush with this man. 'No. I'm Dr Charlotte Flint. I work with the police. I wondered if I might talk to you about the disappearance of your wife.'

His scowl deepened. 'A doctor? From the police? I've never heard anything like that before.'

'I'm what's called an offender profiler. I help them build cases against people suspected of serious offences like rape and murder.'

'Have you found Jenna? Is that what you're trying to say?' His eyebrows lifted and he looked almost happy.

'I'm sorry, Mr Calder. We haven't found your wife. What I'm doing just now is examining some cases where the missing person fits some of the criteria for a known offender to see if we might be able to clear up some out-standing disappearances.' She gave a quick smile, hoping the lie would stand up to doorstep scrutiny.

Calder frowned. 'What do you mean, criteria? What sort of criteria?'

'I'm sorry, I can't tell you that. It's confidential. Possible contempt of court down the line, you see?' Wrap things up in enough verbiage and people would fall for anything. She hoped.

'I'll need to see some ID before I let you in,' he said, thrusting his jaw out defiantly.

'No problem.' Charlie produced her Home Office ID.

'You've come a long way,' Calder said, opening the door and signalling she should enter. The hallway was as bare and cold as the street outside. Plain varnished floorboards without even a rug to enliven them, walls painted cream too long ago. There was a faint ancient smell of cooked meat. The room he showed her into was short on comfort. There was a wooden-framed three-piece suite that looked like it had been a G-plan copy back in the sixties. The cushions were thin and depressed. Half a dozen hard dining chairs stood against the wall. The only decoration was three elaborately embroidered samplers with biblical texts. Even from a distance, Charlie could see the work was exquisite. 'What beautiful samplers,' she said, stepping closer to one to take a look.

'My mother's work.' Calder spoke abruptly, as if the subject was already closed. He waved Charlie to a chair but didn't sit himself. Instead, he stood in front of the unlit gas fire, hands balled into fists in the pockets of his loose grey cardigan. There was no offer of tea or coffee. 'I must say,

I'm glad to see Jenna hasn't been completely forgotten by the police. The locals frankly couldn't care less.'

'It was the local police who suggested this might fit our other cases,' Charlie said. Small white lie, but Northumbria Police had been kind to her. They deserved the return of the compliment. 'I'm familiar with the circumstances of your wife's disappearance,' she added hastily, having little appetite for another rehearsal of the facts. 'I've seen the files. But you knew your wife better than anyone and I'm interested in your theory of what might have happened. What was your first reaction when you realised she wasn't home when she should be?'

His face twisted through pain to embarrassment. 'I know it sounds silly, but the only thing I could think was that she had been kidnapped.'

'You didn't think she might have been in an accident?'

He shook his head. 'I'd have been informed. Jenna always carried her handbag with her personal details.'

It was a curious thing to be so definite about, Charlie thought. 'But why would anyone kidnap your wife?'

'We belonged—' He caught himself. 'I belong to an evangelical Christian church. We campaign actively against the sin we see in our society. At the time of Jenna's disappearance, we were protesting vigorously against the opening of a homosexual bed and breakfast on the front here at Roker. We were gaining a groundswell of support. I wondered if she'd been kidnapped to make us back down. I thought then – and I still think now – that those creatures are capable of anything.'

Charlie always hated these moments where she couldn't

fight back against bigotry because drawing out the information was more important than taking on the prejudiced. Instead, she bit back her measured retort and said, 'But you had to abandon that theory when you discovered your wife had packed a bag?'

Calder chewed the corner of his lower lip. 'It appeared I could have been wrong,' he said.

'So what did you think then?'

He gave a short, sharp sigh. 'I didn't know what to think. As far as I was concerned, our marriage was as strong as it had ever been. I had no indication from Jenna that anything was wrong between us.' He looked up at the far corner of the room. 'But Jenna had not always been in the church. She had left behind her a life of terrible sin before she was born again in the blood of the lamb.'

'You think she went back to that life?'

His eyes slid over Charlie on their way across the room. 'Not from choice. But I've read things about the after-effects of drugs. That people can have flashbacks. Events that alter their perception of reality. I think she must have had something like that. Some sort of mental break-down.'

'And is that what you think now?'

He folded his arms tightly across his narrow chest. 'I think she's dead. I think she had some kind of breakdown that made her leave us. And then something else hap-pened. Someone killed her. Or the Devil spoke to her and persuaded her to kill herself. So she never had the chance to repent and return. What else makes sense?'

'You don't think she left with another man? To start a new life?' He said nothing, simply shaking his head, his mouth clamped in a thin tight line. 'She'd walked away from the past before, Mr Calder.'

'She wouldn't have left the child. She knew we didn't get along, me and Jennifer. She'd have made other arrangements. She'd have made sure Jennifer was sorted out properly.' He turned away and walked to the window, looking out into the street, fists leaning on the sill.

'I've read Jennifer's book,' Charlie said.

He whirled round, his face animated with scorn. 'That disgusting abomination? She had the gall to send me a copy. I threw it in the bin. I won't have the words of Satan in the house.'

'So you won't be aware that Jennifer's account of that last morning was different from the version in the police files?'

'How could I? I wouldn't sully my eyes with that claptrap. Let me tell you, Dr Flint, I wish I had the money to take her to court. That book is a filthy libel from start to finish. So it doesn't surprise me that you've caught her out in a lie. I've prayed over that girl's soul night and day, and that's how she repaid me. But what can you expect from a pervert?'

'She says you and her mother were trying to arrange a marriage for her. Is that the sort of thing you had in mind when you said Jennifer would have made arrangements?'

'Exactly,' he said, triumphant now. 'We were already making plans. Plans, I might say, that would have saved Jennifer from this life of degradation that she's embarked on now. It wouldn't have been long before she was married. Even supposing Jenna had decided she wanted to go, she could have waited that little bit longer. She wouldn't have just run off on a whim. Not without another explanation.

495

Like a breakdown. It couldn't be another man. That could have waited, you see.'

'Jennifer wasn't at school that day,' Charlie said. 'Did you ever wonder if she knew more than she was letting on?'

Calder shook his head. 'Jenna was gone by the time she got back from the dentist. She took to her bed because she was feeling bad so she never noticed her mother wasn't back till I got home. I left her here while I went to check whether Jenna was still down at the Riverdale flats. But the place was empty and locked up. When I got hold of the warden, he said there had only been a couple of them there that day, finishing some stuff off. And he didn't think Jenna had been one of them. When I came home and told Jennifer, she was distraught. I could tell she was really upset. She wasn't putting it on. She was only sixteen, she wasn't that good an actress. You generally knew what Jennifer was feeling,' he added bitterly. 'She left us in no doubt about that.'

'That discrepancy I mentioned, between Jennifer's book and her statement, it's to do with the trip to the dentist. She never mentions the dentist. She says she went to the flat in the morning, only to find it was locked up and nobody was there. But you just said the caretaker told you there had been a couple of people there, finishing off. Why would there be these two different versions?' Charlie had initially dismissed the diverging stories. Now she wasn't so sure that was right.

'Because she's a little liar.' He looked as if he wanted to spit a bad taste from his mouth. 'Anything to make herself seem important. Trying to put herself in the spotlight. She was ruined by the time she pitched up here. If I'd had her from a baby, it would have been a different story. I don't believe she was at the flats that morning. She was at the dentist. Little liar.'

There didn't seem much point in persisting in the teeth of such vehemence. 'Jennifer seems to think her mother ran off with Rinks van Leer. Her old boyfriend.' Charlie kept her voice even and emotionless.

'She wasn't with him. I checked myself. And so did the police. Jennifer got that wrong. Fantasy and lies, all of it. I don't believe she even knew the man before she joined that project at the Riverdale flats. The other volunteers said as much. They were friendly, but nobody except Jennifer thought there was anything going on. But for whatever perverse reason, Jennifer wanted me to believe this man had come out of Jenna's past and spirited her away. Nonsense. Pernicious nonsense. But I expect nothing else from her. Not a word of gratitude for the years I clothed and fed her and put a roof over her head even though she was another man's child. I know my Christian duty.' He came to an abrupt halt, two spots of pink colour on his cheeks.

'I'm sure you do,' Charlie said, the words sticking in her throat. Unbidden, an old memory of Jay surfaced in her mind, standing on the fringe of some group at a party. Sensing Charlie's eyes on her, she'd glanced up, her face as wary as a strange dog on the edge of a clearing. With hindsight and experience, the circumspection that had always lurked at the back of the charisma made perfect sense. Growing up around this man, it couldn't have been easy to find a way to flourish. How many times had he tried to trample Jay's spirit into the dust? Had Jenna felt torn, or had she abdicated everything to the blood of the lamb? 'Was Jenna a gullible woman, would you say?'

'She had allowed others to have sway over her in the past, when she walked in the ways of sin. But after she accepted Jesus as her saviour, she was wholly a woman of God. Her faith was her rock. So she wouldn't have fallen for something that ran against her beliefs.'

Charlie nodded, pretending she was satisfied. 'Well, Mr Calder, I'm sorry to have wasted your time. It looks to me as if it's very unlikely that your wife was a victim of the man we're interested in.'

He bowed his head. 'Thank God for that. Against all the odds, I still pray that one day she will walk through that door, ready to be forgiven.'

Charlie stood up. 'I do so hope you're right,' she said, wishing with all her heart that Jenna had really run off with Rinks van Leer. Or anybody, really. Unfortunately, she couldn't quite bring herself to believe it. But she was done with Howard Calder. Wherever the answers to her questions lay, it wasn't in this shrivelled excuse for a home.

14

Whatever had happened in Roker twenty years before was buried deep, that much was certain. But having come all this way, Charlie couldn't resist taking a look at the place where Jenna Calder had held her secret trysts with her Dutchman. The Riverdale flats were only a mile from the Calder house, but they were down on the seafront. It felt as if they inhabited another world.

From a distance, Charlie could see a brown brick building with faintly art deco lines. Big windows looked out at the heavy swell of the sea. Not a bad place to see out your final years, she thought. But as she drew closer, she realised the place was less charming than it first appeared. A six-foot hoarding extended round the perimeter, and the ground-floor windows and entrance were boarded up. Charlie parked opposite, noticing a sign plastered across the hoarding: *Riverdale. Soon to be a new development of luxury seaview apartments.* And above that, an artist's impression of a generic modern block of flats, all glass and steel. If she'd come a few weeks later, this would have been a building site, all trace of the old Riverdale block gone for ever.

Charlie crossed the road and walked round the perimeter of the hoarding. At the back of the site, away from the road, a pair of gates were held together by a padlock and chain. Charlie shook the padlock, but it was properly fastened. There was some give in the gates; if she'd been the skinny type, like Lisa or Jay herself, she'd have maybe managed to squeeze through. But Charlie had too much padding for that sort of adventure. She walked on and to her surprise, as she rounded the corner, she saw that someone had forced the panels of the hoarding apart. They'd been propped against each other, but there was a clearly trodden mud slick that pointed the way to the breach.

Out of curiosity, Charlie separated the boards and stepped inside. A few yards of churned-up grass separated the hoarding from the flats. The back entrance was covered with a sheet of corrugated iron, but it was juddering in the wind. When she got closer, she could see that the nails fastening it to the frame had been pulled out around one corner and halfway up the side. It was possible to get inside by crouching down and pulling the iron sheet back.

Charlie took out her keys. Maria had given her a tiny but powerful torch at Christmas. Charlie hadn't seen the point but she'd fixed it to her keyring to humour Maria. She turned it on, surprised at how much light it delivered. She found herself in a hallway that smelled of damp, cigarettes and urine. A small scurry off ahead brought rats to mind, which made her think twice about going any further. 'Get a grip,' she told herself sternly. 'They're more afraid of you than you are of them.'

There were doors to either side of the hallway; 1D and 1E. She moved forward cautiously, noticing that the door of 1E was ajar. She pushed it open and shone her torch inside. A pile of crumpled beer cans, some strong cider bottles. Cigarette butts and pizza boxes. It looked more like teenagers than anything more sinister.

Round the corner, and there were the stairs. Solid, made of some kind of composite stone. Charlie climbed past the first floor and on up. As she approached the second floor, the stairwell grew appreciably lighter. She realised that only the windows on the first two floors were boarded up; on the second and third floors, light was still penetrating the building. Now she could see all the doors to the flats were open, the area round the locks bearing witness to blows from some kind of heavy hammer. Someone had clearly gone through the place checking if there was anything worth nicking.

The lock on 4C had given way to violence just like the others. Not quite sure why she was bothering with this, Charlie stepped inside the narrow hallway and continued to what had probably been the living room. It had spectacular views of the promenade and the beach, waves pounding now in a white foam. There was no furniture, but the carpet still held ancient indentations, a presumption of chairs, tables and sideboard. There was a gaping hole in the chimney breast where the fireplace had been and pale squares on the walls where pictures had hung. Charlie looked round the ghost of a room and tried to imagine what it had looked like.

It struck her that there was something odd about the proportions of the room. On one side of the chimney breast was a deep alcove lined with shelves. For books or ornaments, presumably. But there was no symmetry. The other side was flush with the chimney breast itself. At the bottom of the shelving, there was a small metal grid in the floor, where presumably the underfloor heating had vented. But there was no corresponding vent on the other side. It was peculiar, particularly for a period of architecture so obsessed with proportion and balance. Intrigued, Charlie walked out of the room and into the next-door room, to see if a previous occupant had made some alterations, perhaps to create a bedroom cupboard or extra space in a bathroom. But the room backing on to the living room was perfectly plain, completely lacking in recesses or cupboards.

Charlie went back and looked at the wall again. It was odd, no doubt about it. You wouldn't notice it once the room was furnished because it was the logical place for the TV. And there were indeed indentations on the carpet to indicate that's what had been there. But now the room was empty, it was definitely strange. She walked out of the flat and crossed the hall to 4D, which ought to be the mirror image of 4C.

And it was. Except that both sides of the chimney breast were occupied with shelves. This was definitely an anomaly.

Back in 4C, Charlie started tapping on the mystery wall. It didn't sound as solid as the other walls, but equally, it didn't sound completely hollow either. Somewhere in between, she thought. She stared at the wall for a long time, considering. The block was about to be demolished. It wasn't like she'd be damaging anything of value. On the other hand, why on earth was she even considering breaking down a false wall in a derelict flat?

Even as she chewed this over, she was walking back out of the room. The bedroom had been empty. The bathroom likewise. Not even a towel rail she could wrestle off the wall. The kitchen had been stripped of appliances, but in an attempt to remove a granite worktop, somebody had screwed up. Weakened by the sink cut-out, a half-metre chunk of granite had broken off. It was a dozen centimetres wide at the narrow end, about thirty-five at the other. A perfect Stone Age club. Charlie lifted it up and hefted it in her hand. Yes, she could take a decent swing with that.

There was something liberating about the thought of physical violence after the frustrations of the past couple of weeks. Charlie took up a two-fisted stance like a baseball hitter, side on to the false wall. Bending her knees, she raised the club and swung at the wall. With her full weight behind it, the granite hit with a soft crunch, splitting the floral wallpaper and making a sharp-edged depression. A second swing, more splitting paper and a bigger dent. Doggedly, Charlie kept swinging. By the fifth blow, it was clear that the wall was simply plasterboard covered in several layers of wallpaper. After eight or nine whacks with the granite, she broke through. The air that drifted out towards her had a stale, sweetish odour, but it wasn't unpleasant. Through the small hole she'd created at shoulder height there was nothing to be seen, so Charlie grasped the edge of the plasterboard and pulled with all her strength. A chunk came away in her hands, revealing a couple of shelves, one at chest height, the other at waist height. They appeared to be empty.

'Why would you do that?' Charlie said aloud. 'Why seal up a perfectly good set of bookshelves?' She gripped the bottom rim of the plasterboard, hands wide apart, and put her back into it. With a loud rip of wallpaper, most of the lower part of the false wall came loose, making Charlie stagger backwards at the sudden release. Steadying herself, she recovered her footing, looking at the gap she'd revealed.

And then she understood why.

15

The only mummies Charlie had ever seen had been in the Manchester Museum. And they'd been in glass cases. But this macabre relic wasn't some sanitised museum exhibit. Its connection to modern life was all too vivid – the faded tatters of contemporary clothing, the carry-on-sized suitcase rammed against the far wall. Charlie tried to concentrate on those superficialities rather than the all too human remains themselves. But the body demanded her attention.

The skin was dark brown, pulled tight over the bones. The soft tissue had desiccated, giving the head the appearance of a bizarre work of Brit Art – a skull covered in paper-thin leather, the teeth a gleaming grin, the eye sockets dark empty horrors, the hair still hanging lank and coarse. The limbs resembled beef jerky, muscles contracted and contorted into a parody of the foetal position.

At first, she couldn't make sense of what she was seeing.

Then she remembered the description of what Jenna Calder had been wearing on the day she disappeared. The rotted remains of denim jeans hung around her hips. The pink polyester blouse was almost intact, though discoloured where it had been pressed against the flesh. A brown raincoat was bundled under the mummy, its belt buckle clearly visible. The body might look like something that had been there for centuries, but Charlie was in no doubt that this was Jay Stewart's mother. 'Oh my God,' she said, taking an involuntary step backwards and letting go of the plasterboard she'd been clinging to. Without taking her eyes off her gruesome discovery, she reached into her pocket for her phone.

'I don't think so.'

The voice came from behind her. Recognising it, Charlie spun round, disbelief on her face, wanting her eyes to prove her ears wrong. 'Lisa?'

'Hand over the phone, Charlie.' Lisa came in from the hallway.

Charlie couldn't take in what she was seeing. Lisa Kent, in black jeans and black leather jacket, holding something in her right hand that pointed towards Charlie. 'What are you talking about?' she said, uncomprehending.

'Just hand over the phone.' Lisa gestured with her left hand. 'Come on, Charlie, this is not a game.' She held up her right hand. 'This is pepper. It's very painful as well as disabling. I don't want to use it yet, but I will if I have to. Now, give me the phone.'

Bewildered and baffled, clueless as to what she was dealing with, Charlie chose to cooperate. 'I don't understand,' she said, stretching out to put the phone in Lisa's hand. She noticed that Lisa was wearing tight-fitting latex gloves. 'Are you feeling OK, Lisa? What's going on here?'

Lisa tucked the phone in a jacket pocket. 'I'm feeling absolutely fine, Charlie. You were right about those deaths, you know. They were murders.' She spoke conversationally, as if they were chatting in her living room. 'Step backwards, please. I'm not comfortable with you this close to me. And not for the pitiful reasons you'd wish for,' she added, a cruel edge to her words.

Charlie took a step backwards, caught unawares by the sensation of the world tilting beneath her feet. 'I don't understand,' she repeated. 'What's all this got to do with you? Why are you here?'

'You're ridiculously easy to follow,' Lisa said, the chatty tone back in place again. 'Do you ever look in your rear-view mirror? I knew you'd turn up at Howard Calder's eventually, and I just stayed on your tail. I hoped you wouldn't find anything to pursue. But I came prepared to deal with it if you did.'

'But why? What has any of this got to do with you?'

'You really don't get it, do you? All those bodies, those people who stood between Jay and happiness – it wasn't Jay who killed them. I told you: she hasn't got it in her to kill. She needed me to do that for her.' There was no hint of madness in Lisa's sweet smile, which was all the more unnerving.

'Jay got you to kill for her?' Charlie couldn't make sense of this at all.

'No, no. I did it willingly. I did it because it was the only way I could show her how much I love her.' There was something almost radiant about Lisa now. 'She needs to be looked after. But the love between us is so strong, so combustible that she's afraid of us being together. I have to keep proving how much she needs me.'

'You said you hardly knew her. That your paths had crossed at Oxford, but that was all.' The one thing Charlie could cling to in the shifting kaleidoscope around her was her professional skill. Keep her talking, she told herself. If Lisa was talking, she wasn't acting.

Lisa gave a rueful smile and a half-shrug. 'I lied. We were lovers. I was her first. And she was mine. It was so strong, so amazing. Completely transforming.'

A chill ran through Charlie. How in God's name could she have missed this madness? She resisted the urge to shudder. 'I've read the interviews, Lisa. She doesn't mention you. Her first girlfriend was called Louise.'

Lisa's eyelids fluttered in a series of blinks. 'That's right. I was Louise then. But Jay transformed me. And now I'm Lisa. We don't talk about that transformation, you see. Here's the thing, Charlie. Some things are too powerful to share with the world,' she said quickly. 'To know something like the electricity there was between Jay and me is to transcend normal reality. It's impossible to explain to people who have only a mundane experience of the world.'

'People like me, you mean?'

Lisa laughed merrily. 'Exactly, Charlie. Now you're beginning to understand how I couldn't have a relationship with you.'

'As opposed to Nadia,' Charlie said tartly. 'I tell you, Lisa, I am so over you.' As she said it, Charlie knew it was nothing less than the truth. Being threatened and held hostage had a way of putting relationships in a whole new perspective.

Lisa looked momentarily cross. 'That's really of no account to me, Charlie. And I told you already, Nadia was about sex. The satisfaction of a physical urge. There was in no sense a relationship between us. How could there be?'

'I suppose not. But I don't entirely understand how you went from being Jay's lover to being her avenging angel. Presumably she dumped you?' Careful, Charlie, she told herself. Don't make her too angry. Just enough to unsettle her.

'We separated because we couldn't handle the extreme forces between us. My life since then has been about waiting for her to be ready. And taking care of her so she can have the best possible life until that time arrives.'

'And that means killing people who stand in her way?'

Again that brilliant smile. 'Why not? It's not like they were on the same plane as Jay and me.'

'Does she know about this?' Charlie tried to sound conversational too, to hide her intention to understand the pathology of what she was confronted with.

Lisa nodded. 'Naturally. It's important that she understands I'm still as committed to her as I ever was. We remain the keeper of each other's secrets.'

'Each other's secrets?' The echo question. Always a powerful tool. Even with those who had crossed the line.

'She knows I kill for her when it's necessary. And I always knew about this.' Lisa waved vaguely at the alcove and its contents.

'You knew she'd killed her mother?'

Lisa reared back, an expression of outrage on her face.

'Killed her mother? Don't be ridiculous. It was Howard who killed her mother. He'd found out about Rinks van Leer and he followed Jenna here that last morning. He was determined she should die rather than violate his mad Christian principles. By the time Jay arrived to talk to her mother, Jenna was dead. He'd whacked her on the back of the head with his cricket bat. Which he then left lying on the floor beside her.' Lisa rolled her eyes. 'Well, duh. So Jay arrives on the scene in time to see him legging it up the prom. She's scared he's come to put a stop to her escape plans so she runs up to the flat here. And she sees her life falling apart before her eyes. Mother dead, stepfather about to be arrested for murder. What's going to happen to her? The sky's going to fall on her head. The police, the church, the media. She's not going to be sitting her A-levels and going to Oxford in the middle of all that, is she? The lesser of two evils is a runaway mother, right? Am I right?' She paused, waiting for a response.

'Absolutely,' Charlie said. This wasn't the time to try and pick holes in what felt like the authentic version. 'So she hid the body?'

'Exactly.' Lisa sounded as if she were congratulating a particularly slow pupil. 'There were still leftover building materials all over the place. Jay had spent enough of her life in a makeshift existence to know the basics of construction. She took out the bottom shelves and walled up Jenna's body with her suitcase.' Lisa peered round Charlie. 'I don't think she expected to turn her into a mummy, though.' She frowned. 'When she told me about it, it sounded as if she'd sealed Jenna in some airtight environment. But those heating vents, and the chimney – they must have dried out the corpse and carried away any smells up into the roof space.' She wrinkled her nose. 'Old people smell anyway, don't they? You wouldn't think twice about a bit of stink in an old person's flat.'

'She told you about it?'

Lisa nodded eagerly. 'That's how special our relationship is. She's never told anyone else, but one night when we were in bed together, she told me. I had to find a way to repay that trust. So when Jess Edwards threatened her, I did what had to be done.' Again, that smile, so normal it was recalibrating Charlie's measure of crazy. 'The same with that Swedish programmer. I can't even remember his name now.' She shook her head, frowning. 'How odd.' She shrugged. 'Anyway, that was a real help to Jay because I got my hands on all his work too. She told me I'd proved my point, that I didn't have to do this any more. But when I saw her that afternoon last summer in Oxford at Schollie's and she told me about running into Magda and how that had made her feel, I could see she wasn't going to be happy unless she had her sweet little bride to play with for a while. And I can't stand to see her unhappy.'

'You killed Philip Carling? It was you?' This time, Charlie couldn't hide her shock.

'Of course. I was at the same conference as Jay that weekend. We had a drink together right after she'd bumped into Magda. She was on another planet. I did what anybody who really loved her would do. I made her happy.'

There was a long silence. 'You're telling me this because you're planning to kill me, right?'

511

Lisa's reply was forestalled by the ringing of Charlie's phone. Lisa pulled it out of her pocket and looked at the screen. 'Nick Nicolaides,' she said. 'Who's he?'

'Just a friend,' Charlie said, trying for casual.

'A friend? Really? Well, let's see what your friend has got to say to your voicemail.' She waited, holding the phone in front of her so she could keep Charlie in her eyeline. Before long, the voicemail chime rang out. Lisa pressed the icon to put it on speaker and listened intently, her expression darkening as the significance of the message dawned on her.

'Charlie, it's Nick. Amazing, but the telecom people got back to us. Jay made one call from the mountain. She was on the line for twelve minutes. The number she called is the landline for Lisa Kent. Isn't that the woman you were talking to about Jay? I think you might need to cover your back here. Call me when you get this.'

It could hardly have been worse, Charlie thought. Absolutely no prospect of talking her way out of this with a promise of silence now.

Lisa's top lip drew back in a sneer. 'Oh, Charlie, you couldn't leave well alone, could you?'

'What did you say to her, Lisa? Did you talk her into cutting the rope? Was that what the call was about?' Time to go on the attack, Charlie thought. Passivity wasn't going to get her anywhere now.

'She called me because it was on last number redial. She wanted me to alert the mountain rescue because she didn't have a number for them and her battery was low. I persuaded her that if they weren't there within two hours, she should cut the rope and save herself. Then I went shopping.' She grinned. 'It took me at least two hours to get round to calling them. Which was a good thing, because Kathy was being very difficult about the sale of doitnow.com.'

'I don't think cutting the rope made Jay very happy.'

Lisa shrugged. 'Temporarily, no. But it was best in the long run.'

There was no doubt in Charlie's mind that she was dealing with one of the most disordered personalities she'd ever encountered. That she had allowed herself to become besotted with her was deeply shaming. But then the sophistication and consistency of Lisa's delusion and her capacity for concealing it were remarkable. The problem now was that in order to maintain the integrity of her beliefs, Lisa would have to kill Charlie. It was time to start trying to save herself the only way she knew how. 'Killing me's a really bad idea,' Charlie said.

'I don't think so.'

'Lots of people know I've been investigating Jay. Nick Nicolaides. Maria. Corinna Newsam. If I turn up dead here, with Jenna's body, it points straight to Jay. You'd be putting her right in the firing line.'

Lisa laughed. It didn't sound in the least mad; more like an ordinary person who's heard a good joke. 'Good try, Charlie. But not good enough. You see, when Jay hid the body, she also took the murder weapon back home. Wiped it down and put it back where it belonged, in the shed in Howard Calder's yard. It's been there ever since.' She took a couple of steps back into the hallway and reached down with her left hand, never taking her eyes off Charlie. She reappeared, a cricket bat in her hand. 'Until this morning.

And look, here, on the top of the flat side. Burned into the wood. H. Calder. It's probably still got traces of Jenna's DNA on it. Soon to be joined by your DNA.'

'Why would Howard kill me?'

'Obviously, because you found out he'd killed Jenna.'

Charlie shook her head, bemused. 'Why would Howard keep the murder weapon? As far as he was concerned, he left it at the scene of the crime. How would he deal with it turning up in his shed?'

'Good question. Jay reckons he thought the whole aftermath of the crime was God doing him a favour. He must have been baffled by the disappearance of the body and the reappearance of the cricket bat. She always thought that's why he made such a big deal of hassling the police about Jenna's disappearance. He thought he was bombproof because God was on his side. He'd done God's work, getting rid of the sinner. Completely nuts, if you ask me.'

He wasn't the only one, Charlie thought. 'Nick knows about you,' she said. 'He's a police officer. He's going to ask some questions.'

'He'll be a voice in the wilderness. I'll get away with this, Charlie. Just like I always do.' She leaned the bat against the door jamb and took a step forward, raising the pepper spray. 'Goodbye, Charlie.'

'No, Lisa.' The voice came from the hallway. Lisa froze, a look of happy amazement spreading across her face. She half-turned as Jay Stewart walked into the room, the spray still pointing at Charlie but her eyes swivelling towards the door.

It was a half-chance for Charlie, but she didn't dare take

it. She had no idea whose side Jay was on. Was she here to help Lisa or to save Charlie? Or something else entirely?

Jay looked beyond Charlie to the ruins of the wall she'd built nineteen years before and shuddered. 'Jesus,' she said, her face twisted in pain. 'I never imagined . . .' Her voice trailed off and she dashed a hand roughly across her eyes. Then somehow she pulled herself together. Charlie saw her shoulders square and her jaw set. 'It's time for this to stop, Lisa. This isn't helping me. I don't want any more deaths on my conscience.'

Lisa's smile was strained for the first time. 'They shouldn't be on your conscience. They're not worth bothering about.'

Jay shook her head. 'We always end up on the opposite side on this one, Lisa,' she said sadly. 'We're not a superior species, you and me. We're human, just like the people you've killed. I want it to stop. That's what it's going to take for me to be happy.' She moved back towards the door, so Lisa couldn't watch both her and Charlie at the same time.

Lisa's head swivelled between them like a spectator at a table tennis game. 'You don't know what's best for you, Jay. You never have. That's always been the trouble.' She pounded on her chest with her free hand. 'I'm the one who knows. All over the world, people accept I'm the one who knows what's best. They come to my seminars, they buy my books. Because I understand, because I know what's best.'

Jay shook her head. 'I'm not arguing, Lisa. I'm done with this.' She held out her hand. 'Give me the spray.'

Lisa looked as if she was going to cry. The conflict

between what she wanted to do and what Jay was asking of her was ripping her up. 'I can't do that,' she cried. 'You've got to trust me, Jay. Go, now. Just go. You don't have to be part of this. I'll deal with it. Like I always do.'

'I'm not going.' Jay took a step closer to Lisa, closing the angle and making it harder for Lisa to keep both women in her sights.

Suddenly Lisa pushed Jay in the chest, shoving her hard against the wall. 'I'm doing this for your sake,' she screamed, whirling round to face Charlie.

Charlie squeezed her eyes tight shut and threw herself at the floor. But instead of the aerosol hiss she expected, she heard a scuffle of feet, a thud and the clatter of something metallic hitting the wall. Then a voice shouting, 'No, Lisa.' A scream and the sound of bodies moving.

Charlie scuttled backwards till she hit the chimney breast then opened her eyes to see Lisa on the floor, struggling with Jay. 'Let go of me,' Lisa screamed. 'I'm doing this for you.'

Jay wrestled against her, grunting as Lisa elbowed her in the ribs. 'For fuck's sake, help me here,' she shouted.

Charlie hadn't been in a fight since she'd turned six, but the odds were decent and it was her life that was on the line, she reminded herself as she threw her body over Lisa's thrashing legs. She turned her head in time to see Jay land a punch that rocked Lisa's head back to hit the floor. Dazed, Lisa tried to swing her fist at Jay, but Charlie was able to grab her wrist.

And then it was all over. Lisa went limp, all fight gone from her. Without getting off her, Jay pulled the belt from her jeans. 'Tie her ankles up,' she ordered Charlie.

Feeling foolish, like a character in a bad TV show, Charlie did as she was told, then stood up. Warily, Jay eased herself up and away from Lisa, who turned her face away and hugged herself tightly. Her jaw was already red and swollen, a bruise in the making. 'I'm sorry,' Jay said, rearranging her clothes and running a hand through her hair.

'It's a bit late for that,' Charlie said. 'Four people dead because you didn't put a stop to her before now? Sorry doesn't begin to cover it.'

'So what happens next? You're going to wreck some more lives? And for what? Some crazy idea of justice? I know all about your relationship with justice, Dr Flint. There's four dead women whose families know all about it too.'

All the rage that Charlie had been keeping in check suddenly surfaced. 'Putting Lisa Kent behind bars will save lives. Mine, for example.'

'You know that's not necessarily true. Surely it's clear to you that she's mad as a box of frogs? You must have a colleague who'd agree with you that she needs to be sectioned. For her own safety. Look at her.' She pointed to Lisa, who was mumbling incomprehensibly into the carpet. 'If that's how she reacts to the small matter of me turning against her, I think it's safe to say you can demonstrate she's completely off her chops.'

Charlie shook her head. 'Her delusions are too organised. She'll get herself together and convince the powers that be that she's as sane as anyone can reasonably be expected to be. Then she'll be out, and who knows what she'll think is necessary then? There's no way round this, Jay. We need to call the police.'

'You'll be putting Howard Calder behind bars too.'

'It's where he should be. He killed your mother. Don't you care about that?'

Jay sighed and stared out of the window. 'I think Howard's inhabited his own personal hell for twenty years. Prison, punishment, pain – that would be a relief for him. So no, I don't want the law to extract its pathetic price from Howard. I'm happy for things to stay just the way they are.'

'You don't have the right to make that choice. There's a price we pay for being part of society. You don't get to make rules that apply only to you. I don't care how much money you have or how clever a businesswoman you are. The law isn't always fair. Nobody knows that better than me right now. But it's the best we've got. Now give me your phone.'

Jay shook her head. 'I can't do that, Charlie. I can't go to jail. It would kill me. Never mind what it would do to Magda. Who is the real innocent in all of this. When Corinna set you on this path, do you really think she wanted you to destroy her daughter's life? Because that's what you'll be doing.'

'Magda has the right to know the sort of woman she's living with.'

'Jesus,' Jay exploded. 'All I did was cover other people's backs. I never did anybody any harm. Except Kathy, and I tried to save her, I truly did. I'm not the bad person here.' She lashed out with her foot at Lisa's prone body. 'She's the killer, not me.'

'You could have stopped her. You could have saved lives.'

'You could have stopped Bill Hopton. You could have saved lives,' Jay shouted. 'Nobody's sending you to jail though, are they?'

'I couldn't stop him legally,' Charlie said, furious now. 'Because at that point Bill Hopton hadn't killed anybody. Unlike Lisa.'

Jay cast a quick look around, as if seeking inspiration. She turned to Charlie and gave her the full wattage of her charm. 'Look, here's a deal. Give me a head start. Twenty-four hours. Enough time to get out to somewhere we don't have extradition with. Somewhere decent, where Magda can join me.' Jay spread her hands wide. 'I'm not a criminal. Nobody's going to die because of me if Lisa's out of the way.'

Something inside Charlie's head snapped. She was fed up of being fucked around with. She'd had enough of being a scapegoat. She was tired of being dismissed as irrelevant and insufficient. She'd had more than enough of people who thought their desires were the only thing that mattered.

She let the slim metal canister she'd picked off the floor slide down into her hand, unnoticed by Jay, who had walked over to the window. 'You think you deserve that chance?' Charlie said, her voice tight and hard. As Jay turned to face her, she raised her hand and sprayed her with pepper.

Screaming and coughing, Jay collapsed on the floor, her hands over her face. 'You fucking bitch,' she spluttered.

'I'll do it again if I have to.' Charlie backed away from her and stepped over Lisa. She crouched beside her and said, 'You'll get the same if you try anything.' But it was an empty precaution. Right now, Lisa was too far inside her own head to hear. Charlie fished her phone out of Lisa's jacket pocket and moved into the hallway out of the way of any drifting pepper. A sudden tide of exhaustion rose through her, making her legs weak and her head swim. But there was something she had to do first. Wearily she dialled 112. 'I want to speak to the police,' she said. 'I want to report a murder.'

Eight months later

The three people at the table had converged on the Turkish restaurant from very different places. Detective Sergeant Nick Nicolaides had come from the Foreign Office, where he'd been briefed by a civil servant in the Spanish section. Maria Garside had come by taxi from Euston Station; the swift and regular Virgin Pendolino service from Manchester meant she could conduct most of an afternoon surgery and still make it to the capital in time for dinner. Dr Charlie Flint had come from a meeting in Holborn with the providers of her professional indemnity insurance.

'So, is it to be champagne?' asked Maria, first to arrive and impatient for a drink. 'I already ordered a running selection of mezze.'

Nick, who had bumped into Charlie in the doorway,

raised an interrogative eyebrow. 'My meeting was just a confirmation of what we'd already heard. Which is definitely worth champagne. But I'm not drinking fizz unless Charlie got a result too.'

Maria gave Charlie a measured stare. 'Eight years on and she still thinks she can keep her secrets.' She grinned. 'I think it's a bottle of Bolly. Am I right?'

Charlie leaned back in her seat and let out a long breath. 'In the light of the GMC's decision that I acted throughout the Bill Hopton case with professional propriety, my insurers have agreed to settle all outstanding claims from the families of his victims. So yes, Nick, a result. And yes, Maria, definitely worth the Bolly.'

The smile that lit up Maria's face was even more welcome than the news had been. Only when the General Medical Council had dismissed the complaint against Charlie had she fully grasped how much stress her partner had been under. That Maria had asked so little for herself during their time in purgatory was a salutary reminder to Charlie of how lucky she was still to have her.

'Thank God,' Maria said as Nick waved to the waiter.

Once the champagne was on its way, they sat beaming at each other, enjoying the sensation of an ordeal survived. 'So what did the Foreign Office have to say?' Charlie asked.

'Lisa's lawyers tried to have her declared unfit to plead but the court wasn't having it.'

'That's not as surprising as it might seem,' Charlie said. 'When she's not actually rolling around on the floor gibbering, she's capable of simulating a high level of normality. There are very few situations in which she couldn't pass for acceptably normal.'

Nick pulled a face. 'Your idea of normal and mine are clearly not even close.'

'You never saw her at her most convincingly charming,' Maria said. 'You'd have totally fallen under her spell. Like her thousands of NV acolytes.'

'I'll have to take your word for it. Anyway, since the Spaniards were determined to go to trial, her legal team persuaded her to plead guilty. There really was no arguing with the forensics. Her DNA was all over the villa where Ingemarsson was killed. They had records of her ferry crossing and the hotel she stayed in near Santander. There was always a mountain of evidence. But they never had a suspect to test it against.'

'I can't believe she was so careless,' Maria said. 'It's as if she wanted to be caught.'

'Some killers do. But I don't think she was one of them.' Charlie paused as the waiter poured the champagne. They toasted each other, then she continued. 'I think Lisa believed that she was invincible. That her cause was so patently right that she couldn't be stopped. It's a kind of magical thinking that some grandiose personalities indulge in. She was just lucky.'

'Bloody lucky,' Nick said bitterly. 'I still can't believe the bloody CPS, deciding there wasn't enough evidence to prosecute her for the shit she pulled over here.'

Charlie shrugged. 'By that stage, they knew the Spanish would do their dirty work for them. So, how long did she get?'

Nick looked sombre. 'Thirty years. Not much fun in a Spanish jail.'

'That's why her lawyer's already working on trying to

get her transferred to a UK prison. And if he succeeds, I bet you a pound to a gold watch she'll do her time in a secure mental hospital rather than a prison.'

'How come you know what her lawyer's up to?' Nick demanded.

Charlie looked faintly embarrassed. 'Because I'm helping to build the case,' she said.

Nick looked astonished. 'She tried to kill you, Charlie.'

'I know. But she's ill.' Charlie fiddled with the stem of her glass. 'She can't be held responsible. The person who should be held to account and who never will be is Jay. That's why I've been making her sit down and take me through the history.'

'You've been sitting down with Jay Stewart?' Nick's voice rose an octave.

Charlie shrugged. 'Why not? She's got nothing better to do with her days right now. She might only have got a suspended sentence for concealment of a body, but it's made her persona non grata with the 24/7 shareholders. They kicked her off the board and she's having to lie low and lick her wounds. She might as well be talking to me.'

Nick shook his head in wonderment. 'You never cease to amaze me, Charlie. So what's she saying?'

'I finally got the back story. Lisa Kent wasn't always Lisa Kent. She started out as Louise Proctor. She and Jay fell in love at Schollie's and had one of those totally consuming affairs. Jay made the fatal mistake of telling her about Jenna's murder and how she'd hid the body. She says it put her in Lisa's power, but of course, there's an element of bullshit in that. She must have known that the penalties for what she did were negligible compared to what Lisa was doing.' Charlie saw her anger and disgust mirrored in the faces of her companions. 'Even then, it was clear Lisa was completely obsessive and when Jess Edwards started her campaign against Jay, she decided it was her job to protect her lover. So she killed Jess. It was Louise that Corinna saw in the meadow that morning, not Jay.'

There was a moment's silence round the table while they all contemplated the consequences of that misidentification. 'Of course, committing a murder put her under tremendous stress even though she was convinced of her absolute right to defend Jay in any way that was necessary. But then her family freaked when they found out she was in the thick of a lesbian affair so they whisked her off to some extreme Catholic retreat where she promptly tried to kill herself, twice. She had a complete breakdown. She took a year out, then came back to Oxford, but not to Schollie's. She transferred to Univ, changed her name and remade herself. She even tried to turn herself into a nice heterosexual girl.'

'The perfect recipe for mental health,' Maria said drily.

'Well, it worked on a superficial level. She was functioning well enough to synthesise all the therapeutic avenues she'd gone down into a self-help programme that slowly started to take off.' Charlie sighed. 'It would be nice to think that she might have made it if she'd never encountered Jay again. The reality is she'd probably have found someone else to act as an outlet for her delusional fantasies.'

'But presumably she did run into Jay again?' Maria asked.

Before Charlie could reply, the food started to arrive. A

relay of waiters spread a dozen dishes before them and there was a brief pause while they started on the food. 'How did they meet up again?' Nick asked after he'd devoured an entire pitta bread slathered with aubergine caviar.

'According to Jay, Lisa read an article about her when doitnow.com started to take off. Jay arrived at the office one morning to find the place filled with flowers. There was a card with them that had the name of a bar and a time. Jay figured a public place would be safe enough so she went along. And there was Lisa.'

'I bet that totally did her head in,' Nick said. 'She must have thought she was free and clear after all that time.'

'According to Jay, she tried not to get sucked back in. But Lisa's very persuasive. And very good at passing for a normal, sane, sympathetic person. And then there was the small matter of Jess's murder. Jay was well aware that she was the person with the motive and no alibi. She claims she was scared of what Lisa might do if she refused all contact. Instead, she took a leaf out of Lisa's own book and did this big song and dance about how they were destined to be together but not yet. There would be tests and challenges before they would be worthy of each other.'

'Jeez,' Maria said. 'Remind me again, which one's the nutter?'

'Obviously not Jay,' Nick said. 'She's the one who's walked away from all of this with nothing more severe than a suspended sentence. Her stepfather's doing life for murdering her mother, her ex is doing thirty years in a Spanish jail and Corinna Newsam's had to resign her fellowship because she kept quiet about seeing someone in the meadow. But Jay still has her shares in 24/7 and her big house in Chelsea and her lovely life.'

'Not quite so lovely now,' Charlie pointed out. 'She doesn't have Magda.'

'She doesn't? That's news to me,' Nick said.

'Did I not tell you? Magda dumped her right after she found out it was Lisa who killed Philip. She realised Jay must have known that all along and the whole thing about Joanna and Paul was just a stunt to make it look like Jay was totally devoted to her. She was devastated that they'd been put through a murder trial just to make Jay look good.'

'Even though they did do the insider trading that they're still in prison for,' Maria said, less than charitably.

'Poor Magda. Another fucked-up life, thanks to Jay and Lisa,' Nick said.

'Not entirely,' Maria said. 'Tell him, Charlie.'

'Corinna's furious. Magda's hooked up with a lesbian theatre director who's trying to get pregnant via donor insemination. We're all hoping Henry will die of apoplexy when she finally succeeds.'

'So Magda got a bit of a happy ending,' Maria said. 'And she gave all Philip's insider trading money to the oncology department where she works. We took her out to dinner a couple of weeks ago and she told us all about their lovely new facilities.'

Before he could respond, a cascade of acoustic finger-picking emerged from Nick's jacket. He snatched at his phone, swearing under his breath. 'I'm sorry, I've got to take this,' he said, jumping to his feet and heading for the door. 'Work. Sorry.'

Charlie watched him go, an affectionate smile on her face. Then she turned back to Maria. 'I'm glad the trial's over. I know there's still work to be done to get Lisa back to a proper facility in the UK, but this feels like some sort of closure.'

Maria put her fork down and gave Charlie a long level stare. 'You were in love with her, weren't you?'

Charlie felt as if a gaping pit had opened beneath her feet. 'Sorry?' she blurted out.

Maria's smile was edged with sadness. 'It's OK, Charlie. I know it's over.'

'I never—'

Maria leaned forward and put a finger to Charlie's lips. 'Sssh. You don't need to explain. I think she was your demon lover, like in folk tales. The one you have no resistance to. I'll be honest, Charlie. I was scared I was going to lose you. When I saw the way you didn't look at her in Skye, I was sure you were going to choose her over me.'

'I couldn't leave you,' Charlie said, her voice cracking under the strain.

'I know that now. But I didn't then. I'm glad you fell back to earth.'

Charlie swallowed hard. 'Me too.' As she spoke, Nick strode back into the restaurant, a relieved smile on his face.

Maria spoke quickly, determined to say her piece before he reached them. 'And if you ever think about betraying me again, you'll wish Jay hadn't stopped Lisa adding another scalp to her tally.' She gave a grim smile. 'And that's a guarantee.'